THE
RIVER

TRICIA WASTVEDT

VIKING
CANADA

VIKING CANADA
Penguin Group (Canada), a division of Pearson Penguin Canada Inc.,
10 Alcorn Avenue, Toronto, Ontario M4V 3B2

Penguin Group (U.K.), 80 Strand, London WC2R 0RL, England
Penguin Group (U.S.), 375 Hudson Street, New York, New York 10014, U.S.A.
Penguin Group (Australia) Inc., 250 Camberwell Road, Camberwell, Victoria 3124, Australia
Penguin Group (Ireland), 25 St. Stephen's Green, Dublin 2, Ireland
Penguin Books India (P) Ltd, 11, Community Centre, Panchsheel Park, New Delhi – 110 017, India
Penguin Group (NZ), cnr Airborne and Rosedale Roads, Albany, Auckland 1310, New Zealand
Penguin Books (South Africa) (Pty) Ltd, 24 Sturdee Avenue, Rosebank 2196, South Africa

Penguin Group, Registered Offices: 80 Strand, London WC2R 0RL, England

First published 2004
Published simultaneously with Penguin Group (U.K.)

1 2 3 4 5 6 7 8 9 10   (FR)

Copyright © Tricia Wastvedt, 2004

*Publisher's note: This book is a work of fiction. Names, characters, places and incidents either
are the product of the author's imagination or are used fictitiously, and any resemblance
to actual persons living or dead, events, or locales is entirely coincidental.*

Manufactured in Canada.

NATIONAL LIBRARY OF CANADA CATALOGUING IN PUBLICATION

Wastvedt, Tricia
The river / Tricia Wastvedt.

ISBN 0-670-04485-7

I. Title.

PR6123.A88R59 2004   823'.92   C2004-900183-3

British Library Cataloguing in Publication data available

Visit the Penguin Group (Canada) website at **www.penguin.ca**

Contents

Part IV

PART I

1958

❧

Catherine and Jack

Water seeped through the boards and slipped from side to side, folding and breaking in tiny waves. At first only an inch or two round their bare feet, then enough to reflect the clouds and the trees.

Catherine liked the river inside the boat, and as it floated lower the wooden edges became an outline, the shape of a boat drawn on the green water.

They had tried to push to the bank but the oars were heavy and slippery and had gone sliding away. Catherine reached for overhanging branches but the pull of the boat was too strong and she was left with handfuls of leaves.

She sat in the cool water, her skirt puffed around her like a party dress. Jack was in the prow.

Catherine was not frightened, not even when the sides of the boat disappeared and they were sitting up to their waists barely moving in dark, mottled water under a tunnel of trees. But Jack was frightened now and plunged towards her as if he were diving. With the movement the boat disappeared beneath them and Catherine caught him in her arms. He struggled and splashed, climbing up her, his hands over her face, pulling her hair as if he had forgotten who she was. The water churned around them, sending waves to the banks and back again into their faces and mouths.

She held him tighter, holding him up as high as she could and at last he was quiet. He was quivering and slippery. She tried to say things that would calm him.

Treading water, Catherine could feel gentle invisible things stroking their fingers or fins or lips over her legs. Then her feet found a place to stand. It was soft, her toes sunk in and she leaned back against the push of the river. The coldness lapped at her chin and her hair floated out like a cloud of weed. Jack's arms around her neck were too tight but it was not hard to hold him, the water took his weight.

She was standing on the bottom but she could not feel the riverbed in front or behind. There was only a little mound of silt under her feet. She could not move; Jack was too big to swim with and he held too tight.

It was quiet under the trees. The water stretched out around them, smooth now and peaceful. Far away on each side were the banks, and it was strange to see all the secret places under the edges of the river, the wet dark doorways of water creatures, their little harbours and jetties.

The sun going down made slanting gold across the brown water lighting up the billions of microscopic floating things that gave the river its colour.

Jack stopped crying.

'What are we going to do?' he said. He let go with one arm and patted the water, then cupped his hand under a patch of sunlight.

Catherine said, 'Do you want a story?'

Jack did not answer and Catherine let her head lean back on the water. She looked up at the trees, layers and layers of yellow and copper and brilliant green. That is the roof and the river is a pillow, she thought.

Her arms were numb and Jack was slipping down. He rested his head on the top of hers and sometimes whispered things to himself.

Catherine thought of the boat sunk beneath them somewhere, resting like a turtle on the bottom. She felt sorry for the boat and sad that that no one would ever see it again. They were the last two people on earth to sail in it.

1946

⌒∞⌒

Xavier and Adelie

When old Johannes Sevier died, the legacy he left to his youngest son seemed a fortune. Xavier wanted to travel. He had not inherited the vineyard, nor would he have a place of any importance in the family business, so there was no reason to stay. He and Adelie could go anywhere they wished.

Adelie had always wanted to see England and although they planned to go further, perhaps to California, the first stop would be just across the Channel.

The war was over and they married. Celebration on celebration. The world was a beautiful, free, welcoming place and in spite of the devastation they passed from Alsace to the coast, nothing could dampen their spirits.

Adelie had cried when she kissed her mother and sisters goodbye at the station, and for a moment Xavier felt chilled by the responsibility of his promise to take care of her, but they could not be sad or anxious for long. They leaned close, watching the countryside rush past, and felt excitement at all the unknown adventures ahead and all the minutes and hours and years together.

London was not grey mist and sullen people as they had been told it would be. The month they passed there was warm and sunny and Londoners were more like Parisians than the people they had left behind in Alsace. Clothes were stylish and the Thames sparkled.

The war had wounded the city. Where once had been graceful grey-brick terraces there were piles of rubble, broken roof beams and smashed furniture. Sometimes a wall was left standing with its doorways and fireplaces in mid-air, the wallpaper showing to the passersby with ghost shapes where pictures and furniture had been. Adelie thought of the husbands and wives just like Xavier and herself who had decorated these rooms and sat together by the firesides.

But there were plenty of places that the war had not touched. And even when they turned a corner and came upon a bombed building, grass and wild flowers had already taken root.

They stayed in a small hotel near Charing Cross. Their room had a balcony and with the doors open they could hear the noise of cars, shouts of street vendors and the rumble of trains. The habit of sleeping for a while after lunch was not left behind in France. They would lie in each other's arms in the afternoons hearing the sounds of the foreign city through dreams of familiar hills and vineyards.

In the evening they would find a restaurant, looking for the biggest, busiest, brightest they could find. They'd thought only Paris had places like these: high ceilings, chandeliers and curtains that belonged in a theatre—great swathes of velvet and silk, draped and tasselled— scores of white linen tablecloths, silver, crystal and fresh cut flowers. The noise of cutlery on china and the conversation of diners were sometimes so loud that Xavier and Adelie would have to lean towards each other to make themselves heard over the din. But most of the time they were happy to watch. They loved London life, cultured and fashionable, worlds away from the dull tranquillity of their home.

Adelie was very beautiful in her new dresses and Xavier noticed the stares of admiration. He would struggle with English and the waiter would find it difficult to concentrate on his faltering words without being distracted by Adelie's lovely face. But Xavier did not mind, she looked only at him.

They decided to see more of England and forgot their tickets to New York. They booked seats on a slow train from Paddington to Devon. It meandered southwest from town to town, eventually reaching the coast. Adelie wanted to swim in waves, it would be the first time, and Xavier wanted anything that made her happy.

The journey was long and slow. In the afternoon Adelie slept against Xavier's shoulder. She woke when the movement of the train stopped. They were at another country station. Outside the open window there was the sound of birds and the soft hiss of the train. The platform was empty.

'I'm thirsty,' Adelie said. 'Is there anyone selling water or tea?' Xavier jumped down onto the platform, looking up and down then walking away towards the ticket office while Adelie leaned out, anxious that the train might leave without him.

And it did. The train began to move and Adelie, after calling his name twice, jumped down from the carriage and waited for her husband to return with her tea.

They stood together without luggage, or even Adelie's handbag, on the sunny, deserted platform. They had no idea of the name of the place—it was still painted out.

Xavier took her hand. There was no one at the ticket office so they walked out into the lane: in one direction was a bridge and in the other a curve uphill and away out of sight. Bees buzzed in and out of flowers. It was warm and quiet.

On the bridge they leaned over the stone balustrade. The river beneath them was broad and slow; bright weed undulated over the stones. They watched the glittering water slip into shadow under the bridge, and shoals of small brown fish basking in the shallows.

Xavier loosened his tie. Adelie shook her hair, letting the breeze blow through it. The sound of the train faded to nothing.

They were pleased to be having a small adventure. The plan was not unduly upset; they would simply wait for another train and catch up with their luggage further down the line.

They did not know that the next train would not come for six days and by that time Xavier would have bought a house, Adelie would be content to swim in the river, and this place without a name would be their home.

1958

❧

Sarah

Her mother said a husband would come along soon enough. A sixteen-year-old woman so capable would have no trouble at all. But until then Sarah Kathleen was not a child any longer, she must pull her weight in the family, bring in some cash and learn things that would be useful for her future.

Sarah was glad to help but she liked school and was sorry to leave. She had been told that she had a good brain and a sensible attitude so long as she did not get above herself with those looks—she must be watchful of becoming bold. And she was a good pupil when she curbed her tendency to wear the elbows off her arms with dreaming. It was decided she should be of service as a teacher or a nurse.

Sister Perpetua said, but quietly because it was an unusual thing for a Sister to say, that Sarah could be whatever she put her mind to, even a lawyer or a doctor. A woman could make anything of herself these days, there was no limit. The good Lord had given her the wherewithal, and Sarah should go to university.

But that was not possible now. Sarah had a job and she was leaving home. It was so exciting that going to university could hardly be better.

The doctor had chosen her from lots of other girls, he said, and she was the one he wanted. He had no wife to look after him or a pretty daughter like her. Sarah felt sad for him.

His advertisement said his assistant would keep the house tidy, take messages, cook meals and generally do anything that would make his life run more smoothly. She would live in his house and bring some order and comfort back into his life—as only a woman can, Sarah's mother said.

The interviews were conducted at a surgery in town. It was not the doctor's office but he said this was easier for prospective employees. Sarah did not know what he meant. She wore her fawn coat buttoned all the way to cover a dress she felt was too young for her, and her mother's nylons to look her best.

The doctor was elderly. His eyes watered and his hands shook a little. Sarah would start in three weeks.

A car came to collect her and people in the street stood at their front doors to watch and to wave her off. Sarah had never felt so special. She thought the car would drive her to another town, smarter than this one probably with tall, red-brick houses, clipped hedges and iron railings. Instead they turned off the main road when they were still surrounded by fields.

There were cottages and a grey stone chapel. The car stopped outside an ugly, peeling house. The nettles beside the path were waist high, there were leaves in the porch and a row of empty milk bottles.

The place was not at all how Sarah imagined it would be. Now she knew why the doctor had said nothing about where he lived— no one would want to come here, they would die of loneliness in this miserable place.

But the doctor was kind, and it seemed at first as if there was a mistake and he would be looking after her. He had put flowers in her room and a special, expensive bar of soap by the washbasin. There were pink towels laid out on the bed.

Sarah stood by her suitcase with the soap to her nose, inhaling its scent. The room was her own, no little sisters to waste her lipstick and scribble in her books. The doctor said he would make her an omelette when she was ready. It took two whole eggs to make an omelette.

She should give things a chance, stay a least a week. That's what her mother would have told her.

❦

The doctor sat in a fireside chair and Sarah ate at the dining table alone.

'I'm sure you will find plenty to interest you here,' he said. Sarah did not know what to say but she forgave the doctor for not understanding—after all he had no daughters of his own.

'This is delicious,' she said. 'My mother says most men don't know a frying pan from fairy lights.'

The doctor smiled his watery-eyed smile and nodded and watched her eat.

'What a wise woman your good mother is,' was all he said. He poured her a glass of red wine and she wondered whether it counted as a sin to drink it or a worse sin of ingratitude if she did not.

They didn't speak again until her supper was finished and then they washed up together while Sarah talked about her family and the Sisters and her best friends, Maureen, Patsy and Joan. The doctor wiped the plates slowly, listening carefully and asking questions about the things she was telling him. Sarah wondered if she was talking too much.

'Perhaps you would like to look at Joséphine's books,' the doctor said when they'd switched off the kitchen light. 'You're very welcome to borrow anything you'd like to read.'

'Thank you,' said Sarah, wondering about Joséphine.

They went up to the top of the house to a little slant-ceilinged room. There was a pretty bureau and a lamp with butterflies cut out of the parchment shade to look as if they had settled there with their wings fluttering. Sarah could imagine writing love letters in this room.

As if she had asked, the doctor said, 'Joséphine was my wife. She died a while ago but we still talk often.' He must have noticed Sarah's look for he added, 'I expect that sounds odd to you, my dear. When you're older you'll understand.'

Although she had never been in love, Sarah felt that she could understand how you might talk to someone you long to be with, especially if you never would be again, not until you were reunited in eternal rest in the loving arms of the Holy Father in Heaven. There was no harm in it at all. She liked the doctor and she felt happier than when she arrived. Perhaps she would not die of loneliness after all.

⸜∞⸝

When Sarah woke she remembered where she was even before she opened her eyes. There was a different smell to the pillowcase and a weightiness in the blankets that could not have been her own. She turned over and the warmth of herself, familiar and comforting, the same as her sisters', mingled with the strict, polite smell of clean linen.

She listened; the house was so quiet. If she lay perfectly still there were tiny, thin sounds far away. If she moved, she filled the room with noise, the dry hiss of her skin against the sheets, the creak and ping of bed springs. The room was brown shadows. A slice of sunlight split the square of the curtains and made a line like chalk across the floor.

There was a cup of tea on the table by her bed—it was cold and little cracks crazed the surface as if it had set hard. Sarah cupped her hand to catch the drips and drank it down in one. She thought of herself sleeping as the doctor must have seen her when he brought in the tea, and she wondered if he was in the house somewhere.

She dressed, hearing the sounds she made as if she were someone else—the sounds she had never noticed before: the click and rustle of buttons and cloth, the buzz of a zip, like an insect caught inside a jar.

She opened the curtains. Her window looked over a village green with a stone memorial and a bench. Around the green were cottages and houses, all different, and the chapel. There was no one walking by and no traffic.

Sarah sat down at the dressing table to brush her hair, holding up a silver hand mirror to see the back as women in films sometimes do. She laid down the brush and mirror exactly as they had been arranged on the piece of lace.

Her face in the dressing-table mirror was new and unfamiliar, like a photograph she had never seen before. She sat perfectly still and studied the face of the girl who gazed back into her eyes. In the morning light this girl's skin was white and her hair was polished like wood. Behind her in the background was an old-fashioned room—dark furniture and wallpaper with large flopping flowers that made Sarah think of hens in the wet. The rug by the bed was thin and colourless with the years and years of feet pressing into it, and there was a stain round the light switch where fingers had touched the wall, turning the light on and off, on and off, a thousand times.

She wandered through the house, looking in all the rooms and trailing a finger in the layer of dust. The house was filled with furniture. Outside, birds were singing but they were muffled by the heavy silence. Everything was a shade of tea brown, even the watery light, except the bright sky outside the windows, blank as clean white paper.

In the sitting room there was a line of photographs propped on the mantelpiece. Some were new, glossy and white-edged, others were beginning to bend, and some had curled right over and slid onto their backs, too aged to stand up alone. Sarah saw the faces of babies and children and smiling adults, and there were messages written underneath: *'With our grateful thanks, Margaret and David, and our precious daughter Susan Barbara, October '55,'* and *'Thank you doctor, George, Dorothy and the children. Baby John Edward George, born 5th May 1957.'*

Sarah studied the faces of the parents, searching for what it was like to be old, and the babies displayed to the camera like bouquets of flowers or baskets of fruit.

There was a woman in a white summer dress holding a baby in a lace gown. The woman was very beautiful, blond and smooth-skinned. Her lipstick made her mouth look dark in the picture, and she wore pearl earrings and a little necklace that showed up against her throat. Her smile was shy, like a girl's, which was unexpected for someone so elegant. Sarah wondered how she managed to look neat and peaceful when she had a tiny baby to look after—her mother said it was the most exhausting thing on earth second to getting a man to be tidy. Sarah turned over the picture. *'Dear Edward and Joséphine, with our love, Xavier, Adelie and Josef Jacques Sevier, 12th August 1951'*

⚬∞⚬

Sarah's first weeks were not what she expected. She had imagined sitting at a desk to welcome the patients, then showing them into the doctor's office with poise and courtesy to put them at ease. They would confide in her as his personal assistant, maybe even trusting her more because she was a woman and more aware of unhappiness. But the doctor visited his patients and was out for much of the day.

It was only in the evening after supper that she helped him with his work, when the doctor would prepare medicines for the next day's house calls. He unlocked the glass cabinet in his study and measured coloured liquids from the rows of bottles. He weighed out minute heaps of white powder and showed her how to make pills in the little brass press.

The medicines were wrapped in brown paper and sealed with crimson wax imprinted with the doctor's gold ring.

When he took off the ring and put it in Sarah's hand it was warm and heavy. The letters E and J were entwined in curling script: Edward and Joséphine.

Sarah knew she would love only one man in her whole life and it would be for ever, like the doctor and his wife. Edward and Joséphine.

In the daytime when Sarah was alone in the house, there was time to read Joséphine's books and polish the step and bake cakes for tea. She cleaned the house and cooked. She chopped down the nettles in the front garden and swept leaves from the porch.

When the weather was fine she went for walks along the lanes and discovered that she liked the countryside—it was not at all bleak or full of dejected poor people, but it was not like a postcard either, dotted with arrangements of white woolly sheep and jolly farmers.

The lanes were deep and tangled, noisy with birds and the rustles of quick, shy creatures.

1986

Anna

Anna slept for most of the journey home. Through Spain, through France, the ferry, the motorway. Lights seeped their sulphur through her eyelids and the drone of the engine would come and go, her ears popping as if she were underwater. The heat of the Spanish sun was still in her skin and she did not feel cold until they pulled up outside the flat.

'What shall we do?' she said once when she woke. Thomas looked across, his face blank with the hours of driving. He said nothing but took her hand and rested it under his own. When they touched there was the memory in their fingers and palms for a second or two, then a pause and stillness that flattened to nothing.

Thomas moved out and stayed with a friend, although he and Anna still saw each other or spoke every day. They both became stretched thin by the days apart.

Anna could not eat, feeling sick, but her eyes shone. Her stomach wrenched at food and at the loss of Thomas, but secretly she felt a quietness like a smooth pearl inside her that was unconcerned at the anguish in her head.

Thomas came immediately when she said she was going away. He stroked her face but did not dissuade her. Neither believed it was really goodbye—it was like pretending the end of a love story they both knew was not real.

When he had gone Anna found a map and a pin—another game, another scene from a story. She stuck in the pin and it was where she was; that didn't count. The next place was too flat, she wanted

hills and valleys. Once more, this time, this was it. Small black
letters were right under the pin which Anna read, then read again.
She laughed at the name, *Cameldip*—is it a real place? But she could
not cheat a third time.

Beside the name was a winding blue line, a river edged with
trees drawn like puffy clouds on stalks. There was a black railway
and a cross for a church. The place looked plain and uncompli-
cated, it would not notice her. This was where she would bring
up her child.

⌀

Anna was not practical. Her mother and her sister said so,
although Thomas never commented in all the time they lived
together and Anna had begun to think that perhaps they were
wrong.

The pin made its choice but then gave no guidance on what to
do next. Anna could not work out how to organize moving—a
house to rent, money to earn, friends to fill the loneliness and a
child that would fill everything. This time she must make a proper
life that wouldn't slip away from under her. It felt as though the
years with Thomas were sinking, down and down, until soon they
would not hold her up any more.

Anna visited the place later that week. It was a hot September
day. Her skin was still brown from the Mediterranean sun and she
was comforted by the searing heat, it reminded her of being with
Thomas. It had been seven weeks.

Now she was here she realized she should have gone first to an
estate agent in the nearest town to ask about rental and to buy a
local newspaper. It was lunchtime and the village shop was closed,
so Anna went for a walk.

There was a pub at the end of the main street before the road
became a leafy lane. Creeper grew across the windows and hung
down over the door. The place looked derelict. There was a footpath

to the side leading to a river and she could see the water sparkling, pale cool green through the trees.

The path followed the edge of a garden behind the pub and she saw that perhaps the place was not empty after all: there was a freshly dug vegetable patch and the flower beds were banks of blooms. There were arching shrubs and ornamental trees. On the far side was a building partly hidden by trees, its roof covered with tarpaulin below which were pillars of white wrought iron. It looked like an aviary but there seemed to be no birds inside; the doors were wide open.

On the lawn two colossal shire horses, their legs folded beneath them and their eyes closed, basked in the sun.

Anna sat by the river for a while with her feet in the water and wrote a postcard which she gave to the girl in the shop before she left.

'You want to live here?' asked the girl, incredulous, reading the card.

Two weeks later there was a phone call and a woman said, 'I saw your card in the post office. I have a large house and I live alone. There's plenty of space, would you be interested?'

It was not what Anna had in mind. She imagined a cottage of her own where she could be untidy and comfortable with a garden full of toys and a dog. But she said, 'Yes. When should I come to look?' They made an arrangement and Anna liked the woman's voice. They exchanged numbers and names.

'Anna,' said Anna.

'MacKinnon,' said the woman.

の&

The house was four-square grey stone.

When they met at the door the woman took her hand and smiled so warmly that Anna thought she had taken her for someone else. But she said Anna's name before they'd had a chance to speak, so there was no mistake.

Isabel MacKinnon was tall. Her grey hair was pinned up in a ragged bun and her face was lined, but she had an easy elegance even in her faded cords and man's shirt.

They had tea in the flagstoned kitchen with the door open to the garden. The conversation slipped easily from one thing to another and Anna felt drawn close as if the woman saw in her something that no one had noticed before, something overlooked even by those who said they loved her.

Isabel MacKinnon smiled and listened when Anna spoke; perhaps this was what it was to have someone take pleasure in your company with no effort or duty.

'I'll show you to your room,' said Isabel as if Anna had already come to stay.

Anna laughed from surprise when she saw the room. It was a tree house. A walkway from the landing window, like a rope bridge in a jungle, joined it to the house. The tree was ancient and its closeness to the walls had made it grow like a broken parasol. On one side the branches were crooked and twisted with the discomfort of touching the stone, on the other they spread out in an arc of shade as even as if it were drawn on the grass with a compass.

'It can't be cut down,' said Isabel. 'It's the foundations of the house.'

The trunk inside the tree house was still covered with bark. The floor and walls and ceiling were polished smooth, thick planks of some creamy wood. There was a rug, a lamp on the floor and a mattress piled with blankets. Anna could hear birds in the branches above her.

'It's too cold in the winter, but this is a perfect place to sleep in summer,' Isabel said, holding out her hands to Anna as if she were giving her a present.

They could stand up only in the centre of the room where the roof was highest. There was a window in the roof and another low down near the floor, and they knelt to look out. A few overdressed sheep were dozing below them in the shade of the tree. There were no flower beds in Isabel's garden, and meadow grass reached down to the trees on the banks of the river. There was a grassy mound like an earthwork near the trees.

'What is that?' asked Anna pointing.

'It's a blackhouse,' said Isabel getting to her feet. Anna would have asked more, but Isabel was already stepping onto the rope bridge back to the house.

They went up to the attic room that would be Anna's in the winter. Downstairs there was a sitting room and a long, empty room with a polished wood floor and glass doors opening on to the garden.

All the time Anna imagined what Thomas would think if he were with her, but Isabel was one of the few people that Anna did not feel would be happier, would like her more, if Thomas were there too.

She thought Isabel might ask why she was coming to the village when there was no one here she knew, but Isabel asked nothing.

Anna didn't ask anything either. In spite of her warmth, Isabel was not easy to question.

A man came into the kitchen while they talked. He seemed to work for Isabel but she didn't introduce him or make any comment after he'd gone. It was the only time Anna felt uncomfortable; Isabel hardly looked at him. Anna thought how unbearable it must be to be disliked by her.

They made plans for the move and when they said goodbye Isabel kissed her. Anna had thought before she came that she must tell Isabel about the baby, but she didn't.

PART II

Cameldip

According to parish records, only twice has the river been provoked by the English weather.

On one occasion the flood of a December thaw carried away an ancient bridge and heaved up a memory that had slept in the soft, black mud of the riverbed for three decades.

On the other the Camel, bloated and clumsy with summer rain, took a short cut and set an annual project for the art class of St Angela's Infants and Juniors (Mixed).

The village was once only five or six farmworkers' cottages and had no official name by which it could be distinguished from the other huddles of habitation along the stately, meandering Camel. Late one August evening, a steady, weighty rain began falling and continued uninterrupted for seventeen days. The harvest was ruined and the lanes were liquid mud. Hooves, paws and feet softened and rotted in the constant wet.

Although the level rose only to the edges of the banks, the weight of water pressing downstream made the river too ungainly for its usual convoluted route. It abandoned one of its loops and cut across a nose of soft pasture.

For a few months the river was undecided. It gushed impatiently through the new channel and it also still followed the old circuitous route with barely enough interest to get all the way round. By spring the choice was made. The ends of the loop were clogged with silt, leaving a perfect horseshoe of water marooned in the land.

The giant hoofprint was colonized with greenery and insects—floating, skating, buzzing, hovering things. A wooden bridge still pointlessly crossed from one side to the other and a brook passed through on its way to the river, keeping one side of the arc clear while the other was swampy.

In the following spring, trailing streamers of spawn floated in the shallows. The specks wriggled, the water seethed with tadpoles; minute and featureless black at first, then fat, bull-nosed brown. Tiny webbed hands and miniature jointed legs took shape—a nature study lesson perfectly illustrated more than a century before the first stone had been laid for St Angela's.

Generations of toads thrived undisturbed while the nearby village grew. More houses were built; an inn, a chapel. Families swelled and divided, new families fastened to the edges of village life until newer families shunted them inwards. A grocery, a hardware store and a cattle-feed merchant's opened. A sign was erected on the highway pointing an iron finger towards Cameldip and a proper road was laid, which at one point skimmed the bank of the Camel's hoofprint. There had been a track but this was the 1930s and the motor car required a more refined surface.

More cars, then more, and by the 1950s the deaths in March on this quiet stretch of the B3202 had become upsetting. The toads, full of purpose and having no road sense, were squashed in their scores.

In the early sixties a local woman, a ballet dancer by profession, was unable to bear it any more. She spent several days carrying the toads across the road in a bucket, and that was the beginning of Toad Ferry.

The following year people wanted to help and a little organization was needed. Before much longer it came to the notice of the village committee: a meeting, signing up, a rota, a sheet to be completed on which times and numbers must be noted. The police were informed, warning triangles supplied and lighting rigged up in the trees. A relay of people, some residents and some from local nature groups, carried the toads to safety or brought hot tea.

And there was a competition. The children were awarded a prize for the most original container for transporting toads, no rules except that it must give at least three toads a comfortable ride for approximately twenty yards.

There were miniature cardboard taxis, Wild West stage coaches, moon buggies and hollow bombs with sparkler fuses. There were fighter jets, giant cheeseburgers and alarm clocks. The children cut and coloured, stuck and painted for a month of art classes, and put their vehicles to the test on the first Friday night that the toads were in full swing.

There was no specific date when Toad Ferry started or ended: the toads decided for themselves. But when it was over there was an evening of celebration and relaxation in Mrs MacKinnon's dining room, where refreshments stronger than tea were served.

The children were awarded their prizes, then there was music; the adults kicked off their shoes and Mrs MacKinnon's hospitality did not falter. The toads' reckless zest for life entered into the souls of the carriers and for one evening they sang and embraced and pretended to seduce each other in a hot, bright imitation of the slippery, entwining coupling that went on through the night in the horseshoe of still, dark water.

February 1987

⌒∞⌒

Anna

'Why not invite a friend to stay? Your friends in London—they'd always be welcome, Anna. Or your sister—invite anyone you'd like.' Isabel made supper, stirring something in a saucepan.

'Rose is away. I might ask someone.' Anna was drugged with sleep, a leaden afternoon sleep that had not let her go until early evening. Her nose and hands were freezing from the chilly air of the tree house but her pregnant body throbbed like a pot-bellied stove. The tree house was still her bedroom, even now in February. Isabel had said it would be too cold through the winter but Anna piled more blankets on her mattress. She liked being able to get away from the house, from people coming and going, saying 'Hello, Anna' and patting her stomach as if it were not part of her.

She would retreat to the tree house: 'I'm tired. I think I'll go and lie down for a while.' And Isabel's visitors would give each other knowing looks and smile gently as if she were dying.

She sat on her mattress under the blankets with a hot-water bottle, reading a book or writing to Rose by the light of the lamp. With the shutters open it was too cold to sit up so she would lie pinned down by the layers of bedding, looking up through the branches at the winter sky.

When she slept there were dreams of Thomas. He was far away and she called to him with no voice, trying to move her helpless limbs. Then he was close, over her, inside her, his weight pressing down. She could feel the heat and dampness of his skin against hers, his cold breath whispered in her hair and he kissed her cheeks and neck.

But when she woke there was only her own unnatural heat under the heavy blankets and the drafts of winter air on her skin.

◆

A month or two after coming to Isabel's house, Anna wrote to her parents. The replies were slow and when they came, her mother expressed irritation that Devon was an inconvenient journey, and her father's new wife asked only about her job. Neither mentioned Thomas nor what Anna planned to do in a quiet village two hundred miles from London. It was as she'd expected.

She'd said nothing in her letters about her pregnancy; in spite of the proof of her body, somehow it did not seem possible that there would be a baby in April.

Isabel asked for no explanation and showed no interest in Anna's past life or her plans. She came to the hospital for appointments and made sure Anna ate properly, but that was all. She had drawn up the limits of their intimacy, past which she never intruded.

'I like letters better than phone calls,' said Anna once, feeling that she should offer something. 'And friendships change when your life changes. Don't you think?'

'Of course, darling,' said Isabel. 'One cannot keep everyone close.'

London was another life, and the peaceful, uncluttered progression of days with Isabel was all Anna wanted.

She found work in an office in Exeter but the journey was difficult and she was exhausted by midweek. Isabel suggested she give it up, that she should do the paperwork for the village committee instead of paying rent. It was impossible to argue. The paperwork never came to light; Anna gave up asking and gave in to sleepy, swollen idleness.

The days were easy to fill. The house was busy. People called constantly and the telephone rang. The course of village life was steered it seemed by Isabel. The sitting room was strewn with paper:

minutes, posters, fliers, lists, and in the kitchen there was endless
tea-making and committee meetings.

The old dining room with the wooden floor was, it turned out,
the village hall, and Anna became used to a procession of little
girls in leotards, giggling Brownies and scuffling Cubs through the
front door and down the hallway.

Sometimes, instead of fleeing to the tree house, she walked across
the grass to the gardener's earth house, pretending not to see small
uniformed escapees from the dining room playing down by the
river. She would sit in the dusk of the blackhouse and listen to
stories of Robert's life before coming to Cameldip. His voice was
soft like the sound of the sea, and the places he spoke of had names
like mythical kings: Oiseval, Conachair and Mullach Mor.

May 1987

❧

The River

Anna walked to the river, turning along the footpath that followed the bank to the next village. She felt heavy and tired, the day was so close even the sun could not breathe from behind the clouds. The baby slept and Anna's stomach, broad and unfamiliar, sweated where he rested against her in his sling. Her shoulder ached under the weight of the strap.

She looked at her feet walking beneath her. It was still strange to be able to see them. Each step was a thump that jarred her head. She longed to sleep but she had gone out for Isabel. Whatever was wrong did not seem to be surfacing or fading away, and leaving the house to Isabel for a few hours was the only thing Anna could think of to do.

This morning Isabel had come when she heard the baby's wails and for the first time Anna said, 'I'll do it. If you always help me, he won't know I'm his mother.' There was silence and when Anna looked up, she caught a glimpse of something like scorn in Isabel's eyes and a sourness in the patient smile. It was gone in an instant.

'Of course, darling. Call if you need me.'

Anna knew that she tried Isabel's patience like an exasperating but well-meaning child. Isabel handled the baby with a competence that made Anna ham-fisted. When Isabel held him, he settled softly in the crook of her arm, with Anna he stiffened and squirmed, his nappies fell off and he roared with fury when she tried to dress him. She would wait for Isabel to come.

Now, by the river, Anna was glad that her baby was sleeping. When she was alone she felt she could take care of him. Under the trees clouds of gnats followed them and she waved them away from the baby. She stood for a moment, the heat pressing and the silence as thick as if she were inside a room. The tunnel of trees arched high over her head, and beneath the trees the river was tortoiseshell brown. It looked cool and inviting—she would be floating, weight-less—and perhaps her body would feel like her own again, like the one that was hers in Spain a year ago.

She found a hollow on the bank and made a nest for the baby with her dress; she would watch him constantly, he would be safe for a moment. The bank was soft and gave under the weight of her feet, and she slithered into the water, unable to steady herself.

The cold took her breath away and she heard herself gasping, the only sound in the quiet. A few quick strokes and she was in the middle. She turned and saw her baby sleeping in the grass on the bank. She let her head lean back and the water take the weight of her body. She floated. There was only the sound of her own breath in her ears.

This was the feeling she'd wanted. She was light and cool and the disquiet about Isabel seemed to shrink inside until she was more Anna, filled with herself again.

She felt down with her feet but there was nothing. The velvet water flowed round her, colder then warmer on her skin, and thick with floating particles, fragments of the land on their way to the sea. She stretched out her arms, brown with sunburn, but under the water they looked bloodless white. The river stroked her like fingers along her thighs, her back, her breasts and whispered in her ears— there was nothing else, no birdsong, no sound of leaves. The canopy was as silent as a church.

Then she saw her, the child, bending over the baby, a hand outstretched towards him. Anna called out and the girl looked up, a sweet face, open and smiling, with a look of wonder and delight she must have had for the baby. But Anna was filled with panic. She started to swim but the water stretched out and the riverbank was no closer.

The child seemed not to have seen her. She knelt down beside the baby and Anna saw his tiny fist round the girl's finger, which she gently pulled away, then slipped her arms under him and lifted him onto her lap.

Still there was endless water to swim through and Anna shouted, but her voice disappeared as if it was sucked from her mouth and down into the depths of the river. The little girl did not look up again. There was a boy too, a smaller child with bare feet and a quill of hair sticking up from his blond head. He squatted down, leaning his face close to the baby.

Anna's slow arms heaved molten waves of water. It burned silver, stinging her eyes blurred. Then, as if she'd woken, there was nothing, just the leaves high overhead, layers of copper and gold and brilliant green. She was floating, looking up into the trees, out in the middle of the river, and there was the baby still asleep on the bank.

When she reached him she lay down, curling her body around his, and he woke with the wet of her hair on his face. He reached up to tug at it and she wanted to draw him back inside herself where he would always be safe. It seemed that every moment he lived was testing her, waiting to catch her out when she least expected it.

She was freezing but a quietness settled, an enormous weight of sleep that she had no will to fight. Birdsong echoed and the evening sunlight, low and bright, made her eyes close.

When Anna woke the sun had moved only a little but she felt as if she had slept for hours. Her body was numb and she felt ashamed, lying there naked by the river. The peace she had felt in the water had vanished and loneliness for Thomas flooded into her, unexpected and fierce, twisting her throat and making her stomach ache like starvation. She was a mother, a bad mother, and she was a child who was lost. And she was Anna without Thomas.

She wept for the first time since they parted almost a year ago.

∽

Josef Sevier saw her almost hidden in the long grass, and his body froze as still as hers. She was lying on the bank with her feet resting in the shallows. Strings of hair were clinging to her back and her face was pressed into the folds of cloth wrapped round a baby. The baby clutched her hair in each small fist.

Josef wanted to cover her with his jacket, but although he had come closer, he could not touch her, he could not speak. He could only watch—her pale skin, the pattern on the cloth and the tiny face of the baby. They were so still, just the smallest rise and fall of her shoulder.

He had walked along this riverbank countless hundreds of times in his life, searching, and now, late afternoon on an ordinary summer day, he had found something at last.

He came closer and the baby opened his eyes and stared peacefully into Josef's. For a moment or two they stayed like this.

The young woman stirred and Josef saw river water or tears in her eyelashes. She whispered but the words were too soft to hear. He turned and walked away without making a sound.

1958

✥

Isabel and Robert

In the afternoon they made love in the tree house. It was hot dusk inside the little cabin of baked wood. Leaves shut out the sunlight but they could hear the voices of their children playing down by the river and the tiny sounds of the sheep sighing and chewing beneath them in the shade of the tree.

When hunger made them come down, the children had already found food and brought it in from the kitchen to eat while they did some painting. Robert painted too while Isabel sat in a patch of sun, too sleepy to do anything.

And now they were alone, lying on the wooden floor. The room was chaos, the table covered with the remains of tea, cake crumbs and half-eaten biscuits, and boxes of paints, pictures still wet, crayons and brushes. The room was draped with things as if flood waters had receded leaving toys strewn around and trails of summer clothes over the furniture and the floor.

The sun still burned at five in the afternoon and they stretched out side by side next to the open garden doors. Isabel slept flat on her back, her hair spread out on the floor and her hands folded on her stomach. Robert leaned on an elbow reading a book and he stroked her face along the hairline where her skin was damp with the heat.

The children had gone outside again, back to the river, leaving their food and their pictures unfinished.

✥

Catherine held the side and Jack climbed in. He slid head first to the bottom of the boat on his stomach, into a few inches of water. He was wet almost all over but it was so hot he didn't mind.

Josef stood on the bank, uncertain. Then he squatted down pretending to look at something in the grass, not knowing whether to go back to the house and finish his painting, or go home, or play in the MacKinnon's garden by himself. But he wanted to be with Catherine so he stayed put.

He poked at the soft ground with a stick and watched a worm slide away. Catherine had tucked up her dress and she stood in the river up to her thighs steadying the boat. She was taller than Jack and climbed in more easily than he.

Josef tried not to watch but he knew what they were doing and he wished he could be in the boat too.

1958

◦❈◦

Sarah

The night bell had never rung before. It was very faint, ringing in the doctor's bedroom, but it woke Sarah. She sat up, listening for his door to open. When the bell rang for the second time she put on her dressing gown and went downstairs.

A man with a child in his arms stood on the step in the white circle of the porch light. He was tall and broad-shouldered and he filled the doorway. Sarah stepped back. She had thought of telling him that she would fetch the doctor but her voice said nothing.

For a moment it seemed he might speak, then he pushed past her and into the study, and as she pressed back out of his way, Sarah caught a rank cold smell from his sodden clothing.

She watched him through the open door. He sat down heavily in the doctor's armchair with the child on his lap. She seemed to be sleeping and he settled her head against his shoulder very gently so as not to disturb her, then took the hand that hung down at her side and held it against his own chest. He did not look at Sarah. After she opened the door when she thought his eyes were asking her something, he seemed to have forgotten her.

A dark stain spread on the cloth behind his shoulders and on the arms of the chair. Drops of water from his black hair trickled over his face and into the soaked hair of the child. Her cotton dress clung to her legs, streaked with mud and leaves.

The room was soft blackness, only a blur of yellow from the little reading lamp. It sparkled where it fell on the wetness of the man's skin and the shoulders of his jacket and the child's hair. It lit up the reds and golds in the hearthrug, making them deep and warm, and little caves of glowing coal shifted and settled and pulsed in their last burning.

There was the smallest movement as the man breathed, and the child's head dropped little by little against him. When he lifted her chin, this time Sarah saw that her eyes were open but she seemed not to see or hear anything.

Sarah came closer. She was concerned for the little girl; it was not good to be in wet things and she must be cold. But something made Sarah unable to speak. The silence of the man stopped her own throat—his eyes had told her. She was caught with them inside the little sphere of light. The man rested his face against the child's head and closed his eyes and the moments were sliding longer and longer, smooth and even as the slow beating of wings.

The man was sleeping. Sarah need only be still.

But suddenly his body convulsed with a shiver that made him cry out and he opened his eyes with a look of bewilderment as if he did not know where he was. The anguish in his eyes held Sarah fixed and mute and she thought her heart would stop under the weight of it. It was a stone on her chest pressing the breath out of her.

But something seeped up through the frozen moments; the dozens of days and nights that she had looked after her sisters and brothers brought her life back to her.

She took off her dressing gown and spread it over them both. She tucked it round the girl's cold legs and up over the shoulder of the man. Then she kissed them both, the child's forehead and the man's cheek, and closed the door softly behind her.

January 1988

Isabel

It is thirty years since I held my husband's hand. But he takes it now in his and holds it so quietly in spite of all I did and said to him, and we look together at the place where our children drowned.

My mind is silent but full of pictures: my own feet running beneath me in pointed white shoes or in boots, or bare, running along the muddy path where we are standing now. I run past this place knowing I will find them, and I pull them from the water and into my arms, both of them.

They call me and I come to them. And if I run fast enough those hours will not happen, that night will be left behind like the tail of a comet, dust that is lost in the black of nowhere, and I am scorching bright, alive again.

But how could I know I ran past them? That all the time they were in this place under the trees and not down the river caught floating by a fallen branch.

When I ran he would hold me, but I spat in his face and fought him till he let me go. We stand now, the two of us, and we look: the carcass of a boat hauled black and rotten from the riverbed. The bottom has gone but two seats, one in the prow and one halfway, still span the little hull.

There are no words inside me and I am glad my husband is here. I have not held his hand for thirty years.

July 1987

∞

Anna

Josef Sevier was gardening while his horses sunned themselves on the lawn. They were an immense, glossy sculpture, and even lying down their heads could reach his shoulder. But now Vreneli's nose was only just above the grass. She rested on folded legs, her eyes closed, and with each breath a little circle of daisies flattened, then straightened up for a moment or two before being flattened again by the next long, scented gust from above. Her tail fanned out on the grass, a yard of frayed rope, and her coat shone like a conker.

Martha was flat on her side with her back against Vreneli. Martha's huge belly exposed its thinly covered underside where the delicate grey skin showed through. Her legs stretched out with the four silver shoes resting on the lawn in a line of good luck. She was black, as black as her beautiful eyes. Her cheek rested on the grass and she blinked at an ant's eye view of the world.

Josef dug a patch of earth. There was little to do in the garden in high summer but he could find work for himself at any time of the year.

He sowed some lines of lettuce and spinach, and he thought of the young woman with the baby he had seen by the river. He'd seen her again this morning, walking across his garden with her baby asleep in a pushchair.

She moved cautiously, secretively, as if the baby might wake and give her away.

∞

Anna opened the garden gate and wheeled the pushchair across the grass. She did not expect to meet anyone. Every time she walked past on her way to the river, except for the horses, the place was deserted.

Rose had written in one of her letters: 'I've looked up your Cameldip in the AA guide and it says that all you have is a "dilapidated but remarkable Art Nouveau aviary in the gardens of the local pub, unspecified opening, no stars, no food, fine wines".'

Anna stood at the doorway of the aviary. One iron door sagged off its hinges. At first her eyes could make out little. There was a dry whirring of wings above her in the shadows and from time to time birds swooped in and out through the open doorway. A hen clucked softly and scratched at the floor somewhere off in the darkness. Columns of sunlight came through holes in the roof, cutting funnels in the darkness filled with sparkling motes of dust.

As her eyes adjusted to the gloom she saw that she stood in a space the size of a small church. The walls were an avenue of iron saplings with the texture of bark cast into the metal. The branches fanned out and joined like espaliered fruit trees, arching up and over to meet at the ridge of the roof more than twenty feet above her. The roof glowed a rich, deep brown. It was an old tarpaulin lit up by the sunlight outside and it covered the arched iron roof, coming down to a ragged edge where the trees and plants in the garden grew so close that the foliage reached inside. Between the iron branches there was fine wire mesh, almost invisible, that must once have made the captive birds feel free.

The gable walls were tiled with scenes of ferns, curling leaves and huge exotic flowers. The straw-scattered floor was mosaic, as intricate as a Persian palace, but there were patches of bare, dry earth where pieces were worn away. Rust bled through the white paint of the ironwork and tiles were missing from the walls. At one end were bales of straw, some dusty harness and sacks of feed.

The horses stood nose to tail in the shadows, flicking flies from each other's faces. They turned when they heard Anna's footsteps and she held out her hands to them, palms upwards. They dipped their great, heavy heads and snuffed and blew at her, brushing her skin with their muzzles and mouthing her fingers with gentle, bristly lips.

She stroked their bony faces and their heads dropped little by little until she could feel their breath on her feet.

She had left the baby in his pushchair by the door and for once he had not cried when he woke. He gazed spellbound at the glittering pillars of sunlight.

When she left, as she passed the house Anna glanced up at the windows, but as usual there was no one.

✑

'I looked at the aviary yesterday. Isabel? You know, behind the pub?' Anna was feeding the baby while Isabel unpacked shopping onto the kitchen table. 'It must have been very beautiful before it got so run down. Why is it there? It seems such an odd place for it.'

'I hardly remember now.' Isabel read labels and ticked things off a list.

'Why is the pub always closed?'

'I didn't know it was. Surely not.' Isabel didn't seem to be listening. She took foil-wrapped leftovers from the refrigerator and dropped them in the bin. 'Is this off do you think?' she said holding something out to Anna. Anna sniffed and nodded.

'The pub's never open when I've walked past,' Anna said. 'There's never anyone around. The pub is never open,' she said again.

'I'm not sure. I rarely speak to Josef,' said Isabel vaguely, holding a tin at arm's length and peering over her reading glasses.

Anna watched her putting things in cupboards and felt the familiar closing down of attention, Isabel dismissing her. Anna knew she should not go on, it would be an intrusion, but on impulse she said: 'Doesn't he have a family, or friends?'

To her surprise, Isabel turned instantly. She looked irritated, angry, but pained too, as if her head hurt and Anna's voice was too loud.

'I've no idea what Josef Sevier does with his time.' The baby stopped feeding, arching his body away from Anna, stiff and furious in a second. The noise he made filled the kitchen and Isabel winced, turning back to her tidying.

'Oh, poor darling,' she said in her usual voice, 'I expect he's tired. The sun will make him sleep. I'd take him into the garden, Anna.'

It made no difference if she tried or not, it was always the same— Isabel was irritated or bored after a moment or two of conversation. Anna lifted the baby to her shoulder and went outside.

She walked slowly across the grass. The baby made little singing moans. She stroked his back and felt him flopping into sleep with the movement of her walking, and she went on wandering down towards the river and the gardener's house. Robert was up on the grass roof, checking the net and ropes that held the turf in place.

'Can I come up?' Anna said.

'Of course.' Robert held out his hands for the baby and Anna felt grateful for his ease with her and her son. She climbed up the stone steps set into the wall of the house and they sat side by side on the grass roof. She'd not expected Robert to settle the baby in his arms.

He did not make conversation and Anna thought how like her father he was; maybe the same age, kind but remote and inaccessible as if he was always a step back inside himself. He would never be caught out by an unwanted emotion or an irrational thought.

After a while she said, 'I won't ever go back to London.'

'I've not lived in a city.'

'They're mean, exhausting places.'

'All places can be that,' Robert said.

'This garden is very beautiful, more like a park, parkland that's cared for but natural.'

'I stop it returning to its natural state, keep it in check, that's all. Sometimes I wonder if I shouldn't.'

Crickets buzzed in the grass on the riverbank. A blackbird was singing.

'Robert, do you know anything about the aviary behind the pub?'

'It used to house poultry. That was years ago.'

'It seems odd to build it there.'

'It came from the big house at Penquit. When the house was demolished the aviary was sold along with everything else. It was taken down and rebuilt piece by piece by Josef's father. That must be thirty years ago.'

'And Josef Sevier—is that his name? Why does he not bother about it, or the pub? And why does he have those horses? Isabel seems not to like him.'

'Isabel hardly knows him. The pub isn't important to him, he does other things, importing wine. His family has vineyards. And the horses—I'm sure he'd tell you the story himself.'

'I've never spoken to him,' said Anna. What she really wanted to ask was about Isabel, but the question was not clear in her mind. She leaned closer to stroke her baby's face as he slept against Robert. She liked seeing him in a man's arms.

The afternoon was warm and the sheep had packed themselves in the arc of shade under the tree house. From time to time Anna caught the faint subtle smell of the river at their backs, sharp and delicate as a cat.

Suddenly she saw Isabel watching them. She stood at the kitchen door. How long she had been there, Anna didn't know, and she wondered if Robert had seen. She looked up at him, feeling confused. Isabel did not call out or beckon to him as she usually did. For no reason she could name Anna pulled her hand away from the baby as if she were guilty.

Robert's eyes met Isabel's across the expanse of garden, steady and impassive. Isabel turned and disappeared into the house.

'I'm sorry,' said Anna. 'I'm keeping you from your work.'

'You need not apologize,' said Robert. 'It does not concern you.'

August 1987

Isabel and Robert

'Isabel, there's something I think we should talk about.'

'Oh, really. Do you.' Isabel sat at the kitchen table, surrounded by papers. She did not look up when Robert spoke.

'Isabel.'

'I have more than enough to do at this minute, Robert.' She settled her spectacles on her nose and began to write.

'It won't take long.'

She pretended to be engrossed but he could see her hesitating, trying to fix her concentration on the words. Robert leaned over the table. He put his hand on the piece of paper, stopping her pen.

'Don't. Please.' She sat back, looking at the paper until he moved his hand and she began writing again, but he could feel her willing him to go away. He stood for a moment, undecided, looking at the top of Isabel's grey head bent over her work. He knew the line of her parting and the set of her chin, and he knew that she would be biting her lip as she wrote. It was not too late, he could still pull back, but he said: 'I know this is difficult, Isabel.'

'It's not in the slightest bit difficult, just inconvenient. Is that too hard to understand?'

The joints of her fingers holding the pen had whitened and he could see the nib pressing too hard into the paper. It was an ageing hand. The knuckles had thickened and the veins knotted like string. Robert remembered wanting to soothe her once but he did not feel it now.

'Well? Just say whatever it is you can't wait to say, Robert, and
then let me get on with this. I don't want a speech.'

'I think we should talk about Anna.'

'There is nothing to say about Anna.'

'It won't go away, Isabel, just because we don't talk about it.
We've tried that before.'

Isabel put her pen to the paper again and Robert waited, knowing she would answer eventually. She said, 'There's nothing to talk
about because I'm not interested. Isn't that clear?'

'You're being unfair, and you're wrong, Isabel. She's done nothing.'

Now she looked up. 'I know you. You see I know you so well,
and there's no point in discussing this. I refuse to discuss it. I don't
care enough to blame her. Why should I care? She's just the next
one.'

Robert almost smiled. His body felt weak with age and sluggish,
as if the air had weight and the pull of the earth was increasing with
the years, slowly dragging him under. The thought of a lover,
anyone, least of all pale, chubby Anna, no older than a daughter,
was hard to take seriously. And anyway, for weeks he had thought
only of Isabel. He could feel the disturbance in her like static that
crackled constantly in his own head, fuzzing his thoughts and
putting his nerves on edge until he couldn't bear it any more.

'There's no next one,' he said. It was like balancing in the dark
with no way to judge safety.

'Just leave me alone, Robert. I can't be bothered to hear you lying
to me.'

'There is no next one,' he said again even though he knew they
had reached the edge and it was reckless.

'Shall I list them? Shall I? It's in you, you can't help yourself.'
Isabel was standing now, facing him.

'There's no list.'

'Why do you always pick on every word as if it matters? Your
quibbling just makes it worse.'

'She tries so hard, Isabel. Can't you see how she wants you to like her? There's no need to punish her.'

They stared at each other and Robert saw Isabel struggle. 'Don't blame her for her baby,' he said. 'She can't know it hurts you.' He had taken a chance, but it came too late.

'Hurts me? She's ridiculous. She's no idea what it means. She has no idea how to care for a child.'

'And just how should she care for her child—as we did ours?' Anger sparked in him for a second, and he regretted it. Not for Isabel but because 'we' and 'ours' cut his own heart. Isabel's hands clenched, screwing up the paper she had been writing on and she winced, holding the table as if she were unsteady. For a moment he wanted to hold her; he wished he could turn and leave.

'What I did is past. What happened was an accident. We couldn't have known. It was an accident.' He had said these words a thousand times but she never heard him, and couldn't hear him now. 'Anna is lonely, that's all. She brings her child to my house to talk. You don't talk to her now. I know what's happening, and she doesn't understand.'

'Oh, I see. Oh, forgive me. How I misjudge her. How I misjudge you both.' Isabel was shaking with the effort of self-control. She said, 'Can't you leave it? It doesn't matter, I don't care.' Suddenly she looked tired, her face sagged and she sat down heavily. 'Why do you do this to me? Over and over again? Do whatever you want. I don't care, leave me alone. Just go away.'

There was a pause but now there was no way out. He had woken her from the numbness she had nearly perfected and the rage would be as new and fresh as something preserved in ice. He could not stop it now. He did not want to.

'I'm sorry, Isabel. I can't undo what happened.' An apology, a hair's breadth from saying her name; it tempted him, on his tongue, on his lips: 'I am sorry, Isabel. I'm sorry, for Sarah.'

He saw Isabel flinch with the shock of the name spoken aloud, as if it burned her, then gone—snuffed out with the satisfaction of hearing him confess. She was on her feet again and her eyes were shining with spite; this is what he knew, the callous fury. Robert stepped back but the fear was exhilarating like falling.

She shouted in his face, 'You disgust me, our children are your punishment. You deserved it. You made it happen. It's better they never knew you, they would have despised you. Your weakness and your lying. They would have loathed you as I do.'

He could not look at her. She knew he was sorry but she had always known he didn't regret it.

'Hardly older than our daughter. That's what you always wanted, wasn't it, a child, a little girl. A stupid little girl to cry to. A skinny little Catholic skivvy. Anyone would do except me, even an empty-headed French doll.'

'No Isabel, not Adelie. She loved you. You spoiled that, not me.'

'Oh, of course. Me, of course. Ugly, stupid me. It was my fault. I spoil everything, I kill everything.'

'Don't Isabel. You know that isn't true.'

'Pretty little girls, that's what you like isn't it? Even now that's what you like and it always was.' A slow, sly smile. Isabel watched him, measuring her words. 'Why did you bother—we had Catherine if that's what you wanted. Or maybe you did.'

The words did not shock him, their damage had long since worn away and he hardly heard them. He was watching Isabel's hands. She turned her ring round and round and the diamond sparkled under her fingers. It had been a long time, years, but he remembered it would tear his skin. This was the only time they touched.

At the beginning he would hold her wrists, or hold her against him and she would spit and claw, their faces close as wrestlers. When they fell to the floor Isabel wept with fury, the breath squeezed out of her under his weight, and she dug her fingernails into his face or her own, it did not matter. In those days she was strong and almost a match for him. He pinned her down with his body, turning his face away for safety, and with her lips to his ear she whispered nonsense and obscenities in a voice he did not know. She hissed and chortled like a demon in his head.

Sometimes she made a sound so loud it terrified him, like the roar of an animal. The tendons in her neck stood out like wires under the skin and her lips split raw at their edges. As if it were too immense to be contained in her body the sound went on and on until she was exhausted, all the breath gone and her face smeared with blood and spittle. She would lie silently in his arms with her hair spread out on the floor, damp with sweat.

After a while, maybe hours, he would shift his weight to lie beside her, still wary but letting go to wipe her face and pull together his shirt ripped open or her torn dress. Her face and neck and breasts were scratched with her own fingernails or the buttons and buckles on his clothes. She gazed at him as if she did not know who he was and he kissed her, said the names of their children and that he loved her.

'They're gone Isabel. They're gone.'

She always defeated him. He could not bear the indifference in her eyes as if she saw nothing when she looked at him—it was worse than grief, worse than hatred. Eventually he let her go.

She would spring up, wrecked and triumphant, and run out of the house across the grass to the river and he knew that he would find her there whatever time of day or night he went to look for her.

After a while he did not try to hold her or stop her fists. It was a just punishment and of no account any more. He was mesmerized by the viciousness of her words and could not feel any pain.

Now after years, half their lifetimes, it happened rarely—and when it did, there was an emptiness to their fights like reflexes after death. Robert had said his lines for so long they were meaningless; what they made was a thread going back into the past, that was all. He thought of Isabel's anger as a relic, a fragment broken off, displaced but still perfect, which she would unwrap from time to time, struggling to restore its lost meaning.

They had less and less reason to fight, less even to speak. They were bound together so tightly there was no need to acknowledge each other at all. But from time to time Robert disturbed their nullified lives—he roused Isabel's fury, sometimes deliberately, sometimes carelessly; it was the only time he saw the person he had loved, their children existed again, and because of this he needed it.

1958

Sarah

The day after the man, Robert MacKinnon, came to the house with his daughter, Sarah did not get up.

The line of sunlight appeared as usual between the curtains and the white stripe slanted across the floor, but Sarah did not want to leave her bedroom. The great flopping flowers on the bedroom wallpaper were so intricate and beautiful that she needed to study them carefully. She did this until her eyes ached and she had to close them for a while. When she looked again, the light on the floorboards had moved.

Sarah heard voices downstairs.

Later the doctor brought food to her. He looked into her face intently as if he doubted it was really her. He put his cool hand on her forehead.

'Stay here today, my dear. You should sleep if you can.'

'I'm sorry about the children.' The words came out of her mouth even though she had not known she was thinking them.

The doctor patted her hand and got up from the side of her bed.

'It's I who should be sorry,' he said absently, as if it were a thought she could not hear. Sarah did not understand but her voice had sunk down inside her again and she could not ask.

She lay in bed and the sun moved across the room. It could have taken weeks or minutes. It was dusk.

She did not put on the bedside lamp but watched the wallpaper flowers darken to black, then she closed her eyes and slept.

❦

The next morning Sarah got up. Her legs were weak, as if she had been ill. The doctor was already in the kitchen. He stood at the sink with his shirt sleeves rolled up and Sarah noticed that he was not wearing a collar nor had he shaved. He looked tired and very old.

'What happened?' she asked. She had not meant to, but her thoughts and her voice were muddled.

'We will talk in the study, Sarah my dear,' he said. 'I like the morning sunshine in there.' They sat one on each side of the desk as if they were having a professional discussion. The doctor seemed to find it hard to begin and he turned his fountain pen over and over in his fingers.

'I am so sorry you were alone when Robert came,' he said. Sarah shook her head to tell him that it did not matter. She tried to concentrate on his face but she was distracted by the armchair and the hearthrug and the lamp all looking so innocent now as if nothing had happened.

'My dear Sarah, such a terrible thing. Such a terrible thing I have to tell you.' The doctor's eyes were more watery than usual.

There's no need, dear Doctor. There's no need to say. What does it matter now?

'The children—the child you saw and her brother—died last night. Robert was looking for me, but I had already gone.' The doctor watched his hands turning the pen and Sarah watched them too.

'I had gone to Adelie or I would have seen him. He was bringing Catherine to me and I wasn't here.'

The words did not make sense. Sarah listened to the clock ticking, a loud tick then a soft tick like a heartbeat.

'I am sorry. I am a little tired,' the doctor said. Sarah saw that his hands had webs of lilac veins and nails like thick white shells.

You are too tired to talk. You must sleep now and forget.

'Adelie Sevier telephoned me. Little Josef had come home but somehow the others weren't missed. It was very late and you were in bed. I didn't wake you. Xavier and Robert were searching. I went to help—other people turned out too.'

Sarah had forgotten the ticking of the clock. She listened to the doctor's words, each one separate and slow. Time stretched out elastic as dough just as it had in the room with Robert MacKinnon and his dead daughter.

It will go on and on forever. It will never end.

'I called at the house to see if Adelie needed me. And then I saw Xavier and some other men by the river as they found Jack. It was too late. We brought him here together, Xavier and I.' He paused again, longer this time. 'They'd already found Catherine.'

The doctor put down the pen and he looked directly at Sarah.

'I should have passed Robert on the path,' he said. 'If I'd not called on Adelie, I would have met him, perhaps it would still have been possible … They found her first, you see. Perhaps our little Catherine …' He was asking Sarah something with his eyes, searching in her for something.

'It was too late,' she said. 'I knew as soon as I saw her. You couldn't have saved her, it was too late.' She kept her eyes steady, not looking away until the doctor did.

'My dear Sarah.' His hands were clenched together on the desk. He spread them flat and breathed deeply in, as if bringing himself back to the present.

⁕

The fire crackled and a November wind rattled the windows. The sitting room was lit with yellow lamplight and the bleak white light from an overhead bulb that Edward needed for reading. Sarah's face burned with the heat from the fire, and icy drafts chilled her feet. She was listening to *Evening Storytime* on the Home Service. The wireless rasped and whistled not quite on the wavelength: 'Teeny's happiness was short-lived when she heard that Tony Avaford was to marry her lovely cousin Althea. It was to be announced at a grand dinner party given by Mrs Purseglove …'

Edward let the newspaper drape over his knees and picked up his teacup from the arm of the chair.

'What from America?' said Sarah. She leaned over and switched off the wireless. 'I'm sorry, I didn't hear you.'

'These bombs, nuclear they call them.'

'Would you like more tea?' said Sarah.

'It can't be necessary. It can't be right.' Edward held up his newspaper again, tetchily flicking out the creases to turn the page.

There was quiet for a while and Sarah picked up her book. It was one of Joséphine's. The effort of understanding French was too much this evening and the words were nothing more than strings of letters.

She had come across a bookmark, an Easter card made by the child, Josef, the small silent boy who sometimes came to the house. The card was coloured with crayons and on the front was a picture of something that looked like a birdcage with hens inside. Above it was written, *Happy Easter to Tante Joséphine from your Josef I hope you are feeling better soon.'*

The first time she met the boy Sarah offered to look after him while Edward and his father talked. She held out her hand but he would not take it, putting his hands deep in his pockets as if to keep them safe from her. He stood at the kitchen door watching, and his violet eyes followed her. He must be about seven, the age of her youngest brother, and Sarah was happy to have a reminder of home even if this silent, bleak-faced child was nothing like Michael. She talked to Josef and gave him biscuits, but he never spoke until maybe the third or fourth visit when suddenly he said: 'You smell like Mama.'

Sarah could not help smiling.

'I hope that's good,' she said. 'I expect we like the same soap.'

'Joséphine kept the sugar in the blue tin, not that one.' Josef took a step into the kitchen.

'That's what I'll do too then,' said Sarah.

He came and stood beside her and peered into the sink while she peeled potatoes.

'Joséphine made lemon biscuits with real lemons in.'

'They sound delicious.'

'I'm called Josef after Joséphine,' he when on, encouraged by his own bravery.

'It's a very special thing to be named after someone. It means that you will always be very special to them, wherever they are.'

'Yes,' said Josef, 'wherever they are.' But his voice wavered as if the sound of it suddenly unnerved him. Sarah instinctively held out her arms to comfort him. He fled.

⌒∞⌒

Josef's father, a Frenchman, Xavier, brought Edward a case of wine sometimes.

Xavier was not much taller than Sarah, and even though he could not yet be forty, his waist was beginning to thicken and his black hair was greying at the temples. Sarah liked Xavier's broad, hand-some face—a good-natured face, trusting and trustworthy, she thought. When she opened the door, he would raise his battered hat and shake her hand, at once deferential and self-assured.

Josef's mother never came with them. Edward pointed to a photograph on the mantelpiece of a pretty blond woman in white, holding a newborn baby.

'Adelie and little Josef,' he said smoothing the dust off the picture and Sarah could hear the pride in his voice. 'She does not visit much now that Joséphine has gone.'

It was the picture Sarah had seen the first day she came to Cameldip, when she'd wandered through the doctor's house, never thinking that this place would feel like home and the baby was a child she would come to know.

Each time Josef and his father said goodbye, Edward patted the boy on the back or shook his hand in a man-to-man way. Josef's troubled eyes would clear and he looked shy and pleased, smiling one of his rare smiles for Edward.

The three of them, Xavier, Edward and Sarah smiled too over Josef's head as if they were united by a feeling of reassurance and relief.

But we are all thinking of Catherine and Jack, Sarah thought. When we look at Josef we are thinking of them and he pretends for our sakes that he does not know. He pretends for us he has forgotten.

She wondered how his child's mind could defend itself if it was besieged with memories as hers was. His memories would be worse perhaps. And they would become heavier as time passed, not easier to bear.

Sarah sometimes felt her mind had turned against her. She wondered if it was the same for Josef—scraps of the past spliced with the present, scenes lit up like magnesium flashes in front of the eyes, obliterating whatever was solid and real as if it were nothing. Over and over she sorted the fragments, fitted the scenes together in their proper order and calculated their worth, and over and over they slipped into chaos.

Perhaps he could forget. Perhaps his child's mind could do what hers could not. But even if he could forget, the feeling of that night would be rooted inside him like the scent of his mother and the taste of lemon biscuits.

⁐

And on this November evening Sarah thought about it all as she had a hundred times. She pretended to read but in her head it was that night again.

It was hot and airless, and it was difficult to sleep. But she had slept because the night bell woke her. There was Robert with the little girl. It seemed like a dream, as if she had not really woken at all.

The second time she was disturbed by voices, and from the top of the stairs she saw the doctor and the Frenchman, Xavier, coming into the house. Xavier was carrying a small boy. The boy wore blue shorts. His sunburned legs were stocky, the knees rounded with childish plumpness. A lock of hair stuck up from his dark-blond head.

In the back of her mind she knew something terrible had happened, but she went back to her room and switched off the light just as she had before.

Then there was the sound of the front door again and Sarah got up for the third time.

'We don't need anything just now, my dear,' the doctor called up to her. Sarah could see a tall, golden-skinned woman in a summer dress standing in the light of the porch. Her cheeks were livid pink as if the sun had burned her and her hair was loose, to her waist, golden red. The woman's eyes flickered up to Sarah then back to the open study door where the doctor stood waiting. She hesitated then walked past him into the study, gracefully and purposefully like a dancer. The door closed behind her. Sarah heard nothing more.

And inside the room she could see, even though she was not there: the doctor in his dark suit and tie, always neat however quickly he dressed, however serious the emergency. There was the woman, Isabel, and Xavier, and the boy, Jack. And there was Robert sitting in the doctor's armchair with Catherine in his arms. The little girl rested against him with her hand in his.

And now, a year later, Sarah knew. She knew what it was to do this, to be close to him with her hand in his.

Her stomach tightened with a feeling that was anguish and shame and excitement. The Sisters had warned that the flesh is temptation from day one of womanhood (more so entirely for men—but they need less purity). And they warned Sarah in particular of becoming bold, of neglecting to discipline her mind and heart against the underhand ways of the Devil. Now she knew why.

Even though she was careful, even though she did not feel it, she must be sly and wanton. How could something begin with the darkest, saddest memory then twist itself with smirking cunning into a feeling like sparkling light? Butterflies fluttered in her throat and she pressed her lips together to keep her heart quiet. She let the book rest on her lap and closed her eyes to hide from Edward, not daring to move or he would look up and see her face and know. He must have sensed something. The newspaper crackled down again on to his lap and he peered over his reading glasses.

'Sarah dear, you're very quiet this evening.'

'I'm tired. I'm not sure why,' she said, making herself yawn. She could see concern in his eyes and she looked away, closing her book.

'It must be tedious sometimes,' he said. 'Living in so quiet a place with a dull old man.'

'No, Edward! I love being with you—you are the most lovely company I've ever known.'

'Sarah, my sweet girl, I wasn't fishing for compliments. I just wonder sometimes if there's anything … anything amiss?'

'What do you mean?' she asked.

'I wonder if you would feel able to come to me if you were worried perhaps, or unhappy.'

'I'm not worried,' said Sarah. 'And I'm very happy.' Unexpectedly the butterflies in her throat began to hurt and her eyes smarted. She opened her book again, pretending to read.

Edward folded the newspaper and put his spectacles in their case. He said carefully: 'It has been a … a difficult time, a sad time since you came here. I'm so sorry my dear.' Sarah stared at the words on the page. He added gently, 'Perhaps even more difficult than I realize.' There was no disapproval, only kindness in his voice and she wanted so much to tell him, to ask him what she should do. But it was impossible.

'You are a generous-hearted and capable young woman, Sarah,' he said. 'I have been so very fortunate to have you here. But don't imagine you have to look after me all the time. Sometimes perhaps you might lean on me a little.'

'What do you mean?' she said again.

'Forgive me. Forgive me if I intrude where I shouldn't. I say this only because I care for you both, but I wonder … I wonder if perhaps you are more … more concerned for Robert than you need be … more than he should expect you to be.'

'We just go for walks, that's all.' She could hear herself sounding indignant. 'He never expects anything. He makes *me* happy. Everyone thinks of her but she isn't the only one to be sad, she isn't the …'

'Sarah, Sarah, I know, I know. Hush, I don't criticize you or Robert. Isabel cannot find comfort anywhere. She cannot find sense in anything but anger. She blames us all—most of all herself. It's you I am concerned about. I worry for you.'

'There's nothing to worry about.'

'It's good to have faith in love, and you have the boundless compassion of youth. But are you sure?'

'There's nothing to be sure about,' said Sarah. 'I don't love him and I'm not that young anyway, I'm eighteen.' The doctor could not help smiling and Sarah had the grace to smile too.

'We only go for walks.'

Edward regarded her with his mild, kind eyes as if she had reassured him. She had to look away.

After a while he said, 'I'll say one last thing, then I promise I will stop interfering. Robert feels everything is lost, even Isabel—that's how it seems for now. You are … you are very young, Sarah. Life is kind and forgiving through your eyes and we all long for a glimpse of the world as you see it. Forgive me, I'm making no sense at all.'

Sarah looked at her feet. The doctor did not understand anything: life might be kind but lies and slack morals did not go unpunished.

'He doesn't. We don't,' she said, crossing her fingers.

'I know, I know. Robert is a fine, honest man, and I know how much he loves Isabel. I wonder how he endures, how Isabel endures, such loss. But it's you I worry for in this. You are—to me you are …' the doctor's eyes were watery, 'you were like a gift from Joséphine. I could not bear to see you hurt. There. Finished. I'll say no more.'

PART III

1930

Robert

Three peaks: Oiseval, Conachair and Mullach Mhor. Giant tilts of naked rock and rough slopes cut off sheer at the sea as if the land had been chopped with a spade. The pasture edges leaned sickening drops over sucking waves and waited for a sheep or dog or a careless child to forget for a moment.

The houses were a single row, an arc of stone crofts with their backs against the rock and their faces to the Atlantic. Even in the summer there were raw mists, but this day in August was clear.

Robert's mother closed the door. She did not lock it or look round for things they'd forgotten—there would be no one to come in after they'd gone and help themselves to the pots and pictures and furniture they did not take with them. Some people had sold their belongings to souvenir hunters but his father said he would rather give their things to the mice. His mother had laughed, but her eyes were not laughing.

'Say goodbye to your home, children.'

Robert did not feel sad. He was ten. He thought their lives would be better.

The sheep and cattle had gone before. The cows were made to swim behind the boats in which their young had been taken hostage. The calves splayed sea-legs in the rowing boats and stared at the horned faces in the water. At the ship they were hoisted aboard and the children thought it was funny to see cows being fished from the sea.

Now it was their turn to go. Everyone gathered on the pier, sitting on rolls of tweed and bags of feathers which could be sold to help begin their new lives. The children had bundles of things to take care of on the journey. There were a few fleeces and some wool already spun into yarn for knitting, and Robert carried the hand loom which his mother said would always be useful.

When everyone was on board, the children wanted to look back as they sailed out of the bay. They were excited, but the old people were sad and could not look. The parents did not seem interested and kept their eyes forward to the horizon in the east.

It was the last time. The last time Robert did not feel ashamed of his broad bare feet. The last time he spoke his own language without self-consciousness. It was the last time he felt safe in his parents' keeping.

There were clouds around the peak of Conachair. From under the clouds empty pastures tipped down to cliffs, specked all over with thousands and thousands of birds. The gannets and fulmars were rising and wheeling and screaming—for the first time in a thousand years they had Hirta to themselves. The sea heaved slopes of granite green and the boat left a furrow of white longer and longer then disappearing till nothing joined it to the land they'd left.

Robert did not think then that his home was beautiful but he knew now that it was.

⌒∞⌒

St Kilda was cleared of its people. The three dozen had become an embarrassment in these modern times, an affront to the bright new century. They were amusing oddities, and tourists would cross the fifty miles of mountainous Atlantic simply to send a letter with the island postmark. But this had ceased to justify them. The authorities were shamed by the dying babies, the wild, barefoot children and the stubborn, resilient people; if they had given in it would have been simple. It was decided that the remnants must be moved for their own improvement.

They were persuaded with promises of a wider horizon—not the kind they had known, an unbroken seam of sea and sky, a giant hoop around them—but a horizon, it was explained, wider in more important ways: health and comfort and education. They were willing to trust in the wisdom of people who knew about these things, feeling sure that their shoes were proof of their honesty.

On the mainland they were scattered. In time they would adjust, be absorbed and become indistinguishable from true Scottish men and women and children.

At first the St Kildans did not know how strange they were, although they could see and hear their difference. They fitted badly into the lives allotted them, as did their feet into the shoes they were given. Both were gifts of charity that they had not learned the humility to be grateful for; both made them sullen and uncomfortable.

When Robert's family was sent to an estate inland, their things were put in a lorry with a ragged canvas top. The children knew it was for sheep and pigs going to market or to slaughter, and they scrambled in, bleating and honking and shrieking in delight. There was not much to load but their mother watched all the time, counting her possessions, knowing that with each move something was always lost.

The children leaned out over the back of the lorry, thrown around by the thump and judder of the wheels in the potholes. They saw the sea's horizon creep higher as the road climbed. The sea could be relied upon; whether you stood in the waves on the shore or climbed to the peak of a mountain, the sea's horizon aligned with your own eyes. It knew where you were.

And the sea made an edge, a frontier that measured your place on the land so the whole world could be seen in your head. When he'd run and played on St Kilda, Robert could circle above it in his mind, seeing everyone he knew. He did not understand how a person could be lost until he lost sight and sound and smell of the sea. When the lorry turned inland he thought he must memorize all the things he passed, but soon he could not piece it all together. He could not be sure he had each bend in the road, each valley and hill in the right order. He was adrift in the land.

This was the first time in his life Robert MacKinnon knew that the world was bigger than he could imagine.

They were lucky to be housed together as a family. The estate was large enough to employ them all. It was a strange place—there was land in every direction as far as the eye could see, mountains along the horizon and miles of heather and gorse. The herds of grazing animals might be mammoths or yaks, because that was the nearest picture in Robert's *Wildlife of the World* book. There were forests full of tiny cheeping birds, creeping insects and shy, fur-covered creatures with the eyes of seals and branches growing from their heads. *Sparrow, Thrush, Bee, Butterfly, Earwig, Deer*: Robert identified them. He was an explorer in an exotic, teeming land.

There was a river. He envied the river because it knew the way to the sea.

And it was here that he saw a tree for the first time. He was twelve years old. At home on St Kilda, trees had been a puzzle that the pictures in his schoolbooks could not explain. The lumps of driftwood he and his friends fished from the sea were a clue to the mystery. They hauled them out and carried them home for examination, excited and proud as if they were the bones of rare sea creatures.

When they came to Scotland there were coastal trees, gnarled and stunted by the Hebridean winds. But here the trees rose up to the sky and whispered and breathed like a gentle sea. He could not believe what he saw—oaks and pines higher than a barn. It was as if he'd discovered a daisy or a buttercup as tall as himself. And the trunk—he imagined it sinking down through the earth and spreading an upside-down tree of white roots, a ghost mirror of the green one above. Until then he had known only soil a few inches deep, and it was like discovering ships on an ocean when there had been only gnats on a pond. He climbed any tree he could. To be up in the branches inside a swaying, creaking boat of leaves was wonderful to him. Trees were his discovery and his consolation.

He was aware of his parents' suffering; his father's humiliation at being instructed through each day's work with less civility than he would give a collie, and his mother's diminishing strength. She became thinner and thinner, not because food was scarce but because she had no taste for the dry, insipid meat people ate here and no taste for a life in which she was despised.

His anxiety for his parents was a rash beneath the skin, troubling him constantly but only occasionally breaking to the surface. It was an anxiety that had the obsessive self-interest of a child—could they look after him, would he be taken away? He lost faith in them and pretended to need his parents, not knowing how else to belong to them. This was not conscious, it was a watchfulness, an edginess inside him like endless waiting. Sometimes he would search their faces for signs he could recognize, signs of the father and mother he used to have. But most of the time he was taken up in the business of boyhood and could not have said what he was thinking about.

The children found they were hated. This frightened them at first, then puzzled them, and then became as much a part of who they were as the family name. They were astonished at the spite they seemed to deserve at almost anything they did—if they laughed thinking themselves part of the fun, if they kept away, if they joined in, if they were clever in lessons, if they were stupid. But after a while the hate became an identity and a purpose. Robert accepted the pain of fists as proof of his place in things. When a gang of children circled round ready to punch and kick, alongside the fear Robert felt elation, a thrill of wild freedom, like the second before leaping off a cliff. The world had narrowed to a perfect point that was him.

What was worse was being ignored, and at those times he would wonder if he was not a real boy at all but a misty ghost or even nothing at all.

Robert was not lonely but this country, Scotland, seemed more like an island than St Kilda ever had. He had seen it shrinking smaller and smaller behind the ship, but it still encircled him, cutting him off and making him as separate as if he'd never left.

Isabel was his arrival in this world.

1939

❧

Robert and Isabel

'You must move,' she said, after a long moment staring down at him. Even at nineteen, Robert had not learned to be shy. He found it difficult to remember that in this place to be humble is to be polite. He should have looked away. The girl did not know he could not see her face even though they were only a pace or two from each other.

The path was narrow and edged with gorse. It was his route home from work and he rarely met anyone going this way. On one side were black pines, on the other was a line of mountains against yellow sky. Above the mountains the sky had turned glass green, then lilac, up and over his head to starry ink blue. Birds were settling for the night and they twittered and flitted past him, skimming the bushes. His footsteps on the peaty earth made no sound, neither did the hooves of the pony.

The sun was low, shining straight into his eyes, and he did not see the girl until they were a yard apart. The pony was black, made blacker by the glare of the sun. The girl was a black shape too. He could not make out her clothes or her face, it was her hair that was as livid as metal in a furnace. It looked like a great tangle of copper wire lit up round her head. Robert wanted to laugh. If he had known he would fall in love with her he would have been transfixed by the beauty of it, but as it was she was a cut-out with an orange halo. He thought of a lion riding a horse.

'My pony must get past,' she said.

'That will be difficult,' he said. He should have apologized or made some gesture she would have seen as respectful, but he forgot.

The pony filled the width of the path. It stared, its small hooves planted wide apart as if the earth was unreliable, and Robert could hear its breathing as it tried to measure the danger of him. It had a fine line like the mark of tailor's chalk down the centre of its face. He put out his hand to touch the pony's muzzle and the girl flinched, jerking the reins and bringing its head flinging upwards as if he had touched her.

'You *must* move,' she said again, and Robert could hear a catch in her voice as if she were afraid. He did not know if it was panic or her temper that made her act, but she kicked the pony forward into him. Her knee hit his chest and he put out his hands as he fell back into the gorse. Perhaps she thought he was reaching for her for she kicked the pony again and it plunged forward, pushing him aside. For a second, there was a glimpse of the underneath of her chin above him, tender and pale like the inside of his own arm. He saw that she was younger than he'd thought, her hair was dark and her teeth, small and even like a child's, were biting her lower lip.

There was little else to remember of his first meeting with Isabel; some scratches on his back from the gorse, a cut lip he had no memory of and a bruise on his chest where they'd first collided, like the shadow of a fist on the skin.

❧

In 1940, on his twentieth birthday, Robert was called up. But he did not fight. The army doctor put a cross on the clipboard.

Robert stood in line, almost naked with his clothes in a bundle in his arms. He felt thin and dark amongst the white, stocky mainland boys, and he stooped with the anxiety of being so visible. The doctors walked up and down the lines, dismissing pigeon chests or knock knees or wheezing lungs. They conferred when they came to Robert.

'Your feet, laddie—painful are they?' His skin was raw at the heels and toes with the damage of boots that did not fit. Although he put them on each morning without a thought, his feet had never accepted their new life in shoes.

'No, sir,' Robert said. 'They're always like this.' The doctors took a closer look and asked Robert to flex his toes and circle his ankles.

'St Kilda,' one of them read from the clipboard. 'A St Kilda lad. Feet not made for boots.' To be able to march was more vital than loading a gun; the doctors agreed he was not up to it.

But he might be of some use they said, and he was sent to join another queue. This time he was not dismissed before he got to the wooden desk. Three men in uniform shuffled papers between them.

He made furniture didn't he? There was no use for the carving and veneering and inlaid work he could turn his hand to, but a craftsman of his calibre could knock up crates and ammunition boxes no trouble at all. And with so many men away, there were still fences to mend and barns to build. A rubber stamp made a thud on his name: *Accepted.*

So Robert's war was tedious. He laboured and he made boxes, hundreds of them. The workshop was a dozen benches set up in rows in a corrugated hanger. Men worked three to a bench, one marking, one sawing, one hammering. Music played over a loud-speaker hitched on a piece of wire above their heads. All day long it rasped out dance music, and with the sound of saws and hammers and sometimes the drumming of rain on the tin roof, Robert's head buzzed and his ears throbbed even at home in his sleep.

The wood they used was unseasoned and spongy. It split and clogged the teeth of the saw, and Robert knew that dovetailed joints and brass hinges would take weight and movement so much better than nails and leather straps. He did not say so. There was only one way to do the work—quickly. It did not need to last. The men left their own mark; some made a notch with a chisel or groove on the lid. Robert put a pinch of Scottish earth from his pocket in each box and sent it to the front instead of himself.

The invisible war. The mountains, people, towns, all looked the
same but were subtly altered. The world was brilliant, intense but
false and slyly distorted like a mirror's reflection, like the thoughts
in his own head. He had wondered before how it would be to kill a
man but now he could feel the closeness of it. There was a salt taste
in his mouth and a prickling in his veins when it seeped through
from the life he might have had, born in a different place and in a
different body. Somewhere there was excitement and terror and
comradeship, but only its aftershocks, the faint tremors reached
him.

There was a prisoner of war camp in the next valley and he saw
groups of men hunched against the Highland winds and prodding
at the earth with hoes. They waved and laughed, which shocked
him. Perhaps they had killed. Could you still wave and laugh when
you had witnessed the end of another man's life or had faced the end
of your own?

Some weeks he was sent out from the workshop to farms and
crofts that needed help. He hammered and sawed and fixed in the
place of absent sons and husbands. And when a mother or wife
brought him food, he saw in her eyes that his was the wrong face,
his was the wrong voice, and he could not look at her for fear that
she would see the ghost of grief to come.

Robert learned the skills of a dozen craftsmen. He built walls,
plumbed sinks and repaired tractors. He delivered lambs, slaugh-
tered pigs and wired light fittings. But everywhere he went, he
worked quickly, hardly looking at his surroundings, deliberately not
remembering the homes in which he was an impostor. For the week
he worked at a large, prosperous dairy farm he would have taken in
little but the tilt and the tiles of the stable roof he was mending,
were it not for the daughter of the house.

On the first day he saw the girl. She looked up at him on the
stable roof and waved, swinging a bucket. She wore corduroy
trousers, a knitted jumper full of holes and lace-up boots.

She was not beautiful but her smile transformed her face into something close to it. The smile was spontaneous and careless as if it need not be carefully measured out because the supply inside her was inexhaustible. She whistled and a dog came out of the stable, shook itself and went wagging after her. She spoke to Robert later that day.

'Why aren't you fighting?' she asked. She had not said hello or introduced herself. The question came as if it were the first thing she thought of. She was eating an apple, standing beneath him in the yard with the collie sitting in front of her positioned for the core.

Robert nodded in acknowledgement and looked back to his work. She did not seem to know the danger of distracting someone balancing at a height—or she didn't care.

He climbed down. It was time to finish. She stood eating her apple, waiting for an answer and watching him as unselfconsciously as she had smiled. Face to face, she was almost as tall as he. Her skin was pale but not the kind of fine translucence that is delicate and vulnerable. Isabel's skin had a creamy firmness, her nose and chin and cheekbones were reddened by the wind, and she had a scratch at the corner of her eye. Her hair was tied with string in a bundle at her neck, too thick to lie in a pony-tail down her back.

'They wouldn't have me. These.' Robert said, indicating his feet.

'Oh, I see.' She looked disappointed. 'You must have been furious, you must have tried to persuade them.'

'No,' said Robert, and understood the test he had failed. But the girl's seriousness disappeared as if that was now dealt with and forgotten.

'Would you like some food? My mother still cooks too much.'

They walked to the house and Robert was aware of her shoulder almost touching his and the black band round her arm.

They said goodbye after supper and she went with him to the gate. Her speckled eyes did not slide away when he looked at her. Perhaps she had already decided.

Every day Isabel waved and threw her apple cores at him, and the dog raced to catch them when they bounced down off the roof. She drove the tractor and shouted at the cows. Sometimes when they met, Robert saw smears of sweat or tears on her cheeks. Isabel would look him in the eye, defying him to ask or offer comfort. Her brother was dead but her grief did not weaken her, it goaded her to work like a man and it burst out of her in desperate energy.

He saw her heaving bales of straw onto the trailer and carrying sacks of feed on her back. Her hair stuck to her face and she made little gasps with the effort of lifting what should have been beyond her strength. He would offer help, she did not bother to answer him. Silently he worked alongside her.

❧

'Why don't you use the ladder?' Isabel asked one evening as she waited for him to finish for supper. She had watched him climbing the stone walls of the stable more than once.

'Because I don't need to. Where I come from we climb almost as soon as we walk. We caught birds from the cliffs for food. We had to climb to live.'

Isabel seemed satisfied and they walked together towards the house. Then she pointed to the gable wall, two storeys of rough grey stone.

'Why don't you climb that?' she said. It was not a challenge, it was curiosity to know how it could possibly be done. Robert forgot his tiredness when he saw her face. Her eyes were shining as if he was about to do a magic trick for her. He took off his boots and his gloves so that his bare skin could feel the stone, took off his jacket and gave it to her to hold, and stood looking up at the wall for a moment or two, planning the route like a mountaineer. Isabel was quiet, hugging his jacket. Her stomach ached with fear for him and she longed to say no, don't do it now, but she couldn't.

He began and in a few movements, he was higher than her head, higher than he could safely fall. He climbed slowly and evenly, an arm then a leg taking its turn to move outwards and up; finding a hold, testing, shifting his body across, the other arm and leg following. A slow spider zig-zagging upwards, right to left and back again. It was a long time since he had climbed but his fingers and toes could not forget what was born into them. He did not feel anxiety at the drop beneath him, only a clarity in his head that constantly judged his centre of gravity and measured the strength needed to balance his weight against the drag of the earth.

The stone was kind. Dry and firm and full of helpful steps and crevices. He settled into a rhythm—ten feet, fifteen.

Isabel was frightened now. She called but he seemed not to hear. She paced back and forth, wanting to look away but unable to. She felt the hardness of the ground under her feet; he would be hurt so badly if he fell and it would be her fault.

Suddenly she noticed how dark it was. The air was cold and the stars were out, though the horizon was still lit by the sun. She was sure when he started to climb it was only dusk; now when she looked up he was a strange black shape against the stone. The roof made a slanting triangle against the sky and a fat slice of dappled moon was spiked on the wooden point of the gable. He was almost at the top and she saw him reach up and hang something on it.

Then he started down. Slower, more carefully. His arms ached now and his toes were sore from taking his weight. When men climbed the cliffs at home all those years ago, the descent from the cliff edge was first, the hardest part accomplished when one's limbs and concentration were freshest. Coming back, climbing upwards was easier. You see the next move, your path is there in front of you, so no need to lean deadly inches outwards to find the next hold.

He rested for a moment, leaning his head against the stone and he heard Isabel's footsteps below him. He could not wait too long

or his muscles would freeze. He carried on, each movement in slow
motion, inching down to earth and letting himself fall the last six
feet.

He was not hurt and he sat on the grass, putting on his boots
while Isabel watched, white faced, still clutching his jacket.

'It was a good climb,' he said. 'But I'm not going back to get it
for you.'

'What?' A laugh burst out of her. 'What was it?' She looked up,
trying to make out the speck of white dangling from the wooden
spike on the roof.

'Just string,' Robert said. 'I've had it in my pocket for a while.
Do you want it back?' Isabel shook her head.

'I want it to stay there,' she said.

⁓∞⁓

On the last evening, before supper, Isabel led a pony in from the
field to the newly repaired stable. The pony was black and it had a
line like chalk on its face. The sun was low on the horizon and
Isabel's hair, free of its piece of string, was lit up round her head like
a halo. Then he remembered: four years since he had seen her and
now here she was, the same girl with her black pony.

'No,' said Isabel, 'I wasn't frightened. I was angry, but not at you.
I can't remember why.' The pony looked small beside her. 'That was
so long ago,' she said. 'I was fourteen, but I do remember.'

It was strange to suddenly feel an ache in his chest like the pain
he had suffered for months after her knee bruised him so badly.
They did not speak. Isabel looked past him and then at her feet.
Then she pulled him roughly against her and kissed him on the
mouth. Her fingers dug into his back and her teeth caught his lip.
He tasted the smallest trace of blood mixed with his first taste of
her, the inside of her; her saliva, her tongue had a sharp, sleek
otherness. Close to him, her heat breathed up from inside her
clothing. For a second, there was nothing, then a brilliance and a

rushing like the inside of a wave, that made him hold on to her as tightly as she held him.

⚬

When Robert left the farm, they saw each other seldom. For two more years Isabel tried to do the work of her three absent brothers. One of them would not return. Often she was up before sunrise, going on after dark. Robert travelled further each day as men still at home or able to work became fewer.

When they met, they did not talk about the future. He learned to herd cows and she to climb. Together they built a tree house from the remnants of wood from the crates and the ammunition boxes. It was a place to be alone and away from the war that made them so much older than they wanted to be. They made a bed of heather and would lie side by side listening to the wind and the birds, and waiting.

⚬

Isabel's mother decided to sell the farm. Of her two remaining sons, one was unable to walk or see and the other's love of the land had died along with his oldest brother.

'She's selling it,' Isabel told Robert. 'She may as well sell me too.'

In all that time Isabel had never given in, not to exhaustion or to weakness; as good as her brothers. But now it was all lost. Robert saw her beaten, and she was suddenly another Isabel, just a thin, untidy girl.

They sat by the fire in the farmhouse kitchen and Isabel could not look at anything. The chairs and the plates and the pots in the fireplace had all betrayed her. Distractedly she pulled at ends of wool sticking out from the frayed cuffs of her jumper and she rubbed at the frown between her eyebrows. She stared at her feet planted on the hearthrug and thought they looked like dead things. Without socks and boots they were plucked birds, naked and feeble, and she hated them. She tugged at her hair and Robert felt her pain gnawing in his own stomach. He took her hand and stroked it.

'Your life could be in another place,' he said. 'Maybe south, in England. They say the trees are beautiful in England.' Isabel said nothing and Robert hesitated, not sure if he should go on. 'You have your money next year. You could buy another farm. A farm of your own.'

Her head came up and she looked at him levelly, 'You won't get away from me, you know.'

⸎

Sometime later in his life Robert knew it was he who had uprooted Isabel from her home. He had wanted to believe that they shared in the decision, but in truth it had been his alone and he had known that she would follow. Since he left St Kilda as a child it had not mattered where he lived—he was already lost.

She was cut adrift as he had been and although she was happy to go with him, a time came when she needed her mother and her home. He was not enough.

When the war was over Robert wanted to go in search of trees as other wandering people followed gold. He was as selfish and obsessed as any bounty hunter.

They travelled south and eventually came to the valley of the River Camel, full of ancient giants—oak, beech and sycamore. This is where he decided they would live.

They bought a house by the river. It had land for some sheep and a vegetable garden. There was an outhouse where Robert made their furniture.

It was not long before he built another tree house for Isabel. She would not admit it but she missed Scotland and their first home.

The neighbours were baffled by the tree house: young Mr and Mrs MacKinnon had no children yet, perhaps it was a Scottish tradition to have a playhouse ready? They didn't pry but asked politely to see inside, and one by one wobbled across the walkway from the first floor of the grey stone house to the wooden cabin settled like a nest in the branches of a tree.

Robert was asked to build another tree house, then another. At first for village children and then for the parents. Children get tired of adults wanting to share in their games.

He learned to make houses that would move with the tree so the joints would not crack or grind in the wind. Each house and tree must be matched, suited wood to wood, hip to hip, so that in time the two accept each other perfectly. A tree would grow to embrace the house and the house warped and curved to fit inside the tree. Where once they had chafed and complained, they yielded and made peace. Not many years need pass before it was impossible to separate the two.

October 1987

❧

Starling and Gatta

There was a film club in Cameldip started by Frank and Elaine who were at university together and now, in their forties, saw no reason why they should not relive anything they chose.

The chapel was the venue and membership was open to anyone on the understanding that they did not talk during the film and did talk afterwards when there was a discussion. This Saturday it was a classic suitable for everyone except those between two and twelve.

Gone with the Wind blazed its fire and sunsets over the screen. The under-twos slept in the flickering darkness, the over-twelves were dismissive, then astonished then hypnotized by these unimaginable characters, and the oldies, like Frank and Elaine, took their parts and silently spoke their lines.

The heating was on in the chapel. After the first of October it came on automatically regardless of the temperature. This autumn day had been sunny, soaking its thin warmth into the chapel walls. As the sun disappeared the heat stored up in the stony pores leaked into the film show, the radiators scorched like smoothing irons and the chapel sweltered like the Deep South.

Frank and Elaine were satisfied: it had been an authentic experience.

❧

Since the film, and for the first time in her life, Starling was happy with her name. It was almost Scarlett, almost. She knew that her features were pointy rather than delicate and that her hair was black wire rather than ringlets, but from the inside Starling felt pretty. She was fifteen.

It was Monday and she was walking home from school. Her school uniform was green, a shade not unlike Scarlett's velvet-curtain outfit. Alone in the lane, Starling could picture how lovely she looked, just at that moment. If she wanted she could be so Scarlett that Rhett himself would be conquered.

And on a bend in the lane, she met Cat's-pee Cardigan from the pub walking his shires. The horses filled the lane, almost as tall as the overhanging trees and side by side as wide as two steam engines. Their hooves, massive hairy coconuts, cracked down on the tarmac, and they stripped leaves from overhanging branches without pausing in their stride. As usual the horses had no bridles. Josef Sevier walked between them, bumped gently from side to side. They could be guiding him like a foal, rather than him leading them.

They all stopped. Starling smiled at Josef. She could feel a fortunate patch of sunlight on her head—her hair would be gleaming, and her eyes would be gold-brown, just shadowed by her eyelashes. She tipped her head a little to the side and forward and a coil of hair fell over her cheek. She smiled a little more.

The horses chewed. Their muzzles were higher than Starling's head and they gazed over her into the distance. It was quiet in the lane, just the breathing of the shires and the slap of their tails. Josef looked and said nothing.

So Starling hoisted her school bag, giving her the excuse to tilt her hips a little more. Her skirt showed most of her thighs and she knew her legs looked good in black tights. She licked her lips. She slid forward a step.

'Can I give them a stroke?' The smell of the horses was pungent in her nostrils and beneath it she could smell the musty smell of Josef. She could see black stubble growing through his skin, on his chin and down his neck. The collar of his shirt was open and she saw the stained inside and a frizz of hair. Her stomach fluttered. She took a step closer, carelessly, as if she was perfectly unaware of how lovely she was. She reached out her hand and smoothed the chest of a horse. She glanced up at Josef.

He waited. He knew this skinny child. Usually she was with her friends. They would giggle and sneer at him, but they liked the horses and he didn't mind.

Starling felt her heart bumping in her chest and summoned Scarlett to guide her. Then a surprising thing happened. The horses both together started forward. Bored with standing still they resumed their walk, ignoring Starling who was way below their line of sight. Their bulk shoved her backwards and she bounced between them like a cork between two ships. Their hooves were inches from her small feet and Josef caught her up and lifted her out of the way.

They were pressed together between the flanks of the horses— Starling's face was against Josef's shoulder and he had all her weight in his arms. She could feel his chest against her small breasts, his stomach next to hers, his legs against her legs. For a second their faces touched. And this was strange. This feeling was not what she expected.

Josef put her down and she could not look any more. He was concerned and asked her if she was hurt and for a moment his hand rested on her shoulder, then he turned and followed his horses along the lane.

Starling was not Scarlett any more. She stood looking at her feet, trying to give a name to the thing that had happened.

Josef's eyes were not blazing or narrow like Rhett's, they were the darkest, kindest blue that Starling had ever seen. And her body was different, as if he'd left an imprint inside her. She did not know these feelings, she only knew that when she was close to him, Josef's skin smelled of flowers.

⚭

'The filthy old sod. You should tell your dad,' said Gatta.

Starling and Gatta were in Starling's bedroom. She had told Gatta about her meeting with Josef, but not quite. She was trying to rewrite it in her mind into something that would make the feelings go away.

'Did he really feel your tits?' Gatta's eyes were shining and she had a smirk that Starling did not like—as if Gatta had a taste of something she neither wanted to spit out nor swallow, like when they tried to suck chocolate without eating it so as not to get fat. Starling would not tell her dad—he would ask questions she didn't want. She did not know what she wanted.

Except that she wanted to see Josef. He was in her mind all the time, not particular thoughts but a memory that shifted and changed, running over and over. Just to see him might turn him back into Cat's-pee Cardigan, so she had walked to the pub and down the path beside his garden lots of times since. Once he had been digging but he did not look up. She stood for a long time it seemed, waiting for him to see her.

Starling knew he was avoiding her. He was deliberately not being in and not seeing her walking past. She felt impatient and puzzled and anxious all at once, then upset, which was when she told Gatta, just so that she could talk about him to someone.

'You should do something,' Gatta said. 'He's taken advantage, he could get done for assault. You can't let it go.'

Gatta was right, but not in the way she thought; Starling could not let it go.

∞

One evening after school Starling and Gatta and some friends were sitting on the grass outside the shop. Starling had to be ready to run in and get behind the counter if anyone came. Her friends hung around most evenings and she gave them a discount when her dad was upstairs.

And there he was, Cat's-pee Cardigan with his horses walking past. Gatta nudged her.

The horses followed Josef, a few paces behind him today. Josef looked ahead all the time, although both horses turned their heads in perfect unison to meet the stares of the group outside the shop. Neither of the two things that Starling hoped for happened: Josef did not look at her, nor did he go back to being Cat's-pee Cardigan. He was not as old as she had always thought, in fact he was not much older than her oldest brother, it was the battered clothes that made him look miserable. And his name was only because he smelled of French cigarettes, which weren't at all like cat's pee but gave him a dark, thoughtful foreign smell that she used to be too young to appreciate.

Starling felt Gatta on the point of yelling something, something rude most likely.

'No, don't,' she said pulling Gatta's arm.

'You're too kind, you,' Gatta said. 'We'll get him though, don't you worry.'

⁂

Gatta's family lived in two tree houses, joined at the base by a porch and some steps. The houses were tiled and shuttered and built in the branches of a pair of beeches. The trees grew close, side by side and identical, leaning slightly together like devoted twins.

Gatta had two small brothers and a little sister who she often looked after while her mother would sleep or read magazines about how to be beautiful, even though she was. Gatta's father had gone, in fact he had never been: Gatta had no idea who he was. Her brothers' father was fat and kind and lived with them for seven years. That was the best time she could remember.

The little sister's father made Gatta's mind cower at the back of her head or sometimes leave altogether through a hole in the top. The loathing came back even now, a year after he left. He seemed to have soaked into the pores of her skin and she saw him in the shape of her own arms and legs, and her own face in the mirror and sometimes in other things too, then there was a coldness that let her do anything.

Gatta would not have been able to say if she was happy, but when she visited Starling, Starling's family folded her into themselves as if she were one of them—and this was a feeling she thought was happy. Except that when she was there Gatta was shy and sometimes sad for no reason she could explain, perhaps because it was so strange in Starling's home. Starling's mother cooked food for everyone including Gatta. She called her 'sweetie' and 'my love' and asked her to help with things as if that was what mothers and daughters always did. Gatta felt herself melting smaller as if something inside her was giving way.

Starling's family lived above the post office and shop, and they could choose one thing each evening from the ice creams or the sweets. When Starling and Gatta had fudge, they would cut it into tiny squares to make it less fattening while they tried out make-up and did each other's hair. When the fudge was finished, they pinched their thighs and smoothed in their stomachs saying never, ever again.

Gatta would do anything for Starling.

But when Starling told her about Josef, she felt hot and icy at the same time. The feeling that squatted inside her always ready to bare its teeth, pounced instantly on Josef, pushing Starling aside. Gatta fed it with thoughts of their friendship but it was not really Starling who was in her mind. Plans of hurting Josef filled her to the brim and she alone would decide what he deserved.

October 1987

Anna

'For you,' said Isabel, her spectacles on the end of her nose. She handed a card to Anna as they passed in the hallway. Isabel did not look up as she unfolded some letters, crumpling the envelopes and pushing them down into her dressing-gown pockets.

In the mornings she was creased with sleep and Anna was sometimes surprised at how old and frail she looked. Her iron-grey hair was loose. It was thick and coarse and reached to her waist. By breakfast it was put up in a finicky bun held with dozens of pins and the ageing Isabel disappeared beneath the decisive, energetic one.

Anna's card was from the post office to say that a parcel was waiting. She put the baby in his pushchair and walked the half mile to the shop feeling better this morning than she had since he was born. She had heard from Thomas. He said he would visit in a month or so and bring some things he had been storing for her. Isabel suggested he stay if he'd like to, that he would want time with the baby—and she smiled at Anna, kindly and indulgently as one would at a silly but innocent child. Anna felt ridiculous for having said nothing about Thomas being the baby's father. Isabel knew, of course she knew.

The autumn sunshine made the lanes and fields look beautiful and Anna walked slowly, pointing out cows, 'Mmooo,' and sheep, 'Bahahaa,' for her son who stared at her, round eyed and baffled.

'Maahaahaa,' she said louder, and the baby's eyes filled with tears. His small fat hands clutched the arms of his pushchair and his rotund body went stiff with anxiety. Why was he so sensitive? He

84

watched her as if she were a red light or a green light by which the world could be judged. The baby gazed at her, his eyes brimmed and he drew in little breaths like a swimmer preparing to dive. She sighed, forcing away her irritation, and leaned down to him.

'Woof, woof,' she said softly and his face lit up with relief.

The village was deserted. It was too early on a weekend morning for people to be out yet. There was the sound of hooves on the lane ahead and she thought of Josef Sevier and his giant horses, but it was a child on a fat piebald pony who both puffed breathlessly, the pink-faced child and the snub-nosed pony, as they trotted past.

Anna thought of Thomas and wondered if he had changed. It would be more than a year. She looked at her baby's face for traces of him in miniature. There were none. Thomas was fair and fine-featured, his son had dark eyes and black hair. And not like her either, with her pallid English skin and her no-colour hair. This baby was a parting gift from Spain. It had been their last time together and this was what they'd made, a perfect Spanish baby, exotic and Latin, more suited to sunshine than either of his parents.

Anna pushed open the door of the village shop.

'Hello,' said Starling. 'Oh, he's so gorgeous.' She came out from behind the counter and knelt down to unstrap the baby from the pushchair.

'Could you just get my parcel first?' said Anna.

'Anna's parcel!' yelled Starling. 'Can I hold him, Anna?'

Starling's father appeared from the back of the shop with the parcel and a few letters. He beamed at Anna. 'Will you take these home with you?' he asked as if she were a little girl, folding her hand round the letters and patting it closed. 'For Robert—the postman never knows where to leave them at that funny old place of his.'

'Isabel's,' said Anna. 'For Isabel—they're MacKinnon.'

'Robert is *Mr* MacK.,' said Starling. 'Didn't you know? Didn't they tell you—typical of those two. Mr and Mrs, that's what they are.'

So many months and they had not said. And Anna's mind tried to grasp what this meant; all she knew of Isabel and Robert must fit a different pattern.

Starling bounced the baby in her arms, walking him up and down the shop.

'They're married but they don't bother with each other any more. Isabel is stuck up and Robert is best off out of it, if you ask me. He's nice, we all think. He's always nice to us; she's always looking down her nose. And she's bossy. She went funny about her children, my mum says.' Starling rolled her eyes and tapped her head. 'She knew them before I was born and she said they were normal once upon a time. Isabel was lovely once, when she was young, and he was hand-some, but he's a dark horse, Mum says.' Starling giggled and looked sideways at Anna. 'Lots of people think he …'

'Anna doesn't want to know all that,' said Starling's father. Starling looked up from the baby. There was a pause, a second caught in mid-air, then Starling's voice: 'Anna does want to know, 'course she does, she lives with them, she wants to know all the gossip, don't you Anna?'

'We ought to go now,' said Anna. 'He'll be hungry by the time we get home. Come and see us, Starling, if you'd like to.'

'OK, I might, if you like.' Starling looked pleased. She kissed the baby, now back in Anna's arms, tapping his nose with her finger. 'Bye-bye, little darling.' He made a face, which made them laugh.

Anna did not go back to the house but turned the other way towards the footpath along the riverbank. The garden behind the pub was as beautiful as always; the mallow and asters were in bloom and white roses glowed against the stone walls.

She walked along the bank to the place she had first sat when she came to the village. Then she'd thought only of Thomas but this time her mind was full of Robert and Isabel.

Now the memories looked different, as if everything she had seen and heard was a different colour, a different language. Nothing was as she'd thought. She had not seen because she had not looked—Robert waiting for Isabel's instructions, standing at the kitchen door, explaining about a tree or a sheep, and her turning away from him as if she were bored or exasperated with having to listen. They were never at ease or kind, or angry. Nothing: just Isabel, terse, indifferent and Robert, blank and patient. Except for that time in the garden; that once she had seen something more between them.

What should she do? She would find somewhere else to live, not only because of this—it didn't matter so much—but because of the loneliness of living with Isabel. And children, Starling said there were children. They would be grown up but they were never mentioned, no photos, no phone calls.

Anna looked at her baby. He gazed at leaves floating by on the river and his head wobbled slightly as he practised the balance of its weight. He held upside-down with both hands a blue furry duck that Starling had given him. How could it be that your child disappears from your life? It is impossible. It is always possible.

She turned her mind from the thought, wrenching it away before it gripped her tighter. She remembered her parcel: *'Dear black-sheep sister, an early birthday present for you and something for my nephew. Missing you lots, with love, Rosie.'* It was a book and a little striped suit, like an old-fashioned swimming costume, for the baby.

❧

Anna could not sleep. Her eyes would not stay closed, her mind constantly circling back to Thomas. She was tired. The baby had been difficult all day and now he was fast asleep, exhausted by his own bad mood. She thought of putting on the light to read but did not want to wake him.

The moon was full. From her mattress on the tree-house floor Anna had only to sit up against the pillows to see out of the window down across the lawn to the mound that was Robert's house looking like a great beached whale on the grass. The shadows in the garden

were as sharp as if it were sunlight, but blacker, thicker, and everything lit up by the moon was the colour of steel or lead or slate.

Anna listened to the night sounds all around her and little by
little her eyes closed. For a moment or two she drifted, perhaps she
slept. Then something close by woke her. She sat up. On the grass
beneath the tree house someone stood looking up to her window.
Anna did not move. The moonlight through the leaves made
dappled light on the blanket but she could feel that her face was in
shadow. She must be hidden but her heart thumped and her skin
prickled with fear.

The figure did not move for long minutes. Even in the dark
Anna felt the eyes staring into her own and it was impossible to
hide. It came into her head that this might be a dream and she had
only to concentrate on that thought for the shadow to melt into
nothing.

The baby whimpered and the watcher started back, out from the
shadow of the tree. It was Isabel. Her hair was loose and she was
wearing a summer dress, sleeveless and full skirted. She walked
quickly away across the grass towards the river, full of purpose, then
she broke into a run, as agile as a young woman. But after a few
paces she stopped as if she'd changed her mind or was confused.
There was a cry so sharp and sudden, as if something had pierced
her, that Anna's heart jumped. Isabel sunk to her knees on the grass.
Anna leapt up thinking she was hurt but did not go down. Always,
even now, Isabel made her keep away.

After a moment or two Isabel got to her feet. She stood for a
while, then walked out of Anna's sight back towards the house.

1946

⚜

Adelie and Xavier

Adelie concentrated on the rough ground, taking smaller steps than Xavier because of her tight skirt and having to trot sometimes to keep up with him. There was grass growing along the centre of the lane where tyres had not kept it down and the surface was potholed and cracked with wartime neglect. Her shoes were cream calf leather with fine heels, and she thought how sad it would be to ruin them when they were still so new and Xavier had bought them for her in Bond Street.

Xavier held her hand, swinging their arms, and he whistled like he used to when they walked at home. He had not whistled in London, he had not whistled since they left Alsace, and Adelie thought how good it was to be surrounded by countryside and to hear him whistle again. That was how she would know where he was in the vineyard at home—she would follow the songbird sound along the corridors of vines, slipping through from one row to another until she found him. Then she wore faded dresses and a scarf round her hair. It would be nice not to worry about clothes again.

She took off her shoes, pushed them into Xavier's pockets and walked along the grass—her nylons would be ruined but it didn't matter. The heels of her shoes poked out, one on each side of his linen jacket.

It was hot, even in the shade of the trees. Beyond the trees were glimpses of brilliant fields and blue sky. Black-and-white cows grazed against the green. Out there, away from the shelter of the

89

lane, a summer wind made the pasture grass ripple, and the unripe wheat rolled like surf. They saw a pony, its head up and its muzzle to the wind, watching them walk by.

There was a house through the trees, set back from the road and facing down a sloping lawn. It was grey stone with white-framed windows, and doors opening on to the garden. A flagstone path edged with lavender led from an iron gate on the lane up to the front door.

It was a beautiful house, Adelie thought, so peaceful with its long windows and rough stone. The undulating lawn was clipped short as if sheep grazed there, and a tree grew close to the house, shading the windows. She imagined cool, square rooms looking out to the sunshine.

'Should we try here do you think?' she said. 'You'll have to speak though.'

'You know as much English as I do, you just like to hear me get it wrong.' Xavier gave her the shoes and they kissed awkwardly while she wobbled, trying to slip them on. He slid his hand inside her blouse—her perfume, the scent of grass and lime blossom—and Adelie hung on to him, one shoe off, balancing. They almost fell into a hedge.

When Adelie had straightened herself, Xavier pushed open the gate and they walked up to the front door. Through the panels of coloured glass they could see inside—a red staircase, a blue passage-way and a yellow tiled floor. There was no bell or knocker and Xavier called out, 'Good afternoon. Hello. We are visiting you.'

'They won't hear you—they will be in the garden today.' A silver-haired woman had come up the path behind them. She carried a straw hat and a basket, and lifted up her sunglasses to look at them. Her broad, lined face was rosy with the heat and perhaps the exertion of her walk. She leaned on a stick, puffing a little.

'Do you speak French?' Xavier asked, abandoning English hopefully.

'Yes, I do, of course. You are very lucky to have found a Frenchwoman in Cameldip. I'm probably the only one in the county—and the rest of England for all I know.' She shook their hands. 'Joséphine,' she said. 'I didn't know Isabel and Robert had French friends—how wonderful.'

'Xavier Johannes Sevier, and this is my wife, Adèle. Adelie.' Xavier liked to say 'my wife' and Adelie smiled at him, liking it too. 'We're not friends of ... who did you say? Isabel? We got out of our train from London, and we don't know where we are.'

'What a marvellous thing to do, to go exploring, just like that.' Joséphine seemed momentarily puzzled by their city clothes, then she said, 'We'll find Isabel, we'll have some tea. Always tea, but I'm doing my best to change that. Robert might have a beer for us.'

'We need a telephone and a taxi, maybe a hotel,' said Adelie, following Joséphine's wide floral hips along a gravel path round to the back of the house.

'There's no telephone here, but there's one at the post office, it's only five minutes away,' Joséphine said over her shoulder. 'Isabel and Robert will love to meet you, they're new too.'

They came to a tidy vegetable garden where a young woman was digging.

'Isabel. Isabel! Robert. I have brought some friends for you,' Joséphine called out with a flourish towards Xavier and Adelie as if they were gifts she was delivering. Isabel straightened up and it took her a second or two to take in the sight of her elderly friend and the two immaculately dressed visitors standing hand in hand amongst the lettuces.

The young man was stocky and handsome. He was as tanned as a farmer, dark-eyed and black-haired. His suit was expensively tailored, the tie loosened and the shirt unbuttoned at the neck, and he sweated in the hot sun, looking a little uneasy in his smart clothes.

The woman stood close to him, her shoulder behind his. She smiled shyly and shaded her eyes with her hand. She was very pretty, bright and flawless, as unreal as a film. Her blond hair was cut short and her white suit and pearls looked as natural to her as corduroy and boots were to Isabel.

'May I introduce Xavier and Adèle Sevier,' said Joséphine. Isabel brushed her hands on her trousers and held out her hand to Xavier, then Adelie, and kissed Joséphine. Isabel said, 'I'm sorry I'm not dressed for visitors. We thought we'd only be meeting vegetables today.'

Xavier turned to Joséphine helplessly. 'My English is very bad,' he said.

'These lovely young people have come all the way from France to Cameldip. I'm not sure why. It seems they need somewhere to stay.'

While Joséphine was speaking, Isabel smiled at Adelie, and Adelie thought how wonderful it would be to be out in the sunshine like Isabel, wearing boots and growing vegetables to cook for your husband. She could not take her eyes off Isabel's hair. It shone gold and copper in the sun and reached almost to her waist. Isabel wore a man's shirt—how good to have your husband's shirt against your own skin.

They stood for a while, Xavier explaining and Joséphine translating. A young man, Robert, joined them, shaking hands, kissing Joséphine as Isabel had done. Adelie noticed that he looked often at Isabel with kind, watchful eyes. He was not as handsome as Xavier, but taller, thinner and he spoke softly in a strange, lilting voice that she wanted to hear more. He put his arm round Isabel as he listened.

Eventually they understood: Xavier and Adelie had accidentally been left behind in Cameldip, their luggage was still on the train to Plymouth, Xavier had his wallet but that was all. They could hire a taxi, it did not matter about the cost, but they needed to tell the railway to look after their things in the meantime.

Robert went with Xavier to the post office to telephone Plymouth Station, and while they were gone Joséphine asked Adelie about France—how were people recovering, did they have enough food yet, was Paris as beautiful as ever? Isabel caught a few words here and there, listening to Adelie's sweet, clear voice, animated now in her own language but anxious alone without Xavier.

When they returned, Robert said that the stationmaster in Plymouth promised, when the train arrived, to store the Sevier luggage until further notice: one trunk, a dressing case, four suit-cases and a calfskin handbag.

'We will now have tea,' announced Joséphine, in charge of conversation and therefore in charge of proceedings. They walked round the house to the open garden doors and into a long, low room, stretching the length of the house, maybe thirty feet, with windows along one side. Two slender iron pillars supported the span of the ceiling. Sunlight streamed in on the wooden floor—new boards of fawn wood, still bare and unpolished and scattered with offcuts and curls of planings.

'We've not lived here long—Robert is just finishing this room,' said Isabel. 'It will be a dining room and a playroom for our children, when they arrive. And a playroom for us too.' She smiled at Robert.

Joséphine admired the floor, commenting on the colour and the perfect joints and the subtle give of the boards when you walked, and how warm they would be in the winter, and the smell! New wood had such a clean smell, like a healthy, young thoroughbred, or a sow in hay, or …

Isabel took Joséphine's hand and took her through to the kitchen.

'Joséphine is kind, but her compliments are never what you expect,' she said over her shoulder to Adelie. Adelie did not understand but she could see the happiness in Isabel's eyes and hear the fondness in Joséphine's voice. For months she had only thought of

Xavier, their love eclipsed everything, but she missed her sisters and her mother and this was like home.

The house was untidy, sparsely furnished, no carpets, no armchairs. In the kitchen there was a large wooden table but no chairs so they stood while Robert made tea and Isabel talked, not waiting for Joséphine's translation and not seeming to think it mattered that Adelie and Xavier could not understand what she said. The way she spoke sounded a little like Robert, not like people in London, nor the people on the train: perhaps Isabel and Robert were foreigners too. Sometimes Robert turned to look at Isabel, a quiet smile, and she put her hand on his back as he poured their tea. Adelie watched and knew that they were just like her and Xavier.

She followed Isabel upstairs; she took off her stockings and her white jacket and untucked her silk blouse. She splashed water on her face, noticing that her lipstick had gone. The taxi and the hotel were forgotten.

They drank tea outside on the grass. Robert laid out a blanket for Adelie to sit on and unfolded a beach chair for Joséphine. They sat in the shade of the trees by the river where a rowing boat was moored to a willow and some sheep grazed on the bank. Isabel rolled up her trousers and paddled, her teacup in one hand, a slice of cake in the other.

Xavier rolled up his sleeves and lay on his back and Adelie lay down with her head on his stomach, looking up at the English sky.

The same sky, the same sun, but this could not be home. Everything, even the expanse of blue with shreds of cloud and a leafy branch dipping against it, was unknown and undecipherable. Not friendly, only indifferent, the place was not conscious of her, and was exactly as it would have been on this summer afternoon had Xavier not left the train and had she not followed him. They were here of all the places that had passed by the carriage windows and now they were absorbed into it, making no difference other than displacing a scrap of air and adding their infinitesimal weight to the earth.

A bird circled. It was black against the blue. The sun was sinking behind the trees and Adelie could feel the pattern of shade it made on her body, warm and cool.

Robert talked to Joséphine and his voice and the words Adelie could not understand seemed to sift into her head like the sound of the leaves and the birds and the river. Xavier's breathing slowed and he sighed. He was slipping into sleep.

'You must stay with me,' said Joséphine suddenly in French, loudly, as if this were the language for important matters. Xavier sat up and Adelie's head bumped on the grass. 'Edward loves having people to stay and we could have your luggage brought back on Monday's train.'

'We could not possibly trouble you,' said Xavier. 'I'm sure we can hire a taxi, and Adelie would like to see the ocean. We should leave today if we can.'

'No,' said Adelie, her eyes on Isabel, 'I don't mind waiting, I like it here. I'd love to stay. But we really shouldn't inconvenience you, Joséphine.'

'They want to leave us,' said Joséphine, incredulous.

'A taxi will have to come from Exeter, it's late, the soonest will be tomorrow,' said Isabel from the river. 'But do whatever feels right— you had plans, maybe it's best to stick to them.' Adelie did not understand and looked to Joséphine for the words in French.

'I have decided,' said Joséphine, ignoring her job as translator. 'The French cannot be inconvenient.'

'It's wonderful for Joséphine to have civilized company at last,' said Robert. 'You would be making her very happy, can't you tell?'

Joséphine translated this.

Xavier tried to hire a taxi for the following day but there was nothing for a week, when more petrol would be available—longer than waiting for the next train. Another telephone call to Plymouth

Station was necessary: yes, it could be arranged for a fast train to stop at Cameldip but the request must be made in writing in order to get official clearance from Paddington, who would then instruct the signal box at Exeter, and that might take some time.

Joséphine was satisfied; Xavier and Adelie would stay and their luggage would be sent back from Plymouth tomorrow. She would have a beautiful French daughter and son to look after for almost a week.

Adelie paddled in the river with Isabel. They stood in the shallows watching small brown fish dart round their ankles. Adelie's blond head and her white clothes glowed in the shadows. She hitched up her ankle-length skirt, creasing the soft crepe in her hands and still not quite holding the hem out of the water.

'You see, Isabel—the French paddle in Dior,' said Joséphine with satisfaction.

'There's a swimming place further down,' said Isabel.

Robert and Xavier talked—few words and long silences. Robert made furniture. He and Isabel were from Scotland and had come south to buy a farm but when they saw this house with its few acres along the river and magnificent trees they decided that it was enough.

Xavier was … well, nothing right now. He knew the wine business and would bide his time, wait for the right opening to come up. He and Adelie were on their way to America.

And they talked about the war and what might happen now in Europe in this new age of peace and freedom. Xavier's English was better than he thought, the words floating to the surface of his schooldays' memory.

Joséphine settled in her beach chair. She was content; Edward would be happy. She put on her straw hat and closed her eyes.

⌒∞⌒

'It has five rooms at the roof and four rooms under,' said Adelie, floating on her back. Isabel swam round her. The water was icy and she was surprised that Adelie was tougher than she looked. She didn't seem to feel the cold even though they'd been in the water a while.

'We buy the house,' Adelie said. 'Xavier makes the wine business. The brothers of Xavier send wine because here is none, but we are selling beer too. I cook. Xavier knows wine that is good; every one of Alsace.' She rolled over and dived under the water, appearing again further downstream.

Isabel followed her. 'I've only had wine at our wedding. People here don't drink wine.'

'Yes, perhaps,' said Adelie in the way Isabel knew meant she didn't understand.

'I'm glad you're staying. I knew you'd love that house even though it's so run down. And the river's next to you like us. We can use the boat to visit each other.'

'Perhaps.' Adelie swam slowly, just enough to stop the river carrying her on. 'I will make a garden and to have the flowers … and the vegetables … and the eggs.'

'I'm getting out, I'm freezing.' Isabel scrambled up the bank, finding a patch of sun to sit with her towel round her shoulders. She watched Adelie floating. One hand was just above the surface, holding a branch that dipped into the water, keeping her still in the gentle pull of the river.

Joséphine had given her an old petticoat to swim in, *('No, Joséphine, that is fine French lace and hand stitching!' 'Yes, chérie. Look at the size! Who will ever wear it if not you!')*, and it drifted out around her, bubbles of air caught under the white cotton.

Adelie's eyes were open and she looked up into the trees. She seemed to lie on the water without any effort, the river and the cotton and the air between them holding her afloat.

༄

The crates and trunks arrived from France three months later. Adelie and Xavier had expected to buy everything they needed in

London but their mothers decided that the English outpost must at least be furnished with French things.

The Sevier–Zell children would know their heritage by sitting at a French table, drinking from French glass and eating from French china to the tic-tac of Madame Zell's great-grandmother's clock.

1956

⚬✦⚬

The Hen House

'Xavier, do you think we should have somewhere larger for the hens? We have so many now and I can't bear them being so crowded together in that little shed.'

'We only eat them in the end anyway.' He kissed Adelie's neck as she bent over her mending. She held up her hand with a sock glove-wise over it and examined the darn. It was less than perfect, but Joséphine was always kind: 'Chérie, another beautiful spider's honeymoon.'

'Hens taste better if they're happy,' Adelie said and sucked a new piece of thread, squinted and poked it through the eye of the needle. She looked up and smiled at him. On her lap was a small blazer with a torn pocket. She liked to do Josef's things herself, not hand them over to Joséphine with the other sewing, however complicated the damage. She had mastered darning; a rip must be easier. She pinned the pocket in place.

'Will you build a hen house, or should we ask Robert do you think?'

'He's very busy; I'll make one myself.'

Adelie put down the mending in a heap on the rug: 'Good. I'd better tuck in Josef.'

⚬✦⚬

'Adelie! *Adelie!*' Xavier burst into the kitchen, a clutch of glasses in his hand and a bottle under his arm. 'Would you serve for a while, and keep Josef with you? Just half an hour—not long?'

'Joséphine's arriving in a minute. Xavier, we need to cook, I'm behind with everything today.'

'Please, Adelie, please. I need you just half an hour, that's all. Joséphine will understand. I know she will.'

'Why now, can't it wait? What is it?'

'I'll tell you soon.' Xavier put the glasses and the bottle on the kitchen table. 'Please, Adelie, I must go *now*.'

'But what about the customers, they'll be expecting food and they won't get any, what will I tell them?'

'Tell them it's my fault.' Xavier was halfway out of the door.

'The shearers are here from Penquit. And the school inspector,' Adelie shouted after him. 'I promised I'd soften him up with something special. Xavier, no, not now.' But he had gone. She wiped her hands on her apron and hung it on the hook behind the door. There was a mirror on the wall in the passageway; she patted her hair and licked her lips.

In the bar, the table for lunch was already pulled into the centre of the room and three men, two in labourers' overalls and one in a brown pinstriped suit, sat in companionable silence.

'Messieurs,' said Adelie, with a smile for each of them. 'Forgive me, but today lunch will be a little later. Perhaps another beer?' They said nothing, gazed at Adelie, forgot their stomachs. 'Or perhaps something more interesting. Something special for you gentlemen.'

Adelie brought a bottle of red wine and four glasses to the table.

'I will join you,' she said, sitting down opposite the sheep shearers and next to the school inspector.

⸙

Josef waited by the garden gate, looking out for Joséphine. A lorry with a cloth top had stopped outside but it wasn't Joséphine, so although it was interesting he went back to keeping a lookout.

Joséphine would be here soon. He would eat his lunch at the kitchen table while his mother and Joséphine chopped vegetables that hissed in the frying pan like horses peeing.

'Sit with me, Josef, before you go back to school.' Joséphine would pat her knees for him. Her front sat on her lap so there was not much space left over for him. She smelled of onions and soap, and she had to hold on to him or else he slipped off her slippery knees like a slide. She and Mama talked like songs, using the right words for things, not words that made their voices slow and strange. English. He knew more English than Mama because he was five and Catherine said he was an English boy now. School was English. School was St Angela's. Sometimes Mrs Lamb asked him to tell everyone the French word and he would stand up, sometimes special and sometimes squirming because later they would tease him and say you have to spit and cough up your throat to speak French. French sounds like being sick, Jack said.

Once, a long time ago, the French word was a thing's real name, but he wasn't sure any more. More and more things had only an English name and no name in French, then if his mother didn't understand, he would have to wave his hands to make the shape. They were stuck if it was a word like frogspawn or plimsol. Joséphine knew every word.

He looked down the lane to where Joséphine would come. Any minute she would be there in a blue dress with flowers or a yellow dress with flowers or another yellow dress with smaller flowers. She wore a hat and her sunglasses twinkled and her walking stick was a cane that spanked you in storybooks, but never in real life. Josef kept his eyes fixed on the lane because he always missed what happened between when she wasn't there and when there she was.

'Josef.' His father was behind him, scooping him up off the garden wall. 'Help Mama for a while. A surprise for her is coming and you must help me keep it a secret.'

'What is it?'

'Promise you won't tell her?'

Josef nodded.

'It's a hen house.'

'Oh.' He didn't think a hen house could be surprising, but Papa must know. Josef had forgotten to keep his eyes on the lane. And there she was—Joséphine was there and he'd missed it again, how she came round the corner. She waved to him and he could see the underneath of her arm wobble in a friendly way like milk pudding.

∽

'No, this is not for me,' said Xavier when the canvas top of the lorry was rolled back.

'Mr X. J. Sevier. Cameldip. Lot 43. Art Nouveau Aviary,' said the driver.

'I bought a bird house,' said Xavier, looking at the typed list on the delivery book. 'It was forty guineas. It's for hens.'

'Same thing: hen house, bird house, aviary.' The driver clapped his book shut. 'You've got yourself a bargain, mate.'

Xavier watched the men unload ironwork from the lorry. It took four to carry each piece and lay it on the lawn behind the house. There were twenty in all and they'd done only ten in the half-hour he'd promised Adelie. Xavier went to see how things were indoors. From the garden, through the kitchen window, he could see Josef standing on a chair at the sink washing potatoes. His sleeves were held up with pegs, his hair dripped, and he was wearing Adelie's apron like a full-length frock. Joséphine had pulled a chair up to the stove and was stirring something in a pan.

Xavier walked round to the front of the house. He put his face to the window and cupped his hand against the glass. He could make out the back of Adelie's blond head and three faces turned towards her. He heard her voice, the sheep shearers and the school inspector laughed. Two wine bottles stood on the table between them with a plate of cheese and bread. Everyone was fine.

The men finished unloading sacks of nuts and bolts, crates of glazed tiles and two iron doors. The lorry went off to collect the next load: iron arches, ridge plates, more tiles, more bolts, rolls of netting, it said on the delivery docket. The garden looked like a scrapyard.

By half-past three the diners were still eating and Josef was home from school.

Adelie called out, 'Xavier, I *must* get on with things. Joséphine needs to go home and these poor gentlemen have missed an entire afternoon's work.'

The three looked unconcerned. Another bottle had been emptied before Joséphine served the lunch and they had long since ceased to feel competent in the use of shears or in the assessment of arithmetic and spelling.

Xavier barred the kitchen door, but he could see that his time was up. Adelie had better have her surprise.

For a moment she was speechless. 'What is it?' The chaos covered the lawn from the house to trees by the river, a waist-high tangle of jutting white ribs; an elephant's graveyard.

'It came with the saucepans.'

'What?'

'From the auction where I bought the copper pans and the wine racks and the oak barrels, the ...'

'Yes, I know. I know about those things. What about *this*?'

'My bike's underneath,' wailed Josef.

'It's going to be magnificent,' said Joséphine. 'Absolutely superb. What is it, Xavier?'

That was the question he'd asked the man standing next to him three days ago. Xavier was about to leave the auction room, having got most things he'd bid for. He pointed to the catalogue, a list headed 'Livestock Equipment Misc.'—sheep pens, hurdles, feeding troughs, pigsties, those words he knew.

'What is it? Aviary?' he asked.

'For birds. For keeping birds,' answered the man distractedly, jotting figures and making calculations on a notepad. He had been buying furniture.

'Hens?'

'If you wish.' The bidding started and when the hammer came down at forty guineas, Xavier was pleased that this afterthought had solved the hen problem so neatly. He had not inspected this hen house—it must be large and of the best quality; just what Adelie wanted. It was expensive, surprisingly so: the bidding had started at eighty-five guineas, but had come down to forty when no one else had raised his hand—that was the luck of an auction.

⁓

It took eight months to build the aviary, from September until the following June. Robert and Xavier cleared a space to the side of the garden, levelled the ground and dug a trench for the brick foundations. A gang of men was hired and they started work by building wooden scaffolding with a rope pulley to raise the upper sections. It took five of them to haul up, manoeuvre, hold steady and bolt a single arch in place. A stonemason was employed for the gable ends and he agreed to finish the job by lining the walls with the hand-coloured tiles.

The ironwork was painted, the wire netting fixed in place and the doors were hung. It was almost complete.

The last job to be done was the most difficult: the floor. The mosaic design had been complex and the pieces taken up hastily. Only a rudimentary record of the pattern had been made. The restoration required the skills of an artist, a historian and a craftsman, someone with infinite patience. A local man was known to fulfil these requirements. He also possessed the dexterity of a lacemaker and the gift of healing. He was a retired surgeon, Her Majesty's Royal Navy.

He was a resident of Cameldip and arrived each day on his bicycle. The work was undertaken on the understanding there would be no fee but neither would there be consultation on the design; his decision would be final.

An assistant arrived each day at noon, also by bicycle, with a picnic lunch, and they sat together in the aviary saying little, contemplating the expanse of dry earth to be covered. The assistant stayed for the afternoon, standing at the surgeon's shoulder to receive instructions.

They worked from January, into spring and summer. When they started Xavier offered to cover the roof with a tarpaulin to keep out the wind and wet, but the surgeon insisted that the light must be excellent and if this were done, electricity would be necessary. A temporary cable was run from the house and a dozen light bulbs were strung from the roof.

The surgeon began by marking out three circles to be left bare and in which trees would later be planted. He then counted and catalogued the thousands of pieces, sorting them for colour into barrels, re-sorting into buckets for shade, then again into bags for shape. There was no hurry. He researched designs of the period, took measurements and made calculations. He drew diagrams, made ink sketches and watercolour paintings. Finally he put on his gloves, mixed the lime mortar and got down on his knees. At his side, the assistant referred to the master plan, selected the next tiny fragment from the four dozen bags and placed it in his hand. The surgeon fitted piece to piece until the earth was covered.

It was finished.

The aviary measured thirty-two feet in length, fifteen wide and twenty-four feet high at the apex of the arched roof. Inside, the mosaic floor sparkled, so vivid and luminous, especially after rain, that people thought they stood on a carpet of glass beads. The tiled walls at each end seemed part of the living vegetation growing close by, adding huge impossible blooms to the laurel, hawthorn and willow outside.

Seen from the river the ironwork shimmered like a curtain of bleached lace in the trees.

Adelie's hen house had cost eight hundred and seventy pounds. Half the cost of the house in which she and Xavier and Josef lived.

1958

∽

Frank and Elaine

Frank and Elaine came together by way of an egg flan, a missing copy of the *Radio Times* and a cello.

When they met, they had two things in common: being twenty and being at the same university. Frank was seeing a first year botanist and Elaine was not seeing anyone. She shared a flat with the botanist and had heard Frank on many occasions late at night when she would rather have heard only the thud and gargle of the immersion heater.

She had never seen him nor he her, until the botanist mistakenly bought an egg flan made with mushrooms to which she was allergic. The reaction was not serious—an hour of vomiting and eight hours of sweats—but the botanist wasn't up to the Christmas ball Frank had asked her to.

'You go, Elaine,' she said knowing that Elaine was no threat and, if anything, a contrast likely to increase his appreciation. Also, he would be tethered to a partner of her choosing, leaving her free to concentrate on being poorly. 'It'll do you good and the ticket won't be wasted.'

'I suppose,' said Elaine. 'As long as there's nothing on TV.' She searched for the *Radio Times* and failed. It was under the botanist's bed and Elaine never did discover what she'd missed. She agreed to go as a favour.

She didn't have a ball gown and decided that Frank would just have to lump it. This was fine with the botanist. She didn't offer to lend Elaine anything, not from meanness but because tall and narrow does not adapt easily to short and wide. But she did press Elaine to a diamanté handbag and matching earrings at the last minute, and was a little unnerved to see how beautifully the earrings sparkled against Elaine's olive complexion.

❦

Frank was handsome, a good sportsman, and had been toughened up by his four sisters. Family life in his teens was testing—a pubescent boot camp—you did not show fear, or else you were done for. Breasts, periods and complicated underwear must be met head on. The teenage Frank was spaghetti thin and his jaw unpromising but he could handle anything as far as the opposite sex was concerned.

By the time he went to university he had filled out and squared up. Girls did not unnerve him. He looked them in the eye whatever they confided or confessed. They interpreted this as maturity and on this foundation Frank built himself the reputation of being considerate, dependable and broad-minded, with thighs to match.

He never met a girl who surprised him. He never met a girl who was mysterious. All there was to know he'd found out long ago. And (Elaine could not have known) he wasn't used to lumping it. Frank had assets and was generous; what he asked for in return was run-of-the-mill perfection, visually at least. Elaine did not know this either and was therefore unusual material.

The botanist telephoned Frank to explain; her understudy needed a nice time and did music. He picked up Elaine from the flat on the dot as was his habit.

When Frank followed Elaine down the path he tried not to look at her fleshy shoulders or the matronly bustle of her rear or her sturdy calves that seemed to plummet, ankle-less into scuffed white kitten heels. She had not understood the deal and Frank was disorientated, but he would be gentleman enough to see it through.

He opened Elaine's door and she reversed in with surprising grace. Her underwear creaked softly and she smiled up at him.

'I'm in. Chocks away.'

Frank noticed that her long hair was luscious and her dark eyes were very pretty.

∽∾

The evening was not what he expected. Elaine did not stick to his shoulder and blink at him when he spoke to her. She talked her way through dinner, pulled crackers with her neighbours and told a rather good joke. They moved away from the tables and into a hall where a rock and roll band twanged into key against a backdrop of tinsel. Elaine topped up her glass, scanned the crowd and said: 'Don't think I'm going to cramp your style. I'm fine. See you later.'

From time to time he caught sight of her with a group of musical friends. They looked dull but Elaine seemed fine, as she said she would be, so he beamed in on a philosopher who turned out to be deliciously flirtatious but had a laugh like a duck, even over the noise of the band. It was almost two o'clock when he thought he'd better find Elaine.

She seemed to have disappeared so he asked around. What followed was nothing compared to romantic fiction, a non-event by the standards of erotic cinema, but it changed Frank's life.

Elaine was playing the cello. She and her friends had gone off together to an upstairs room, one of the practice rooms, and had been jamming their way through a selection of Vivaldi concerti. They had taken a couple of bottles of vodka, some Babychams and a candelabra from the dining table. The room was small and sound-proofed. The temperature rose, the boys took off their jackets, unfurled their shirt-tails and let their bow ties dangle. The girls' shawls and little evening cardigans slipped to the floor. As Vivaldi took hold, their shoulder straps slithered and skirts were hitched up to let the air circulate. And so it went on through Beethoven and Bach. Eventually they discarded any clothing that wasn't too complicated to get out of. The candles burned lower and there were

some interludes for drinking and familiarization. People fell asleep
at their instruments or in each other's arms.

By the time Frank found them, only Elaine was still playing. The
slow, deep chocolatey sound of the cello filled the room. It took a
moment for Frank's eyes to adjust to the near darkness. Gradually
he saw.

Elaine was sitting, turned slightly away. The candles on the piano
at her side caught her profile and sketched her in strokes of liquid
light and charcoal shadow. An earring sparkled in her hair. Her eyes
were closed and the little flames thumbed gold on her cheek, on the
rim of her lips, on her generous shoulder and her hand. So blissful
was the look on her face that it took a moment for Frank to regis-
ter that Elaine was without her dress and also without whatever had
creaked beneath it. Her solid thighs straddled the cello, and as she
moved, the candlelight caught the lavish curve of a breast and the
dot of a nipple, lit for a moment then gone in velvet shadow, velvet
shadow down to her belly and down.

Frank, for all his early training, was caught off guard. For the first
time in his life he was unprepared. This woman, Elaine, astonished
him—a secret illuminated, but still as mysterious as the arcs and coils
and serpentine curves of a golden hieroglyph. Frank backed out of
the room and returned, dazed as one converted, to the dance floor.

An hour later, Elaine tapped him on the back. The philosopher
was hanging on to his lapels, serious now and weepy.

'I'm knackered,' Elaine mouthed. 'Can we go?'

They walked to the car, Elaine weaving a little but not requiring
assistance. When he dropped her off she said, 'Don't worry, I didn't
see a thing.' Frank was still in shock and missed the irony of this.

He married Elaine two years later. It took him that long to learn
the difference between *vivace* and *lento,* and for her to adjust to the
unconventional way in which he liked her to practise the cello.

❧

In 1971 when their first child, Beatrice, was nearly four, Frank took up a teaching post at Exeter University and Elaine, three months pregnant, decided that she would take the plunge and teach music from home. They searched for something rural but accessible, within reach of Exeter but beyond the orbit of pub-going students. It all fell into place. They house-hunted from the time Elaine was her normal Rubenesque girth until she could barely fit behind the dashboard, and just in time they found a cottage in Cameldip.

It was one of the original dwellings near the chapel with low ceilings and underwater light. There were steps up and down between the rooms, a quaintly dangerous staircase and ceiling beams at the level of Frank's eyebrows. It seemed perfect until they moved in.

The tiny windows cut off the outside world and the walls and ceilings heaped their weight on the air inside. The deep, vibrating voice of Elaine's cello was as compressed as a seventy-eight through a cardboard megaphone, the piano became muffled in a fog, and Bee's flute produced only a piping chirrup.

It was a cottage that liked quiet, and Elaine despaired. So they decided to build an extension, a timber-and-glass music room with plenty of light and space enough for the notes to breathe. They looked up a local builder, a furniture-maker by trade but who, to Elaine's amusement, specialized in tree houses. She took it into her hands to organize things.

'It's all organized,' she told Frank. 'He's a nice, quiet Scotsman. He likes building tree houses but he's willing to build our music room on the ground. He'll start in the spring, and I'll have had the baby by then so that'll be good.'

'Splendid,' said Frank. He shuffled the frying pan and flipped over some fish fingers with a spatula, jockeying them back into line. Beatrice sat at the table, a fork and spoon at the ready. 'Stand by, Bee, nearly done. Ketchup or nothing?'

'No,' said Bee. 'Thplendid.'

'He lives in that big grey house down by the station,' Elaine went on. 'You know, past the post office and down that way about ten minutes, by the river.' She kicked off her shoes and lowered herself onto a kitchen stool. She was six and a half months pregnant; her ankles were swollen and her back ached. 'Well, I say in the house, he seems to live in the grounds somewhere; a nice woman called him in to see me, Scottish aristocracy roughing it I'd say, looked like his sister. She's Isabel and he's Roger. He's coming to price up next week.'

'Peas, Queen Bee?'

'Apparently the baby ballet classes are in her place, in her dining room. Her actual dining room in her house is the village hall. Frank? Did you hear me? Her dining room's the village hall!'

'On your marks, Bee. Tuck in.'

'I've signed up Beatrice. I thought it would be good for her but she's not so sure, are you, Bee?' As she turned, Elaine's sleeve picked up a slice of buttered bread. In one swift movement Frank leaned across and caught it before it fell to the floor.

'Anyway,' Elaine went on, 'before we were through our first cup of tea she had it out of me that I play the piano and I think I'm down for the Christmas panto. What do you think?'

'Splendid,' said Frank.

'Er, I mean … us. I mean, *we* are. On the list, for the panto. I couldn't say no.'

'Just a sec, Bee. Let's just organize those fish fingers.'

'I'm sorry, Frank. You couldn't help liking her but you wouldn't cross her in a million years. Anyway, she'd volunteered us before I realized. You'll have to tell her yourself if you want to get out of it. I just can't.'

Frank, with his hands over Bee's fists, divided a fish finger into mouthfuls.

'Frank? I couldn't say no. Don't clam up on me. What do you think?'

He straightened up and looked at her, his forehead furrowed: 'You always ... I don't know ... you're so ...'

'What?' said Elaine anxiously, her voice rising a minor seventh. *'What?'*

He leaned over Bee's head and kissed Elaine on the lips—which was the last thing she expected him to do.

November 1987

~❦~

Starling and Gatta

Starling had decided. This time she would talk to Josef—if he wasn't in she would find him and speak to him today because she had thought up a good reason to and she would lose her nerve if it wasn't now.

It was raining and cold and Starling wished she had something nicer to wear than a plastic mac, but at least it kept her suede jacket dry and she could take it off straightaway when she arrived. A rain hat was out of the question; frizzy was better than stupid.

There were too many puddles to avoid and in the fifteen-minute walk from the shop where she lived to the pub, the frayed bottoms of her jeans sucked up the rainwater and flapped wetly round her ankles. She kept her head down. A voice said, 'Hello, Starling,' and it sounded like Mrs MacKinnon, but she pretended not to hear, not wanting to get involved in explaining anything or being polite about having a nice half term.

It was nearly a month since Josef had almost kissed her. The feeling she'd had after it almost happened had gone from inside her but the memory stayed. Except now she could imagine it into a whole conversation and a beautiful embrace where she had not hung in his arms like a stunned sheep with her eyes crossed because his face was so close, and her school skirt rucked up and her feet accidentally kicking his shins.

Surely he had scooped her tenderly right up against him and she had leaned her head on his shoulder, a little faint with the shock of the dangerous, rearing horses. He had put her gently down and held her face in his hands looking into her eyes, bewildered and astonished at the feelings she inspired in him. And he had asked if he might see her again.

Starling paused in the lane, sniffed and wiped the rain off her nose. The pub looked especially bleak today, the windows were dark and rainwater gurgled in the downpipe from the gutter. The creeper that covered the stone walls and most of the windows was a dense mesh of black stalks with a few dead leaves dangling here and there. For an odd moment Starling felt her back prickle as if someone was watching her, and she turned round, but the lane was deserted, only the sound of drips plopping from the bare trees on to sodden piles of leaves.

Josef's place was surrounded by trees. They lined the river and looped a noose round the pub and the aviary and the garden. They arched over the roof and edged into the flower beds. It was only the clear green space of the lawn at the back and the tarmac lane in front that seemed to keep the trees from closing right in. Starling imagined the branches growing in front of her eyes, slithering in and out and weaving a huge lobster pot that would trap her and the house inside. Her and the house and Josef.

She walked up to the door—she had never done this before—lifted the heavy latch and pushed. Starling expected the door to be locked, it was mid afternoon on a Tuesday and the pub was closed, but the door swung open.

The bar smelled of old smoke and beer and dust. There were wooden tables with chairs left pushed back askew as if people had just gone, and the flagstone floor was so uneven it made dark hollows and silvery crests like moonlit water. Lines of bottles twinkled on the shelves. The counter was a long trestle with wooden barrels underneath and on the top were three wineglasses in a little cluster still with stains of red inside. Starling pushed at one with her finger. It moved a fraction, leaving a purple crescent on the bare wood.

She coughed to show politely that she was there, but no one came so she took hold of the rope on a brass bell above the counter and gave it a tug. The sound of the bell split the air and clanged round and round like a dropped saucepan. Starling's heart thumped until the quiet settled again. The odd feeling had returned and she felt a small, cold fear in her stomach. She would have abandoned her plan, turned quickly and left this hushed, listening place, but there was a sound just through the doorway to the back of the house.

Footsteps, soft as if the person had bare feet or was wearing socks, came nearer, almost to the doorway, then the tiny rattle of a latch lifting, a pause, a door closing gently, then silence again. Starling did not know what to do. Josef must be in the next room, so close, but he might not want to see her after all. Suddenly the memory of his blue, indifferent eyes came back to her: no, he had not really asked to see her. And another memory, clear now in her mind, of Josef leaving her, walking away along the lane and not turning even once to look back.

But she had to talk to him, she could not bear it any more. She walked round the bar, through to the passageway and tapped on the door.

It was even darker in the passage. The walls were wooden planks, polished or varnished sparkling black as if they were wet, and there were other doors and a staircase going up into shadow. Starling leaned closer to the door, turning her head a little to catch any sound. The fist that had knocked was still raised and as she leaned forward she opened her hand and rested the palm against the wood. It was as warm as her own skin.

'Hello,' said a voice above her head. Starling's heart jumped and she turned with a great rustle of wet plastic. Her heel and her elbow banged on the door behind her. Josef stood on the stairs, his feet level with her eyes. Starling's mind fluttered between fear and guilt and shyness.

'I've come about a job,' came out of her mouth. Then: 'I met you with your horses on October the fourth but you probably don't remember.'

Josef came down. He carried a cat in his arms and it started to struggle when he got near to Starling. He let it jump and it landed with a thud and shot away into the shadows.

'Yes, of course I remember.' Josef reached over her shoulder and opened the door. Light streamed through and Starling blinked. Her face felt tight and hot with the dried rainwater and she knew that her cheeks must be very pink, but Josef was not looking at her. She followed him into the kitchen. He took two glasses from the dresser and without asking, poured wine for them both from the open bottle on the table. He pulled out a chair for her.

'Please, won't you sit down?' he said formally and politely as if she were grown up. 'As for a job, I'm afraid the pub is never very busy. I don't really need help, I'm sorry.'

He went back to the dresser where he cut some bread, opened cupboards and drawers and put some things on a plate. 'At this time of year there are so few visitors, some days I don't even bother to open up. Christmas might be different.'

Starling took a sip of her wine and sat quietly. She had wondered what Josef's house would be like; it was untidy. There were piles of things, sacks and boots, cardboard boxes in the corners. Crockery was stacked in the sink.

But it was very peaceful, a place where you need not be careful of spilling things when you helped or being in the way when you didn't. The room was square, low-ceilinged with beams crossing from one side to the other. Above the sink a window looked out over the wet garden.

Along one side of the kitchen wooden shelves were lined with blue painted plates and on the other was a stone fireplace, the opening almost as high as Starling. Ash spread over the hearth, glowing red in the middle and giving off a warm bonfire smell.

Cobwebs looped across the ceiling like Christmas decorations and swayed in the warm air.

Starling felt sleepy in spite of Josef's being just across the room. How old was he? Thirty or forty or twenty-eight like her brother?

'How old are you?' As soon as she said it, Starling wished she hadn't.

'Very old. More than twice as old as you,' said Josef over his shoulder. He brought some things to the table, some bread and cheese, two plates and a knife. 'Thirty-six.' He put a piece of bread on her plate and cut some cheese. The backs of his hands were hairy.

'Thank you,' said Starling, instead of 'that's too much,' which is what she always said at home. She had taken a bigger mouthful of wine than she'd intended. It was horrible, bitter, but she swallowed and waited for the warmness. It spread up from her stomach, up her chest and her neck and into her already hot face. She would get off the subject of ages.

'Well perhaps you'd like a cleaner, then.'

'Do you think I need one?' Josef was smiling and Starling could not look. He was too handsome.

'I just thought you might, and I need to earn some money,' Starling said to her wineglass.

'I'll think it over. Perhaps I should talk to your mother, just to make sure it's OK.'

'Yes,' said Starling. Now she felt silly and it was clear that Josef thought she was just a silly schoolgirl who needed her mother to check up on her. She wanted to go home but could not think how—she had hardly started her food, although the wine was almost gone.

'Do eat,' said Josef. 'I'm sorry, of course you're perfectly able to make your own decisions, it's only if you were my daughter I would want to make sure you were doing the right kind of job.'

Somehow Starling liked Josef saying this and found she could look at him again.

'She'll say it's fine, I know,' she said, taking a mouthful of bread and cheese. 'She thinks I should get a job and cleaning your house would be exactly her idea of what's good for me. The point is she's always saying I don't appreciate what she does.'

'I see.'

'Anna says that women make work for themselves and there's no sin in being untidy and my friend Gatta's mother doesn't bother much either so my mum's in the minority.'

'Yes, I know Gatta's mother.'

Starling stopped chewing. 'Do you? She doesn't go out much, she just sleeps and cuddles Linnet. That's the baby. My mum says she's got more children than she needs what with Gatta and Spike and Pete and Linnet and no husband.'

'She used to do a lot of cleaning and cooking once. She was a housekeeper when she was about your age; did you know that? She was very organized. That was a long time ago.'

Josef was looking into the air over Starling's head; she should get off that subject too. Josef's chin was bluey black and his eyes were kind but sadder than she'd remembered.

'You're easier to talk to than I thought,' said Starling and Josef's eyes came back to her.

After a moment he said, 'You talk to Anna a lot?'

'Yes, we do. She lives with the MacKinnons with her baby. She says a tidy house means a dull woman.'

'Does she like it there?'

'I dunno. I suppose so. Why not? They're weird but they're OK. You could ask her yourself. She's going to the fireworks.' Why did he want to know about Anna? 'She's got a boyfriend in London,' said Starling emphatically.

'Anyway, you're friends, you and Anna.'

'Well, we are, but she's older than me so it's different. She comes to the shop. Her boyfriend's coming to see the baby but she won't say if he's the one, you know, the baby's father. I don't know why she won't say. I wouldn't tell anyone if she told me. I know how to keep my mouth shut. And be discreet.'

Josef seemed to be thinking of something else now. He tipped back his wineglass.

'Would you excuse me a moment? I must feed the animals, they've already waited too long.' He put on a coat and opened the door to the garden, letting in a draught of the outdoors. It blew in the smell of mud and leaf mould and the swishing of the wind in the trees. The sound cut off when Josef closed the door behind him and there was only a faint rustling like tissue paper and sometimes a spatter of raindrops on the window. It was almost dark outside.

Starling was happy to sit alone in Josef's kitchen. She tried to plan what she would start on first but it was difficult to think—it seemed a big, complicated room to clean. The wine tasted nasty but the feeling was nice. It made her smile and feel that it did not matter what she did because anything would be all right.

There were two rocking chairs, one on each side of the fire. One was high-backed and almost black, the other was the same shape but in miniature as if it were for a child. It was made of some golden wood and letters that Starling could not quite read were carved on the back. She thought how nice it would be to sit by the fire and rock but it was not as easy as she thought getting up and walking the two yards to the fireplace. The floor heaved like the deck of a ship and she was tipped one way and then the other. The little rocking chair moved, always slipping away from her hand, just out of reach. Starling concentrated and caught it.

She sat hunched, rocking. The chair was a tight fit around her hips and her knees were up under her chin when she rested her heels on the rockers. The room swayed wildly, the flames in the fire danced, the saucepans twinkled and the colours of the plates glowed clear and bright in the shadows. It was so beautiful, everything stretching and tilting like things under water.

Starling closed her eyes and rocked and looked forward to Josef's coming back. She would ask him if he had ever been in love. The blackness behind her eyelids was beautiful too, and if she tipped forward just a little more, she could lean her head on her knees.

When Josef came in, shaking the wet off his coat and stamping the cold from his feet, he found Starling sleeping in Catherine's rocking chair.

He had forgotten that English children, even grown children, are not used to wine. Starling's cheek rested on her bony, blue-denimed knees, her small hands rested on the floor. She was snoring slightly. He felt uneasy—perhaps he should telephone her parents. Not yet, she had drunk so little. She would wake soon and it might be better for her if they did not know.

Josef hesitated, then picked her up and carried her into the sitting room. He had not held her since her christening, and now twice in less than a month. He put her down on the sofa and covered her with a blanket. Her hair was still damp and he smoothed it back. Her face was pinched and thin, older than she was, but her mouth was childishly plump, the lips full and smooth, delicate pink. Her mouth was open a little and her tongue rested between her lips like a baby.

∞

Two babies, wrapped in white. They are pass-the-parcelled from guest to guest up and down a table set out on the grass. A summer wind is bending the roses and stirring up the trees. The white table-cloth undulates, overturning wineglasses, clattering china and silver dishes. People laugh and grab at things, mopping up spilled wine, rearranging knives and forks. Bread rolls and napkins cartwheel over the grass chased by children and dogs.

One baby sleeps through it all. He holds her in his turn, fascinated by the minute, fastidiously curled fingers and the curved black eyelashes, too long and thick for someone so small. He bends down, his face close to hers, looking for signs he can recognize. He prays she won't wake before he passes her on but it is hard to let her go.

The other baby cries furiously or stares, round-eyed and astonished, depending on the face in front of her. When she is put in Josef's arms, she studies him, then her eyes fill with tears. He gives the baby Starling quickly to Adelie; his mother's smile can pacify anyone. She cradles Starling in the crook of her arm and continues round the table, filling glasses, leaning over each shoulder, smiling.

And his mother asleep on this sofa, the pain in her face smoothed away by sleep.

And longer ago than anything, at the beginning of time, he sleeps here wet and dazed too. He is seven years old. He has fallen in the river and walked all the way home alone. His mother wraps him with this same blanket.

⌒∞⌒

When Starling woke it was black outside and the rain tapped and hissed against the glass. It sounded like people whispering. Her face felt sore where it pressed against the rough upholstery which smelled of dust and feathers and ancient dampness. She could see shadowy furniture in the half-light from the passageway. Her head throbbed and she wanted to go on sleeping on the gently rocking sofa.

She remembered Josef and sat up. The air was freezing. She staggered up and pulled the blanket round her.

The kitchen was warm. It was lit by firelight and by some candles in saucers on the windowsill and the table, and a tinny radio voice was talking softly and indistinctly. Josef sat in the big rocking chair with a thin, grey dog curled at his feet.

'Are you feeling better?' He got up. 'You look like a squaw in that blanket.' He put his hands on her shoulders and sat her down in his chair.

'What time is it?' said Starling.

'About five. You've only been asleep for an hour. I'll make you something to drink and walk you home.'

They did not talk as they drank tea. Starling's head was empty. She could not remember why she had been so awkward with Josef or why she had wanted to make up things that weren't true. She had meant to ask him something but that had disappeared too.

He helped her put on her mackintosh, gave her a scarf and some gloves and put a woolly hat on her head with a rain hat over that. She did not protest.

They walked along the dark lanes following the beam of Josef's torch through the rain. Starling hooked her arm up through his and leaned in to his shelter. When he left her outside her own front door he did not mention the cleaning job, or speaking to her mother. But Starling did not mind. When she closed the door, this time Josef had turned to watch her.

⌀

Gatta found it easy to hide. But she did not conceal herself in the usual way—or very rarely. She became invisible by merely giving herself up to the things around her, becoming part of them, so still and neutral that even her heart slowed and her breathing flattened almost to nothing.

If she sat for a while in a field or on the bank of a lane, little by little animals and birds would resume their normal comings and goings and she could be as much the scenery of their lives as a tree or a blade of grass. They seemed even to forget the scent of her.

She did not know when she had first learned to do this but for as long as she could remember she could eavesdrop on any conversation, watch almost anything she chose, without being noticed. She would become silent inside, nothing and no one, and it seemed that life could happen around her as if it were a film or she a ghost.

When she was small it never occurred to her that she was spying; she did not need to be out of sight but only be of no more account

than a carpet or a chair. The deception was in seeming so lifeless
that sometimes even her mother's eyes would slide over her. It was
at those times that Gatta would see a face that did not belong to her,
a woman with thoughts of her own that Gatta could not guess, a
mother who might even forget her children.

When Gatta was very young she would find it almost too much
to bear and would burst out of her bubble of stillness to bring her
mother back to her. But gradually she came to like riding the wave
of panic to watch this woman's dreaming, searching eyes. She could
see that her mother's real life was elsewhere and that the love that
she gave to her children was perhaps only at the edge of something
that Gatta would never know.

Pete and Spike had each other and did not notice. It would be
harder to fool her little sister, to deceive Linnet into thinking she
was safe. She would make sure that Linnet was always seen.

Sometimes Gatta was exasperated with her mother and sometimes, more often, she was tired and longed to be just an ordinary
daughter like Starling. But Gatta loved her mother and could not
let her forget Linnet in the way that she had been forgotten. Even
Linnet's father had made no difference to that.

As Gatta grew older it was more difficult to be invisible. She
could not have said why it was ever necessary to be so—she never
discovered anything she could not already guess. Except that she
could watch people live their lives away from her, the secret selves
they would not have shared, and in this she lived more lives than
just her own. She never feared being discovered, her heart never
thumped with nerves. Her eyes and ears would be all of her and the
cold on her skin or the numbness in her limbs would be nothing.

So when she followed Starling through the rain, watched from
the garden yellow-lit scenes inside the house, Josef pouring wine,
everything, and then walked with them back to the village, she was
soaked and frozen but did not begin to shiver until Starling had
closed her front door and Josef had turned for home.

November 1987

Anna

When Anna opened the shutters, the trees were glittering and the sheep standing in the sunshine were matted beige against the silver grass.

Anna puffed a breath, testing the temperature, and thought with regret that she would have to move out of the tree house, it was too chilly for the baby even in his knitted coat. He was awake. His cheeks were pink with cold and he was in a good mood. Anna could feel his woolly little body relaxed and placid when she carried him into the house, through the sting of fresh air, past Isabel's closed bedroom door and down to collect the post. The house was cold but the kitchen was warm. Robert came in early to light the stove and it was always warm by the time she and Isabel got up.

Isabel appeared late, shuffling in her ethnic socks and ragged dressing gown with her hair a mass of grey wire. She didn't speak but seemed more tired than aloof. Anna asked if she'd like tea but Isabel filled the kettle herself and stared at it absently while it boiled.

The unease between them was no more than usual. Isabel was somewhere far off, distracted and still half dreaming.

Anna switched on the radio to hear the news. After a while she said, 'Isabel, I'd like a friend to stay if that's convenient.'

'Of course.'

'I thought I'd invite Thomas, you know Thomas? You spoke on the phone once or twice. I thought he might come this weekend and he might want to stay.' There was a flicker of interest in Isabel's eyes.

'Of course. Take whatever you need from the linen cupboard.' Isabel put the teapot on a tray with milk and a mug. Anna heard her go back upstairs to her room.

Anna called Thomas at work from the telephone on the kitchen wall. She rested the baby on her hip and dialled the number she still remembered.

'It's fine, Tom. You can stay here, Isabel says you're welcome.'

'I'm not sure if I can get away, Anna. It's difficult at the moment.' He sounded distracted and Anna could hear someone speaking in the background. The receiver was covered and she heard his distorted voice saying, 'Yes, yes, that one and that one, I'll be with you in a minute.'

'Please come. You keep cancelling, if you don't want to see me, just say.'

'I do, I do want to see you,' he said flatly. 'I'm not sure if I can stay though. I may have to get back.'

'Is there someone to get back for?' Anna felt a twist of jealousy. After more than a year, how did old habits survive?

'Yes,' he said with the directness she had loved in him. 'Actually there is.' The shock silenced her; her throat tightened and her eyes watered. The baby clutched at the silver chain round her neck and made a little murmur of interest.

'What's that noise?'

'It's a baby,' said Anna.

'Oh.'

Her skin prickled. She hadn't planned to tell him now but perhaps this was as good a time as any. He would have to know soon and surely he would have to come if she told him. But Thomas was speaking again to someone in the office: 'The number's in the file, haven't a clue where it is,' then to her: 'Anna, I do want to see you. I'll come after work on Friday. I'll leave early and drive down so it will be late. I'll phone you when I leave.'

'Don't come if it's difficult.'

'It is difficult but I'm coming. I'd like to see you.'

'You can't drive down after work then go back again. You'll be driving all night. Maybe we should leave it.'

'Then I'll stay.'

'Only if you really want to. There's fireworks in the village on Saturday.'

'I'll see you on Friday. Anna? I'll see you on Friday. OK?'

'OK.'

Thomas arrived after ten. Isabel had already gone to bed and the house was peaceful, smelling of woodsmoke and coffee. Anna had tidied the sitting room, piling up Isabel's village committee paperwork that covered the sofa and the chairs.

Thomas looked smaller and thinner than she remembered. His hair was longer and he was wearing a suit she hadn't seen before. The tie was one she had bought him years ago and it looked more familiar than he did. She saw his eyes go quickly over her body and she was suddenly conscious of the pads of flesh on her hips, the curve of her belly and her swollen breasts that had been almost flat when he saw her last. She was bigger and fatter, he was smaller and thinner; and the thought came into her head that if they were naked they would feel like strangers to each other now.

They sat on each side of the fire with a tray of tea and whisky and biscuits between them on the hearthrug.

Anna did not know what to say. Now that he was here, telling him he had a son she'd concealed from him seemed brutal. She felt sorry for him but not ashamed. She had made her decision; she was a mother now, she had to decide what was best for her child and Thomas must understand that.

'I'm fatter, as you see,' she said needlessly.

'You look good, Anna. It suits you.'

'How are you?' she said, crossing her arms over her chest. It was the third time she had asked.

'I'm fine.' Thomas leaned down to pour a drink and they clinked glasses but did not propose a toast to anything. They talked about his new job and their friends in London.

'Everyone's wondering where you've disappeared to, Anna. What do you get up to here? It's a lovely place but you're miles from anywhere. Where are you working?' Thomas took a swig from his glass and waited.

Anna's stomach turned over. A hard heat in her head that might have been the alcohol smothered the past year when she had missed him only once or twice. She forgot their final grating, gruelling holiday in Spain. When she looked at him he was reassuring and familiar and he was a stranger in his new, affluent city clothes. She wanted him again. They would be tied to each other when he knew.

'I've got something to show you,' she said, hearing her own voice brittle and bright. Maybe it was too soon but what was the point in trying to do this carefully, to not blunder when they were already in an impossible situation? He had made it so.

Thomas looked mildly interested but wary, like he used to when she'd bought a present for him.

'I won't be long.' She went upstairs and lifted the sleeping baby from his cot. He whimpered and rubbed his fists in his eyes but was asleep again on her shoulder by the time she got back to the sitting room. She closed the door behind her and came forward into the lamplight by the fire.

Thomas hadn't heard her. She saw him sitting, peaceful and oblivious, staring into the fire, the nearly empty glass in his hand and his shirtsleeves rolled up, and it struck her how separate he was from her now. The bond between them this past year was only an idea in her head. They were not parents together; she had been a mother from the moment she knew, and even before that she had changed inside. But Thomas was no different, neither in his body nor his mind—until she told him, a second from now. She hesitated at the edge of the moment, then time ticked forward and she said, 'This is Matthew John.'

Thomas looked up, his eyes going back and forth from the baby to Anna.

'He's yours,' said Anna. 'Ours.' Thomas drew in breath but said nothing. 'I didn't tell you before because you never wanted babies so that's what I decided.' She felt the baldness of the words—her clumsy accusation and excuse delivered alongside the shock—and she was sorry for it. But it was the quickest way to the other side of this chasm. Now it was said and Thomas knew. They would start from here. 'I'm sorry I didn't tell you.'

He still didn't speak and coldness seeped into her stomach.

'I'm sorry. You wouldn't have wanted him and we'd decided to be apart. It happened in Spain. I decided this was best. Tom? Say something. What are you thinking?'

'He can't be mine. You would have told me.'

'I couldn't. What would you have done?'

'Don't joke with me, Anna. He's not mine.'

This was not the scene she had imagined.

'He is, Tom.'

Thomas looked at the baby, disbelief then confusion, one after the other. He got to his feet.

Anna said, 'There was nothing you could say. Or do. We'd decided. I didn't want that—you being with me just because of a baby, so I took responsibility for him.'

Thomas yanked at the knot of his tie as if it were strangling him and the whisky slopped on the hearthrug. The little splatter of drops seemed to make him furious.

'*Just* because. He's a baby for Christ's sake, it's not for you to decide who owns him. He's not a … a hi-fi or a garlic press. And what about me? What about him?' He jabbed a finger at Matthew.

Anna stared. Thomas paced a circle round the tray.

'Anyway, you've made a mistake. He can't be mine.' He picked up his jacket from the back of the chair. 'I'm sorry. I've got to go. I need to get back.'

'No, Tom, please. We won't talk about it any more tonight.'

'You're unbelievable, Anna. How can we not talk about it? How can I sleep here now? You've either deceived me for a year or you're lying to me now. Which is it? Well? Which? Deceit or lies?'

'Please don't go now.' She started to weep. It was not a strategy. 'Do you want to hold him?' This was.

'For fuck's sake.' He never swore. On the other side of the chasm was a landscape she didn't recognize. Thomas had his jacket on but he poured himself another drink and handed one to Anna, avoiding her eyes. He turned his back and distractedly poked at the fire. She stood sipping and swallowing her sobs which even to her sounded self-pitying.

Suddenly the sitting room door opened and Isabel came in. She didn't hesitate when she saw them, Anna red-eyed and Thomas with his back turned. It was as though she assumed she couldn't be interrupting; they were expecting her or even waiting for her. Her hair was pinned up neatly and her dressing gown was tied with its proper cord.

'Hello, Thomas. It's lovely to meet you at last.' Her eyes went quickly to Anna and the baby. She smiled at Thomas, taking his hand in both of hers, and there was the Isabel Anna had met the first day she came to Cameldip, warm and charming and smiling into your eyes as if you were the person she most wanted to see in the world.

'I hope you've eaten, both of you.'

'Thank you, we have.' Thomas seemed glad of the diversion.

'It's very late, Anna darling. Thomas looks exhausted. You both do. Let me put Matthew to bed and you two can relax.'

'I'm not staying,' said Thomas abruptly.

Isabel went smoothly on, 'Oh, what a shame. But promise me you'll come again when you can, Thomas.' She held her hands out for the baby: 'Up we go, little one.'

'He's fine here, Isabel,' said Anna. 'Thomas has only just met him.' Isabel seemed not to have heard and lifted the baby out of Anna's arms. She took Thomas's hand again and said goodnight.

They sat in silence watching the dying fire. The room grew cold and the clock in the hall gave a single chime for the second time. It could be one o'clock or half-past one.

Eventually Thomas said, 'I'm too tired to drive. I'll stay if you like and you can tell me the truth tomorrow—or not, whichever you like, it's up to you. Where am I sleeping?' He picked up his bag.

'I'm sorry, Tom.'

'Just leave it, Anna. Don't say any more. I'm tired.' Upstairs, she opened the bedroom door and waited. He kissed her on the cheek before he closed his door.

In her room in the attic the reading lamp was on and the covers turned down for her. Matthew was asleep and she tucked him in under the little quilt embroidered with rabbits that Isabel had given her months ago.

⚶

The baby was gone when Anna woke. She had slept late the four nights she had been in the attic bedroom and every morning Isabel came in while she was still sleeping and took him downstairs. Anna wished she wouldn't, it always frightened her for a second or two to see the empty cot. In the tree house he had slept on the mattress beside her and it was strange to be sleeping alone. She missed him and he seemed to mind less than she did.

The house smothered her. She slept heavily and woke with a headache, feeling cut off from the birdsong and the November air, forgetting where she was for the first time since coming here.

Last night the longing for Thomas had kept her awake. He was so close, in the room below with not much more than air between them—through the mattress and the floor, lying in his own bed, closer than he'd been for more than a year. Anna had slept on her stomach trying to remember the feeling of lying on him as she used to sometimes when she would fall asleep on his chest with the thud of his heart in her head.

As she woke, last night's conversation surfaced in her mind and cringing embarrassment made her dread going downstairs. When Isabel had come in she knew exactly what was happening. She had probably always known how it would be when Thomas arrived, and now she would be even more sympathetic and patronizing.

They were in the kitchen and Anna could hear Thomas's low voice and Isabel laughing. Anna pushed open the door.

Isabel was at the sink with her hair as neat as last night, and Thomas sat at the kitchen table holding Matthew in his arms. The baby leaned back to examine the new face. He had breakfast smeared round his mouth and a pendant of dribble dangled from his chin. His fists gripped the neck of Thomas's cashmere jumper.

'We're waiting for you.' Isabel was cheerful. She wiped her hands and kissed Anna. 'Darling, you look very tired.'

She made more toast and coffee—they had already eaten—and Thomas glanced across the table to Anna from time to time, not unkindly, but cool and neutral.

'I thought perhaps you'd like to go off together today,' said Isabel. 'I'll have Matthew and you can just come and go, do whatever you feel like doing.'

'Thanks, but it's fine, we'd thought we'd …'

'Thank you, Isabel, we'd like that.' Thomas cut across her and Anna trailed off. She realized the wisdom of leaving the baby with Isabel. If last night had been different it would have been good to be together with Matthew, but it was too much to expect to have a family day when Thomas had been a father for less than twelve hours.

They decided to walk. Thomas borrowed some boots from the porch where there was a heap of all sizes from small children's red and yellow up to enormous mud-covered ones that must be Robert's, and a coat from Isabel.

The sky was the colour of clay and the air was bitterly cold. Winter had taken hold. Cameldip was messy with rotting leaves and semi-clothed trees, and soaked through from the constant on-off autumn drizzle.

'We'll go through the village then up over Tye Hill, then back along the river and we could call in at the pub on the way if it's open.'

Anna wanted to ask how long he was staying, if he'd forgiven her, if he believed her, but she said, 'Does that sound OK?'

'It's fine, Anna. Don't look so worried, I'm better this morning.'

They called at the village shop. The bell over the door jangled.

'Someone wants to meet you,' said Anna. 'Starling, this is Thomas. Thomas, Starling.'

'Hello,' said Thomas. He seemed to fill the little shop. Starling's eyes flitted to his face and away.

'Oh. Hi,' she said. She giggled and pulled at her T-shirt, then recovered her usual nonchalance. 'Where's Mattie?' she said to Anna.

'Isabel's looking after him today.'

'He's so cute. And cuddly. Don't you think he's so cute?' Starling's eyes slid to Thomas. He picked up a newspaper from the rack.

'Go and see him if you want to, Isabel won't mind,' Anna said. Starling gave her a patient look as if she had said something ridiculous: 'I can't. We're going into town shopping.' She looked over to a girl sitting on the stairs.

Anna hadn't noticed Starling's friend. The girl leaned back on her elbows, her feet tipped delicately on the wooden edge of the step and her smooth brown hair tucked behind her ears. She was watching Thomas, unashamedly studying him. She glanced across at Anna and the expression in her grey-green eyes might have been contempt or simply boredom. She returned her attention to Thomas.

'Oh, well. Maybe we'll see you tonight at the fireworks.'

'OK.' Starling almost missed as she dropped the change into Anna's hand. She was watching Thomas over Anna's shoulder; he was reading the newspapers, scanning the headlines.

'You make me feel invisible sometimes,' said Anna when they left the shop.

They turned out of the village by the chapel and took a footpath uphill. It was wide enough to walk side by side but Thomas went striding ahead, Isabel's coat flapping and his feet in Robert's boots making rhythmic gulping sounds that Anna could follow even with her head down against the wind. They crossed some sloping fields then up through a copse of dripping trees and out onto rough pasture. By the time they reached the summit of Tye Hill Anna was gasping trying to keep up, and it struck her how familiar this was, all the times he had refused to wait or noticed she was way behind. He wasn't angry, this was normal, and the thought was unexpectedly soothing.

When she caught up he was sitting looking out over the dun-coloured fields. Anna sat down beside him, hugging her coat against her. The river below them curved round the foot of the hill from the meadows upstream to the east and Isabel's house, then down into trees to the west and the pub at the other end of the village. Behind them, south, in the shelter of the hill, was Cameldip.

Thomas said, 'I do believe you. Isabel told me.'

'Told you what? I haven't told her anything.'

'I can't believe you'd do this to me.' He was incredulous. 'Even that girl in the shop knows. And what about your sister? Am I the last one to be told about my own son?' She could hear the anger seething in him again and she kept still as if that were less likely to provoke him. When he spoke again his voice sounded tired and flat.

'I haven't a clue about babies, I don't know how old he is but Isabel said he was born in April so the dates work out.' He paused. 'Isabel says you're a wonderful mother.'

'Does she? Did she really say that?'

'She said that you haven't met anyone else since you came here and that you're really trying to do your best for Matthew.'

For no reason she could understand, for a moment Anna hated Isabel. 'And what else did she say?'

'Don't sound like that, Anna. Isabel is a wonderful person. She's very fond of you.' Anna felt herself shrinking into the Anna she thought she'd left in London.

'We talked it through and Isabel is willing to go on helping you.'

Isabel had told him that Anna didn't pay rent, there was no need until she was working again, and Thomas would send her money too. It had all been straightened out.

Anna thought of saying that she didn't want to live with Isabel any more—Isabel didn't help—and she didn't want his money either, but she was listening to the crows in the trees by the river. They sounded as if they were laughing.

She heard Thomas say, 'I'll come when I can but I'm seeing someone—since last Christmas. She'll find all this pretty difficult.' He took Anna's hand and patted it.

The wind in her eyes made hot watery lenses that stuck in her eyelashes. The water swelled and squeezed out in blobs, dripping off her nose and splashing on her knees like a cartoon character crying.

'I wish you hadn't called him Matthew,' said Thomas. 'It was the name of a boy at school I hated.'

⌒∞⌒

'God, this is dreary. A good piece of vernacular architecture left to rot.' Thomas looked up at the façade of the pub.

'It's supposed to be nice inside.' Anna pushed open the door and it screeched on the flagstones. The midday winter gloom was barely more than dusk inside. The fire was alight and there were candles on the bar and on the tables. It looked rustic and festive. A middle-aged couple sat at one of the tables, and a woman on a stool by the fire, surrounded by bags of shopping, warmed her hands round a mug.

Josef Sevier leaned on the trestle bar reading a book, a glass of red

wine on one side, a candle on the other. He had looked up when
the door announced them.

'Oh, I see, I hadn't realized. This is nice. Very nice,' said Thomas
looking around. 'Sensitive conservation and appropriate materials
and there you have it, an authentic, naive interior. What would you
like, Anna? All it takes is attention to detail and the right lighting.'
They stood at the bar and Anna wiped the wet off of her face.

'Ginger wine,' she said.

'Apologies for the power cut,' said Josef. 'The generator's having
an off day.' He put her drink on the bar. His eyes caught hers and
he smiled politely. She couldn't tell if he'd heard what Thomas said.

She turned away to find somewhere to sit and the couple swivelled to look at her. He was handsome and greying, she was stout
with a broad face that must once have been beautiful and dark eyes
that still were.

They looked content and easy with each other, everything that
Anna and Thomas were not.

'Ah,' said the man from his table, 'you're Anna.' He tapped his
nose. 'Process of elimination.' He didn't explain. 'I'm Frank, and
this is Elaine. We know all about you from old Izzie MacK, and at
last we meet.'

'Hello,' said the woman, leaning over the table. It scraped on the
flagstones, the drinks teetered and the man expertly grabbed them.
'I've seen you at the house but you probably don't remember. I'm
Elaine.' She squeezed Anna's hand. They both smiled at Anna as if
she were a camera, Elaine leaning into Frank's shoulder, his arm
around her, she with her hands folded in her lap.

'Hello,' said Anna. The last thing she was in the mood for was
being sociable. She could hear Thomas talking to Josef—no
draught beer, no cold lager, but the wine list was impressive.

'I've seen you at Isabel's,' Elaine went on. 'I play the piano for
the Little Butterflies and the Old Camels' Keep Fit. I ought to be
working out with the ancients rather than sitting at the piano, but

there you are, that's life.' Elaine patted her front where her cardigan buttons gaped and her waist should have been.

'I do remember you now,' Anna said. She edged round them and their faces followed her.

'There's a film next week at the chapel, why don't you come?' Frank said. '*Zulu*. Seen it a dozen times but great stuff. Isabel tells us she's quite happy to have that baby of yours any time you want to get out.'

'Do come,' said Elaine. 'You don't get space to breathe with a tot hanging off you all hours. God, don't I remember. If Isabel's on tap for minding, make the most of it—it'll do you good.'

'Yes,' said Anna, and could think of nothing more to say. Elaine turned away.

Anna stared at her hand holding the glass in front of her. She could hear Frank's voice, muffled as if he were behind a curtain: *'Busy, eh, Josef? Fireworks bring the punters in?'* Elaine was laughing.

The little glass of green liquid was as pretty as poison. She could put it down on the table and walk away, leaving Thomas and forgetting him. She could go home to her baby and take him from Isabel, and Isabel would know that this time she had lost.

It was Isabel's eyes that would defeat her, flecked and shining, eyes that made her feel so loved there was no reason to fight and nothing at all to fear. Or they would slide through her as if she were made of glass, searching for some other thing that did not disappoint.

'Where's that pretty daughter of yours, Sarah?'

'She's gone into town with Starling.' The woman's voice echoed after Frank's bass like voices underwater. Anna shivered and a chill drenched her like ice water. She should not have left Matthew with Isabel and it was Tom's fault. No, not Tom's, Isabel's. Isabel had got her way as she always did. But she had kept Thomas here, he would have gone back to London if not for Isabel. Was that good or bad?

There was the sound of Elaine's voice: *'Steffie's gone with them. Honestly Frank, she told you this morning—in one ear ...'*

The green in the glass. It would fold her into itself like a fly in a bead of syrupy sap and carry her back to Isabel. Whatever she did would bring her back to Isabel.

'Anna? Anna. Is there anything wrong?' The sound of her name cut through.

'No, nothing. I'm fine thanks, Elaine.' She sat down at a table in the corner. Two small boys pelted through the front door to the woman by the fire.

'Steady, boys. Quietly.' They started delving in the carrier bags. 'Pete, no. That's for tea. Put it back.'

'But I want it.'

'There's Penguins in that one, Spike. Pete, I'm warning you. If you open that, no fireworks.'

Anna watched the three of them bent over the carriers, the boys' rough blond heads and the woman's smooth, silver-streaked hair falling forward as she looked in the bags. A happy little family.

Thomas was swilling tasters of wine and smacking his lips. He seemed not to have heard Elaine ask if anything was wrong, he was enjoying himself and in no hurry to sit down. There were uncorked bottles lined up on the bar and Anna watched Thomas talk and Josef listening attentively. Josef glanced over to her and she saw the amusement in his eyes.

She took a sip and the ginger wine warmed her. Thomas was ridiculous and Josef knew it. At least she was sharing a small joke on this dismal day.

'Zulu next week, boys, sharpen your spears,' said Frank.

She took another sip and held up the glass. It had a fine stem and a small rounded bowl etched with stars, each one different as if they were cut by hand. Through the glass she could see a scene in minia-ture all shades of jewel green—an empty table with the bright dot of a candle, the edge of the fire and a stack of logs, clear and glittering as if they were inside a tiny aquarium. And there was a child, a little girl standing just to the side of the fireplace. She wore a summer dress, smocked over her chest, and one bare foot rested shyly on the other. Her face, sweet and open, looked to Anna through the watery green.

Anna moved the glass and there were the golden flames and the black slate of the floor and the wooden table. And the empty space by the fire.

'What an astonishing place,' said Thomas loudly, sitting down heavily beside her. 'The most interesting wines I've come across outside Islington.' He put his arm round her and kissed her ear: 'Fine wines and film clubs in deepest Devon. What a find.' His face was flushed. His hand slid under her coat to her breast and his fingertips stroked through the cotton of her shirt. A little current flickered inside.

'I miss you,' she said. Thomas said nothing. He withdrew his arm and held up his glass, twirling it in his fingers and looking through the red wine as she had done the green.

What had she seen? What could he see? The red and the green: blood and water, fire and water. She hated him and she needed him to touch her. The red and the green: opposites that cancelled each other. The anxiety was gone, smothered by fatigue.

Thomas bought another round, and another. The door scraped open from time to time and more people came in. The pub was noisy. People talked louder and the voices tangled, rebounding off the slate and the stone.

The boys leaned over Frank and Elaine's table and they set up a xylophone of lemonade in tumblers. Elaine pointed out a tune, 'Pom, pom, pom,' and the boys banged with teaspoons. Their mother sat watching them.

'Ready for tonight, Josef?' Frank bellowed. 'Us oldies rely on you to keep us from freezing to death.'

When they left, Thomas waved to Josef as if they were old friends, and he stood at the door buttoning himself into Isabel's coat. Anna put the little glass on the bar.

'It's very pretty,' she said.

'Will you come to the fireworks?' Josef said to her. 'I'll bring it—the glass—if you like it. Residents have their own, this could be yours.' Anna did not know what to say. There was something in his eyes she could not interpret. She looked over her shoulder. Thomas was waiting.

'I don't know. I'm not sure.'

'I see. Perhaps …' Josef paused. It seemed as if he would go on but instead he said, 'Bring your baby, won't you.'

∽∾∽

The river path was the long way home. Anna said it would take them an hour at least so they decided against it and turned back through the village. It was bitterly cold and the drink had made them feel lazy and chilly.

Thomas's arm was a dead weight on Anna's shoulders. She put her arm round his waist under his jacket, and hooked her thumb in his belt to save the effort of hanging on. This was comfortable, familiar, like all the years of being a couple.

'I've got a son,' said Thomas. 'Well, well. I've got a son.'

'We have,' said Anna. They leaned together in chummy affection, weaving along the lane and stumbling sometimes. Anna was suddenly happy and also absent-mindedly carnal—the last time was more than a year ago in Spain and Matthew had been the result. It occurred to her that she could get pregnant again and the thought made her laugh. Then unexpectedly the open neck of Josef's shirt and the blue-black stubble on his chin came into her mind.

'I'm going to call him John,' said Thomas. 'That's his second name, isn't it? That all right with you? Jack. That's a nice name, Jack.'

'His name's Matthew,' said Anna.

'You feel gorgeous,' said Thomas stopping and turning her to face him. His hand searched vaguely under the lapels of her coat as if he were trying to find something inside a bag.

'It's too cold.' Anna said, pulling her coat together. 'Let's get home. Isabel will be wondering.' Isabel's name cleared her head.

It was beginning to get dark when they reached the house. No lights were on. Anna opened the front door and called out. The fuzz of alcohol had left her.

'Isabel!' She called again, going along the passageway, opening doors and switching on lights. Thomas followed her into the kitchen.

'Good,' he said. 'No one home. Come here, delicious one.' He pulled her against him and his hands slid inside her coat, inside her shirt.

'Thomas, for goodness sake.' She pushed him away. 'Where's Isabel? She's got Matthew.'

'Yes? So? She's looking after him, Anna. There's no need to panic.' He grinned and leaned against the sink, his arms crossed. 'She's a big girl, she can cope.'

'She should be here. Why would she be out now? It's dark.'

'Well she is and it's a good thing too.' He pulled her to him again, gentler this time. 'Anna, it's fine. What is there to worry about?'

'I don't know.'

They kissed and for a while there was nothing else but being close. The sensations were the same, no different from a time when they loved each other, as if they loved each other now. The ghost of their past dissolved and Anna pushed him away.

'I'm going to ask Robert, he'll know.' She unbolted the kitchen door and ran out into the gloom, across the grass. It was icy now and the stars were out. She banged on Robert's door.

'Do you know where Isabel's gone? She's looking after Matthew and I thought she'd be here—not here with you, but in the house. Did she tell you where she's gone?' Anna did not know what she expected but his reaction, though calm and measured as always, filled her with panic. He said nothing, but reached in for his coat and pulled the door closed behind him.

'What? Robert? What is it?' He was striding down towards the river. She ran after him.

'They'll be on the path somewhere. Isabel likes to walk by the river.' He stopped suddenly.

'It's all right, Anna. Go back in case she comes home. You should stay here or we won't know. Wait for me in the house, I won't be long.'

'It's not all right, is it? You think something's happened.'

'Nothing's happened, I promise you. I'll find them. Go inside and get warm. You look frozen.'

'No, I …'

'*Yes,* Anna. I won't be long.' He turned and continued down through the trees, disappearing in the dusk. Anna stood alone on the grass. The frost was beginning to whiten. Her breath puffed out in quick white clouds and her heart thumped with unnamed terror. She turned towards the house, then back to the river, then back again. Her body ached to run or fight or scream. She ran back to the house and flung open the kitchen door, and there was Thomas sitting at the kitchen table with Isabel. Their faces turned to her.

'Where's my baby?' Her voice burst in her head, belligerent and desperate like someone crazy.

'Darling, whatever is the matter?'

'Where is he?'

'He's asleep, darling. He's in his pushchair,' said Isabel getting up. 'There's no need to disturb him, Anna. Why don't you leave him, he'll be cross if you wake him.'

Anna ignored her, pushing past to the passageway and there was Matthew, his head lolling to one side, his padded coat up round his ears. She undid the straps over his chest, fumbling in her desperation to hold him. He whined and waved his fists irritably even before he opened his eyes.

'We've just this minute come in,' said Isabel. 'I thought I'd get his tea ready before I woke him.' Anna hauled the baby up against her.

His foot caught in a strap and the pushchair tipped up and clattered on the tiled floor; his wails changed to roars of outrage.

'He's fine, darling. We only went out for a little stroll. He's been perfectly happy.' The crying soared to full volume.

'I wish you'd told me,' Anna said. Matthew squirmed in her arms, heavy and warm and full of his own fury. She hugged him tight, breathing him in. Thomas put his arm round her shoulders.

'Here he is, Anna, see? He's fine. I'm so sorry, Isabel.'

Anna ducked under his arm. She wanted to get away from them both. She sat on the stairs, unzipped the baby's suit and pulled his arms out of the sleeves. He was sobbing and she wiped his face with the cuffs of her shirt. She lifted him up under his arms so the suit dropped onto the floor. She held him higher and tipped him over until their noses touched and he beamed at her with teary eyes.

She could hear them talking in the kitchen. There was the sound of the garden door and then Robert's low voice. He came out into the passageway.

'I'm sorry I worried you, Anna,' he said. 'I think Isabel may have said she was going for a walk. It was stupid of me to forget.'

'It's OK.' Anna could not look at him. He stood for a moment then went back into the kitchen. She heard the back door close.

Isabel and Thomas must have thought she'd gone upstairs, because she heard Isabel say, 'Anna's very tired. One is always exhausted with the first.'

And then Thomas: 'She seems different. A bit edgy. Bad-tempered.'

'Perhaps you can talk to her, Thomas, persuade her to let me help a little more. It would be good for the baby, too.'

1958

✦

Lions and Swans

There was a shared party for the crop of birthdays in August: Isabel, Xavier, Joséphine, Catherine and Josef.

'That makes us Leos. We're lions,' Catherine told Josef. When she said this he thought of orange fur pressed flat under his tight-fitting human skin, a skin in the shape of a boy which could be peeled off like a diver's suit. He would roll it down to his feet and step out, like his mother did when she took off her nylons. She often shook her hair—he would shake his mane then drop down onto his hands with their new, magnificent claws, leaving the empty skin of Josef lying on the ground. It was thin and crumpled like old pyjamas. He was seven, Catherine was nine, Papa and Isabel were too old to know and Joséphine was with Our Lady in Heaven and didn't need birthdays any more because she was in a state of bliss and had all the presents she wanted.

✦

Four months ago, Joséphine had woken tired. Too tired, she knew, even to reach the kitchen to make tea. Edward had left early and the house was so quiet the silence was singing in her ears like a glass bell. She came down the stairs, single step by single step, holding the banister with both hands. At the bottom she lowered herself down to sit for a rest. The morning streamed through the glass of the front door, and across the passageway Edward's study was filled with sunlight the colour of lemons. Joséphine wanted nothing more than to sit in his armchair until he came home for lunch.

She heaved herself up—it seemed such an effort. In the armchair, she put her hands on the worn cloth and noticed that this morning it felt smooth, almost silky. And there was a coolness on her forehead where, even though she had been asleep, she remembered that Edward had put his hand when he'd left that morning.

The clock ticked and something fluttered against the window, caught in the curtain. The pattering on the glass was powerful and desperate like a bird. Joséphine knew it would have to wait for Edward to come. But after a while it stopped and the room was quiet again.

❧

Adelie wept for days, clinging to Isabel. When she stopped it was as if not only her tears but her whole being had run dry. She was white-faced and sullen, insisting that everything must go on as usual and daily life should not even pause. There were hours then whole days when she would seem herself again, full of remorse for the times she had ignored Xavier and given Josef only the most cursory attention. But she refused to talk about Joséphine, turning her back even on Josef when he mentioned her name.

Isabel tried to help with the practicalities of Adelie's life without Joséphine. They cooked the customers' midday meal and looked after the children together. Much of the time Adelie seemed to find comfort in no one but Isabel.

Isabel tried to bring Joséphine into their conversation and sometimes Adelie would respond with some small comment or a brief smile, but the question of the birthdays was met with silence.

'Adelie, we must talk,' Isabel said. 'It's not fair for the children, they don't understand. They don't see why we can't have birthdays without Joséphine.' She waited, watching Adelie's thin shoulders tense as she tidied the dressing table. 'Adelie?' A picture frame fell to the floor and the glass shattered.

'Leave it now,' said Isabel softly. 'It doesn't matter.' She pulled Adelie to her, as she did her own children, folding them close, pressing love into them.

'Not a party,' Isabel whispered. 'We needn't pretend to be happy—we'll eat together like we always do and the children can have their presents, that's all. We'll think of Joséphine all the time, we won't forget her for a moment.'

They sat on Adelie's bed. It was late afternoon and it had been a sunless, oppressive day. The light was fading early and the bedside lamp was already on, a parchment shade with birds cut into it, their wings folded up as if they were flying.

Isabel leaned her face against Adelie's hair and felt her giving way, sinking softer against her. The heat was stifling but Adelie shivered and Isabel lay back on the pillows, pulling Adelie with her.

'Lie down, just for a while,' she said. She pulled the bedcover up and around them both, wrapping their bodies close together.

❧

Since the building of the aviary it was the place for celebrations. The hens' straw was swept up, the big table carried out from the restaurant, and Xavier's wind-up gramophone brought out from the house.

The three trees growing inside were now, two years after planting, almost shoulder height, the peach tree a little taller than the fig or the cherry. The trees were decorated with candles and it took careful positioning to make sure that the leaves or the blossom or the fruit, depending on the time of year, did not scorch when the candles were lit.

The shared birthday meal was on a day in August. There had always been nine of them—Xavier, Adelie and Josef, Robert, Isabel, Catherine and Jack, Joséphine and Edward. This time, Edward had written a note:

My dear young friends,

I'm sorry I can't be with you this year—you can be sure I'll raise a glass to your health and happiness, as Joséphine will wherever she is.

Sarah has been here such a short time. I would love her to meet you all but I think perhaps it would be too much to foist upon her all at once, wonderful as you are! None of us is quite ourselves just now and I would like it to be a happy meeting for her.

I know you will take her under your wing and she will love the children. Thank you, Izzie, for bullying me into finding her—she is a sweet girl, far cleverer than I shall ever be, and, as you told me, she will stop me becoming a tetchy old man!

Happy birthday to all. To my Isabel, I have so much depended on you these past months, to the young Lady Catherine, to our fine linguist and cyclist, Josef, and to you Xavier—Joséphine always said you are our son (and Adelie, our daughter, of course), delivered pain-lessly on the 3.15 from Paddington.

Yours,

Edward.

It had been hot for days but the weather seemed to be breaking. The evening was cool and starless. Sometimes the moon caught a hole in the clouds and the wind cuffed the tops of the trees in the garden and along the riverbank.

Inside the aviary, Xavier and the children lit and relit the candles on the three small trees until eventually the wax melted in the wicks and the flames were strong enough to survive. Even then a gust would flatten them, leaving curls of white smoke. By the time they sat down to eat, the breeze had settled. The dozens of dots of flame plumped out, fine-tipped and still.

They ate almost in silence but the quiet was different. Since Joséphine died, whenever Adelie was present there was a tense, stifled reticence. Now it was peaceful as if they found themselves together after a storm, with Adelie rescued unharmed. The aviary was filled with candlelight, lighting their faces, their hair, their hands. It glowed like a huge lantern set down in the trees.

When they finished eating, Jack and Josef rode their bicycles far out round the table, making a road of the mosaic pattern. Catherine leaned against Isabel, playing with her hair.

'Mind the candles, boys,' someone said from time to time.

'What about presents?' they shouted back. Jack had something too; his birthday was near Christmas and he pointed out that everyone got things on his birthday, so if he didn't now it wasn't fair.

They opened the presents. The biggest came last; Catherine had a paintbox, Xavier a camera, and Isabel a summer dress. Josef whooped at his telescope. His high voice shot up through the candlelight and echoed in the trees, setting the birds twittering.

They drank to Joséphine, then to Edward, then:

'To France.'

'To Sarah.'

'To peace.'

'To the grape.'

'To Mrs Lamb.'

'To Buddy Holly.'

'To my newts.'

When it started to rain they sprinted to the house, leaving everything but the gramophone. The candle flames fizzed and disappeared one by one but it was only a shower and within minutes the clouds were gone and the moon appeared. Droplets hung on the aviary netting, dripping on the wreckage of the meal, tapping on plates, into half-empty glasses, and making fat, shining beads on the polished table.

꩜

The following day Robert had a thick head. From what he remembered he had not drunk much, but Xavier refilled his glass as soon as it was empty or wanted him to try another bottle, pouring a new glass. By the time the rain started he had a collection of four lined up on the table. He was beginning to acquire a taste for wine but he did not have Xavier's head for it. He would learn a tolerance for hangovers, that was a start.

He wandered across the garden, squinting in the sunlight and aware that he was ravenous. It was nearly lunchtime and Isabel was still asleep. The thought of her made him forget his hunger.

Last night when the children were in bed, they had gone swimming. Robert hardly felt the cold of the river or the rain. The red warmth of the wine fooled him, and Isabel too it seemed. They clung to each other in the water, going under sometimes, laughing and breathless. Isabel's wet skin slipped against him, and when the moon appeared between the clouds, splashing raindrops glittered round her face. Sometimes, if they were quiet, they'd hear a rustle in the undergrowth or the tiny splash of a creature into the river. High up through the trees Jack's nightlight glowed.

When they finally went to bed they heaped on blankets and were still racked with shivers. The last thing Robert remembered was holding Isabel tightly in his arms, enfolding her so that his skin touched hers. He was worried for her even though she was sleeping peacefully. Her breath was hot but her body was too cold, hard and icy, sucking the warmth out of him.

This morning, asleep, she looked filled with life again. Her skin was golden, in some places rose-pink with too much sun. Her hair was its usual wild tawny mass. He kissed her and left her sleeping.

∽◯∾

Robert made a slow circle round the house and the sun boiled his head. The sheep stood in the middle of the vegetable garden, puffing and sun-dazed. He shooed them out, closed the gate and walked back across the grass towards the open kitchen door. He should get food for everyone—little Josef was here too, he remembered.

Down by the river the rowing boat was upturned on the grass and Robert made a detour to inspect the repairs on the hull. Last night's rain had dried, the wood was parched again and cracks had started to appear. There was more work to be done but the heat-wave had already lasted five days and the wood was shrinking. If it wasn't back in the water soon the joints would be beyond hope and repairs would be useless. He pulled the boat down to the river, rolling it into the water, and it swivelled in the shallows, suddenly full of life. He tied the rope to a tree, tugged on the knot and watched for a few minutes. Water bubbled up through the bottom. The boat would not be riverworthy until the wood expanded, but empty it was high in the water and would fill only a few inches. He fetched the oars and threw them in. He must tell Isabel not to use it yet.

The kitchen was chilly and in semi-darkness, like diving into water, but his head continued to throb and his thoughts were slug-gish. He sliced bread and began to butter it, realizing that although he felt hollow he couldn't face eating. The children came in and he directed laying the table and getting food from the cupboards. He must have said 'quietly' a dozen times. By the time Isabel appeared they had almost finished. She was wearing her new dress, her hair was tangled, and she yawned.

'What do you think? My one and only dress.'

'Lovely, Mummy,' said Catherine.

'You look like a dinner lady,' said Jack. 'That's good.'

'What do you think, Joe?'

'It's got flowers on,' said Josef thickly, his cheeks bulging with bread.

Catherine took her plate and sat outside. When the boys had finished, they went outside too, and Robert and Isabel sat alone in the cool of the kitchen drinking tea.

In the afternoon they slept and made love in the tree house. It was hot dusk inside the little cabin of baked wood. Leaves shut out the sunlight but they could hear the children's voices as they played down by the river and the sounds of the sheep, sighing and chewing beneath them in the shade of the tree.

When hunger made them come down late in the afternoon, the children had already found food and brought it into the dining room to eat while they did some painting. Robert painted too while Isabel sat in a patch of sun, too sleepy to do anything.

And now they were alone, lying on the wooden floor. The room was chaos, the table covered with the remains of tea—cake crumbs and half-eaten biscuits—and the children's things; boxes of paints, half-finished pictures, crayons and brushes. The whole room was draped with things as if flood-waters had receded leaving toys strewn around and trails of summer clothes over the furniture and the floor.

The sun still burned at five in the afternoon and they stretched out side by side next to the open garden doors. Isabel was sleeping again, flat on her back, her hair spread out on the floor and her hands folded on her stomach. Robert leaned on an elbow with a book in one hand, and he stroked her face along the hairline where the skin was damp with the heat.

The children had gone outside again, back to the river, leaving their food and their pictures unfinished.

⌒∞⌒

Xavier looped the camera round his neck and strolled towards the village. The heat had softened and the air carried the scent of scorched pasture and the perfume of England—cut grass of garden lawns. He turned off the lane at the chapel and took the path up Tye Hill.

Shadows were beginning to lengthen and the landscape was bronze-tinted. He stood at the summit, took out the camera and steadied it against his chest. In the square of glass was an inverted picture of deep blue sky and golden fields with the metallic ribbon of the river. With the sun at his shoulder, he moved the camera slowly from the west and the setting sun. His own house was just visible in the trees with the white aviary close by, then eastwards, he followed the arc of the river round the foot of the hill to the meadows and Robert's place. Xavier pressed the shutter and it made a smooth, satisfying click. He looked down at the distant grey stone house with the tree against it visible even from here, and a patch of yellow-green grass sloping to the river. Josef was there today with Jack and Catherine, and Xavier thought of strolling down that way to meet him. It was nearly six—Josef was probably already heading home.

Xavier clicked the shutter again, moving across the panorama, clicking then moving to frame the next view. The cows in the meadows had moved close to the water, some tilted on the bank and some waiting on the path. He wondered if the lens would pick them up. Through the viewfinder they were clearer than his own eyesight.

There were swans, minute white figure twos with V-shaped ripples fanning out behind. The swans bobbed on bigger ripples that caught the sun as they broke against the banks. Something else moved on the river. It was a boat. Xavier caught only a glimpse of the stern before it disappeared under the trees.

❦

When Isabel woke on the dining-room floor Robert had gone. There were long shadows in the garden. She sat up. Her head ached and her body convulsed with a spasm of cold. She could feel the river, freezing her skin as it did last night. It pressed around her body, draining the warmth from her. She wanted only to be in her bed, wrapped in blankets and sleeping.

The floor under her feet was clammy and the new cotton dress scratched on her skin. She knew in some part of her mind that she wasn't well, perhaps the wine or the sun, perhaps the river, but they were distant thoughts that were buried under a longing to be lying down warm and still in the dark.

The house was quiet. There was no sound of the children or of Robert. She closed her eyes as she went up the stairs, trying to shut out the smell of the house which was suddenly overpowering— dust, soap, children, food—and the sickly, oily slide of the banister under her hand.

She must have slept because when she opened her eyes it was dusk and the bedroom window was a deep blue rectangle. Someone had put on the light in the hallway and Isabel listened, wondering where everyone was. She needed a drink of water but it was hard to move.

Then Catherine was standing at the bedroom door. The light caught wisps of her hair and shone through the skirt of her summer dress.

'Hello, darling,' said Isabel.

But Catherine had gone.

She pulled the blankets closer round her shoulders. The air was cold on her skin. 'Has Josef gone home?' she called. There was no answer. The stairs to Jack's room in the attic creaked softly. The house was silent again.

Isabel did not wake until Robert came in.

'It's a beautiful evening,' he said, switching on the lamp and drawing the curtains.

'Where have you been?'

'To see Edward. Are the children in bed yet?'

'I heard Jack go up. Come here, please, I need you to warm me up.' She sat up, reaching out her hands to him.

'Catherine?'

'She's fine, she came in to see me just now—no, a little while ago I think. Lie down for a while.'

'It's only nine o'clock,' he said. He sat on the bed, leaning over her, and she lay back on the pillows.

She kissed him and his lips chilled her.

'You feel so warm,' he said. 'Do you want all these blankets? Are you not well?' He put his hand to her face. 'I'll say goodnight to them, I'll be back in a moment.'

She kissed him again. 'They're fine. Please come to bed.'

It was past ten when Robert got up to get water for Isabel.

Catherine and Jack's beds were empty.

1958

The Blackhouse

At first, there were perfect memories, precise as scalpels. He would gasp, winded by the kick of grief and the joy of recognition both in the same split second. But however hard he tried there was never more than an instant, a glimpse lit up like lightning, too quick to bring comfort.

He chased down black tunnels in his mind and found that other children wore the bright familiar clothes he followed. And when at last he thought he'd found them, his children's faces grew grotesque before his eyes, the features swelled and rotted, gaping the joke at him.

More and more, Robert found his own childhood coming back to him. At first he fought the memories down, wanting no distraction. He would strive to make in his head the most precise, the most intricate likeness of his son and daughter before they were lost to him for ever. He would catalogue them, the size and shape and weight of them, not just faces, but fingers, knees, feet, everything.

They refused to help. Even now they were too full of life to be examined like specimens on a board. But when he gave up and let his exhausted mind slip back in time, there they were. They chose to be part of the past that did not belong to them. Again and again they turned up like merry gatecrashers and he could see them playing barefoot on the grass of St Kilda where he had been a child, more clearly than in the Devon garden where they'd lived.

The more he tried to force the memories into order, into their proper sequence, the more they'd weave and slide through time, unwilling to stay where they belonged. His beginning and end were spliced together and the years between fell away, useless.

At night Catherine and Jack were closest, soft voices, small hands in the dark. But by day the present burned like a blowtorch and stripped them away along with all the years before they were born, and he had neither a childhood of his own nor children he could be sure of.

He came to realize that the life he'd lived could rearrange itself into anything, and only in darkness could he see clearly.

So he built a house without windows. Stone walls and turf roof held with net and weighted with stones, and inside, quiet, still twilight. A blackhouse built to the pattern of boyhood memory, the time in his life where his children now lived.

Sometimes Isabel would watch him work, arms folded, indifferent. She made no comment. She had her own ways of finding her children and had no need of him now.

November 1987

❧

Spike

At school, Spike wrote in his Everyday Book:

November the Fifth is Fierworks Night when Guy Fawkes tried to explode the Prime Minister and so real gunpowder is used to explain it. Our Prime Minister is the first Britaish woman in history.

There were jam jars along the riverbank with candles inside to mark the water's edge in the dark. They were the lights on an aircraft carrier, or landing lights for a UFO.

The sky was huge and black, speckled with stars. Any single star could be a spaceship on its way from a distant galaxy where they didn't need oxygen, on its way to capture humans for experiments.

If aliens came, Spike would break into an airbase and find an F15 Streak Eagle and he would shoot them down, picking off the pods first then calling in back-up to destroy the mother ship with Exocets. Or maybe he would finish them off himself with a GBU concrete-blasting laser bomb.

Spike could feel his socks creeping down to the toes of his wellingtons. His bare heels stuck to the cold rubber.

There was a crowd of people round the bonfire with their faces lit up. Spike looked for his brother, but Pete had lost him on purpose again. There was his mother and his little sister. His mother waved a sparkler in front of Linnet, who stared and leaned away with her mittens out to fend it off.

'Spike, do you want a sparkler?' Mr MacKinnon said. Spike pulled on his gloves and his fingers went into the wrong holes. He took the sparkler from Mr MacKinnon and the empty thumb of his glove stuck out from his wrist, but Mr MacKinnon didn't point this out, or offer to help put it right as if Spike was only in Class One.

Instead Mr MacKinnon held out a candle to light the sparkler and Spike waited for the hiss and sputter that would make him want to drop it. Mr MacKinnon didn't say, 'be careful' or 'mind your hand', which showed that he trusted Spike to know those things by himself.

Spike stood with his sparkler a little way away, and Stephen Briggs and Adam Tay from Class Three came and lit sparklers too.

Adam said fireworks were giant farts. Hiss and bang. Piss and fart. They waved their sparklers in circles and the sparks got nearer their hands until Spike could feel them through the gloves like pins on his skin.

They dropped the dead sparklers into a bucket of sand, then they ran round the bonfire, in and out of parents and fathers and other people.

Not last year, or the year before, but perhaps the year before that, Spike's father had been there. Spike had just started at St Angela's Infants so he stayed close all the time holding his father's hand. And Linnet hadn't even been born.

He was Pete's father too, but not Gatta's—or Linnet's either. People thought this was complicated but it wasn't. It was just that they all had a different father except him and Pete who had the same.

His dad, and Pete's, had given their big sister her special name. She was Gabriella Josephine but he'd said a girl so smooth and quiet with green eyes must be a little cat. *Gatta* is Spanish for girl-cat.

Spike thought about this often. Gabriella was the girl angel Gabriel who visited Our Lady to bring her an immaculate conception. And Gatta said she could see in the dark, see people doing secret things and they can't hide their sins. So Gatta was both; an angel and a cat, half and half at the same time, like he was Sebastian and Spike, and he and Pete were English and Spanish. Everybody was two things at once.

Gatta said one day she would grow claws—or wings.

∽∾

'What about a sausage, you boys?' said Steffie's mum, who was also called Elaine. 'Help yourselves. Don't bother about forks, chaps, just keep your gloves on if it's hot, I would.' Spike took one and said thank you. The sausage got fluff on it and burned even through his gloves.

The fireworks were lit on a platform tied to a boat out on the river. The men in the boat hauled the platform close to the boat to light the fireworks then let it float a little way away, and the rockets exploded in a zillion stars going out to the edges of the sky.

People said, 'OOOO' and, 'AAAHHH.'

There were whirls and spouts of tiny, vicious sparks, copied upside-down in the black river.

Behind the trestles the cows' white faces swayed in the dark. They jostled and shoved, and with each firework their heads shot up and they trod on each other's hooves like clumsy people.

'Hello, Spike,' said Josef Sevier.

'Hello.'

A woman with a baby in a pushchair was standing beside the barrels and bottles. Spike saw Josef Sevier look across at her softly and carefully like his mother looked at Linnet, but the woman didn't see.

Josef had given Spike a badge once and Gatta said he was creepy. She said Josef Sevier fancied her. Like chocolate. Sometimes his mother said this too.

'Oooh, I fancy some chocolate, Spike, don't you?'

In the daytime the river was clear. Green weed waved over brown pebbles. But at night the water was as black and shiny as bin bags.

A rocket went up with a tail of silver, and somewhere high above Spike's head it boomed so deep and strong it pressed inside his ears and echoed off the distant hills. The sound rolled like a wave across the meadows and thundered inside the bowl of the sky.

November 1987

Anna and Robert

Anna wanted to stay at home, but they watched the fireworks in the evening. The lunchtime drinking had made her tired, and then there was the incident with Isabel. Anna wanted to curl up on the mattress in the tree house with her baby and sleep. But Thomas was in a good mood and it was difficult to refuse to go. Isabel went on ahead to do her usual organizing.

They walked along the river path to the field where trestles of food had been set up. Starling and her friends crowded round Thomas. There was the girl with the silky hair, Gabriella, and Frank and Elaine's youngest daughter, Steffie. They passed the baby between them but he wailed and reached out for Anna. She didn't mind when the girls took Thomas to try the food.

She wandered around with Matthew, content to be alone. The upset of earlier had faded but there were too many people. Perhaps Thomas was right and she was getting wound up over nothing. She was imagining things.

She came across Elaine, who was dishing up food, and then Josef Sevier. She stood next to the barrels and crates of bottles and she ate a baked potato off a paper plate. He gave her a brandy in the little star-cut glass.

She surreptitiously held it up but this time there were only the lights of the fireworks on the other side of the glass.

'What can you see?' Josef was standing behind her. He reached over her shoulder and put his hand over hers to hold the glass higher.

'Nothing,' said Anna. 'Just colours.'

Later, Thomas came to find her and they walked home with the baby asleep on his shoulder. He came up to her room, carrying Matthew to his cot, and didn't go down again. It seemed natural to get into bed together.

They woke sometime in the night. Even blind in darkness Anna could not forget herself. She felt as if she were floating above her body, which was enjoying itself without her. She wanted a rush of memories that would join her to the past if only for a while, like the kiss in the kitchen. Disconcertingly she heard every moan and sigh and creak of the bed. In the past they had seemed to match but now her body was heavy and clumsy and Thomas was sinewy thin. As she'd thought the first moment she saw him again, they both had the bodies of strangers.

On Sunday morning he could not disguise his restlessness to get back to London. Anna wanted the weekend to be over. They had run out of things to say.

'I'll come back soon—as soon as I can,' said Thomas. They sat in the kitchen after lunch. Isabel had left them to say their goodbyes, taking Matthew with her for his afternoon nap.

'I can't have any more leave until Christmas, maybe a few days then.' He took Anna's hand.

'What about what's her name. Will she let you?'

'She's Clare. Of course she'll let me, I have a child. But I have to consider her feelings.'

'What feelings?'

'Anna, I've been honest with you. Please don't give me a hard time.' Sometimes, unexpectedly, Thomas sounded kind and unguarded like he used to. 'She helped me get over you,' he said.

'I'm sorry,' said Anna. 'I'm sorry it was all so difficult. I mean it, Tom. And it was wrong of me not to tell you.'

'It's OK, let it go. You did what you thought was right. I think he's great. He's terrific. I want to be a father to him, I really do.'

'Yes,' said Anna. They looked at each other across the table and they both knew they had no idea how Thomas could be a father to Matthew or how they were going to manage to be in each other's lives again.

'I'll phone,' said Thomas.

'Yes, do.'

'I'll see you soon.' He picked up his bag and his keys.

'Yes, I know. Tom, it's OK. Let's see how things go. I didn't tell you but I want to move out of here so things may not be settled for a while. Don't worry about getting away again soon.'

'Moving?' He put down his bag. 'Why?'

'It's complicated.'

'But you're settled here. You can't. We discussed it.' His voice was patient as if she needed the situation explained simply.

'Can't what? What do you mean I can't?'

'We discussed it, Anna. You need Isabel's help. You must think of Jack.'

'He's not Jack, he's Matthew.' Her anger erupted in a second. It was just as it always was. He tripped her up and she was never ready. Always she fell on her face, fell into being exactly his idea of her— silly and illogical. 'Who discussed it? I didn't. I am going to move. And I don't want Isabel's help. I can't stand it any more. She takes him over, she takes me over.'

'What?' Thomas was momentarily taken aback.

'I don't know. I don't know what it is but she makes me feel I shouldn't have him—Mattie—sometimes. Not always.'

'I'm sure she doesn't think that at all, Anna. Why would she? She's just a human being with her own moods.'

'I can't explain. Sometimes she's wonderful and other times she looks at me as if I don't exist.'

Thomas looked at her dispassionately. 'And that's why you want to move.' He shook his head. 'You really are selfish, Anna. Do you know that? Do you ever think of anyone but yourself? I want my child to have some security, God knows he doesn't get much from you. Isabel is capable of giving him stability. You can't only think of yourself now, you know.'

'Don't tell me what I can and can't do,' Anna shouted over him. Thomas went on as if she hadn't spoken.

'Face it, Anna, you're disorganized and over-emotional. You've had him sleeping in a tree house, Isabel tells me. A baby in a tree house in November! Yesterday you lost it completely—over nothing. I do have a say you know. I have a responsibility for his welfare.'

'You make me emotional. I'm fine without you.'

'And what about money? And work? I can't pay for everything. You're on your own, through choice I might add, miles from your own mother, who could have given you a bit of guidance and financial support.'

'Don't lecture me. I don't want money. I can look after my own baby,' Anna yelled.

'Isabel said you're overwrought. You are, look at you. She has experience with kids and you should be grateful for that. For God's sake, Anna, she couldn't do more. She's brought up her own children, you could learn a lot from her.'

'Did she tell you that? Well, she's never said anything to me. And you know why? Because they don't have anything to do with her, they don't come near her. Where are they then, these perfectly brought-up children?'

They heard footsteps coming along the passageway.

'I don't know what to say,' said Thomas quietly. He sounded exasperated. 'Things are never perfect, Anna, people aren't either. For once in your life, accept it.' The kitchen door opened.

'Oh, you're still here, you two.' Isabel dropped an armful of laundry onto the floor by the washing machine. 'I don't want to rush you, Tom. I'd love you to stay, but the forecast says the roads will be icy.' She smiled at Thomas and she put her arm round Anna's waist. 'Matthew's asleep, darling. He went off straight away. He's exhausted with all this excitement.'

Thomas said, looking at Anna: 'Thank you Isabel. We really appreciate all you do for our son.'

Anna picked up his bag. 'Icy roads,' she said.

⁂

Robert unlocked the workshop and switched on the light. It was just after four in the morning. The machinery and tools looked strange lit up unexpectedly.

He stood with his hand on the switch. For an instant he thought he'd seen a flicker of movement. The thought was gone almost before he could name it. It was as if the light went on a millisecond before everything froze—something vanished or hid from him in the same breath as he saw it.

He knew this feeling. It was one of those echoes of childhood that surface in the early hours when the senses are raw and stripped of their insulating logic. There is a certainty that things have secret lives of their own, and for a second the mind is caught in the balance, hanging between terror and longing. The eyes might be saved from a nightmare—or only just miss seeing magic.

The moment passed. Robert looked at his workshop. It was no nightmare nor was it magic, just ordinary, overdue work in progress. The air was still warm; he had stayed up until gone midnight to finish a table which was to be delivered to a customer in Cornwall first thing this morning.

Everything had gone badly for the last few weeks and the work was behind. It was difficult to concentrate. The materials and tools picked up his disquiet like sensitive animals and were obstinate and unyielding.

Isabel was partly the cause. When Anna moved into the house he expected things to get worse, but instead there was a lightness in Isabel, a mood in her he could barely remember. Her old self, loyal and generous and warm, seemed only just under the surface. She did not speak to him more, but when she did her voice was softer.

This made him uneasy. It started up an ache he'd thought was buried so deep he was safe from it.

And something other than Isabel disturbed him. Somewhere in his mind he always thought of his children, but over the years he'd learned to accommodate their absence by observing his life from a distance. He had taken a seat in the gods, high up, far back, as removed from the world as they were. The course of his life did not matter to him. He watched himself moving through the weeks and months and then the years.

But something had changed since Anna came to the house. It happened so gradually he did not know when he became conscious of it. At first it was a clarity of sight as if a film of dust was wiped away, and the air carried something of the sea or the mountains. He sometimes had a sensation like a rush of fear but shot through with sparks of joy, anticipation. Now he knew what it was, it was too strong to doubt. Catherine and Jack. Everywhere he went they were near him.

He knew it was his children he had expected to see when he turned on the light in the workshop.

⌥

Robert smoothed his palm over the tabletop, feeling the flaws in the beech wood more by instinct than touch. It needed another couple of hours' work even though to the eye the surface was perfect, blond and vulnerable. He lit the gas heater and put the kettle on, then he went out again into the dark and across the yard to the house.

He made no noise opening the kitchen door. It was bitterly cold. Isabel and Anna would not be up for hours but he would light the stove early and for once it would be properly warm when they came down.

The house was silent. There were empty coffee cups on the kitchen table and some clothes on the airer over the stove. Most were baby things, miniature suits with the feet and sleeves looking full and stiff as if they were still occupied. He recognized one of Isabel's shirts. The other things must be Anna's.

He laid paper and kindling in the stove and looked for matches. The box was empty so he went out into the passageway and along to the sitting room to fetch the matches kept by the grate. He knew his way by touch.

He pushed open the door and was surprised that the sitting room was not in darkness. A reading lamp was on and Isabel was lying on the sofa.

She was asleep in her dressing gown, wrapped in a blanket. Under the blanket with her was Anna's baby. He was sleeping too, on his front with his arms outstretched and his small fat hands on the collar of her dressing gown.

Robert looked down at her, careful not to make any sound. The lines round her eyes were smooth, the frown between her eyebrows disappeared. He had not seen his wife sleeping for longer than he remembered. He picked up the matches and went back to the kitchen.

Every morning now he saw her, though never before so early. Since Anna moved out of the tree house and into the attic room, Isabel was always downstairs with the child when he came in at six to light the stove.

She seemed not to mind their early-morning encounters, she hardly noticed him. She would walk up and down the kitchen or sit at the table, absorbed in the sleeping baby. Once, the baby had woken.

'Hush, Jack. Hush, darling,' she whispered to him.

'Izzie, he isn't Jack,' Robert said. The moment he spoke her head came up and she said, 'His father calls him Jack.'

Robert thought he'd angered her but instead there was faint amusement in her eyes.

'His parents still can't agree on a name,' she said. 'Didn't you know?' For a moment there was an understanding. He had caught a glimpse of Isabel, the first for what seemed a lifetime; and now here was another this morning when he found her sleeping.

He lit the stove and went out into the cold again back to his workshop. The dawn was hours away and it was still pitch black.

He tried to forget Isabel so he could concentrate on his work, but it was impossible. He was distracted by an odd creeping warmth somewhere inside him, almost pleasant but with an agonizing edge like the feeling of blood beginning to flow into a deadened limb.

He'd thought she came downstairs not long before he let himself into the house each morning. Now he wondered how early she went into Anna's room to take the baby from his cot, how many hours of the night Isabel slept with Anna's child in her arms.

⟡

'Thank you for being so understanding about the other day,' said Anna. 'I'm sorry I disturbed you for nothing.'

Robert stood at the door of his house in his shirtsleeves and he looked edgy, as if she'd disturbed him again. She'd not been inside his house for months. The long talks they used to have he seemed never to have time for any more. He didn't look willing to invite her in.

'It's all right, Anna.'

'I'd like to talk to you, Robert. If you're not busy.' She took a step forward.

'Of course, come in. I'm sorry.' He glanced up towards the house. 'She's out,' Anna said.

Robert made tea and Anna sat in one of the ragged armchairs. She settled the baby on her lap with his back against the arm of the chair. He wanted to sit up and look at this place he'd not seen before.

Although it was daylight outside, the lamps were lit. The earth walls were ridged with shadows, and without windows to let in the sounds of wind and birds the quiet had the stifled hush of a cellar.

The clicks and rattles of the kettle were made louder by the stillness. There was a smell of the dry earth of the floor under the rug. The house felt snug and secure and oppressive. Anna thought of a story-book house, the woodcutter's house, but she could not remember if he was good or bad.

Robert handed her a mug of tea.

'The other day—I think I didn't help,' he said. 'I worried you.'

'I feel silly about it now.'

'It was a misunderstanding, that's all.' He stirred his tea. 'You'd like to talk to me about something in particular?'

'I think I want to move,' she said quickly. 'You've both been very kind but I think Isabel isn't happy with me here any more.' Robert did not look surprised. He took a drink of tea.

'Did what happened make you decide this? Isabel understood your concern about your baby, I know she did.'

'No. Well, yes, partly.'

'I would be very sad if you left us.'

'I'll stay in the village,' said Anna at once, though she'd not yet given a thought to where she'd go. He'd wrongfooted her. She had not expected him to express his feelings.

'Anna, please don't leave.' Robert's unaccustomed intensity was unnerving and he must have realized, because he sat back in his armchair. 'Of course you must do whatever you think best. Is there anything I can do to help? Perhaps I could talk to Isabel?'

'I don't think so,' said Anna. 'And anyway, there's other things too.' Since Starling told her they were married she had wanted to say something. She had no right to know about their lives, but it was belittling to have them conceal it from her as if she were too silly, too unimportant to be told.

'Robert, I know about you and Isabel. About you being married. I don't know what happened between you, it's none of my business, but I know that Isabel doesn't like me. I bother her, I irritate her; and I think I should go.'

'I see,' said Robert. 'I see.'

'It's affecting me, and I need to get away.'

'I'm so sorry, Anna. It's too quiet for you here.' He sounded concerned but for the first time she was unsure of him.

'It's not that, I like the quiet. I don't know,' said Anna cautiously. 'It's just that … I can't say exactly. Sometimes things feel odd here. Perhaps it's having a baby that's done it.' Robert was watching her intently.

'What feels odd? Something odd about this place?'

'It's me, Robert. I just need to get away.'

'Isabel wants you to stay, I know it,' he said. 'Sometimes she isn't easy to be with, but she would want you to stay.' He sounded certain but he seemed troubled. He got up and paced back and forth across the room. Matthew's head swivelled like an umpire to watch him.

'Robert, I'm sorry. You've both been good to me but I think I should have somewhere of my own now. I'm sorry.'

'It's not your fault, Anna. How could it be? We should have told you. Isabel and I are so used to it, it isn't strange to us any more.' Suddenly he seemed to come to some decision because he stopped pacing.

'We are married—you know that. For forty years. We had two children. They died. Our son was seven, our daughter was nine. Jack and Catherine. Isabel and I could not live together afterwards—as you see.' He spoke in his ordinary voice, as if he'd given her some incidental details of his life.

Anna could not take it in. She stared at him and he began pacing again.

'Isabel has found it hard having a child in the house again. But she's adjusting now and it's making her happy. You do understand?' Anna nodded. 'If you go I don't know what she'll do. I know it's not fair to ask you to stay, but I am asking—just for a while, Anna. Please.'

'Nobody told me,' she said.

'No one talks about it. We never did—Isabel refused to.'

'How did they … ? Were they ill?'

'It was an accident.'

'It's so terrible, Robert. I'm so sorry. If anything happened to Matthew it would be the worst torture, I couldn't bear it, I couldn't live.'

'I know, Anna, I know. Please don't be upset.'

'But she'll never want me to leave,' said Anna. 'She would never want my baby to leave.'

'I'll help her when the time comes. But not yet, she needs a little longer.'

'How do you bear it? You don't even have each other.'

'In a way we do,' Robert said. 'Anna, please don't cry. It was a long time ago.' He sat on the arm of the chair and took her hand in both of his. 'Will you stay? For a while, a few months? For Isabel?'

'Yes. Yes, of course I will.'

'Thank you, Anna. Thank you.' He stood up and let go of her hand as if their conversation had come to an end. Then something seemed to occur to him: 'There is one other thing, for Isabel,' he said.

'Yes?'

'If you leave the baby with her, would you tell me first?'

'Yes, if you like.'

'I should be near in case she needs me. She shouldn't be alone if she is upset.'

'Yes, of course.'

Robert was restless and Anna could not read in his eyes what he was thinking.

'It must have brought it all back to you,' she said. 'The other night, I thought—I feel so terrible now—I thought she had taken him and you knew something, but you wouldn't tell me, and you were frightened. But it was because of your children, wasn't it?'

Robert did not answer, nor did he look at her.

'How stupid I am. Of course it was. I'm sorry, I can't imagine …
Robert, should I stay for a while? Maybe you shouldn't be alone. I'm
sorry I made you tell me.' He shook his head as if to clear away the
thoughts.

'It's never been difficult to talk about them. Not for me.'

'Will you tell me about your children sometime? What they were
like. Do you have pictures?'

Robert seemed not to be listening any more.

'I think Isabel has one or two,' he said. 'She'll be home soon.'

'Yes,' said Anna. 'I'd better go.'

November 1987

❦

White and Blue

Anna walked back to the house. Isabel had said she was going to see Elaine and Frank about something or other. Village business, Anna thought: Isabel did not visit people for the pleasure of it. But the habitual anger that came with thoughts of Isabel had lost its edge. Even the memory of Isabel's face was different now. The months of difficulty, Anna knew now, were really nothing at all to do with her; it had all been sadness for her children. Perhaps it would be possible to stay. Perhaps things could be better now that she knew.

The baby was asleep again. He was always tired. He slept so much and never woke her at night either. But Isabel said he was fine—a baby who sleeps one should be grateful for, she said. Isabel must know.

Anna carried him upstairs. Something made her hesitate at the landing: three doors, all closed. One was Isabel's bedroom, the other two were guest rooms, the white room and the blue room—impersonal names because they belonged to no one.

Anna turned the handle and pushed open the door: white walls, a chest of drawers and a wardrobe, a striped rug on the floor. There was a suitcase stand at the foot of the bed, piled with folded blankets, and a picture of heather-covered mountains above the headboard. The air was freezing, stale. The plain, unpolished furniture was sober and frugal. There was nothing of a child in the room.

The door of the blue room was ajar. She pushed it with her fingertips. The chintz curtains printed with forget-me-nots hung stiffly at the window, the furniture was painted dull yellow and a patchwork coverlet was folded on the bed. She closed the door. Which room had been Catherine's, which had been Jack's? She should not pry; if she should know more, Isabel must tell her.

Anna shifted the baby to her other shoulder. His cheek was cold and wet with dribble and his face slipped against her neck. The house was quiet. On impulse she turned back along the landing to Isabel's room and opened the door. There must be some sign of the children; there might always have been clues she'd missed.

The room was familiar. When she first came to the house Anna had often stretched out on the huge, soft bed in the afternoons. Isabel would sit in the cane chair with a pile of village paperwork at her feet and a cup of tea in her hand. Anna would cradle her pregnant belly, sleepy and empty-headed. They talked. About what, Anna couldn't remember. They used to talk easily. Isabel's presence was comforting—she smiled her cool uncritical smile, asked nothing, gave occasional advice. Sometimes she would lower her spectacles to her nose, sort through her papers and attend to the business of Cameldip. Isabel was the mother Anna wished she belonged to.

Isabel's room was full of things—three chests of drawers all different woods, a wardrobe and the big carved bed that Isabel told her long ago Robert had made. There were clothes over the backs of chairs, across the bed, and every surface was cluttered with things— books, shells, stones, beads, scarves, china. It was dusty, and the dust dulled the colours like an old photograph.

Anna looked slowly over the room. There were no pictures of babies or children, there was nothing she'd not seen before. There were paintings of mountains, heather and deer and an ugly print of a custard sunset over a turquoise sea. Over the bed was a crude tapestry of a black pony with a white line on its face. A piece of string had been sewn on for a bridle. It was the only thing that might have been made by a child.

Anna went into the room. On the bedside table was a lamp with a ragged shade. In a cup was a bunch of winter blossom and beside it a silver candlestick with a stub of pink candle, a bottle of tablets, an earring and a notebook open, face down. Isabel's things, beside her when she went to sleep in the big carved bed and when she woke in the morning.

And there was an old square photograph in a plastic frame that Anna had seen but never looked at. She picked it up. It must have been taken with a good camera, the smallest details were clear.

The picture was yellowing: a view from the top of a hill looking down over pasture and trees to a river flowing through meadows. It was evening, long shadows stretched out over the grass. Cows stood on the riverbank, some half in the water, their bony haunches tilted, their forelegs in the shallows, and a pair of swans were gliding past. The water rippled behind the stern of a boat almost hidden by the trees. A moment after the picture was taken the swans would be gone. In the distance were meadows, hedges, slanting shadows, a hazy line of rounded hills.

Anna studied the picture. The scene was idyllic, perfect, but it was of nothing in particular.

She knew the curve of the river and the little shingle beach where the cows stood—it was an old picture of the Camel taken from the summit of Tye Hill. Whoever took it was looking out from the place where she'd sat with Thomas and cried for the loss of something she'd never really wanted.

It seemed odd that the only picture Isabel kept close to her was of the countryside on an ordinary summer evening, that she chose to have this at her side rather than the faces of her children.

There was a sound on the landing. Anna jumped and hastily put down the picture.

'Isabel,' she called thinking it better to speak up rather than be discovered. There was the sound of the wind in the trees then a pattering on the landing like the paws of a cat on the carpet.

'Isabel,' she called again going to the door. The landing was empty and the wind gusted through the wide-open door to the tree house. It must have been a cat.

She shivered but not with cold. The house was filled with raw, intoxicating November air, pure as oxygen. The sinking sun stained everything—the walls, the carpet, the sky—orange, pink, lime and scarlet, flamboyant as a carnival.

Anna stood at the open door, the baby held tight against her. The wind was exhilarating, pressing down into her lungs, and she saw Robert walking across the shimmering garden below. He did not look up. The sun through the trees made his shadow flicker and dart as if he were not alone.

The wind did not drop and the sunset blazed but the sudden elation that had filled her ebbed away, emptying her out and leaving her desolate.

She closed the door, leaning her shoulder against the push of the wind to lock it. She would tell Robert that the catch was loose again.

Upstairs in her room, she put Matthew in his cot. She covered him with the quilt Isabel had given her.

One afternoon, just before he was born, Isabel had so casually gone to a drawer in her bedroom.

'Would you like this?' she had asked, kneeling with it in her hand, holding it out to Anna. It smelled of lavender. 'It's rather old, I'm afraid,' she said. 'Could you make use of it, darling?' Anna had taken it, politely admired the embroidered rabbits and the little bunches of appliqued carrots at each corner.

'Thank you. It's lovely,' was all she'd said.

'I didn't ask you,' said Anna aloud. 'I didn't think to ask.'

Downstairs the telephone was ringing. Anna ran down the three flights to the kitchen.

'Hello?'

'Anna, it's me,' said Thomas. 'I've only got a minute, got a meeting at four. Look, I thought I'd better tell you, I spoke to Isabel about you wanting to move.'

'Oh no, Thomas. Why?'

'Because I can talk to her easier than you can. I don't know, I just thought after what you said, I could help maybe, smooth things over a bit between you. Anyway she …'

'Everything's different now. I'm not going yet. I don't want to any more.'

'You're not going? Well I wish you'd told me. Why didn't you tell me? I can't keep up with you, Anna.'

'Everything's changed and I can't go. I like it here—with Isabel—I'm OK.'

'I should have known you two would patch things up. Another bloody drama over nothing.' He laughed.

'What did she say, Tom? Was she upset? When did you speak to her?'

'A few days ago, Tuesday, no Monday, I think. Anyway, she said she understood and that she'd let you tell her whenever. She said you have to make your own decisions and she'll carry on helping you out even if you do move. So she's OK with it. No worries. OK? Anna?'

'She wasn't upset?'

'No, not at all. She cares about you, I told you.'

'Yes, maybe she does.'

'Got to go. How is he? My little man?'

'He's fine, Tom.'

'Good. Great. Got to go, speak soon.'

❦

'I've cooked something for us,' said Anna. 'I'll make some tea and then we'll eat.' Isabel unwound her scarf and unbuttoned her coat. Her eyes were bright with the cold and her cheeks were pink. She looked happy.

'That's lovely of you.' She kissed Matthew and he put his arms up to her. Anna looked away.

'How are Elaine and Frank?'

'They're well,' was all Isabel said. She sat next to the baby's highchair.

Anna had rehearsed what she would say but now they were together it was hard to speak. It was as if this were the first time they'd met. Everything she'd thought she knew was false and the truth was there in Isabel's face. It had always been there but Anna had not seen—the children had always been there.

Anna could think of nothing to say but Isabel seemed not to notice. She commented on the oddness of the weather, clear skies and freezing wind; that the wood pile wouldn't last the winter and perhaps she should order coal to keep in the stove at night. They had almost finished the meal.

'Isabel, I talked to Robert today,' Anna said at last.

'Yes?' Isabel held up a spoonful to the baby and he swayed towards it with his mouth open and his tongue out like a fledgling. She smiled, all her attention on the baby. She pretended to chew and he smacked his lips. She opened her mouth, he opened his for another spoonful.

'Robert told me,' said Anna. 'He told me what happened. Isabel, it must have been so terrible. I just wanted to tell you how ... how sorry I am.'

'Of course,' Isabel said lightly. 'Of course.' She pushed away her plate and dabbed her mouth with a napkin. 'It's such a treat to be cooked for. Food always tastes so much better.' She got up from the table and stacked the dishes by the sink. She filled the kettle.

'I'm so sorry,' Anna said again. Isabel took cups and saucers from the drainer and milk from the fridge. She turned on the tap until the water ran hot and filled the bowl. After a while Anna said, 'Tom phoned me today and I think there was a mistake. It's my fault.'

'Oh?' Isabel's back was still turned.

'He told you I wanted to move, but that's not true. I was wondering about it but now I've decided I'd like to stay here with you. If that's all right. If you think so.'

'Of course, darling.' Isabel sat down and passed a plate and bread to Anna. 'And Robert?' she asked unexpectedly. 'What else did you two chat about?' Anna did not know how to answer. It was impossible to speak of the children; Isabel made it impossible.

'He said that I should stay,' said Anna impulsively. 'Because of you.'

'Me?' Isabel gave a sudden laugh. 'Oh, of course, he wants you to stay for me.'

'Isabel,' said Anna desperately. 'Please can we talk about it?'

'Anna, darling. We are talking. Don't be so intense about everything. Now you know; Robert has my best interests at heart, of course, and I'm glad you're staying. So, we're all happy, aren't we?' She reached over and patted Anna's hand.

'He told me their names,' Anna said and was suddenly frightened though of what she didn't know. Isabel showed nothing. She cut some cheese, cut it again, then again, into cubes, then quartered, quartered, smaller and smaller. The knife slipped and the blade screeched on the china plate. She put down the knife.

'He had no right to,' she said quietly. 'I'm rather tired this evening.'

'Don't go, Isabel. I'm sorry. I wanted to say how terrible it must be, I'm so sorry. It's worse than anything I could imagine. And you and Robert, that too. I couldn't bear it.'

Isabel listened impassively. 'Shall I tell you something, Anna? If you are going to talk to Robert then you should know. Robert speaks from guilt, not kindness. He was responsible, his stupidity, his neglect. Not only him—I was equally to blame. I've shouldered my guilt, but he was too weak to deal with the ... the situation we found ourselves in and he deceived me. He betrayed us all. A cunning, lying girl, that's what he ...'

Isabel stopped abruptly as if she'd said too much. She shivered. For the first time Anna saw her laid open.

'You can't be to blame, either of you,' Anna said. 'You aren't to blame, Isabel, I know it.'

Isabel had already recovered her composure. Her face showed nothing. She lifted Matthew out of his highchair, sat him on her hip and wiped his mouth. It was absent-minded, instinctive. Matthew grasped her hair and leaned his chin on her shoulder. This time Anna did not resent it. It seemed natural.

December 1987

❧

Water of Life

In the first week of December the weather changed. It was cold but the wind had dropped and the sky was overcast. There was a sallow semi-dusk from morning till night. The countryside was quiet. The forecast was snow.

Anna stood in her coat and hat in front of the bathroom mirror. The glass was rust-spotted and stained with age.

She twisted up a lipstick and sniffed; it smelled sour. Poppy red. She smoothed it on with her finger but it was hard to see if the colour improved her. It was more than a year since she'd done this.

'Goodbye, Isabel,' she called out, manoeuvring the pushchair out of the front door. Four small girls in tutus and wellingtons ran past her into the house.

'Hold your horses, girls. No boots in the dance room.' It was Elaine coming up the path, carrying a stack of sheet music and a handful of haloes. 'Hello, Anna. Hello, Matthew John. We'll have those little feet in first position before much longer.' She bent down and pinched his nose. He swatted her away.

'Anna, are you going far?' Isabel appeared from the kitchen. 'Hello, Elaine. Would the children not dance on the new floor-boards. They'll get splinters—Robert hasn't varnished them yet.' Without waiting for Elaine to speak, she said, 'Anna? When will you be home?'

'Not long, I'm just going for a walk.' She saw Isabel notice her lipstick.

'Matthew's tired, darling. Are you sure it's a good idea?'

181

'He's fine; we won't be long.' Anna squeezed past some waist-high shepherds and a king.

'Anna,' called Elaine. 'Come for lunch or supper or something. Come and see us—Frank keeps asking me to get you round, the old goat.'

'Thank you, I will,' said Anna but Elaine had disappeared after the cast of the Little Butterflies Nativity ballet.

On the path, Anna met Constance Lamb, Tutor in Deportment and Elementary Dance.

'Hello, Constance,' said Anna, automatically straightening and licking her lips. Miss Lamb dipped her head with its perfectly disciplined bun and clasped together her gloved hands under the resolute shelf of her bosom.

'My dear, hello. All's well?' She smiled and her apricot lips flexed.

'Yes, thank you,' said Anna, wrestling the pushchair round her and back onto the path. Miss Lamb watched her. 'And you? How are you, Constance?'

'Very well, my dear.' The aquamarine eyes swept down to Matthew. 'What a striking child he is. Not at all your colouring. But they're all beautiful at that age, in their own individual way. Don't you think?'

Anna smiled and waited to be dismissed. Constance nodded and her suede gloves clapped in satisfaction then wound together again as neat as a pair of nesting hamsters.

Inside the house squeals and shrieks crescendoed until an up-tempo, almost calypso 'Silent Night' was struck up on the piano. Elaine's voice trilled above the din. 'Neat toes, children. In a line … and one, and two and YES! *Off* you go.'

'Goodbye,' said Anna.

'Do come to our little show, won't you,' said Miss Lamb.

'Of course, Constance, I'd love to,' said Anna. With the village hall on the premises such things were difficult to avoid.

Out in the lane Anna could hear the piano and the squeals and Elaine's voice calling instructions, '… and hop, hop, SLIDE, and uppity-up, POINT.' There was a sudden silence at about the time Miss Lamb would have entered the room.

⟨∞⟩

Anna walked to the village memorial. 'To the fallen of two …' was carved in the stone below a mossy angel. The remaining words were hidden under a poster:

Little Butterflies Christmas Ballet, Unto Us a Child Is Born
Friday, 19th December, 7.00 pm

and underneath was the end of the inscription:

AND THEIR MEMORY IS ENSHRINED IN THE HEARTS
OF THE PEOPLE OF THIS PARISH.
'AND HE SHEWED ME A PURE RIVER OF WATER OF LIFE,
CLEAR AS CRYSTAL, PROCEEDING OUT OF
THE THRONE OF GOD'
REVELATIONS CH 22 VERSE I

She circled the memorial clockwise, past the shop where Starling lived, a cottage, then Constance Lamb's bungalow, the chapel, the footpath to Tye Hill, Frank and Elaine's place. Then a big empty house that used to belong to a doctor, still with its two doorbells, one for day, one for night, two more cottages, back to the shop.

She sat down on the bench and tucked Matthew's mittens under his cuffs. He was asleep again.

She'd thought of going to see Josef. She thought about it every day. At the fireworks he had invited her. She self-consciously sucked at her red lips. He was friendly, that was all.

'Hi,' said Starling.

'Hello, Starling. I've been thinking about you. We haven't seen you for ages, not since the fireworks.'

'I know.'

'You're home early, how's school?' Anna noticed that Starling's lips were glossy pink.

Starling shuffled. 'I've got mock Mocks,' she said.

'Oh, of course. Good luck with them, you'll be fine,' Anna said.

'Thanks.' Starling shifted her school bag and looked past Anna's shoulder.

'Why don't you come for a walk with us? Mattie would love it and I could do with some company. I was going to call in on Josef Sevier but I think I'll go that way instead.' She pointed to the lane beside Frank and Elaine's cottage.

'He's out anyway,' said Starling.

'Oh, I see.' Anna was puzzled. 'Well, it doesn't matter. I'll wait if you want to change and dump your school stuff.'

'I've got History tomorrow, I'm revising. He's got a girlfriend,' said Starling.

'Well that's OK. I know you like History. Has he? I'll call in tomorrow, shall I, and see how you got on?'

'Yes, if you like,' said Starling vaguely, 'bye then.' She sauntered off.

Anna took the lane beside Frank and Elaine's cottage, away from the river and away from the two houses that pulled at her, one at each end of Cameldip.

It was too cold to be walking but she would not go home yet. She'd told Isabel she would be out for a while and she must go through with it. When she thought of Isabel she did not feel helpless any more. Isabel needed her, and Robert too—Anna held their lives in the balance while she decided how long to stay. Now it seemed a small thing to be asked, to share her child for another month or so.

She and Isabel understood each other. No more would be said of Catherine and Jack, or of her leaving. But silently they would bargain, *'You have him now, but in an hour—in two hours—he's mine.'*

It was beginning to get dark and the temperature was falling. Anna put on her gloves. The lane ran alongside the wall of Frank and Elaine's garden then between hedges. In this direction, to the north of Cameldip, it was hilly. From the top of the steep incline Anna looked back over the village. It was not a spectacular view like the one from Tye Hill out over the water meadows and miles of distant countryside. Here she looked down on the tiles and thatch and slates of Cameldip. Already there were Christmas lights strung along the eaves. People were beginning to draw their curtains and light fires. White smoke hung above the roofs.

She could see Josef's place in darkness and next to it the mound of the old aviary covered with tarpaulin. She'd not seen him for more than a month. The pub was closed on the afternoons she'd walked past.

She went back down the hill and home. It felt like home in spite of everything.

1958

❧

Josef

'Why? Why does he have to come with us?'

'Because he can. I say so,' said Catherine. She held the side and Jack climbed in. He slid head first to the bottom of the boat on his stomach, into a few inches of water. He was now wet almost all over but it was so hot he didn't mind.

Josef stood on the bank, uncertain. Then he squatted down, pretending to look at something in the grass, not knowing whether to go back to the house and finish his painting, or go home, or play in the MacKinnons' garden by himself. But he wanted to be with Catherine so he stayed put.

He poked at the soft ground with a stick and watched a worm slide away. Catherine had tucked up her dress and she stood in the river up to her thighs steadying the boat. She was taller than Jack and climbed in more easily than he. Josef tried not to watch but he knew what they were doing and he wished he could be in the boat too.

Catherine called, 'Joe, untie the rope and we'll pull you in.'

He jumped up, throwing his stick on the ground, forgetting the worm instantly. The rope was wet and the knot had got tight with the pull of the river. It was difficult to untie it and he felt tears coming.

'He can't do it, he can't do it,' said Jack. 'Now we're stuck. I knew he couldn't.'

But Josef managed and waded into the water with the end of the rope in his hand. The boat was free and slipped away from the bank out into the river's flow. The rope tightened and before he knew, it had pulled him over. He swallowed water and his hair stuck to his eyes but he did not let go.

'I'll pull you in,' he heard Catherine shout. 'Don't let go.'

And they were going faster, out into the middle. The little boat gathered speed and Josef was sliding along behind like a fish on a line. Catherine stood up pulling on the rope as hard as she could but the boat swayed and it was difficult to keep her balance. Jack shouted but Josef's ears were full of water and he couldn't hear the words. Then suddenly the rope wasn't in his hands any more and the boat had gone a long way down the river just in the time it took to wipe his hair out of his eyes. He saw Catherine still standing up with the rope in her hands.

'I'll come back, I promise,' she called. And she waved to him.

Josef stood up. The water was only up to his chest, the river was wide and shallow here. It pushed him hard but he could easily wade to the bank. It was strange being left on his own even though all the time he had half expected to be forgotten. He sobbed a little; dry, short sobs that had no real heart. He knew that Catherine had tried and he should wait for her on the bank so she would find him when she came back. He walked a little way down the river path, finding things to throw in, bits of stick and leaves to watch sailing downstream after the boat.

He wandered on, forgetting that he should be waiting. The sun began to go down and Josef was cold in his wet clothes. He had left his shoes at the MacKinnons' but he was nearly home now. The river path ran behind his own garden and he remembered that the boat would have passed this way a long time ago. He felt left out of the adventure, but he did not mind any more. It would be nice to see his mother instead and have something to eat.

He ran across the garden and Adelie smiled when he came into the kitchen, not minding about his shorts, which were torn as well as wet. She did not ask what he had been doing or about Catherine and Jack until after it was dark and Isabel telephoned.

That night no one reminded him to go to bed. Robert and Isabel arrived, Isabel wild and frightening. She held his arms too tight, shouting in his face and he said, yes, it was he who had untied the rope, that was all, nothing else happened except that Catherine had waved. His mother was speaking on the telephone and his father found the lamp and the torch, then he went out with Robert. Although Adelie begged Isabel not to go, she followed them.

When Josef and his mother were alone, it was so quiet. She pulled him to her and hugged him tight saying that it was all right, but her eyes said something different.

Later, more people arrived and asked Josef again what happened. This time he cried. He did not know what they wanted him to say. After that he must have fallen asleep because the next thing he knew it was morning and he was on the sofa covered with a blanket. He was still wearing the same clothes and they smelled of the river. The house was silent and he went into the kitchen.

'Did you find Catherine?' he said.

'Yes,' said Adelie. 'We found them both.'

1958

∞

Josef and Isabel

Josef was in the kitchen, standing at the table. There was a glass of milk on one side, a tractor on the other and a plate of bread and Marmite in the middle. His mother said she must run to the postbox so he was alone in the house. Papa was mending the car which meant lying on the ground underneath it. Josef would go and help him when the bread and Marmite was finished.

It was suddenly darker and Josef turned to see what was making a shadow on the table. Catherine's mother stood at the kitchen door.

Josef had taken a bite and he must finish the mouthful before speaking, but he would not have known what to say anyway. Isabel was different now that she had no children.

She came into the kitchen. He chewed then swallowed, waiting for her to say something. When she didn't he looked at his glass of milk. The last piece of bread was in his hand and he could not eat while she watched him. He closed his fist around it, squeezing tight so the butter oozed under his fingers.

Isabel stood behind him and he heard her breathe hard as if she had been running. He could feel the hair moving on the top of his head with the warm blowing from her mouth. He kept very still and waited to see what she wanted him to do. It would be telling something about Catherine and Jack. Something important he'd forgotten. He had already said what happened, everything he could remember, but perhaps the words were wrong and he had better find other words or else she would ask him again. He would never tell about Catherine though, that she said she would come back for him.

He kept on looking at his fist wondering about the squashed bread inside but knowing that he should not look now. Butter trickled under his cuff. Out of the corner of his eye he could see the folds of Isabel's dress and they moved in time with her breath as if the dress were breathing too.

Then her arm reached out quickly and she took hold of his wrist, the hand with the bread inside. He had thought she was sad but now he could feel she was angry. She held so tight it hurt and she pulled him hard towards the door as if she was impatient and he must hurry. He banged into the table and the milk tipped over and splashed on the floor.

Then he heard his mother call out, and Isabel was gone.

Josef looked at the puddle of milk. It had been Isabel's fault but she had not meant to do it. He would say that he knocked over the milk by himself.

❧

Adelie put plates and some food into a basket. She sat down to write a note, scribbling, crossing out, tearing up three or four pieces of paper. Finally she wrote: 'With love, Adelie.' There was nothing more to say. She thought of Catherine with her arms around Isabel, and Jack on his bicycle in the candlelight. Anxiety contracted her guts like nausea.

'Josef,' she shouted. 'Josef, come here this minute. I want you here now.' Almost immediately Josef appeared at the door, the toy tractor in his hand. His eyes were big with fear. 'I don't want you wandering off.' She bent down to him and shook his shoulders hard. 'Josef. Look at me. Stay in the garden where I can see you, you hear me?' Josef nodded dumbly.

He sat on the path outside the kitchen door. There was no point in looking out for Joséphine. He let the tractor roll away on its own down the slope. It veered and bumped into the wall of the house and he wondered if his mother would be angry with him for letting it crash. It didn't matter, she was angry anyway and her mouth had thin lips. When she wasn't angry she looked at him with watery eyes and hugged him too tight. Too tight like Isabel, he could still feel her hurting hand round his wrist. Was it because he let go of the rope? Or was it because he should have been in the boat too? Or was it because he came home on his own?

He heard his mother's shoes clicking on the path.

'I'm taking some supper to Isabel and Robert,' she said. From where he sat on the ground her shoes were up close and he studied them instead of looking up to her thin lips. 'I won't be long, my darling. Papa will be finished soon.' She bent down to kiss him but he turned his face away.

Everything was different. Since Catherine died he'd slept in Mama's bed between her and Papa.

'I can't sleep, I *must* know he's safe,' he heard her say.

What would happen if he slept in his own room? How could he drown in there? Perhaps when it was dark and everyone was asleep, it would fill with water. No one would know when the water came. First his bed would float like a boat then it would sink down to the floor, so gentle and quiet it would not wake him. That was how he would drown.

When his mother had gone, carrying the food in a basket, Josef wandered across the lawn. He kicked his bicycle lying on its side. He thought his father would call him back long before he reached the hole in the fence but he didn't, and Josef didn't care. He ducked through the hole and stood on the deserted path. The trees swished and the river made sucking, gulping sounds like something swallowing.

Isabel was there. He had not noticed her at first. This time she held his hand softly and they walked together beside the river. After a while he felt he should say something about Catherine and Jack because that was what she was thinking.

'We were sailing to the sea,' he offered. Isabel squeezed his hand and looked down at him. Her eyes asked him to go on. 'We were going to find the kingfishers and then the whales.'

'The kingfishers and then the whales,' she said. Her voice rasped as if she needed a drink.

'Mama told me the story and in it there are French children: Pierre and Vreneli and Jacques and their dog Martha. Two boys and a girl like us but we didn't have a dog so we thought we could get one on the way. In the story they sail to the sea because all rivers go to the sea however far away it is, and on the way you have adventures.' Josef looked up at Isabel to see if she was still listening. 'Catherine said it was too far to the sea in one day but she said we might see a king-fisher. And the story was French so I said it in English so that they would know about the adventures—so that they could understand.' He paused for breath. 'We were sailing to the sea,' he said again so that Isabel would understand about untying the rope.

Isabel did not seem interested any more. She was looking at the river. She stopped at a place where the bank went down to a little shingle beach. Then she did an unexpected thing, she walked to the edge then into the water, still holding his hand, not stopping when her skirt was wet and then the edges of Josef's shorts. He pulled back and tried to twist his hand out of hers but she held firmly and did not seem to notice her dress floating out and the water up to Josef's waist.

'I'm here now,' she said and her voice was kind, like it used to be. Josef did not want to go further into the water, he knew that it was too deep to go even one more step. He tried again to get his hand free but he slipped and went under. Isabel neither helped him nor let go of his hand. He slipped again and water filled his mouth, and Isabel took another step even though the riverbed sloped steeply and the gravel rolled under their feet.

Then suddenly there was a great rushing and bubbling in his ears and someone was lifting him out of the water. His father was holding him up out of the river and Josef found that Isabel's hand had gone and he could put both arms round his father's neck. His father did not look back, he carried Josef along the path towards home, holding him close and comfortable.

Josef leaned his head on his father's shoulder and watched Isabel come out of the river. She started to walk in the other direction, towards her own house, then she broke into a run as if someone were calling her.

1958

❧

Robert

Robert walked up to the doctor's front door, noticing that the nettles were cut down and that the brass step had been polished. His mind watched as he noticed these things, it watched his hand reaching for the bell, it looked down at his shoes standing beneath him on the tiles of the porch.

He was somewhere far back inside, unmoved, undeceived by the pattern on the tiles or the prettiness of the brass bell in the sunshine. *Press,* it said slyly, as if that were all. He looked out through the holes of his eyes, shifting the body that was his to look up at the blue summer sky. The world was a crystal of light and jewel colours, a sublime, luminous world where his children no longer breathed.

'Good afternoon,' said the girl. His memory had made her younger than she was. This girl wore a woman's summer dress and a housewife's overall. After a moment in which Robert should have spoken, she added, 'I'm sorry, the doctor isn't here.' The sleeves of her dress were rolled up to the elbow and her hands were covered in flour. She waited for him to speak, pushing back her hair with her wrist and leaving a smear of white on her face.

'I'm baking, but you can wait if you'd like to.'

'I've come to see the doctor, is he here?' Robert saw a flicker of alarm in her eyes and he was suddenly ashamed of frightening her. He still wore the same stinking clothes, five days old, and his too-long hair was tied with string. He knew from the mirror that his eyes stared like a lunatic and his face had fallen inward, collapsed in on itself like wax.

'I'm sorry. You just told me he was out. I would like to wait, though, if you don't mind. If I'm not in your way.' His voice forced up from his lungs.

'You won't be at all.' She clapped her hands softly together and they made a thick, patting sound. She brushed them on her apron—it seemed a gesture too old for her—and opened the door wide for him to go in.

He followed her along the passageway past the doctor's study, feeling its memory pressing on the other side of the door like a weight of water dammed up inside the room. The girl walked quickly ahead of him and he saw her back tense and her head dip as if she did not want to be heard.

The sun streamed through from the back of the house. The kitchen was small and full of colours—yellow tiles, red tins, blue cupboards. The curtains were printed with bowls of fruit and the tiles over the sink had pictures of vegetables and saucepans and cutlery. It was like a child's playroom where everything can be used for naming games.

'If you sit there, I won't get flour on you,' she said going round to the other side of the table, which was covered with bowls and packets and utensils. A patch of flour marked her work space. 'I'm making scones, and a Madeira for Sunday. The scones are for today though.' Robert sat on a chair with his face to the sun and his back against the warm wall.

'I'll make tea. You must be thirsty,' she said. And suddenly he was. The first sensation he had recognized for days. This was thirst and she would give him tea.

Sarah filled the kettle and lit the gas. She turned back to the table and with both hands scooped yellow dough from a bowl, flattened it with her palms, patting it down into the flour, cupping the edges where they cracked. With each roll of the rolling pin she rotated the dough, each time a deft quarter turn; a sprinkle of flour, roll, turn. Robert watched her. She leaned over the table and a strand of glossy hair slipped from behind her ear.

The kettle boiled and she clapped her hands again, filled the
teapot, set out their cups and some biscuits on a plate, the milk
in a spotted jug, the sugar in a blue bowl. Then back again to the
table—all one movement, smooth and quiet in the yellow
sunshine.

She cut the dough with a circle of steel, pressing circles all over
the surface, lifting out the little soft disks, peeling away the surplus
with her fingers and laying each one in its place on a baking tray.
Then she squeezed the dough again into a ball, patting down,
rolling, turning, pressing the rings side by side. She was absorbed in
her work. He watched her hands and her floury arms with the
sleeves slipping down and the strands of slippery hair.

'Please drink your tea,' she said stopping suddenly. She had only
a small piece of dough left to cut but she hesitated and for the first
time seemed uncertain what to do next.

'You must drink,' she said evenly. 'You are very tired and you
must at least drink.'

All the movement in the bright kitchen halted. Robert's eyes
watered and the colours split open, sparkling like Jack's kaleidoscope.

'I'm so sorry about your children.'

He saw her in her long white nightdress reaching to the floor
and a child's dressing gown too small for her girl-woman's body.
The sleeves were too short and a teddy bear was embroidered on
the pocket. He could not move, Catherine was so heavy in his
arms.

'I didn't know when you came the other night that your little girl
was dead,' she said. 'I saw your son too, when Mr Sevier and the
doctor brought him back. The doctor told me their names were
Catherine and Jack. Catherine and Jack. I am so sorry they died.'

It was said. He tipped the tea into his mouth and the warm
sweetness was like nothing he had ever tasted before.

∽

The doctor and Robert sat in the sitting room with an untouched plate of scones on a table between them. There had been a little eddy of greetings and conversation when the doctor returned.

Sarah took the doctor's bag with her floury hand and kissed him on the cheek, with her other floury hand on his black-suited shoulder. The doctor admired the baked scones and dipped his finger in the Madeira cake mix, and Sarah scolded him, patting away his old, veined hand.

'I'll bring you tea in the sitting room,' she said. 'It's sunnier in there than the study. And I'll be hurt if you don't eat what I've made for you.' Robert saw their eyes meet, his old friend and the young woman conspiring to take care of him.

Edward settled back in an armchair and Robert did the same. Perhaps they had rehearsed the scene all these years just for this moment, to be at ease in each other's company knowing there was nothing more to be done. They would discuss the cricket, the newspapers and maybe politics, like father and son. And Joséphine would come in, too large and bright for the sepia room, her silver hair coiled perfectly at the nape of her neck and her high French cheekbones rosy from the garden or the kitchen. She would tease them for being so English—'always cricket'—and ask about Isabel, 'your fine Isabel', and 'the little ones'.

Everything changed except the two of them sitting in this shabby, comfortable room.

Sarah brought in a tray. She moved a plate of scones to the arm of Robert's chair and put another cup of tea in his hand. He could not help smiling at her persistence. She opened the doors to the garden and drew one of the curtains a little way across to shade the doctor's eyes.

They sat in silence for a while, hearing the sounds of her busy in the kitchen again.

'We don't sleep, but I suppose that's natural,' said Robert eventually.

'My dear Robert, who can say what's natural? Such things are not natural. Would you like me to give you something to help?'

'Isabel won't believe it. She looks for them. All the time, she goes looking for them and I can't stop her. She won't let us sleep.'

'She must make sure. She needs your help in that.'

'But it's like madness. She won't say it; she thinks if she doesn't, it won't be true.'

'If you feel I can help, I'll talk to her, Robert. Bring her here if she will come, or I'll come out to the house. But we can't force her, we must just take care of her until she knows for herself.'

'But she saw. She saw them both. How can she not face up to it?'

'What she saw, she could not understand. She will understand in her own way, when she's ready.'

Edward talked as if this were a puzzle, a riddle whose answer was itself. It was no riddle when he grasped Catherine's hand as she floated with her hair caught in a branch, or when Xavier plunged into the river searching for Jack.

When Robert left the doctor's house, Sarah was sowing seeds beside the path in the garden. She wore huge yellow gloves and four little packets were arranged in a line on the earth, perhaps as she planned to sow them.

'The nettles are all gone now,' she said. 'Bare flower beds are so sad, I thought these would be nice, if there's time—the summer's nearly over. Weeds will grow if there's an empty space.'

⊷∞⊶

Instead of walking home through the village, Robert turned the other way, towards the river. It would take him an hour to walk home this way but there was no hurry. When he passed Xavier and Adelie's house he did not think of calling on them. But his mind noticed: everything had changed. Josef's bicycle was on its side on the lawn.

He expected to come across Isabel somewhere along the path but he met no one. They had found the children further downstream and he wondered if she was there. When he said he was visiting the doctor, she had been incredulous—why, why? They must keep looking or Catherine would miss her ballet class.

Catherine had not been to ballet for more than a year but time flooded outwards, obliterating landmarks, and this small fact had disappeared.

It was not only Isabel, he too had thoughts that made no sense. If he turned now and walked downstream, perhaps he would catch up with the little boat before whatever had happened could happen. But there were other memories he could not forget, the ones that Isabel refused to remember, and he was angry with her for keeping the craziness for herself. She was forcing him to be the one to know the truth. He wanted his mind, like hers, to tangle itself in a knot of ridiculous hope.

The river curved lazily round the foot of Tye Hill and out onto the meadows of Cameldip. It was shallow here, edged with reeds and willows. The water was clear enough to see the stony bed in the places where the undulating weed had not found a hold. Some cows basked on the path in the late afternoon sun and Robert skirted round, not wanting to disturb them.

By the time he reached home, it was getting dark. The sun had gone down but the air was still warm and birds twittered in the trees as he walked up from the riverbank across the grass to the house. There were no lights on and the garden doors were wide open. He did not go in and sat for a while on the step with his back to the room. It was just as they had left it, tea plates, paints, clothes. It would not be long before their things were covered with dust. He saw that his hands shook as he lit a cigarette. He wondered where Isabel was.

The house was silent and he went into the kitchen, switching on the light. There was a tray on the kitchen table covered with a cloth. It was a saucepan of soup, some bread and ham, and there was a note tucked under a bowl: *With love, Adelie*. He folded it and put it in his pocket. He drank some water and switched off the kitchen light. Perhaps he could sleep for a while. A flat calm had settled on him and with it, exhaustion.

As he climbed the stairs there was a knock at the front door and it took a step or two before he halted and came down again. It was Sarah. She held out a small package to him, wrapped in paper and sealed with wax.

'You forgot this,' she said. 'It's such a beautiful evening, I thought I'd have a walk, so it was no trouble to bring it.' She put it in his hand. 'The doctor says to take two with water before you want to sleep and to keep the bottle in your pocket.'

'Thank you, I will. Please tell Edward, thank you.' Sarah was turning to go and he suddenly thought how much he wanted her to stay. If he had been able to feel anything, he would be consoled by her grey eyes and her smooth brown hair. He would be comforted by her neat cotton collar and her town shoes.

Sarah buttoned her summer coat and her heels scuffed softly on the flagstones as she walked down the path into the summer night.

He found Isabel sleeping on Jack's bed. She was on her stomach, her face in the pillow. The dusk and the shadows hid Jack's toys and pictures but he could see the colourless shape of Isabel's dress and the backs of her legs. The soles of her feet were black. A breeze lifted the curtains and Robert leaned over to close the window.

He lay down in the narrow space beside her, edging his body close to hers. She keened and whined in her sleep and he rocked her. Her hair against his face smelled sour, like something decaying.

December 1987

The Citroën

'It's from my sister,' said Anna. She sat on the stool by the sink to read her letter.

'How is Rose?' said Isabel after a while. She was in her dressing gown, her hair loose. It was nearly midday.

'Her contract's finished.' Anna pulled on her boots. 'But she's not coming for Christmas after all.'

'What a shame, darling. You must be disappointed. What will you and Matthew do?'

'We'll be here,' said Anna. Isabel looked pleased.

'His first Christmas.'

'I hope he'll be good with you today, Isabel. Robert says he'll be in the workshop if you need him.'

'We'll have a lovely time together, won't we my sweet?' From Isabel's arms, Matthew's eyes followed Anna. He looked glum and watchful, making up his mind whether this was a crisis.

'Thank you for having him. Are you sure you can manage? You're not …'

'Just the two of us. We'll have a lovely day.'

'Don't forget the Camel's Keep Fit is in the dining room this afternoon, Isabel. Don't get trapped in the kitchen in your dressing gown.'

'It doesn't matter.' Isabel tipped out a game of plastic shapes on to the table for the baby. She looked content.

Anna watched; she was not anxious for Matthew any more—soon, after Christmas, they would leave and then she'd be his only mother—it was Isabel. She seemed vague and preoccupied, like an invalid turned in on herself. Often she did not dress, wandering the house in her dressing gown. She was equable, but there was an edge to her Anna could feel that was more guarded and watchful than ever. The old Isabel appeared sometimes, when visitors came, with Robert or when some small annoyance provoked her, but mostly she seemed to have let go her hold on things. Anna cooked and shopped for their food. They hadn't spoken again of the children.

'I'll be back at about six if the bus is on time. Can I get you anything in town?'

'No, darling, nothing. Yes, I do need more Christmas cards— have I still got time to post them? Two weeks, that should be enough shouldn't it?'

'It's six days, Isabel.'

'Would you choose for me? No robins or angels but apart from that—or Father Christmases, and not coaching scenes either. I'll leave it up to you. And nothing with glitter or nativities.'

'Snow?' said Anna.

'Yes. I like snow.'

Anna walked out to the lane. The bus would stop for her if she held out her hand. It usually came too fast, the driver unable to resist the thrill for his passengers when they were momentarily airborne at the hump on the bridge.

Anna looked for the best place to wait. One must stand well out in the road to be noticed—the dilemma was between being passed by when standing safely in the hedge or being driven over when standing in the road.

There was the sound of an engine. Anna stepped forward, then stepped back. But it was not the bus. A yellow Citroën came over the bridge. The top was rolled back in spite of the cold. It was Josef Sevier. Beside him was the woman, Sarah, her collar turned up and held tight together by a gloved hand. Her silver-brown hair flickered round her face with the turbulence of the air. Anna saw her glance across at Josef, leaning a little to say something over the noise of the engine. He laughed. Anna watched them pass. They did not notice her.

The bus was close behind. Although she was standing in the hedge and forgot to wave, the driver had seen her.

∞

Exeter was busy. By three in the afternoon the light was beginning to fade and Anna was dazed by the endless motion of people and traffic and winking decorations. The heat in the shops and the cold of the air outside made her face burn. A sprinkling of wet snow fell, the tarmac glittered and the feet of the shoppers slapped on the pavement.

She bought everything she needed except for Isabel's cards—and it occurred to her how much Isabel must hate Christmas. The cards all said 'Merry' or 'Happy', had childish pictures or worthy messages. In the end she picked up a pack of ten all the same, a single star over an empty desert. The message was 'Peace'.

There was a café by the bus station. Anna sat down at a table by the window where she could see her bus arriving and ordered hot chocolate. The place was full of people, groups of students, women with children, couples shopping for Christmas. It seemed she was the only person alone.

She stacked her carrier bags on the seat opposite, put her coat beside her and got out her diary for no reason other than to have something to do. She made a list of the things she'd bought. Her chocolate arrived. She made another list of people she'd phone before Christmas and those she should write to. She started a letter to Rose. There was no sign of the bus. She ordered another chocolate and picked up her pen, gazing out of the window. The lights across the road twinkled through her black reflection. Suddenly she was looking out at Josef Sevier's face instead of her own.

He came into the café and over to her barricade of carrier bags.

'Anna? I thought it was you. I was walking past and I recognized your coat.'

'I'm waiting for the bus,' said Anna.

'Yes, I thought you might be. I'm meeting someone or I'd give you a lift back,' he said.

'Oh, it's fine,' said Anna quickly, 'I like the bus, I wasn't expecting ...'

'Would you mind if I join you? I could do with a coffee. I'm early for once.' Anna pulled the bags over the table onto the chair beside her. Josef sat down opposite. He ordered a coffee, took off his scarf, unbuttoned his jacket.

'Are you shopping?' said Anna. 'No, of course, you said you're meeting someone.' She looked into her chocolate and stirred the froth with a spoon.

'Yes, in a while.' He leaned back in his chair and she felt him watching.

'It's strange seeing you here,' he said. 'I expect you're more at home here than in the village.'

'No, not really. I like London, but I like it in Cameldip. Christmas in London is frantic.'

'I'm never sure about Christmas,' he said. 'I always think I'm missing something, that I must be the only person in the country not playing charades with friends or waking up on Christmas morning with a lover.'

She looked up and smiled. 'Do you?'

'Where will you be for Christmas? Doing just that, I expect.'

'Oh no. I'll be with Isabel,' she said. 'And you?'

'Working, I'm sorry to say.'

'I saw you today, in your car with ... ,' she began.

'Look, your bus. It's here. I'd better give you a hand with all this stuff.' He got to his feet.

'What about your coffee?' said Anna.

'I can come back. I'll give you a hand and come back.' There was confusion; Josef could not reach the bags so she collected them up herself while he waited.

'It's fine, I can manage. I've got everything.'

'You've forgotten your coat,' he said. He took the bags out of her hands and Anna struggled with her coat. He put down the bags to help and when she was ready, they shared the shopping between them. They found a way through the packed tables to the door then Anna remembered she hadn't paid.

'Don't worry, I'll get it,' said Josef. 'Don't miss the bus or you'll be here for another hour.' He hurried her across the road. A few passengers were waiting to get on. 'Call in if you ever have time,' he said.

'You're never there,' said Anna. 'I mean, when I've walked that way.'

'I've been in France,' he said.

'But you're back now?' said Anna.

'I think so,' he said, patting his chest. 'Yes, this is me, I'm back.' Anna got on the bus and paid for her ticket. When she turned to say goodbye, more people were getting on behind her and she couldn't see him. The bus started and she rubbed a circle on the misty window. In the café, their table was empty. He must have already gone to meet his friend.

⌘

Gatta was lying on her bed in her school uniform with her feet up on the wooden ceiling. It was the last day of term and she was waiting for relief to kick in. She heard her mother come home. A car came up to the house, then there were voices, and the car drove away. Her mother's heels tapped on the wooden steps and the front door banged closed. Gatta did not need to look out of her bedroom window; she knew Josef Sevier's car—it sounded like a hairdryer.

Gatta's bedroom was at the top, the highest room in the house. When she was small Gatta loved the house but now it was

embarrassing to bring friends to a place like this. They said it was
'different', which was patronizing. What they meant was there
was nowhere comfortable to sit and no television.

When you came to the house you turned off the lane at a gap in
the hedge and into what you thought was a wood. And there it was,
mossy and grey and looking almost like a tree itself on its stilts with
its rooms skewered by the trunks of two trees and its roofs amongst
the branches.

There was no path or garden. In the winter the house was
surrounded by leaves and mud. As the months went on it was prettier. There were snowdrops, then crocuses, then bluebells and grass.
Wooden steps went up to a long porch and the front door, which
opened straight into the kitchen. The bathroom was at the back and
a place for outdoor things like boots and screwdrivers.

The trunks of the trees came up through the floor of the kitchen,
with shelves and worktops built around them, and they were
pinboards for Spike's paintings and a place to display the sticky
coloured things Linnet made at nursery. There was a calendar and
notes from school that her mother forgot to look at.

The trees disappeared through the kitchen ceiling. At each end
was a staircase, one going up to the room that would be Linnet's
when she was old enough to sleep by herself, then up again to her
mother's bedroom. The other staircase was more of a ladder, to
Spike's room, then up to Pete's, then up again to hers, Gatta's, which
was not much bigger than the size of her bed, a crow's-nest with a
roof.

Gatta's bedroom looked down on her mother's. It was not difficult to climb out of the window across to the other tree and down
to a branch where she could sit and watch through the window. It
was an easy climb for Gatta, although she did not bother much now.
She used to climb anything when she was young but now she was
nearly sixteen it was annoying to ruin her jeans and break her nails.
Anyway, there wasn't much to see in her mother's room these days.

Gatta could remember when she was small and there had been only the two of them living in the house. She liked it then. They had just the kitchen and a room above it.

When she was four a man whose name she'd forgotten stayed for a while. He never remembered her name either, he called her 'the child' however often she said, 'I'm Gabriella Josephine.'

Later there was Dario, who called her Gatta, his own special name for her. She was seven. When Pete was born, they had to make another room.

'Eets no fair for my Gatta not have room for her own,' Dario said in his husky Spanish voice. 'Good, I think, yes?' She wanted to sleep in her mother's bed as she always had but Dario was kind and he made Gatta feel like a real daughter, so she couldn't say no.

Mr MacKinnon from the house by the river came to build the new room. He'd built the whole house for them, her mother said, before Gatta was born, so he knew how to do it without harming the trees.

Then another room was needed for baby Sebastian who was Spike. Dario said this time Robert MacKinnon should build two new rooms, one for Spike and a spare for the next baby who was sure to come.

Then Dario left.

When Gatta was eleven, there was a man who had laughed when he caught her on the branch outside her mother's window.

'A little girl who likes to watch,' he said, pulling her close and tickling her.

She said to her mother, 'He smells like the weedy water in the frog pond and he smells like an old bonfire.' Her mother laughed quick and hard, like the squawk of a bird, and said not to tell him.

He was the only one who'd ever caught her watching, and he could see her even when she was no one. She did not breathe, she was as quiet and small as a lost sock, but it was useless, he always found her.

'Here's my special little girl,' he would whisper. And his sour stench smothered her. 'My pretty, secret girl. Here she is.'

After a year he left them too, but he left them with Linnet so that was something good. Gatta hoped no one else would ever live with them.

In all that time and in all those people, even Gatta and her brothers and her little sister, it was only Robert MacKinnon whom her mother baked cakes for. When Robert MacKinnon was there, her mother was as calm and safe as the deep grey sea and her eyes followed him everywhere.

He was the only one who never stayed, not even for a while.

'Gabriella.' Her mother's voice wavered up through the wood of the house and the bare branches of the trees.

'Fuck,' said Gatta. But she got up and climbed down through the chaos of Spike and Pete's rooms.

Spike's had an aviation theme. He'd made his windowsill into an jet fighter's console with fruit-gum warning lights and bottle-top dials hammered through with nails.

Pete's was full of cardboard boxes, homes for anything injured he happened upon when out roaming. Toys and clothes were everywhere. Their mother rarely came up here.

Gatta climbed down into the kitchen. 'What do you want?' she said.

'Oh, nothing. I thought you weren't home yet,' said Sarah. 'Seeing as you are, could you pick up Linnet? I can't face going out again.'

'If I must,' said Gatta, picking up her jacket. 'But I can't look after her this evening, I'm seeing Starling. And anyway, how is old creepy cardigan? I hope he's not next in line.'

'Josef's a friend of mine, Gabriella. He's not the "next in line", and I don't need to explain myself to you.' Sarah did not sound annoyed, she never did. She sat down heavily on a kitchen chair with her coat on.

'Well you always look kind of fussed-up when you see him,' said Gatta. 'You go off in his pathetic car every blue moon and that's it. Believe me, it's going nowhere. He never comes round. He's using you. You need someone reliable.'

'Gatta, not now, I'm not in the mood. He's a friend, he is reliable—it's not a question of going somewhere.'

'Anyone living in a dump like this at his age must be a loser.'

'His business is here.'

'Business! Huh! He's not right for you,' said Gatta. 'I'm telling you because I care even if you think I don't.'

'My little girl.' Sarah pulled Gatta's face down to her and kissed her. 'I know you care. I'm fine. Now go. Linnet gets cross if you keep her waiting.'

'I haven't been your little girl for ages. And you're never fine and you never tell me anything,' said Gatta. 'I never know what you're going to do next. He's weird and I hate him.'

'Gatta, I'm too tired for this. You don't hate him. You hardly know him. And I won't do anything without telling you. I promise.' But her mother had turned away. She was thinking of something else and Gatta could see she didn't mean it.

❦

'Pearlized plumps the lips,' said Gatta, squinting into Starling's dressing-table mirror. 'And matt reduces.'

'Mine are narrow and thick, one of each, so what am I supposed to do?' said Starling, watching Gatta stretch a letterbox smile and apply Poochie Petal. 'I need pearly and unpearly.'

'Gloss,' said Steffie. 'You've got a cupid's bow and it's your best feature. Accentuate your best and accept the rest.'

'Which one, Gatta? This is important.' Starling held up two lipsticks at Gatta's back.

'In your left hand, no the other one, your right.' Gatta's eyes in the mirror glanced at Starling's hands. 'He won't notice anyway—

he's not into looks, you can tell, he's too old.'

'Who?' said Steffie, looking from one to the other.

'No one,' said Starling, and frowned at Gatta in the mirror.

'I know who you're talking about,' said Steffie. She wiped her mouth with the back of her hand and put on her blazer. 'I know who you mean.'

'We won't see him tonight anyway, he won't be where we're going,' said Starling.

'Where are you going?' Steffie stood by the door, waiting for an answer.

'Bye then,' said Gatta still intent on the mirror.

'Give up violin, then you could come out with us more,' said Starling.

'I can't,' said Steffie, 'or the band will fold.'

'Why? It's so boring,' said Starling. 'They should do without you.'

'You can't have three in a quartet. I'm violin, Mum's cello, Bee's flute and Dad's page-turner. Bye then.' They listened to her heavy footsteps on the stairs and then Starling's mother calling out goodbye. The front door slammed.

'I don't understand you,' said Gatta. 'One minute he makes you vomit and the next you're obsessed.'

'He's not how you think. You don't know him.' Starling took off her school blouse and her bra and tied on a halter-necked T-shirt.

'Yeah, yeah, of course he's not. You worry me, Starling. You let him do all sorts to you and you don't like it and then you go back for more.'

'What do you mean?' Starling fiddled behind her back and shrugged her shoulders to make sure the knots were secure. 'That stuff I told you was nothing really. He made a mistake with his hands, that's all. I gave you the wrong impression.' She took off her tights then unzipped her skirt and let it fall on the floor. She sat on the edge of the bed and crossed her legs, admiring their shape. 'He's nice. He's mature. He knows your mum.'

'Take my advice, Star, forget my mother's taste in men.' Sometimes Gatta sounded much older than she was. 'Anyway, you know what I'm talking about—not that time.'

'I don't know what you mean.'

'Oh yes you do-oo,' said Gatta in a sing-song voice.

'I don't, I swear,' said Starling.

Gatta turned round. She smacked her lips. Her mouth was fondant pink and her green eyes were edged with spikes of black like two iridescent insects.

'You went to see him, I know you did. It's all over your face.'

'I didn't. It isn't. What?'

'"I didn't. It isn't",' Gatta mimicked. 'I know so don't be all baby innocent. I know what he did the other day. I saw you. You should think about pulling the curtains if you're going to get up to stuff. Anybody could have seen. You're lucky it was only me.'

Starling looked at her blankly.

'We talked, that's all, God's honest truth and hope to die. He gave me some wine then I went to sleep.'

Gatta paused before she said, 'Asleep? Asleep you say. I rest my case.'

Starling grinned but her voice was edgy, 'What did you see? Tell me.'

Gatta's mouth turned up at the corners. She put her finger to her lips.

'I won't breathe a word. I shouldn't worry about it if I were you.' She turned back to the mirror. 'Anyway, he's got his beady eye on your friend Anna and I should leave them to it if I were you. Come on, let's go out.'

'He likes me,' said Starling bleakly. 'It proves it. What you saw proves it.'

'You don't know what I saw. Put your clothes on and let's go.'

Starling stood holding her jeans. Her bare legs were goose-bumped and her nipples made two small buttons under her T-shirt.

'What did he do?' she said.

Gatta reached over to get her jacket off the end of the bed and as she did, she pinged the elastic on Starling's pants.

'Don't ask,' she whispered.

⁂

The last bus from town was full. There was patchy fog and the bus slowed to walking pace when they left the street lights. By the time they reached Cameldip there were only the two of them and a man asleep. It was ten-thirty—late—but Gatta was unconcerned about her curfew; she could always make her mother doubt what time she'd said. Starling worried all the way home.

When they got off the bus Gatta suggested they hang around for a while, that it was stupid to be in so early when it was the holidays.

'I'll tell my dad I'm back.' Starling disappeared into the fog, her shoes clacking across the road to her house. Gatta sat down on the bench by the memorial and after a few minutes Starling appeared beside her, rummaged in her bag for her tobacco tin and rolled herself a cigarette.

'You should give that up,' said Gatta. 'You'll age prematurely and be unpleasant to snog.'

'It's freezing sitting here. Let's walk while I finish this then I'm going home,' said Starling. They ambled along the main street, arm in arm in the middle of the road. The tarmac sparkled with frost. There was one street lamp in a swirling halo of orange fog, then house lights, dim and far away in their invisible porches, then darkness as the lane went on out of the village. The girls giggled and shrieked, taking mincing steps. They clung together, they slipped on frozen puddles. It made no difference if they closed their eyes or kept them open, there was nothing except the tip of Starling's cigarette.

After a while the fog seemed thinner and a light appeared high up on their left.

'It's the pub,' said Gatta. 'It's closed and it can't be eleven yet. He's useless. What's the point of a pub when you never know if it's open.' She let go of Starling's hand and felt her way along the path to the garden.

'I'm staying here,' Starling called.

'Don't you want to see what he's up to?' said Gatta. Her voice was loud in the silence. 'You know you want to see him. One of us could be ill, we could be lost. I'm going to knock on the door.'

'I'm not doing it.' Starling sounded far away now. 'Come back. Gatta? I can't see a thing.'

Gatta went round to the back of the house. She stopped to peer in at the kitchen window but all she could make out were the embers of the fire in the hearth. The sitting-room window was blank, the curtains were closed this time.

She passed the old aviary and heard the horses making their small night sounds in the darkness like a couple in bed—rustle, sniff, cough, sigh.

The yellow car was parked on the other side of the house. It stood out pale in the blackness and Gatta caught the oily warmth of the engine and the feral scent of nettles that must have been crushed by the tyres. The car made tiny metallic clicks. The bonnet was still warm.

She tried the door. It was not locked and she got in behind the steering wheel, putting her hands where Josef put his. She felt the seat beside her where her mother had sat, and found a lighter. The keys were in the ignition. She slid down in the seat, stretched out her legs to the pedals, but her skirt was too tight. She pulled it higher, one foot on the right pedal, one on the left. For a moment she thought of starting the engine; instead she pulled out the keys and jingled them in her hand.

His keys. A bunch, all different, in a soft leather case that he kept in his pocket or held in his hand, as she did now. They smelled of leather and ashy smoke and man's hands. She played with the keys in her hand, letting them slither through one by one, slick and well-worn, and notched on their undersides. She tipped them over, they clattered softly and she let them dangle in her fingers, trailing them along her thigh. They made her skin tingle like being stroked with feathers or grass or the lightest touch of cold fingers. Suddenly the feeling sickened her. Josef Sevier sickened her. They all did; Starling and her mother and all of them.

She scrambled out of the car, not caring that the seat creaked and the door slammed. She was glad of the nettles stinging her legs. She pressed the point of a key into the yellow paint.

'Yes,' she said and scratched a slow, halting line along the side of the car. The key stuck over the seams in the metal, it scraped and jerked and squealed softly until the scratch encircled the yellow car. On the boot she carved lines that she guessed would make letters but it was too dark to see. She threw the keys into the undergrowth and walked out into the lane. The fog had cleared a little.

'Let's go,' she said to Starling who had tucked herself under the hedge.

'You've been ages—what were you doing? Did you see him?'

'No,' said Gatta. 'But I've got you a present.' The lighter was in her hand. She held it out to Starling. 'Go on, it's for you. I don't smoke.'

'How did he give it to you if you didn't see him? You nicked it.'

'Suit yourself.' Gatta dropped the lighter on the road and starting walking.

'You didn't see him at all?'

'No, I told you. I didn't see him. I left him a message.'

'What do you mean. What about? About me?' Starling picked up the lighter and hurried after her.

'Yes, about you,' said Gatta. 'About you and other things.'

June 1971

Sarah

Except for the study, all the windows were wide open and a breeze blew through the house. It was satisfying—everything was clean and polished but unchanged, which was how Edward liked it.

Sarah kicked off her sandals and climbed up onto her dressing table with the pressed curtains draped over her arm. She stretched up, one foot on the windowsill, to hook the curtains on to their rings.

The cloth was old heavy linen. The curtains had been sent out to be laundered because they were too big for the washing machine and they had come back with the colour and the pattern almost gone, like the ghostly flowers on the wallpaper and the faded rug by her bed. And Edward, he too was growing fainter, more indistinct. His skin was transparent, his eyes were cloudy sea-washed glass, his hair was no more than wisps of silver. He and his house full of Joséphine's things were slowly being bleached away by the light of passing years.

Sarah wrestled with the folds of cloth. She stood high up at the window and felt the heat of the sunshine outside. For a moment she rested her arms and looked out over the view that was hers again after so long, across the village green to the chapel and the foot of Tye Hill. The colours were startling. The grass was saturated green, the sky cornflower and the stone of the chapel sparkled with flecks of granite.

She could hear the muffled voices of children in the school play-ground and the sound floated in the air with the cawing crows and the bleats of sheep on the hill.

The years of parties and study and bedsits did not belong to her, they were another life.

Today was Friday and the fish van was parked on the verge. The driver sat on the grass smoking while he waited for customers, and Constance Lamb was weeding her garden. There was a young man in jeans carrying a rucksack. Sarah briefly registered his long hair and his loping walk and that she did not know him.

The doorbell rang. She let the curtains sag over the dressing-table mirror and climbed down. As she ran down the stairs she hoped that whoever it was wouldn't ring again and wake Edward.

'Josef! It's you! I saw you but I didn't recognize you with your hair so long.'

'Yes, it's me. Don't say I've grown.'

'I wouldn't.' She kissed his cheek. 'Oh, how wonderful to see you. Come in, come in. Let me make you some tea, or coffee. Are you just back?'

'Yep, I got the train.'

'You haven't been home yet—to see your parents? Adelie?'

'No, I thought I'd see you and Edward first. I phoned her this morning and she says she's feeling good today and not to worry.'

'I'm sorry, Joe. It must be hard for you being away just now.'

He looked at his feet. 'It's OK.'

'Edward's having a nap in the study, he'll be so pleased to see you. How's college?' Sarah said.

'Good.' He followed her into the kitchen.

'Tell me about everything—I want to know how you are. How's your girlfriend?'

'She's fine.'

'And work? Exams?'

'So-so.' He swung the rucksack off his shoulder and onto the floor. He watched her as she washed some mugs in the sink; she was wearing shorts and he looked at the smooth backs of her legs. He could see that she wore nothing under her T-shirt.

'While the kettle's boiling could you just help me do something?' she said, smiling at him over her shoulder.

'Yes, sure.'

'I shouldn't be using you the minute you arrive.'

'It's fine.'

'I can't reach the window over the stairs and I need to put the curtains back up. I want to get it done while Edward's sleeping or he'll fuss.'

They went up to the landing.

'If I stand on there and reach over, all you have to do is hold me.'

'I'll do it, I can reach,' he said.

'But I can't hold you, you're too big—it'll be easier for me.'

She climbed over the landing banister and stood on the ledge over the staircase.

'Hand me the curtains would you, and just hold me so I don't fall.'

Josef hesitated then he leaned over and put his arms round her waist. Countless times he had imagined the feel of her. She reached up and began hooking up the curtains.

'How are you?' he said. 'Are you glad to be back?' It was easier to ask when she was not facing him.

'Me? I'm fine.'

'Fine?'

'Apart from Edward being under the weather sometimes, I'm fine.'

'What's it like coming back here? I wouldn't, not unless it was for a reason.'

'Oh, I want be here, there is a reason ... for Edward. That woman was hopeless. I've told Edward he should have told me sooner and I would have come.'

'He was always talking about you. About what you're doing.'

'He wants me to qualify, but I can anytime. I can go to Exeter Hospital when I've got things straight here.'

'He's proud of you.'

'I wouldn't have done it without him.' She stretched up, leaning against his arms. She swished the curtain to one side.

'Done,' she said. He passed her the other curtain and she reached out over the stairwell again. He watched her slender arms reaching up, and her sunburned hands.

'Have you … have you seen Isabel? Or Robert?' he said.

Her body tensed. 'No, not Isabel.'

'Robert?' He thought he could sound casual but in an instant he felt hot with jealousy.

'Yes,' she said evenly.

'Robert's still living with her then?'

'Of course,' she said.

'He must be crazy. Why doesn't he leave her? They aren't happy, so why stay? I wouldn't.'

'Perhaps we couldn't understand. We couldn't know what it's like.'

'He should sort it out or leave her. Why is he wasting his life?' He felt the insistence and the clumsiness of his questioning but he couldn't stop, the words came spilling out. This was how she made him feel.

Her breasts brushed his arm through the T-shirt as she leaned forward. He let his other arm slide down around her hips and his hand touched the skin at the hem of her shorts.

He wanted to stop this conversation and make her laugh, but most of all he wanted to know.

'What do you think? You know Robert better than any of us,' he said and he hated himself for saying it.

He held her tightly. He had no reason to be angry and even less to hurt her. She had almost finished.

'You can let me go now,' she said, and he realized that he was holding her too close. She climbed back over the banister and her eyes avoided him. 'Thanks, Joe,' she said, going down the stairs in front of him. 'That's done.'

They took their coffee mugs into the garden and Sarah lay on her stomach on the grass. Josef sat a little way from her. The ease between them returned as they talked. He made her laugh. She was prettier than all the featureless, tedious girls at college. She was twenty-nine and more beautiful than any of them.

Before he left, he went into the study. Edward was sleeping in his armchair, and Josef leaned down and touched his arm to wake him.

'Hello, my boy,' said Edward. 'What a pleasure it is to see you.' They shook hands as they always had since Josef was small.

Josef heaved his rucksack onto his back and Sarah stood on the front step to wave him goodbye. She kissed him again on the cheek and he resented the joy he felt. There was nothing in her eyes to tell him he could hope.

He waved to her from the gate and when he turned Robert was there, walking across the green.

'Josef, you're home. Good to see you.' He embraced Josef and clasped his hand. 'Come and see me, won't you? Come to the black-house, any time. Call in one evening and I'll give you a taste of real whisky.'

It was impossible to feel angry when Robert was there in front of him.

'It's good to have you back. We've got you for the summer? Until September?'

Josef nodded.

'Good. That's good. We miss you.'

Robert walked up the path to Sarah. He stood close to her and she smiled; they did not touch or kiss.

Josef closed the gate and turned towards home. He wished he'd not seen. That was the look he wanted for himself. Her smile for Robert told him everything.

⁂

One fingertip, light as a leaf, circled the curve on her shoulder, along the jawbone, the cheek and the chin, then down under the throat and the breastbone. His finger traced the cold nipples, the creases under her breasts, the softly covered ribs. Down over the slight curve of her belly. His hand slid between her thighs and his fingers opened her.

'A flower in the rain,' he said.

Sarah laughed. 'You say things so beautifully.' She rolled onto her back.

He found her hand. 'Feel. You are beautiful.'

'Listen to it. Listen to the thunder,' she said.

The rain pattered on the roof. They heard it splash on the leaves of the beech trees above them and the soft creak of the new joints of the tree house as the branches moved in the wind.

'I'd want to live here—if it weren't for Edward.'

Robert pulled her closer. Her body was cold against him. The light was fading and in the dark, with the sleepiness and utter calm, his mind drifted back in time. He was woken by an instant of illusion that vanished as he tried to hold it—that this woman in his arms was taller, broader, that the hair against his shoulder was coarse and abundant, spreading out red and gold on the pillow.

'I love you, Sarah,' he said, and it was true. The pieces of his life did not overlap, they existed on different planes between which he passed without contradiction or regret.

'Are you glad I came back?' she asked him.

'Of course.'

They must have slept because when Robert sat up and looked at his watch it was dark. His eyes made out the glow of the hands. He reached for his clothes.

'Don't go, not yet,' Sarah said.

'I must.'

'But she won't even know you're not there. Now we have this place, she won't know.'

He could feel her tense, trying to stop the words, but she said: 'Joe said something today, he said you're wasting your life and you should leave.'

'Life is what it is, waste or not, it is as it is.'

'But we can make it change. It's been so long. If we want to, we'll make it change.'

'It's too long, I know.' He could say no more. He wished he could be generous in the lie and tell her that one day it would be different.

She sat up and her voice had an edge of anguish that seared him.

'Isn't there anything we can do to help her face it? You could be happy even if she can't. You could have children. We could have children.'

He lay down again beside her and she was shivering. He kissed her but something had disappeared inside him, fled to some place that left him insensible. He knew he had ached for her but at this moment he felt nothing at all.

'I love you.' And then, because it was no longer his voice that spoke: 'It would be wonderful to have a child. You can't imagine how much I want that.'

He tucked the blankets round her and he got up and dressed in the dark. 'It's too cold to sleep here; I'll walk you home.'

'I'll stay for a while,' said Sarah.

She listened to him climb down to the ground then his footsteps disappearing into the sound of the rain.

⸙

The morning was misty and the sun, already high, turned the air a thin pearly white. It would be hot again, and Sarah felt oppressed by her dark dress and tights and shoes. The village was still sleeping and she closed the front door quietly with the key. Edward always woke early but few people would be up yet on a Sunday morning.

She was already rehearsing, trying out the words she'd not spoken for years: 'Forgive me, Father, for I have sinned ...' There was a decade to confess, and the wrongs had accumulated as the Sisters always said they would, to a weight from which there was no escape.

'You have a dangerous weakness, Sarah Noone,' Sister Mary Thomas had said. 'You have a gluttony for happiness that is insatiable and slovenly, and you will suffer for it.'

Her sins bound her tight, the renouncing of one ensuring the committing of another. 'Sin is slack, it is content, it is lying on your back. Sin is procrastination and excuse.'

She started the car and drove out of the village. There was no other way but to pass Isabel's house. As she came closer, Robert's nearness was a physical sensation dragging at her and she was ashamed; even on her way to church her body longed for him.

She could not see more than a few yards, and she peered into the bright mist. Suddenly a figure was there in front of the bonnet of the car. She stepped on the brake and the car slewed on the wet ground, shuddered and stalled.

It was Isabel. She stood in the road, seeming unconcerned that the car had nearly hit her. She was wearing a summer dress even though the morning was chilly. The hem was torn and the front was stained.

Sarah's heart thudded. She had not seen Isabel for years but the fear of her was as powerful as ever. The lane was silent except for a bird singing somewhere high up above the mist.

Isabel rested her hands on the car and Sarah pressed back in her seat. It came to her that she must lock the doors, but she could not move. The window at her side was open and there was the bird, still singing in the shining silence.

The summer mist settled on the windscreen and Isabel's face was blurred by droplets of moisture gathering on the glass. Sarah could see the ragged outline of her hair and her bare shoulders, and Isabel leaned forward as if she was trying to see Sarah more clearly. Then she spoke. Her voice was soft through the glass and deadened by the water-laden air.

'You'll make no difference, you know. You can give him nothing. You do not exist in our life, mine and his. Not now or ever.'

She straightened up, smoothing her hands over the filthy cotton of the dress. Then she walked past the car, so close to the open window that Sarah saw freckles on her sunburned arm. And inside the folds of yellowed cotton the sprigs of printed flowers were fresh blues and greens on pure clean white.

'I can make him happy and he wants me!' Sarah shouted. Her hands were shaking. 'He loves me!'

But Isabel had gone.

After a while Sarah started the car and at the main road she did not turn towards Exeter and the church, but drove aimlessly through the lanes until she found her way back through a string of unfamiliar villages to Cameldip.

It was still early. She let herself into the house and went up to her room, taking off her Sunday clothes and dropping them in a heap on the floor. She stood naked by the bed and drank down a glass of water left from the night before.

On her bedside table was a pile of textbooks, her rosary beads and the card of yellow pills with almost a month of days pressed out, leaving little empty bubbles and lips of torn silver foil.

She gathered them up, the books, the beads and the pills and went down to the kitchen. She tipped them into the rubbish bin under the sink.

⌘

Josef ambled up the lane. He'd thought of going into town but it seemed too much trouble. He'd been back for almost a month and he was bored out of his mind. He thought of Sarah and wondered when he would see her again.

Then there she was. She was coming along the lane towards him, looking at the ground, deep in thought, and she hadn't seen him. He stopped and waited for her to look up, but she didn't. She nearly ran into him.

'I was coming to see you,' she said. 'Will you come for a walk with me, Joe?' She had been crying.

He fell into step beside her. She said nothing for a while, then she pulled at his arm: 'Let's go in here.' They turned through a gap in the hedge and into some woodland where Josef knew Robert had been building a tree house, though he didn't know who it was for. They went up wooden steps to a porch that opened into a room through which the trunks of two beech trees grew. There was a ladder on one side and he followed Sarah, climbing up to a small room above. She sat down on the mattress on the floor. The bed was neatly made with blankets and two pillows. He knew now who the tree house was for.

'I'm pregnant,' said Sarah. Her eyes spilled over with tears. He did not know what to say, or what she wanted him to do. He reached out and took her hand but she snatched it away. 'No, don't be nice to me. It's my own fault. I did it on purpose.'

'What did he say when you told him?' Josef couldn't unravel the tangle of feelings. He heard his voice sounding reproachful and harsh but there was a spark of elation inside him as if this conversation, here with her, had in it some hidden possibility, some promise that could not be guessed at.

'I can't tell him. I thought it was the right thing to do so I let it happen. But it's not right. It's not.' She wept openly.

'Are you sure you're … you are?' he said.

'Yes, yes. I didn't take my pill. I threw them away and now I'm late, over a week.'

'It's not long,' he said. 'You can't be sure yet, especially if you've been on the Pill.' She looked up, a sharp look as if she was only now aware of him. 'You're a doctor,' he added, 'but I do know about these things.'

'I expect you do,' she said coldly. 'And I'm not a doctor, not yet.'

They sat for a while. Sarah stared at nothing and sometimes she shivered. He moved next to her and pulled a blanket round them.

'What will you do?' he asked. 'Will you keep it?'

'Of course. How can you say that, what do you think I am?' She sounded furious.

'I'm not suggesting, I'm only asking.'

'It's a sin, the worst there is.'

'He'll know then, sooner or later.'

'I could lie; it could be someone else's. That's what I deserve.'

He had never heard her sound bitter. He couldn't follow what she meant.

They sat in silence for a long time and Sarah wept and leaned against him. He stroked her hair and struggled to keep his mind on the problem in hand.

'He loves you and he will want it,' he said. He hesitated, then he said, 'I know he will because … because I love you and I would.' At last he had laid open his heart to her. She sat up and looked at him hopefully. 'Do you think he loves me? Do you think he feels that?'

He could see her thoughts racing then her face crumpled, she lay down and tears trickled down into her hair.

'I'm making him leave Isabel. He'll never forgive me. And he'll never leave her.'

There was nothing more to say.

Josef searched for words to comfort her but he knew what she said was true. He was angry and her tears broke his heart, but he was glad. Robert would never leave Isabel.

He stroked her hair and her face. He kissed away the tears and she did not stop him. She put her arms around him and he held her as he'd longed to. He tasted salt tears on her eyes and her cheeks and her lips.

PART IV

＜◈＞

23 December 1987

Constance Lamb had a friend coming for Christmas. Lydia Arbamount would arrive on the twelve-sixteen from Plymouth, just in time for a sherry at The Inn—Constance disliked the word 'pub'—before sitting down to a ham salad lunch at the bungalow.

As Constance prepared their food that morning, she felt herself moving a little more fluidly, with more verve than usual. Her dancer's body, although ageing and grown rather heavy, was still quick to pick up her moods. She could feel her spine arching perfectly from cranium to pelvis as she bent over the cutting board to slice the cucumber, and her wrists gracefully loose as she shook the lettuce dry in a tea towel. Constance was excited.

Lydia had been her friend since the age of eleven. They had met at the Marjorie Barton School of Ballet. Both girls were blond and bespectacled and long-legged. They each wore the ends of their plaits tied together for neatness, and home-knitted pink cardigans. At first meeting they paired up like matching ponies. It went without saying they were best friends.

Later, the plaits were changed for a topknot bun and the pink cardigans for black leotards. Together they danced up through the Marjorie Barton ranks from sunbeams to fairies to princesses. Side by side, Connie and Lyddie felt the first flutters of vanity before their twinned reflections at the barre, their admiration of them-selves and of each other inseparable.

That was almost sixty years ago.

Lydia's husband, Gerald, had died that autumn so she was coming to Constance for a change of scene. They had not met up for years.

The table was set with the salad cling-filmed and the bread and butter under a pie dish. A modest (with respect to the recent passing of Gerald) table decoration of holly and gold berries was placed centrally between their empty plates, and Constance put the matches ready to light the candle.

She buttoned her coat and slipped on her ankle boots—flat, fur-lined, zipped and perfect for snow, though they were years old and it was the very devil of a job to find a pair these days. There was no snow, but there might be.

Before she left she impulsively switched on the fairy lights in the porch. This was a celebration.

Constance stood on the platform, her eyes moving from the clock to the bend in the track where the train would appear, back to the clock, the bend, the clock. The train was only six minutes late, not late enough for her excitement to have peaked and slumped, but quite long enough to be teetering uncomfortably between anticipation and impatience.

The train appeared and Constance smiled spontaneously at the thought of Lydia's face (aged somewhere between eleven and her present age of seventy-one), so shortly to be a reality before her. Three passengers got out at Cameldip, but Lydia was not one of them.

Constance looked up and down the train. No more doors opened, the train hissed and clunked and moved off. She walked the length of the platform and back to the barrier unable to take in the problem. How could Lydia not be on the train when she had telephoned three days ago to say that her seat was reserved and should she bring the port?

The train disappeared and the winter quiet settled. A few flakes of snow fell. Constance decided to enquire at the ticket office although she was unsure what to enquire about. Yes, that was the twelve-sixteen from Plymouth. No, there was no message for her. Yes, it had left on time with nothing unusual about the departure. No, there was no other train stopping today.

Constance walked out of the station alone; it was something she had not visualized and it was oddly difficult to do. She felt self-conscious although no one was watching, and muddled because the lane outside was suddenly unfamiliar, and anxious as though she was lost. She started to walk home then realized that her bungalow was behind her and she was heading for The Inn. Her body had sensed something wrong but was still set on the day's plan. It had carried her past her own front door and onward to the sherry.

A small spark of anger at herself for being so dizzy as to miss her bungalow and at Lydia for letting her down, made Constance brazen enough to do what she would not normally dream of doing: enter a public house alone.

It was dangerously dark inside and with the uneven floor, Constance wondered how Josef Sevier avoided being sued for the accidents that must surely occur. She concentrated and trod elegantly, smoothly to the bar in spite of her boots and the undulations.

Josef was drying glasses. His face registered surprise, but he quickly recovered.

'Hello, Constance. How are you?' he said. She was relieved that his first question was conventional. It put her on firmer ground.

'Well. Thank you.' The fire was lit and the place was cosy. Out of the corner of her eye she could see people seated in the shadows. They were familiar—Cameldip people she thought—but naturally not in her sphere. It was horribly quiet. They were clearly waiting to hear what she would order.

'A small Amontillado,' she said, and her nerves gave way. She could not turn to find a table because they would see her tears, and in any case she was next to blind in this dratted gloom with her eyes brimming. She dabbed with her handkerchief and summoned all her rusty strategies for dealing with stage fright. She breathed deeply and slowly from the diaphragm, but the tears kept coming. Josef had seen, damn him.

'Let me get you a seat,' he said. He fetched a stool and positioned it just to the right of centre of the trestle bar so she would have the warmth of the fire and the other customers at her back. He held it steady while she got on; a difficult manoeuvre, not unlike mounting a horse side-saddle, with the heel on a rung of the stool and a quick lift of the rear. With perfect timing Josef removed his hands as she sat. It was easier than she'd thought.

When he'd poured her sherry, he picked up the glass cloth again and he talked to her. He had just returned from Alsace, a routine visit to buy wine for his contacts in London and to see his father. It was cold, his father had a cough and a little arthritis, but was in good spirits.

Constance had known Xavier Sevier for years and it was soothing to listen and nod and hear about someone her own age. The boy, Josef, had his father's looks, handsome but a little rough and unnecessarily scruffy, and his mother's extraordinary navy-blue eyes. *And her charm,* thought Constance with a mixture of pique at the memory of Adelie's intimidating prettiness and solemnity for the dead.

Constance's mind faltered as if somehow it could not go on; Mrs Sevier, her waist like a girl's and her sweet French voice. Adèle Sevier, with a husband and a son.

And dear Xavier, gallant, respectful, in spite of his nationality. He loved his wife so *openly*—foreign doctors and whatnot as if Exeter General wasn't good enough, and then, at the end, she wanted to go home and that was that. Up and off. Adèle Sevier left her son, her own flesh and blood. Her son.

'I had a few days in London, just business,' Josef was saying. 'I like the place. It's a great city. Do you know London, Constance?'

The sound of her name jolted her mind unstuck and the thoughts in her head vanished. Perplexingly, she could not recall what had annoyed her so a moment ago. Constance was calm. She was warm and at ease in this surprisingly agreeable place.

'Have you spent any time in London, Constance?' Josef asked again.

She noticed a miniscule lag between her intention to speak and the sound of her voice.

'Oh, indeed yes. I had some marvellous times there as a young girl. My parents allowed me to rent a nice little flat just off Fitzroy Square with some other girls and we had such fun. Such fun. Independence but limits, you see. We learned self-discipline—an invaluable lesson. It must be learned, you see. Self-discipline is vital and I'm so grateful for it. So grateful.' The words jostled and surged like a wayward corps de ballet from the wings. 'We reaped the benefits, we did indeed: the rewards of discipline and self-control. We worked, we played and we performed. It was a golden time. Oh yes. Golden, indeed yes.'

The memories lifted Constance's eyes up to the sparkling row of optics behind Josef's head, lit like a stage in the darkness and she suddenly felt herself tipping too far backwards. She reached out with her free hand to steady herself on the trestle and refocused carefully on his face.

'I was at Covent Garden in '34,' she said. 'I was nineteen years old. The youngest to dance ... Lydia and I ...' Unexpectedly the tears welled. This time Josef could not pretend he'd not seen. But, more of a gentleman than she would have given him credit for, especially at his age, he said nothing.

'I'm so terribly sorry,' she said. 'I think I'm a little squiffy, do forgive me. My friend was coming for Christmas but it seems she's changed her mind. It's very silly of me. She wasn't on the train. I feel so very silly.'

'Not at all, Constance.' He poured her another sherry.

'Lydia and I have known each other since ballet school. We arranged the visit in November.' Constance took a large sip and smudged at her cheek with her hand. Her handkerchief was on the floor and it would be impossible to get down off the stool to fetch it. She sniffed and then to her horror she heard herself say: 'It's very hurtful. Lydia is my best friend. I don't know what I should do.'

Josef hung up the clean glasses.

'I wonder if I could offer you a coffee, and perhaps a small brandy?'
he said. Thankfully he did not humiliate her by responding to the
outburst. 'I'll have to leave you for a moment and put the kettle on.
Unless of course you'd like to come through to the kitchen?' He
helped her down from the stool and held her elbow firmly, guiding
her round the bar. In the kitchen, he sat her in a large rocking chair
(the place was full of perilous seating) and filled the kettle.

Constance gripped the arms of the chair, wishing she could grip
her eyeballs. The tears would not stop and now she was making
snorting sobs and unpleasant gurglings in her nose.

'Would you excuse me, Constance? I won't be long, I think
there's someone at the bar,' said Josef, closing the kitchen door
behind him.

Constance bawled as she had not done in years, not because of
Lydia or because she would spend another Christmas by herself, but
because after thirty-two years in Cameldip she had finally braved
The Inn alone, and because little Josef Sevier, after that dreadful
thing, had turned out to be such a nice young man.

∽∾

It was two o'clock and the pub was empty. Josef closed the door and
hung the cloth on the pumps. The grey dog got to its feet, shivered
its skin and stretched its hind legs.

Josef hoped that Constance Lamb felt better by now, although
she had still not emerged from the kitchen. He decided to give her
another half an hour.

To avoid the kitchen, he went the long way through the house
and out to the back. There was a flurry of snow and the thinnest
covering was settling on the ground.

In the old aviary, the shires came to him, dipping their heads.
Josef fetched the one set of harness, slapped off the dust and slung
it over his shoulder. The horses followed him out into the garden

single file through the door, Vreneli always first, and Martha falling in behind.

He laid out the harness, untangling and unbuckling and reminding himself what went where. Martha wandered off and Vreneli waited, standing square and still with her head helpfully lowered. This was more familiar to her than it was to Josef. It took a while.

When it was done, he led her into the lane and hauled the cart from the nettle patch beside his car. The car was out of use, not because someone had wrecked the paintwork, but because the keys were missing.

As he pulled at the cart he avoided looking at the scar on the yellow paint and the letters scratched on the boot of the Citroën. An ancient fear heaved inside him, unformed and unanchored to anything he could name. It broke the surface for an instant too brief to see clearly then sank again and disappeared. The only hatred he'd known in this place had gone cold long ago.

It took all his strength to get Vreneli between the shafts. She swivelled and sidestepped, her hooves grinding on the tarmac lane. She tried to cooperate but his obvious lack of practice confused her. He'd done this only half a dozen times in the ten years since he bought her.

When the harnessing was done, Martha took her usual place at Vreneli's side and a little behind. Martha looked suddenly naked and aimless, like someone who'd wandered up from the beach to meet a friend in working clothes.

Josef clicked his fingers and the dog jumped up on the cart. The snow was falling steadily now and he would have to go in to Constance, if only to fetch his coat. He couldn't put it off any longer.

Then he saw figures coming up the lane from the village: it was Frank and Anna with a grey-haired woman between them who was very much like Constance, although of course it couldn't be. Anna's baby looked over their heads from his carrier.

'Tally-ho!' called Frank predictably. 'We've found the chariot, now all we've got to do is find the Queen.'

'Hello,' said Anna. 'You haven't by any chance seen Constance have you? She seems to have gone missing, she's not at home or at the station where she was supposed to be.'

'It's my fault,' said the woman. 'I got off the train too soon. I don't know how I made a mistake.'

'She's here,' said Josef. 'She's been here some time. Come in. She'll be pleased; I think she assumed you weren't coming.'

They found Constance washing up at the sink. Her make-up had gone and her hair wisped untidily round her face. She looked flustered, an expression that no one—Anna, Josef, Frank or any one in Cameldip—had seen before on Constance Lamb's face.

'How do you do it, old boy?' Frank said to Josef, whacking him on the back. 'Elaine hasn't found her way to the sink in twenty years.'

'I'm so sorry, my dear.' Lydia opened her arms and waited for Constance to gather herself together. 'I got in a muddle. Gerald was always telling me—he'd say to me, "Lyddie," he'd say, "one day you'll turn into a batty old trout." And I have. Come here, Connie dear, it's so wonderful to see you.' They embraced. Constance straightened up and recovered her starchiness.

'I've been waiting since midday, Lydia. You might have let me know. How could you possibly go wrong, didn't you keep my instructions handy?'

'I did, I don't know why I got out too soon. I'd just dozed off and I thought we were there. You must have been telephoning all over the place, thinking I was dead in a ditch.'

Constance smoothed back her hair and by some subtle means she'd perfected, wordlessly let Josef and Frank know that one of them should help her on with her coat.

'What a friendly place you've found for yourself, Connie. This lovely man gave me a lift,' Lydia went on. 'He passed me on the road—I'd almost got here. I was walking you see, it was only three miles according to the signpost. And dear Anna and her baby were just passing your bungalow and came to help. So, Connie dear, we've both been looked after.'

'Looked after?' said Constance sharply, knotting her headscarf. Her face looked bleached. 'I'm here merely because I thought it sensible to stick to the arrangements.'

'Of course,' said Lydia, linking arms with her friend. 'Of course you did.'

❦

When Constance and Lydia had gone, Frank settled himself in the rocking chair, waiting for Josef to offer him a hospitable tot of something as he usually did.

'I'm sorry, I've got to go,' Josef said. 'I promised your wife I'd drop off your tree this evening and the weather's closing in.'

'What tree?' said Frank.

'Elaine asked me to pick up a tree for the music room, a ten-footer, which won't fit in your car. She sorted it out with Penquit—they've been felling. I could have used mine but it's off the road at the moment. I'm taking the milk cart.'

'Seriously?' said Frank. 'A ten-footer? For us?' He beamed. 'It must be a surprise. Well, well, what a girl she is.' He shook Josef's hand. 'I'd better get off and sort out the lights.' He kissed Anna's cheek, tweaked the bobble on the baby's hat and disappeared, whistling.

'I should go too,' said Anna. They walked out to the lane. 'Your horse looks beautiful in the harness. I didn't know you ever used them, I thought they were—well—pets.'

Josef smiled. 'They'd hate to hear you call them pets.'

'I hope it settles,' said Anna. 'The snow. We might have a white Christmas.'

'We might. It's cold enough.' Josef took hold of the reins lying over Vreneli's back. He stood with them in his hand.

'I used to ride,' said Anna. 'When I was small, with my sister. I'd like Mattie to learn when he's older but he probably won't want to. Did you ever learn to ride?'

The grey dog circled the cart, wagging in anticipation. Snow was settling on the horses. Josef put on his gloves.

'Would you like to come with me?' he said. 'It won't be comfortable, but you're welcome to.'

'Are you sure? I don't want to be in the way. It might be difficult with the baby.'

'It's fine. We'll manage.' He got up onto the cart. 'Pass him to me. Put your foot there.' He took her hand and pulled her up beside him. The seat was a wooden bench with an iron backrail and Anna held Matthew on her lap. She thought he would start to cry, but he flapped his arms and bounced with delight. They were high up, looking along the horse's back, as wide as a dinner table, mahogany brown and spotted with snow. The horse shifted and the cart lurched. Anna wished she had a hand free to hang on.

Josef spoke and Vreneli's ears flicked back to catch his voice, her head lifted and they moved off. The other horse followed behind.

'Put your feet up here, Anna. It'll balance you. You'll feel safer. We'll go slowly. Just a walk.'

They left the village behind them, turning away from the river and along another valley. They were high enough to see over the hedges and across the fields already turning white. The snow fell in huge dry flakes. There were huddles of sheep and a pony in its ragged winter coat but the countryside seemed empty, stunned into silence at the suddenness of its own transformation. There was no sound of traffic, nothing but the rhythmic thud of the hooves on the snow, one horse in front and one behind, and sometimes a bird clattering out of the hedge as they passed.

After a while Anna said: 'This is what travelling should be like.'

'It isn't usual, I'm afraid—a last resort with the car out of action.'

'Is that why you keep them? For emergencies?'

Josef looked amused. 'The horses? No. They were an accident of sorts. I bought this one, the bay, and the cart at auction—auctions are a Sevier weakness,' he said. 'She came from a holiday farm, a tourist place closing down.'

'You wanted a horse though?'

'No, not really. I suppose I bought her because no one else did. I can't remember what I was there for—chairs I think for the pub. She was in foal with the other one, Martha, but I didn't know at the time.'

They turned off the road and onto a broad track through pine trees.

'I expect Sarah loves coming out in this,' said Anna.

'Sarah?'

'Don't you go out like this sometimes just for fun?'

'No, I don't think we ever have. You're the first.' Josef looked at her. 'What made you think of Sarah?'

'Isn't she your … I saw you both, in your car when I was waiting for the bus. You drove past. I thought you two were …'

'What did you think we were?'

'Starling told me you were with someone so I thought it must be Sarah.'

'No,' said Josef. 'Starling told you that? No, I'm not with Sarah.'

They lapsed into silence again. Snow floated down. The air was empty of everything but the warm smell of the horses. Vreneli's mane flapped with the nod of her head, her back swayed from side to side and the leather harness creaked. The pines were black on either side, fading to grey through the snow ahead, then merging to white nothing. The sky was the mauve of a bruise.

Josef said, 'We're nearly there. How about a trot? Just the last few yards so the old horse can stretch her legs.' He put his arm across Anna and the baby, holding them in like the bar on the chair of a big dipper. 'I'll do this and you can't fall out. Ready?'

He flicked the reins and Vreneli's back heaved into a trot. Not the mincing, tapping trot of a normal-sized horse but a huge, striding gait, mane streaming and legs pounding like the pistons of a train. They were moving fast. Matthew clutched Anna's sleeve in astonishment, not knowing whether to scream with delight or terror. His nose and his hands were shrimp pink, his mittens had gone. The snow stung their faces. It felt like flying.

Martha passed them at a gallop with her ears flat and her neck stretched out. She looked wild. The grey dog raced after her. Vreneli threw up her head, tense with the urge to follow and Anna saw the reins tugged through Josef's hand. If the horse decided to go, she would not even notice him, or the weight of the cart.

'Can we stop?' yelled Anna but the snow in her mouth smothered the words.

Josef had heard her, or guessed what she said. He pulled Vreneli back to walking pace and Martha slowed down to a rocking-horse canter. She turned and ambled back to them, looking herself again.

The snow was falling heavily now, settling on their clothes and covering the tracks they'd made.

They stopped at a clearing of felled trees. Josef jumped down and walked round the heaps of pines, choosing two and hauling them to the cart. He tied them with rope and whistled to the dog who'd disappeared into the forest. They turned for home.

It was getting dark by the time they left the plantation and were out on the road. The snow stopped and as the light faded the cold hardened to a mean, penetrating chill. Anna's boots and her long skirt were soaked and her legs were numb. Her head ached with cold. The pink in the baby's cheeks had gone and there was a faint bluish line round his lips.

'He's not warm enough,' said Josef. 'Here, wrap him in this.' He took off his scarf.

'It's all right. He'll be fine.'

'Take it,' said Josef. 'He doesn't look fine.'

'He's hungry,' said Anna, 'that's all. I should have thought, he ought to have been fed an hour ago.' She tucked the baby's hands in her coat and pulled down the flaps of his hat over his ears.

'This took longer than I thought,' said Josef. 'I'm sorry, it's my fault, I shouldn't have asked you to come with me.'

'It's no one's fault,' said Anna.

Josef stared into the winter half-light. The snow was lying deep enough to obliterate the verges and ditches. There'd been no traffic and the road ahead was smooth and glittering like sugar.

Every moment it grew colder. The clouds cleared and the sky was a dome of stars above them. Anna wondered how they would see when the light failed, but the moon rose brighter than the dusk.

The night was smooth, deep blues. Sometimes the clouds were laced with silver, then the moon would appear, lighting up the fields the palest lilac. The horse's mane lifted and fell like a slow wave.

'How long?' Anna asked. The baby's eyes were half closed and she shifted him on her lap to rouse him. It was too cold to sleep.

'Half an hour, maybe less.'

The snow was deeper as they neared Cameldip. Where the trees did not shelter the lane there were deep drifts, and for the first time the horse used her strength to pull them. She moved slower and started to slip on the ice compacted in her hooves. She grew hesitant, wary of treading where she could not see, lowering her head and blowing on the snow, trying to sense what was hidden. She stopped, took another pace, and stopped again.

The silence was complete. There was no help nearby, or likely to come. No cars had passed since they set out. Anna wrapped Matthew inside her coat.

'We'll have to walk,' she said.

'Stay there.' Josef lowered himself down into the snow. It creaked as he waded with his arms out like someone in water. When he was ahead of Vreneli she started again and step by step they moved forward. The horse slithered and struggled, her huge head lunging and dipping. Josef did not hold her bridle or speak to her, but pushed on ahead knowing she would follow.

Anna leaned down over the baby, making a tent of her coat and Josef's scarf, her wet hair falling forward. She closed her eyes and thought of nothing but the odd warmth that crept through her if she did not shiver. She listened to the horse's breath, the huge bellows of the lungs sucking and blowing, in with icy air, out with horse heat. Anna breathed, out and in, long and slow. Warmth flowed out and was lost in the night, ice cold slid down inside her. The night was softly drowning her, emptying her out and filling her with itself. Mattie's breath on her cheek was quick and warm. He did not know how to welcome in the cold.

'Anna?' The movement had stopped and Josef's hand was on her arm. 'Anna. We're home.'

In the kitchen the fire had gone out and the air was as cold as the lane outside.

'There's hot water,' Josef said. He turned her round and led her up the stairs. In the bathroom she sat on the edge of the bath with the baby still inside her coat.

'We must get him warm. And you're soaked too.' Josef pulled off her boots and unwound the scarf.

'He needs to be fed,' said Anna.

'I know, I know. This first.' He stood up with her boots in his hand. 'Should I try telephoning someone, a doctor? What about the hospital?'

'There's no need, and in any case no one could get here,' said Anna. 'He'll be fine. He will.' She would have smiled but her face was numb.

'If you're sure.' Josef stood for a moment. He touched her with his fingertips, her cheek and her chin, then he turned and closed the door behind him. She heard him going downstairs and outside again.

The bathroom filled with steam. There was a gulp from the tank and the pipes shuddered when she turned off the taps, then silence. In the warmth, her hands and feet and face throbbed, and the baby turned rosy again though he barely woke.

Anna closed her eyes and listened for Josef. There was only the sound of the tap dripping into the bath water, each drip followed by the smallest echo. She could feel her hair floating out around her and her baby almost floating on her stomach. If she'd not been holding him, she could have drifted into sleep in the water—and she thought of Isabel and that she must tell her they were safe. She should get out of the bath and telephone, but the thought slipped away.

It was hard to rouse herself. She wrapped the baby in a towel and put on Josef's dressing gown hanging on the door. She wrung out her wet hair.

Downstairs in the kitchen the fire was alight and Josef was sitting at the table with a glass in his hand.

'It's snowing again,' he said. 'I think you should stay.'

'Should I?'

'You can't take him out in the cold again.'

She said, 'I should call Isabel. I must let her know I'm here.'

The telephone rang for a long time before Anna heard Robert's voice sounding far away and indistinct. 'Isabel's not here. I'll tell her you're safe.'

'Is she looking for us? I'm so sorry, it took so long to get home, we got stuck coming back from Penquit. Where has she gone? I said I was going to the shop, did she go there?'

'No. She's …' The line crackled.

'I can't hear you, Robert.'

'She's with me. She's at my place.'

'With you? What happened?'

'Nothing, Anna. She came to me when you didn't come home, that's all. We're having supper. I heard the phone and came up to the house.'

'I should speak to her,' said Anna. The line buzzed. 'Will you tell her we're at Josef Sevier's and we'll get back in the morning?'

The line went dead.

'Isabel was looking for me,' Anna said.

Josef handed her a glass. 'Brandy,' he said. 'It seems to be my day for plying women with brandy.'

'Constance?'

'Yes. Drink up.' He tapped her glass with his. 'Against best medical advice, but if it's good enough for the Swiss rescue, it's good enough for us. *Santé*.'

Anna went to the fire and stood with her back to it, sipping the brandy. Josef's eyes followed her.

'Are you warm now?' he asked. 'You look as though you've been swimming.'

'I am warm. Thank you. And I'm sorry I—we—worried you. I cornered you into inviting us, I think. It wasn't fair of me.'

'We're here now.'

'For a while I thought we wouldn't get back.'

'Not as romantic an outing as you'd thought?' he said. They smiled at each other with open relief.

Anna let her eyes wander over the room. The cupboards and dresser, the rows of blue plates, the cups on their hooks, all had an air of peaceful neglect, as if they were untroubled by dust and damage. The years of use—stains under the glaze on the plates, chips on the cups, the dents in the wood, had not worn them out but given them permanence. They were as much a part of the house as the roof and walls.

'*C. M.*' Anna read the curling letters carved on the back of the small rocking chair.

She tipped the chair with her fingers and it began to rock.

'*C. M.*—not you. Someone in the family? Someone who didn't want to be forgotten.'

'Her father gave it to me,' said Josef.

'A boy gave me his scout cap once,' Anna said. 'I was nine. I had to look after it even when we went off each other because he wouldn't let me return it and it was too important to throw away. It was only a scout cap but it was a token of love. I think I've still got it somewhere. You must still be friends to have her chair in your kitchen and she must have been very small when it was made for her. Was she in love with you? I expect she was.' Anna stopped, suddenly conscious that she was talking too much.

'Robert made it for her fourth birthday,' said Josef.

Anna looked at him uncomprehending. The rocking chair rocked silently, still moving as smoothly and evenly as when she'd touched it with her hand.

'Robert?' she said.

Josef got up from the table and went to the stove.

'It was Catherine's chair,' said Anna. 'So she was Catherine.'

'Let's eat,' Josef said. 'And I think we could do with a bottle of wine.'

'I'm starving.' Anna sat down at the table. 'So you knew her, both of them? I hadn't thought, but you must have been about the same age. What were the children like, do you remember? Perhaps it's too long ago.'

'No, it's not too long ago.'

'I didn't realize you grew up here. And you've known Robert and Isabel since you were small. They must have been different before.'

'I've brought in the cushions from the sofa so you can put the baby down while we eat. Unless you want to wake him up to feed him.'

'I'll let him sleep. I'll feed him when he wakes.'

'The soup's hot. Have your soup.'

'They've never got over it, have they. Especially Isabel. I wish I could help, but I expect everyone wishes that.'

'We used to wish that.'

'Robert says it's good to have a child in the house again. He says it's helping Isabel.'

'I should be careful of Isabel,' said Josef. He stood up to fetch glasses from the dresser and he opened a bottle of wine.

'What do you mean?'

'I brought a couple of cases of this last week. Tell me what you think.'

'Isabel does this,' said Anna. 'She acts as though she can't hear me. Don't you do it to me too.'

'I won't.' Josef put down the wine bottle. Anna started at the noise it made on the table. He sat down. 'If you want to know, I'll tell you.' He tore some bread. 'Well? What is it you want to know?'

'It doesn't matter.'

'Ask, Anna.'

'Could you tell me what happened? How did they die? Isabel isn't just sad, she's angry with Robert. I think she hates him. I shouldn't ask. Perhaps you don't know.'

'I can tell you—none of it matters now.'

Anna wished she'd not spoken. The relief they'd shared at being home had gone. 'You needn't tell me if it's difficult, but I feel as though I've been living with it but not knowing since Matthew was born.'

Josef leaned back in his chair and pushed the plate away. He lit a cigarette.

He said, 'I'll tell you. I want to tell you. Isabel makes us all live with it.'

◦∞◦

From time to time Josef put more wood on the fire as he talked. The baby woke and Anna fed him some soup, then he slept again. Once Josef put on his boots and coat to go out to the horses. The grey dog was let out and in, and when the door was opened the step of snow against it was deeper each time. The thick silence outside came in with the cold air.

It was after midnight when he stood up and took their plates to the sink.

After a while Anna said, 'They drowned. They drowned in the river. How terrible, for all of you.'

'I don't remember it clearly, I've told you what I think happened. My father said Isabel was out of her mind. She thought we were all to blame. And as for now, well, things became fixed.'

'How could she blame you when you were only a child—and the doctor and your mother and father, and Robert, and even Sarah?'

'She doesn't blame Sarah, she loathes her.'

'Isabel was kind to me—in the beginning especially,' said Anna. 'It's hard to believe she's so bad.'

'She's not bad.'

'So you forgive her?'

'It makes no difference now.'

'I don't know what to do. What should I do?'

'There's nothing to do. I've told you because I'm tired of Isabel pulling our strings. And yours too, now. She laid down the truth and perhaps at first she had a right to, but she couldn't stop. She made weapons of her own children. Perhaps we were responsible, all of us.'

'You were seven. How could anyone blame you?'

Josef drank the last drop from his glass. 'I wanted you to know because she'll keep you where she wants you. Whatever you say, somehow she'll do it.'

'And that's why I should be careful?'

'I meant you should take care of your baby.'

'But it wasn't Isabel's fault. I know she was a good mother, better than I am. She's so careful and gentle with Mattie, she never upsets him.'

'Isabel would never let you see her feelings.'

'Sometimes she wishes Matthew was hers, I know that, but she'd never hurt him, she couldn't. She loves him.'

Josef said, 'I think we should go to bed.' He stacked more logs on the fire. 'You need to be warm tonight too,' he said to the dog, which thumped its tail.

'And Sarah. Why didn't she go away?'

'Edward persuaded her to leave for a while. But she came back. She would have been a doctor but when Edward was dying she came back. And she stayed.'

'Why do you stay? You don't have a wife or anyone to stay for. I don't understand why you don't leave. She won't stop me leaving.' Impulsively, Anna took his hand. 'Let's not talk about it any more. Let's forget it.'

He pulled his hand away, not unkindly but instinctively, as though the feel of her was uncomfortable.

'You must be tired,' he said. He stood by the door and Anna followed him upstairs to a room at the back of the house. There was a high bed, a sofa and linen curtains with only the ghost of a pattern. The chest of drawers had a freckled mirror and china handles. There was the smell of damp and a faint animal staleness as though the things in the room still remembered their beginnings in a forest or field or on the back of a sheep. Without the interference of polish and perfume and daily human authority, the soft subtle scent had crept out in the quietness.

'Does he sleep with you or should we make a bed for him?' Josef asked.

Anna hesitated. 'He sleeps with me,' she said. 'Josef, if this is your room ...' But he had disappeared along the passageway.

'I'll get more blankets.'

Anna got into bed, and it was comforting to have the baby sleeping beside her again as he used to in the tree house.

Josef came back with an armful of blankets. He stood over her, shaking out each one, letting it fall, tucking it in at the foot and turning it over at the top. Anna watched his face above her and a disconcerting memory came into her mind of her mother performing the same ritual.

Anna would lie in her bed, combed and tidy in pyjamas with her doll tucked in the crook of her arm. She would concentrate on her part in the display of maternal care and wait for the kiss that would be the flourish, the seal of authenticity at the end. As her mother leaned over, her eyes avoided Anna's, fending off the moment of intimacy, then she would straighten up, hands on hips, assessing the neatness of her work.

Rose was tucked in too. Their mother repeated the smoothing and patting with a lisp of her nylon slip as she stretched. It was a secret sound you heard only when you were quiet and good inside the invisible tent of her smell—heavenly perfume that must be like angels. At last the kiss like a pebble would tap on Anna's forehead as the lamp was switched off.

Josef leaned over her, turning and tucking the blankets with absent-minded gentleness as if practical care was in his nature in a way that was never in her mother's. Anna searched his face for some chink in the glaze of neutrality but there was none. Earlier, she'd sat on the side of the bath and he had touched her. He had smiled straight into her eyes when he tapped his brandy glass on hers.

He straightened up and turned away to the window. He leaned his arm on the lintel and looked out into the blackness.

The snow had stopped. The garden and the trees by the river were ghostly and the light from the window made a golden lozenge on the ground. Close by was the roof of the aviary, the only blemished patch of white—where the tarpaulin sagged with the weight of the snow there was a ragged smudge of darkness that could have been the shape of a cat. Josef watched but it did not move and the shadow dissolved into nothing.

He closed the curtains.

'I hope you sleep,' he said. She heard him go into the room at the end of the passage and close the door.

⟡

Isabel hammered on the door of the blackhouse. She went on hammering until Robert opened it.

'Is she here?' she said tersely.

'No.'

Isabel looked past him into the room.

'Anna's not here, Isabel. I haven't seen her today.'

'I telephoned Elaine, and Frank said he left her with Josef Sevier just after two.'

'Then that's where she is.'

'But it's six o'clock. The baby needs feeding. She's irresponsible and I'm going to fetch her.'

She turned on her heel and started towards the lane. She had no coat. The snow had already soaked her trousers to the knees. Robert caught up with her in a few paces and held her arm.

'Don't, Isabel. She'll telephone if there's any difficulty. We know where she is.'

Isabel looked at his hand on her arm.

'Let go of me, Robert. This discussion has ended.'

'I'd rather you didn't go.'

'You know as well as I do she should be home. That baby needs his supper and his bed, and I'm not prepared to stand back and let him bear the brunt of her selfishness.'

'The baby's with his mother,' said Robert. 'And his mother is with her friend. There's no need to go looking for her.'

'She must be told. She has no concept of time and she must be told.' Isabel pulled against his grip but he didn't loosen it. She looked furious.

'I know. I know,' he said. 'He's the worst person she could be with—after me that is.'

Isabel looked astonished.

'Let's not pretend,' said Robert. Isabel opened her mouth but the words wouldn't come. He was ignoring the rules and something began to slide away from under her. She shivered.

'Come back inside. It's too cold to be out here.'

'I simply think she should have let me know. She should. It's extremely thoughtless,' said Isabel peevishly. She stopped straining against his hand. Her body shook and her teeth clacked together. She clamped her jaw tight.

'I'm just about to have something to eat. Why don't you join me?' said Robert.

'How formal.' She looked at him stonily. 'What do you eat these days—sea bird, I suppose.'

'Wait and see.'

Isabel was still rooted to the spot and Robert let go of her arm. He put his hand on her shoulder, noticing the thinness of the flesh on the bones. She looked past him and sighed as if she was suddenly too tired to argue.

The sky was black. Beneath their feet the snow gave off a phosphorescent glow, shadowless and sparkling. It was a world tipped upside-down, with the earth lit up and a solid sky.

Robert turned back and Isabel followed him. He pushed open the door. It was the first time she had come into his house.

∽◌◌∾

Isabel woke, wondering where she was. The bed was too hard to be her own. There was a smell of woodsmoke and earth, and total silence; no ticking of electricity or the creaks of joists and floorboards.

She remembered she had accepted Robert's invitation to stay as if the journey home was long and dangerous and not just to the other side of a slope of snow. She accepted because she did not know any more how to be in her house alone.

Robert had held out a pair of pyjamas to her and Isabel had taken them, still talking about the fundraising for St Angela's new classroom as if they were at a village buffet. He made a bed for himself on the floor by the fire.

She'd thought she would not sleep because of the jumble of thoughts plucking at her mind, but the next thing she knew was the voice waking her.

The moonlight came in at the one small window high up under the roof, and her eyes made out the wooden frame and curtains round the bed like the bunk of a ship. Her clothes were folded on a chair. She was stiff and it was difficult to bend down and sort through them, and to dress without sitting on the edge of the bed, which might creak and wake Robert.

She did not mind the ache in her body—it matched the sluggishness in her head. She thought of last night and the tide of her own talk, dull and unstoppable. Robert had listened and for once his patience did not irritate her. She saw papery creases in his skin and hollows in his cheeks she'd never noticed before.

They had heard the telephone ringing faintly in the house.

'I'll go,' Robert said. 'That'll be Anna.' He was out of the door and had closed it behind him before Isabel could answer. When she thought of Anna her mind tangled and she lost her way.

'She's with Starling,' he said when he came back. 'She'll be home in the morning.' They had said no more about Anna.

Isabel dressed in the dark and her mind moved placidly, thick with sleep (when had Robert's eyes become filmy and his stubble turned from black to silver?), but alongside the meandering thoughts, a shrill, chattering voice spewed out from a fissure in her brain. The voice had woken her and urged her out of the warm bed; it was Jack's birthday. It was her son's birthday tomorrow and she would be neglectful, she would be careless if she did not bring him home. Isabel listened to the voice and tried hard to remember which birthday this was—was it seven, or eight? But he was still so small, no more than a baby. It puzzled her.

✢

The night was like a snow scene inside a plastic dome. Tiny flakes floated on the air, almost too light to settle.

Isabel walked out into the lane towards the village. When she came to the memorial she sat down on the cushion of snow on the bench. Opposite was the shop with blank, black windows above it. One was the room with Anna and the child inside. All she needed to do was to wait until morning and they would appear.

It was odd and rather pleasant to be sitting outside on a moonlit night with Cameldip sleeping around her. The only sign of life was a faint glow in one of the windows of Constance Lamb's bungalow.

Isabel settled back. She was not cold. The voice in her head had ceased and she felt a twinge of embarrassment at herself. It was quite ridiculous to be sitting here in the snow, and the sensible thing would be to go home. She wondered what time it was.

Then she saw that someone had come along the lane, had almost reached her and she'd not noticed. The person was tall and slender. Her shoulder-length hair fell forward round her face. She had the collar of her denim jacket turned up, her chin tucked down and her arms were folded tight across her chest. A line of bare skin showed at the waist of her jeans. The girl kept her eyes fixed on the ground but she glanced up and started when she saw Isabel. She did not pause, only slightly altered her direction to steer away from the bench.

It was the woman's daughter.

'Your mother should be ashamed, letting you wander about at this hour of the night.' Isabel's voice rang out in the silence. The girl's eyes flickered up with a mixture of furtiveness and irritation. She tucked her chin lower. 'Do you hear me, Gabriella? Does your mother know you're out at this hour?'

'What?' said Gatta.

'I should have known she would have no idea of control.' Isabel got to her feet. The girl stared, unmoved. 'All you children run wild, but it doesn't surprise me.'

Isabel had never been near to the girl before, and unexpectedly Gabriella's face stirred something in her. The anger curdled like old milk, separating into thin, bitter spite and an almost forgotten feeling that caught in the throat with piercing sweetness. The delicate chin and upturned nose made Isabel's heart leap and she wanted to take the girl in her arms and kiss her hair.

'You don't know anything. Fuck off and leave me alone, you old hag,' said Gatta. She started walking again. 'And if you're looking for Anna, she's up the lane with him,' she said over her shoulder.

∽∾∾

Lydia was finding it difficult to sleep. She missed Gerald at night more than any other time. For years his snoring had kept her awake. She would prod him harder than was kind and loudly insult him, using the foulest words she knew.

'You buggering old skunk,' she would say to his silhouette. Gerald would heave and groan like a dugong, smack his lips contentedly and dive down into his underwater world again. At night she hated him with a molten fury she came to treasure. Every annoyance, every irritation, every smallest disappointment was aired. Every last scrap of marital debris was hauled up and flung out at the comatose Gerald—so, by day, there was nothing left to pollute the peaceful lake of Lydia's love. He was her friend and her companion and the most handsome man she had ever seen after Errol Flynn.

And now there was no Gerald to keep her awake, she could not sleep. The sweltering heat did not help. Connie had turned up the central heating to a temperature that was clearly unusual. A smell of scorched dust filled the bungalow, the pipes pinged and the furniture tapped restlessly.

Lydia peered at her bedroom radiator and longed to hear Gerald's voice booming from the other side: 'Don't worry with that, Lyddie. I'll adjust the thermostat.' Thermostat was a word that had masculine magic and now made her sad.

She leaned on the windowsill and closed the curtains like a tent behind her. It was delightful in the little cubicle of freezing air and Lydia pressed her forehead against the glass.

Connie's small front garden had turned into a fairy grotto. Mounds of heather peeped out from under thick white hats and the miniature conifers dipped their branches prettily. In the centre, a stone obelisk-cum-birdbath-cum-sundial rose up like a tiny alpine castle. The scene was all silver lights and iron shadows in the moonlight.

Then Lydia's eye was caught by a movement. People were standing just beyond Connie's hedge. Two figures faced each other. One gesticulated wildly and the second turned suddenly and walked off towards the lane where nice Frank lived with his family. A woman with long, silver hair stood staring after the other, with arms held out and fists clenched in a strange gesture of supplication and threat.

Lydia held her breath with a sudden impulse to hide. It came into her head that the woman was not a woman at all but a lonely Ice Queen conjured up by the magical, snowy night. If she turned now and caught Lydia spying, something terrible would happen, some horrible spell would be cast. And when people looked in the morning there would be no footprints—nothing that mortals could see.

But when the woman put her hands to her face in a way that could only have been human, the illusion vanished and Lydia knew that she should go out to the poor creature and see what was wrong.

She put on her dressing gown and went to the front door, slipping into Connie's boots which were propped on their toes on a sheet of newspaper.

'I say,' called Lydia. 'It's terribly cold to be out here.'

Isabel looked as if she, in her turn, doubted that Lydia was real in her capacious dressing gown (Gerald's) of a deafening tartan (even in moonlight), below which poked the frill of a nightdress and stout ankle boots. 'It's gone two, did you know?' said Lydia. 'I was just wondering if I could help at all.'

Isabel wanted to speak but found that the words fluttered like bats in her head. They dived and swooped, refusing to keep in formation. The eyes that gazed into hers were calm and kindly and filled with sorrow, and Isabel thought how much she would like to be with this woman for a while.

'I'm Lydia Arbamount,' said Lydia, holding out her hand.

'MacKinnon,' said Isabel grabbing a word in flight and finding it was the right one.

'Mrs?' asked Lydia. Isabel looked puzzled. 'Well, it doesn't matter. Doesn't matter at all,' Lydia went on. 'Let's go in and get warm.'

Constance met them at the porch. She gasped.

'Good gracious. Isabel! Lydia, this is Isabel MacKinnon. I said this is *Isabel MacKinnon*.'

'We couldn't sleep, Connie, that's all. Isabel—Isabel, is that right dear?—Isabel, was out walking so I invited her in. Perhaps when we've warmed up, I thought we might telephone her husband if she has one, to fetch her so she doesn't have to walk home by herself. Or I'm sure that nice Frank wouldn't mind.'

Constance's long, cold-creamed face swung from Lydia to Isabel. She composed her features into an expression, she hoped, of hospitable gaiety.

'What a pleasant surprise,' she said. She noticed that Isabel's shirt was buttoned askew and the belt on the trousers dangled. She failed to control her eyebrows when she saw Isabel's bare feet. Surely not. Had poor Isabel MacKinnon starting roaming again, after all these years?

'Earl Grey or China? Do you mind Lydia? The kettle?' She jutted her chin towards the kitchenette.

'Cocoa I think,' said Lydia.

'Do come into the lounge, won't you?' said Constance. 'I'll just flick on the gas. *Voilà!* We have heat.'

'It's quite cosy enough I think, Connie dear. I'd save the gas,' said Lydia.

Isabel sat on the edge of the wing chair with her eyes fixed on the doorway where Lydia was preparing cocoa.

'Are you and your husband in a nice snug bungalow, Isabel?' Lydia said. There was the sound of whisking, then a clatter. 'As we get older, it's so important to be compact, I think. And well insulated.' She brought in a mug of cocoa and put it in Isabel's hands.

'My house is large,' said Isabel clearly. She paused. 'I have four bedrooms and one in a tree house. And my husband, Robert, lives in the garden.'

'I see,' said Lydia brightly. 'What an unusual household. Well, I often wished Gerald at the other end of the garden—or further. Does he snore, your Robert? What is it Connie?' Constance was making dry coughs and arching her eyebrows.

'I'm glad you've popped in, Isabel,' said Constance. 'I've been wanting to speak to you about the horticultural show.'

'The what?' said Lydia.

'Surely you know what horticulture is, Lydia.'

Isabel looked from one to the other—two elderly ladies with thin grey plaits and large horsy faces, one imperious and one baffled, one in lilac candlewick and one in riotous tartan—and she giggled. Laughter gripped her stomach and clutched at her throat, and she was helpless.

Lydia put an arm round her shoulders and gave her a tissue for the tears that were streaming. Constance got up and went to the telephone.

Christmas Eve

The snow continued through the night, small, dry flakes like scraps of down, falling through black air, falling thousands of feet from cloud to earth in countless, unhurried millions. As each speck of frozen cloud came to rest, it added its infinitesimal weight and thickness to whatever it touched—a twig or telephone wire, a gatepost or the rim of a cattle trough.

The ground swelled up like dough. What stood above it was reduced to simple blocks of light and dark. Houses, cars and outbuildings were topped with tilting slabs of white. Roads and paths disappeared, ditches closed, and the intricate wounds of human habitation healed over flake by flake.

By the time Josef left Anna and the child in his bed and made a last visit to the horses, the tracks left by the cart on the lane from Penquit to Cameldip had disappeared.

Josef was reluctant to go to bed. He had a dislike of the small bedroom, from something that had happened so long ago, he'd forgotten what it was, and Anna's presence in the house was hard to ignore. He wondered if he wanted her. How could he not know? But the feeling was not desire, it was something else about her that touched him and made him restless—more longing than lust, something harder to satisfy.

She irritated him. Neither her face nor her body had characteristics he loved easily—she was large-breasted and heavy, her hair was neither brown nor blond and her skin was pale. She smiled too easily, talked too much and looked at him with childish coyness.

But since the summer, when he'd found her by the river, he'd thought of her constantly. He felt compelled to take care of her as if somehow, with her muddled naive trustfulness, she had dug into a place inside him he'd learned to ignore.

She was not a woman he wanted always in his mind, and he had fought against her intrusion into his thoughts.

He already had a lover, a Frenchwoman he stayed with several times a year. She lived in Paris; she was beautiful, slim and dark. She wore white silk underwear, linen suits and blond calf-leather shoes. They had intense, intoxicating sex, their desire for each other always at first insatiable, but then in a few days dissolving to nothing. He had never asked her to come to England and she showed no curiosity to visit.

Once she had said, 'If you must live in England, why do you not at least live somewhere civilized? Why not in London?' And he answered truthfully and unexpectedly that he could not leave the people he loved. She looked at him, an open, bleak, questioning look from which he turned away.

'A woman?' she persisted. He answered no, again truthfully: Catherine would never be a woman. He had been unable to deny to himself that he'd meant Sarah and Robert too, and their child, the daughter who was as sly and spiteful as Catherine had been good. But the same features had been given to both and he could not help but see Catherine in the arrogant, pretty girl who either ignored him or looked at him with an incomprehensible hatred that froze his heart.

Anna was not part of that, nor was she part of his pointless, loveless present. Perhaps that was why he longed to be in his own bed, with her sleeping next to him, quiet and untroubled by the past that circled him like a wolf.

Inside the aviary it was pitch-black but he did not light the lamp hanging by the door; there were no matches and he had forgotten that his old silver lighter was gone. He found his way to the horses by the warmth of their breath, reaching out his hands and finding their faces stretched towards him. He felt over them like a blind man—they were dry now and warm, as he'd hoped.

He went back to the house. There was no light in Anna's room. He stood in the kitchen, undecided, waiting for the pulse of feeling that would propel him one way or another. He went into the sitting room and lay down to sleep on the sofa, still in his coat, and pulled the blanket over him.

◦∞◦

He woke because of the cold and lay listening to the silence. He wondered if he could sleep again or if he must get up and go to bed. From habit, he tuned in to the soft thud of the generator, separating it out from the silence. The sound was uneven—it would probably not make it through the night. He heard the dog on the floor beside him let out a yip and a whimper in its sleep. Its paws scratched on the rug. The stairs creaked one after another from top to bottom, quick, light steps he often heard when he woke in the night.

Then there was an unfamiliar sound, a heavy tread which must be Anna coming down to the kitchen. He'd left the light on in the passageway and he saw her shadow on the carpet, the latch on the kitchen door rattled, a light switch clicked and footsteps padded across the flagstones.

Then there was silence. He waited for the sound of the tap going on and water splashing. He lay still, straining his ears to hear. She must be looking for a cup.

Perhaps a minute passed. The light in the passageway flicked off then on—the generator faltering—then off again for longer this time. It flashed on for a second, then there was utter darkness. The tone of the generator dipped and stopped.

'Anna,' he called. 'It'll come back on in a moment.'

'I can't see anything.' Her voice wavered.

'It's OK. Stay where you are. I'll light same candles.' As he felt his way across the room, he heard her crying softly, sobbing under her breath, and he was surprised then bewildered by her fear. 'I'm coming to you. I'm nearly there. One, two, three steps, here I come,' he said as if she were a child. He felt the kitchen door, pushed it open and stretched out his hands to find her. Suddenly everything was drenched in hard bright light.

Anna stood by the table. Her face was white with a dab of hot pink on each cheek like a doll. She stared at him. There were deep shadows under her eyes and the dressing gown sagged off one bare shoulder.

'There's someone here,' she said.

'It's only the house. There's only us. Don't be frightened.' He folded her into himself, wrapping the dressing gown round her, smoothing her hair.

'I saw someone.'

His mind stopped. He hugged her against him. 'You were dreaming,' he said and the words sounded like a script playing from his mouth. 'You imagined it. You were dreaming.'

'She was at my bedroom door and I followed her down the stairs. She was sitting in the rocking chair. It's Catherine.'

'Let me put you to bed. Look at you, you've nothing on your feet.'

'I've seen her by the river, and Jack, and I've seen her here—before by the fire and now. Three times. I've seen her three times.'

'Tell me in bed.' He half pulled, half carried her up to the room.

'I'm seeing things. I'm going crazy. She wears a little dress like it's summer. Don't leave me. I don't want you to. Why do I see her?'

'I don't know.'

In the bedroom he picked up the pillows scattered on the floor and lifted the covers for her to climb in. He watched her curl herself round the baby just as he had seen her by the river, then he took off his coat and lay down beside her. He turned his body close to hers, his face in her hair and she reached for his hand.

Outside, the wind was rising. It rattled the window. A door shut downstairs. As it blew round the house the wind made a gentle note, rising and falling like someone singing. Josef stared into the darkness. He would not sleep now.

He whispered: 'What is she like? Did you see her face? Anna?' Her breathing slowed. Her grip on his hand loosened and she sighed. In sleep, she was as still and peaceful as he had known she would be.

⌘

'Coming out? I've got something interesting to tell you,' said Gatta. She looked flushed with the cold—pink cheeks, white skin, and her grey-green eyes sparkled with the brightness of the snowy sunlit morning. Unusually she was wearing a warm coat that Starling knew was Sarah's: black velvet almost to the ground with a fur collar and cuffs.

'You look like a prat in that coat,' said Starling. 'Wow! Look at it. We're going to be cut off for Christmas, or even longer.'

'Coming up Tye Hill? Please, Gatta. You can have a go on my sledge.' Spike had broken away from a gang of boys carrying old milk crates and plastic bags and had struggled through the snow to his sister. He took hold of her hand and pulled her. 'It'll be better if you come. Oh please, Gatta.'

'I might later,' she said. 'Find the best place and I'll come later.'

He wobbled off again back along his own tracks: 'Oy, wait for me. Pete! You can't have a go. I mean it. Pete!'

'We're going visiting,' said Gatta to Starling who was pulling on her boots. 'And on the way I'll tell you something you just won't believe. It's brilliant. Everyone's going nuts. Fucking snow madness.'

'Want some gloves?' said Starling. 'Where's my smokes? I'm gasping.'

They staggered out into the brilliant Christmas Eve morning. They threw snowballs and flopped headlong into drifts. They shrieked and screamed across the glittering whiteness, both of them forgetting about whatever it was Gatta had to tell.

Later, they were lying on a snowdrift and Gatta said, 'Anyway, get this. I saw old MacKinnon last night—in the middle of the night, with her hair all sticking out and no shoes, lurking around your house.'

'My house?' said Starling. 'What were you doing out?' she asked reasonably.

'Tell you that later. So I didn't say anything, though she had a go at me, winding me up as usual, but I got away from her and hung around to see what she'd do.'

'What time?'

'Oh, I don't know. Late. I said it was late.'

'What were you doing ...'

'For fuck's sake. Do you want to hear this or not? So the next thing, some old biddy comes out of Miss Lamb's house, trots over to MacKinnon, ushers her in and all's quiet for twenty minutes or so. Then Robert turns up, poor sod, goes in and it's all quiet again. Then the whole lot of them come out: Robert, Miss Lamb, the other old girl and MacKinnon clinging on to her; Robert standing there like he always does, like he's on another planet, and Miss Lamb flapping her hands and gibbering. Then MacKinnon lays into him and she's screaming, "You knew, you knew she was there! You lied to me!" Blah, blah, blah on she goes, on and on. Then she thumps him round the face so hard I hear the whack from where I am. The old girl manages to stop her doing it again. Robert just stands there, calm as Jesus Christ, turns round and walks off and the three of them go in again.'

'Poor Mr MacKinnon. He's so nice.'

'Then guess who comes along next: Steffie's pa. Old Frank puffs up to the front door, in he goes and it's all quiet again. I tell you, Star, it was crazy last night. In the end they all came out, Frank and MacKinnon and the old girl—not Miss Lamb, the other one—and went off, arm in arm, to Steffie's place, right past me. And that's it. Show's over.'

'Wow.'

'They're nuts, the lot of them.'

'Oh, wow. Poor Mrs MacKinnon.'

'She's mad.'

'She's never grieved properly, my mum says. She says Mrs MacKinnon's got grief that's never been done properly,' said Starling. 'About her children.'

'What's that supposed to mean?'

'She should be sad but she can't be, so she's angry—I think. Or is it the other way round—she should be angry but she can't be?'

'But she is—she always is.'

'I dunno.'

They lay on their backs in the snow and looked up at the cloudless blue. Then Gatta said, 'I told her that Anna was with Josef Sevier.'

Starling sat up. 'Why?'

Gatta looked at the sky.

'Why?' said Starling.

'If you must know, because she was.'

'How do you know?'

'I'm sorry, Star. I saw them. I climbed up on the old bird-house stable thing and looked in. She was in bed and he was standing at the window, then he pulled the curtains.'

Starling was quiet. She lay down again on the snow and turned her face away.

'That's men for you.' Gatta leaned up on an elbow to watch Starling. 'Take what they want and that's it. You've lost him I'm afraid, Star.' She could see Starling's cheek. She saw the eyelashes blink wetly. Starling sniffed.

'Let's go. It's best to face it. Get over it and move on. Come on.'

'I hate her,' said Starling. 'I hate him.'

'That's it. *That's* how to take it. Fuck them both, let them get on with it, the fuckers aren't worth it.' Gatta hauled her up and brushed the powder snow off Starling's back and her hair. 'We're going to get ourselves a job. We're going to be barmaids. It'll be a laugh.'

Starling's face had lost its flush of pink. She looked pinched with cold and miserable. 'I think I'll go home.'

'Oh, no you don't. You can't chicken out, you've got to face him—and her.' Gatta hauled on her sleeve, then hooked her arm through Starling's.

They trudged along the lane. It looked broad and unfamiliar without its verges and ditches, blinding white in the sun. Even keeping their eyes low, the glare made them ache. The sunlight bounced up from the snow, up under their eyelids so that closing them completely and walking in blood-red blindness was the only way to get relief.

Gatta held Starling's arm all the way to Josef's kitchen door. She banged hard then pushed Starling forward. They could see inside, the glow of the fire and his shape at the table.

'Hello, girls.' To their surprise he was holding Anna's baby.

'We've come to ask about bar work,' said Gatta. 'You said there might be something at Christmas or New Year maybe.'

'Oh. Yes, of course. I did.'

'And she's come to see Anna.'

'Hello, Starling.' Anna appeared at Josef's side, in a dressing gown. She looked sleepy. 'How did you know I was here? And your friend too. Hello, Gabriella.'

'Sorry if we got you up,' said Gatta.

'Isn't it fantastic snow?' Anna said, smiling at them. She reached out and took Starling's hand. 'Come in. We're having hot chocolate for breakfast. I'll make you some.'

They brought in the cold and the fresh air. The kitchen was warm and filled with light, white and gold from the snow and the sun outside.

'We got stuck yesterday,' said Anna getting cups from the shelf. 'We went to Penquit in the cart to get a Christmas tree. What have you two been doing?'

Starling stood by the fire and Gatta perched on the edge of the table with her feet on a chair. She looked slowly around, taking in everything. Her eyes moved over Anna, she studied her briefly and without interest, then moved on.

'Hold Mattie if you want, Starling,' said Anna. Starling shook her head.

'I could do with someone at New Year, Starling,' said Josef. He sat down at the table and settled the baby against his chest. 'It would be a great help to have someone collecting glasses, if you're interested.'

'OK.' Starling looked glum. She scuffed the toe of her boot on the floor.

'I'll come too—if you'd like me to,' said Gatta. She smiled at Josef, turning a little to look down at him from her seat on the table.

He had never seen her smile. She was more like Catherine, more like Sarah than he'd noticed before. She was pretty. Her creamy skin was dusted with rose on the cheeks and the tip of her nose, and her green-grey eyes were shining with the brilliance of the winter morning. Tiny crystals of melting ice sparkled on the fur of the collar and in her hair.

'I can be useful,' she said with a little laugh. She tucked the coat up over her knees and the skirt of the coat trailed down like black wings on either side. It was hard not to stare at the girl who sat like a glittering bird in front of him.

Gatta looked away. There was no need for more. Just as she knew how to be no one, she knew how to be everything too. She could fill a room so completely that everything else would shrink to nothing. As she'd grown older she discovered this flip side, the reverse of the trick she had learned when small—to spread out to every corner and be everywhere was as easy as being nothing.

'Would you like chocolate too, Gabriella?' said Anna. She looked from the girl to Josef and back to the girl again, whose smile was for her now.

'Oh, yes, please. That would be lovely. Thank you.'

'Second thoughts. I don't want to work on New Year,' said Starling loudly. 'I'd rather go to a party.' She sat down in the small rocking chair. Her face and hands were red with cold. She took a pack of cigarettes and a silver lighter from her pocket. Her eyes flickered to Josef. She held the lighter up high, clicking up the flame three times as if it were not working, then lit her cigarette. Josef watched her. She blew out a long breath of blue smoke. 'I'd be bored wandering round collecting glasses all night,' she said.

'Well that's a shame, but never mind,' said Anna. 'Would you like to take Mattie out and show him the snow this morning?' Josef was not absorbed in Gabriella any more, he was watching Starling, who played with the lighter on her knee, turning it round and round in her fingers. He had a different expression, one that Anna could not understand.

The girls had somehow broken the sweetness of the morning, the slow waking in the dark, lying close with the baby asleep between them, with need for no more than to take off the clothes they'd slept in and share warmth. They had slept late and woken to the dazzling, breathless day.

Now Anna was cold, as cold as if she could never be warm again. Her head ached. She thought how ugly she must look in Josef's dressing gown with her tangled hair and her face raw from yesterday's wind. 'I should get dressed,' she said to no one in particular.

They sipped their chocolate. Gabriella played with Mattie and took him onto her lap. She bounced him and tickled him, making him laugh delightedly. 'I think we should go,' she said after a while. 'I told my little brother I'd go up Tye Hill with him.'

'I'm not ready yet,' said Starling. But she got up out of the rocking chair.

'Come to Isabel's this afternoon. We can talk and play with Mattie, just us,' Anna whispered as she kissed her goodbye.

'I've got things to do. I'm busy,' Starling said and pushed past and out into the sunshine.

Gabriella stood by the door, waiting. She smiled at Anna and leaned forward for a kiss. She smelled sweet and clean as a child.

Then Josef; she put her hands on his shoulders, lifting up her face to him, touching his lips with hers.

∞

'I must go home. I'll be getting in your way,' said Anna. They could hear Gatta and Starling squealing and calling out in the lane. It sounded like a snow fight.

'I should open up soon, though I don't suppose there'll be many in until this evening.' Josef sat down at the table again. He had seemed preoccupied but now he smiled at her. 'There's no hurry.'

'But I should go?'

'Not if you don't want to.'

'But you'd rather I did.'

'No, Anna. You can stay as long as you'd like to. What's the matter?' He reached out and took her hand. 'You don't look too good, you know.'

'I know I look awful, you don't have to tell me.'

'I didn't mean that. You look lovely to me.' He hadn't known until it was said that he meant it. 'You look as though you might be coming down with something, that's all. Do you feel OK? Maybe you should go back to bed for a while.'

'I'm fine.'

'What is it? Tell me. Those girls upset you, didn't they?'

'No. And they certainly didn't upset you.'

'Oh, Anna, they're just little girls playing at being grown-up,' he said gently. He pulled her to him and sat her down, the baby on one knee, her on the other, and she hated him for knowing, for humiliating her by understanding.

'I could see it. You loved it,' she said angrily.

'No, that's not true at all.'

His kindness made her ashamed. 'You couldn't keep your eyes off that girl.' She got up, wanting him to keep hold of her hand, but he let her go.

'I don't know what they're up to and I really don't care.' He got up too, with the baby settled against him, and went to the dresser. He took down some plates with one hand, still holding Matthew. 'Do you want toast?' The conversation was over.

'More secrets. I'm sick of it. Tell me, Josef.' His back was turned and he did not answer her. Even the set of his shoulders made it clear that she should say no more.

'You're not doing this to me,' she said.

'I've done nothing, nor will I do anything to you,' he said dryly. He sat the baby on the edge of the dresser and Matthew hung on to Josef's sleeves, watching his hands as he sliced the bread. The two of them together looked absorbed and peaceful, as if she didn't exist. Anna willed herself to stop. Her head ached. She sat down heavily in a chair.

'This morning was so nice,' she said feebly.

'Yes, it was.'

'But you didn't want me.'

'It was good to wake up with you, Anna.'

'It's not Sarah, it's that girl isn't it.'

Josef turned round at last. He looked exasperated. 'Gabriella's sixteen. I was there when she was born. I was at her christening, both of them, Starling's too, out there in the garden.'

He put bread under the grill and felt in his pocket for the lighter. 'Damn. Damn her,' he muttered furiously. 'They're babies to me, Anna—just children. This is ridiculous.'

'Well, there's something you're not telling me. And Starling, she was upset and I don't know why.'

'I've upset her it seems—unintentionally. I just hope she gets over it quickly.'

'What did you do to her?'

'Nothing, absolutely nothing. And as for Gabriella, I hardly know her. I can't remember the last time she spoke to me. I'm fond of her because of … because of Sarah, that's all.'

'Were you and Sarah …?'

'I'm tired of this. I've told you about Isabel, about Catherine and Jack, because you asked, but I'm not willing to explain Sarah's life to you—or mine.' Josef showed no inclination to comfort her now. The baby had started to cry when he sensed the anger in their voices and now he sobbed quietly with his fist in his mouth, his dark head under Josef's chin. He looked at her resentfully.

'But there is something isn't there? About that girl. And Sarah.'

'Sarah and I were lovers once. One time, one night. It was not a mistake—I hate that English excuse, that cliché—and I've no need to hide it from you, nor do I see why you should know.'

'And Gabriella. What about her? Either she's yours or you wish she was, don't you—in one way or another.' Anna had not meant to say it. The fever in her head made her reckless and as soon as the words were out of her mouth she knew how sorry she would be.

'Gatta is my friend's daughter. And I dislike being questioned as if I owe you some explanation, as if I'm guilty of something.' Josef stood looking down at her. Even the blue of his eyes had changed. 'You really don't look well, Anna,' he added. His voice was kinder. 'Do you see? It's not for me to tell you about Sarah and her daughter. Things that have nothing to do with us.'

'Us?'

'You're cold. I think you should get dressed. I've time to walk you home if we leave soon.'

'I'm sorry,' she said.

'I know.'

Anna longed for him to say *it doesn't matter,* or *I'm sorry too;* anything other than, *I know.*

'I've hung your clothes in the airing cupboard,' he said. 'They'll be dry now and warm too, I hope.'

⁓

He left her at the gate. The house looked deserted and Anna wondered if Isabel was still at the blackhouse with Robert.

'Will you come in?' she asked.

'I'm sorry, I must get back. I need to get Elaine's tree to her somehow.' He kissed her quickly on the cheek. 'You should try and get some rest. Will you call me later, let me know how you are?' She nodded.

He walked away, back along the lane, hands deep in his pockets, collar up, and she wanted to go with him.

The kitchen was freezing. The stove had not been lit, the fire not even laid ready. There was a little wood and some coal. She went into the sitting room. A Christmas tree had been decorated and there were presents under it.

The baby seemed to have completely recovered from his ordeal of the day before; he reached out his hands towards the tree and struggled to get out of her arms. She sat him on the floor with some toys and forced herself to light the fire, then she lay down on the sofa. She closed her eyes and listened to the wood crackle and the little murmurs of her baby playing on the rug. The air was cold and filled with the scent of the tree.

Sometime later there were footsteps in the hall and she heard Frank's voice: 'I'll nip across and call old Robert. Through here, isn't it, Isabel? It's brass bloody monkeys in this place—excuse me, ladies.'

Then a woman's voice: 'Gracious me. Your boiler's out, my dear. Let's get ourselves organized.'

Anna didn't want to open her eyes or to move but she got up. In the kitchen Lydia Arbamount was on her knees by the open stove. She knelt on newspaper with the washing-up gloves on and was dipping into the coal scuttle with tongs. Isabel stood watching. Her hair hung down, dull and damp, and her face was sunken with exhaustion. She wore a festive scarlet coat with gold buttons that Anna knew was Elaine's. It hung in folds round Isabel, the cuffs high above her wrists, and the hem, usually at Elaine's calf, above Isabel's knees.

For some unaccountable reason Anna started to cry when she saw her. She put her arms round Isabel. 'I'm so sorry. I'm sorry I worried you, Isabel.'

'Oh, darling, don't cry. Don't cry, my darling. It doesn't matter, all that matters is that we're home now.' Isabel seemed thinner, as though in twenty-four hours she had starved, but her eyes were peaceful and she smiled her magic smile as though nothing in the world mattered but the two of them.

'Isabel has been rather upset but we've talked it over, haven't we, Isabel dear?' said Lydia. 'She's much better this morning.'

'Where have you been? I thought you were with Robert,' said Anna. Isabel seemed not to have heard. She said, 'All together for Christmas. I'm so pleased you came home.'

'I must get Mattie. I've left him on his own in the sitting room,' said Anna. When she returned to the kitchen with the baby, Frank and Robert were there too. Robert had taken over from Lydia lighting the stove.

'Well, we'll leave you to it,' said Frank. 'Merry Christmas everyone. Call if you need anything, old boy.'

'Just a minute,' said Lydia. 'Let's just make sure that everyone is happy and that Isabel won't feel the need to go out on her own again. How are you feeling now, Isabel? Would you and Robert like to come and have Christmas with us, with Connie and me? Or with Frank and Elaine?'

'It's a madhouse at our place—I mean, er, it's no place ...' Frank shuffled closer to the door.

'She's told me all about your poor dear children, Robert. I won't intrude, but I know what a difficult time Christmas is. We've talked about it, haven't we, Isabel—my Gerald and your little ones.'

Isabel was suddenly decisive. 'Thank you, Lydia. You've been most kind. And Frank, please thank Elaine for putting me up last night. Goodbye and Merry Christmas to you.'

'Stay with her, Robert. A woman needs a husband,' said Lydia briskly, buttoning her coat. 'Good. Now I must get back to Connie or she'll think I've deserted her again. And you need some aspirins and a hot-water bottle, Anna dear, I can see that much without spectacles.'

❧

After Frank and Lydia had gone, there was quiet. The three of them and the baby were not often together in the kitchen. Isabel looked uncertain and watchful, as if weighing up the situation.

'I'll make us something to eat,' said Robert. There was a purple bruise and a cut at the corner of his eye. 'Would you like a bath and a rest for a while, Isabel?'

'Why did you lie to me?' She took a step towards him, her hands clenched into fists. 'You told me a lie.' She turned on Anna, suddenly more perplexed than angry. 'He said you were with Starling. Why did he say that?' They both looked at Anna, Isabel accusing and Robert expressionless. The seconds ticked.

'He couldn't hear me,' said Anna quickly. 'The line was bad then we were cut off before I said. He didn't know.'

As if she had forgotten her question, Isabel sighed. 'I'm too tired to talk any more,' she said.

'It would be nice if Robert stayed, wouldn't it, Isabel? For

Christmas?' said Anna. 'Please let him stay.' She suddenly knew that she did not want to be alone with Isabel.

'There's absolutely no need, darling. Robert has things to do, I'm sure.' The old Isabel was back, icy and unassailable, but she gave him a brief smile, reached out with her fingers and touched his face. 'I'm sorry,' she said simply. 'Thank you, Robert, you've been kind.'

After he'd closed the door, Isabel said, 'I've got everything planned, darling. Robert will be here tomorrow, if that's what you'd like. This evening it'll be just the three of us.' She kissed the baby. 'I was so sorry to have missed his birthday.'

'But it wasn't his birthday. He's not one until April, Isabel—don't you remember?'

Isabel seemed not to have heard. She went to the kitchen door, turned the key in the lock and put it in the pocket of the scarlet coat.

'You look very pale, my darling. Why don't I take Jack and you can have a rest?'

'I'm fine, thank you.'

'Well, if you're sure. I'm going upstairs for a while, I've got some things to wrap.' And she went out of the kitchen.

Anna heard the scrape of the bolt on the front door and the oily click of the old iron key.

⁂

She listened to Isabel's steps on the stairs, up to her bedroom then back across the landing to the bathroom. The bath taps turned on and the door closed.

Matthew squirmed in her arms and Anna tried to hush him as she picked up the phone. She had no number for Josef, and Robert had no telephone. What was the name of the pub? She had never seen any directories in the house and she had never known Frank and Elaine's name. She put down the receiver.

The ache in her head had frozen with the cold and it was hard to move or think. She must get out, she must get Mattie out—

through a window or force the door, or shout across the garden to Robert. Or she could lie down on the sofa by the fire in the living room and sleep and let whatever would happen just happen.

She pushed open the door to the hallway. Upstairs, there was the sound of water trickling into the bath and Isabel singing softly. Anna had never heard her sing before—her voice was true and clear and the sound of it echoed in the empty house. Then the water stopped and Isabel was quiet.

The telephone rang in the kitchen.

'Hi-ee! Merry Christmas, Anna, it's me, Elaine. I just wondered if you were ...'

'Isabel's not well, Elaine. She's locked us in,' Anna whispered. 'Please come. Elaine, please tell Frank to come now.'

'Blocked you in? Where?'

'Isabel's locked the doors and I can't get out. You've got to come quickly, I can't talk much more or she'll hear.'

'No, no, we *told* her to.' Elaine laughed. 'Quiet, you lot, I'm on the phone,' she bellowed straight into the mouthpiece. 'Sorry about that, I've got a house full—Bee's home with the boyfriend and Steffie's lot have descended *and* Frank's mother to put the icing on the cake—literally I mean, to ice the cake not to finish us off, but she might, I wouldn't be surprised.'

'Elaine, listen to me. What shall I do?'

'Do? You don't have to do anything. She told Lydia she didn't like being at home on her own, so we said to lock the doors.'

'You told her to? When?'

'Yes, last night. They were here, Isabel and Lydia Arbamount, Connie's friend. Poor old Constance was out of her depth with it all, but when you've got daughters you get used to dealing with fits of the vapours at three in the morning. Frank was going to take Isabel home but she said she didn't like being in the house on her own, so I made up the spare in Bee's room and shifted her in with Steffie, which didn't go down too well, putting the boyfriend on the sofa. So, we said, lock yourself in, Isabel.'

'You told her to.'

'It seemed the best thing. She's just had a funny turn, Anna. It's age. Hormones. I'm just the same. What I wanted to suggest was ...'

'You think she's OK?'

'*Yes*. She's fine. Now what I phoned for was to see if you wanted me to have the baby tonight. I heard you and our gorgeous landlord are getting along rather well so I thought you'd want to be unencumbered for the evening. And Isabel's not her best, I grant you, so I just thought I'd offer.'

'I don't know. I can't think.'

'Oh, go on, Anna.'

'I think I've got a temperature.'

'Well you'll be nice and rosy then. And warm.'

'But you've already got a houseful, you said. You don't want Mattie too.'

'I'm up to my neck in teenage girls, they'll be fighting to look after him. Starling's coming over later, Matthew loves her—and Gatta, she's wonderful with little ones. Anyway, the offer's there. If Isabel can't, I can.'

'Isabel can't.'

'Well there you are then. Drop him off on your way. We'll be up late, so go to church if you want.'

'Church?'

'Didn't you go last year? Christmas Eve, people fall out of the pub and walk along the river path to the church at Penquit. Anyway, we'll be up till God only knows when, so go if you like. We'll put Mattie to bed when he's tired.'

'And you think Isabel's OK and she'll let me out?'

'Of course she will. You're over eighteen aren't you? Tell you what, if you don't turn up by nine, I'll send Frank along with his wrench.'

'Thanks, Elaine.'

'Now off you go and dig out your sparklies. It's time you had a bit of fun.'

∽

'Isabel?' Anna tapped on the bathroom door. 'Isabel, could I have the kitchen key? We need more coal.' There was silence.

'Isabel?'

'Of course, darling. It's in the door—or on the hook, I can't remember.'

'You put it in your pocket. The pocket of that coat you were wearing. Can I come in and get it?'

'Did I? How odd. Yes, of course.' The bathroom was full of steam and Isabel was lying with her eyes closed. Anna sorted through the clothes on the floor and pulled out Elaine's coat. She waited for a moment, wondering if Isabel would speak.

'Don't fall asleep, Isabel,' Anna said softly. 'You must be so tired.'

Isabel's grey hair floated, her skin was bloodless and slack like something emptied out.

'I am ugly in red,' said Isabel without opening her eyes.

When Anna came downstairs to the kitchen, she noticed that the iron key to the front door was still in the lock. There had been no reason at all to be frightened of Isabel.

∽

They ate supper by the fire in the sitting room. Robert came in and although Isabel did not welcome him, neither did she seem to mind when he closed the sitting-room door behind him and sat opposite her in the other armchair by the fire.

Anna played with Matthew on the floor and Isabel gave him a present from under the tree. It was a toy radio that made animal noises when the fat red buttons were pressed. The baby sorted through the wrapping paper, turning it over in his hands as if it were some mysterious treasure.

They ate cheese and cold meats and mince pies from a tray, and Robert had brought with him a jug of mulled wine. The candles on the Christmas tree were lit, fixed in little silver cups that clipped to the branches.

'How lovely to have real candles,' Anna said.

'Adelie gave me the holders,' said Isabel.

'Who is Adelie?'

Robert looked across at Isabel but she sipped her wine and watched the baby play. 'I'll put you to bed soon, my sweetheart,' she said. 'It's a big day tomorrow.'

'Well actually, I'd like to take him with me this evening,' said Anna. 'I'm thinking of going to the pub and I thought I'd take him. A late night won't hurt just this once.'

'Oh, darling, he'll be much better here. You have a lovely time and I'll see to him.'

'I'm taking him,' said Anna. 'I want him with me this evening.' Isabel looked up from the baby and her eyes narrowed. Anna saw that she guessed a lie, though could not be sure what the lie was.

'Perhaps we should join you, Anna,' said Robert. 'Shall we go too, Isabel?'

Isabel did not reply, and it seemed that exhaustion washed over her again. She sank back in the armchair, closing her eyes. A tear trickled down her cheek and she licked it from her lips.

⚬◯⚬

'So you escaped,' said Elaine. She opened the door with a large glass in her hand, wearing what looked like a beaded bedspread. The noise of the house blasted out with the hot air. There was thudding rock from upstairs, a flute somewhere in the attic and jazz from the music room, mixed with the sound of laughter and the clink of glasses.

'Thanks for this, Elaine. I'll be back—well, I don't know when— later.'

'It's snowing *again*,' said Elaine, scooping Matthew out of Anna's arms. 'You look gorgeous, you naughty girl. Josef brought round our tree this afternoon and I told him he should get cracking and women like you don't expect to be kept hanging around.'

'Elaine! You didn't!'

'No, I didn't.' She beamed. 'Off you go. How's Isabel?'

'I can't tell really. Tired. Robert's with her. She said she wanted to see Lydia but I don't know if she'll go.'

'Well, don't you worry about her, or this little chap. Bye-bye, Mummy.' They waved as Anna walked down the path. She stood at the gate until Elaine closed the door.

∞

Anna pushed open the door of the pub and the scene she expected—a few quiet drinkers, the lighted fire and Josef leaning on the bar reading a book—disappeared with the crush and the noise.

She had an impulse to turn and go home but someone arrived behind her and she had no choice but to go inside. People were standing and talking loudly. Coats and scarves were heaped on the chairs, and the floor was wet with melted snow. The place was warm and Anna wished she'd not worn a wool dress that was too hot and too tight for a country pub. She had not worn it since London with Thomas the winter before Matthew was born; then it had not stretched over her stomach or gaped at the cleavage. Perhaps she would keep her coat on.

She couldn't see Josef, but over the crowd of heads was a Christmas tree in the corner. Its top touched the ceiling and it was lit with candles in silver holders.

Anna squeezed her way through. She said hello to people she recognized from the village committee and the film club, and parents of Brownies and Little Butterflies. There was Starling's father and the men she'd seen repairing the bridge. They must be unable to get home for the snow. From time to time she caught sight of Josef.

He did not see her at first. He was standing beside Sarah with his hand on her shoulder as she poured a drink for someone. They were smiling, talking to whoever was there at the bar in front of them. Sarah's head leaned back against Josef's shoulder. She held out the glass and turned away to attend to another customer.

Then Josef saw her. 'Anna. You're here. I'm glad you're feeling better. I didn't expect to see you tonight.'

'I'm not staying long.'

He took her hand across the bar. 'Come into the kitchen and take off your coat. It's pretty busy—luckily no one can get out of the village so they're all here. Sarah will be fine on her own for a while.' He kept hold of Anna's hand, along the bar and round to the kitchen. He closed the door behind them, shutting out the noise. The peace of the house enfolded them: the half-light and the big dusty kitchen, the dog stretched flat on the flagstones by the fire.

'I was worried about you. I thought you were in for a bout of something,' he said.

'I think I am.' She took off her coat and she saw him notice her dress, though he said nothing.

'Shall I sit down?' she said at last.

'Of course, I'm sorry.' He went to the dresser. 'I've got something special I think you'll like. It's wine from home. My father sent me a case of it and I can tell you it was a big sacrifice for him, he thinks this is the best we've had for years.'

'Is this a celebration?'

'I think it is.'

In the quiet they heard the noise on the other side of the door. Sometimes there was laughter or a voice would rise above the rest.

Josef pulled a chair from the table to sit beside her, and Anna sat in the rocking chair. Her skin was stinging with the fever and her face burned. The wine tasted strange, delicious and bitter.

'I must get back soon,' said Josef, but he didn't get up. They sat in the firelight, the two of them and the grey dog.

After a while there was a tap at the door.

'Hello,' said Sarah. 'I'm sorry, but I've got to go now. I told Gatta I'd be home by half nine.'

'Yes, of course.'

'She wants to go to Steffie's party and I don't suppose the boys will be in bed either.' She smiled at Anna. 'I'm glad you're here; Joe told me you might come.'

She pulled on her coat, the one her daughter had worn. She had the same grace, the same slipping, silky hair, but her face was softened by the lines round her eyes and at the edges of her mouth. How old was she—forty? Perhaps more? Anna wondered if she had ever been as pretty as Gatta. Sarah's eyes were kind, a look that had not been passed to her daughter.

'Josef was hoping you'd make it tonight,' Sarah said. 'He's told me all about you and your little boy—and that you're living with Robert and Isabel.'

Anna looked at Josef, but he was picking up the bottle on the hearth and the wine glasses. 'I have a baby daughter,' Sarah went on. 'Linnet's older than your son, she's four. We could meet up sometime. There aren't many little ones in the village.'

'I'd like to.'

'Please call in if you can,' Sarah said to Josef. They gave each other a perfunctory kiss. Sarah pulled on her gloves. 'Linnet made you something at nursery and she wants to give it to you herself. Call in tomorrow—both of you.'

'We will,' Josef said.

'Happy Christmas.' She left by the kitchen door, waving as she ran past the window.

Through the evening Anna pretended not to see when Josef watched her, or when he noticed people looking at her in the red dress.

To everyone's surprise, Constance and Lydia called in for an hour. They arrived arm in arm in matching boots, Lydia's being Constance's old ones and Constance's being the ones Lydia had bought her for Christmas and given to her early.

'I know what she likes,' said Lydia with satisfaction. 'She wore boots like that before the war.'

'This style of boot is perfect for snow. I see no point in chopping and changing,' said Constance. 'A port and lemon for myself, and what would you like, Lydia?'

'Rum,' said Lydia. 'Gerald would always have rum at Christmas and so shall I.'

⌘

Everyone had gone—to Frank and Elaine's party, or home, or setting off along the river path to the church at Penquit.

Josef took the lamp from the aviary and they walked across the white garden. He ducked through a gap in the fence to the river, holding up the lamp for Anna to see.

They turned downstream, away from the snowy meadows and Isabel's house, and followed the track of footprints. Ahead were flickering beams of torches and voices carried on the air.

As they walked, the river threw back an arc of glittering gold from the lamp and the sounds in the distance became fainter. They talked easily and softly, all the tension falling away, walking in step, Anna's arm through Josef's.

Perhaps the awkwardness had been all hers—now that she had seen them together there was no doubt that Josef and Sarah were simply friends, familiar and close as brother and sister, no more or less than that.

A branch laden with snow dipped down close to their heads and Anna reached up to it with her hand. Snow spattered down on them. Josef reached over her head and shook a bigger branch. She shrieked under the small avalanche. The sound of her voice was swallowed up in the night.

There was a moment when they faced each other, then they fought like children.

Josef fought harder than she expected. He aimed well and let her fall heavily when he tripped her. Anna laughed with the shock of the snow in her face and the thud of the ground that came up to meet her over and over again. Eventually she could not scramble up any more and lay gasping for breath and looking up at the stars. The earth shifted beneath her as if she were shaken loose from its hold.

Josef held out his hand.

'Have I won?' he said. He pulled her up and dusted the snow from her hair. She could feel the warmth of his hands.

They stood on the bank and he held the lamp, his arm outstretched over the dark water. Unexpectedly, under the circle of light the river was as clear as glass and they could see down through the shallows to the stones and weeds and drowned, broken branches on the riverbed. Dead leaves moved slowly along, pirouetting in eddies, catching on stones then sliding on. Under the water the ground sloped steeply away into darkness, and here and there were blurred shadow-shapes of larger things sunk into the mud, too heavy for the current to carry away.

Anna thought of the little girl kneeling in the summer grass and the blond boy in shorts. She thought of Matthew's tiny fingers reaching up to them. Suddenly it did not seem strange that the children were Catherine and Jack.

'I went swimming here once,' she said.

The heat inside her burned and she imagined slipping now into the black water and warming the whole river with her body.

Ice crackled in the trees. The moving water made her lightheaded and Josef's arm on her shoulders pressed the woollen dress into her tender, scorching skin. He felt heavy, as if he leaned all his weight on her and her aching limbs would give way if she had to take another step.

He put down the lamp on the snow at their feet. There was no need to walk further tonight.

∽⊗∽

'Hi,' said the young woman who opened the door. She turned her
back and started up the stairs, leaving Anna on the doorstep.
'They're in the music room,' she added over her shoulder.

'I've come to collect my baby,' Anna called after her. 'Do you
know which room he's in?'

'Oh, you're Anna.' She came back down the stairs. She was large
and lustrous and heavy-footed. 'I'm Bee, hello.' She pushed her
thick hair off her face and rubbed her eyes with the cuffs of her
enormous sweater. 'Um, I don't know where Mattie is.' She yawned.
'My sister was looking after him, just a sec.' She went off up the
stairs, leaving Anna in the hallway.

It was past two and there were still piles of coats on the floor. The
music room was at the back of the house and she could hear voices
and laughter and the sound of a cello. Anna wondered whether to go
through uninvited and find Elaine, but Elaine would ask about Josef;
she would see Anna's face and guess. For a while Josef was a secret.

There was a scuffle and squeals at the top of the stairs and
Starling came leaping down with a tall, thin boy bounding after her.
He lost interest halfway and disappeared upstairs again. Starling
stopped dead, pink-faced, breathing hard and giggling. She had
tinsel in her hair.

'Hello, Starling. Good party?'

'Yep. OK.'

'It looks better than OK.'

'He's after me with the mistletoe, but my mum and dad are here.'

'Oh. I see.'

'We're all in Steffie's room,' she said, as if in explanation. 'He
likes me better than Gatta.'

'Perhaps you should let him catch you then,' said Anna.

'I'm not bothered any more, about him. I told him that. I'm not
interested any more so you can have him.' Her speech was slurred
and she hung on to the banister swaying a little.

'Who?'

'You know who.' Gatta had come down the stairs.

'Me?' said Anna. Perhaps it was a joke she'd not caught up with.

'*Me?*' whined Gatta. 'You think you can twist him round your little finger, don't you?' Her face was pushed up close to Anna's. She smelled of alcohol and her eyes were smudged with make-up.

'Who are we talking about?' said Anna.

'Are you stupid or something? He's working his way round anyone who'll let him. Star got caught but I won't. I know what you've been up to tonight. He'd have anything he could get his hands on, so don't think you're special, you fat cow.'

'Josef? You mean Josef?'

'Don't say that to her,' said Starling, as if Anna hadn't spoken. 'It's not her fault she's fat, she's had a baby.'

'She thinks she can come here and push everyone around—well, she sodding well can't.' Gatta sniggered at Anna. 'My mum's the one he really likes. You've got no chance, she's better looking than you even if she is older.'

'They're friends,' said Anna. 'He told me.' But the girls seemed to have forgotten her.

'That's a really mean thing to say.' Starling's voice shrieked and croaked in turns as though she'd lost control of it along with her legs. 'He likes me as well. And don't swear at her, she's nice. And she's from London, so what do you know.'

'Well fuck her, if she's so *nice,* with her *nice* poxy designer clothes and her *nice* stuck-up prat of a boyfriend.'

'You liked him. You said.'

'You cowing liar, I never did.'

'You did. I swear, cross my heart.' Starling staggered and hung on to Gatta as if they were the best of friends. 'You said it when we were having sausages.'

Gatta snorted. 'I couldn't fancy a dick like him if you paid me.'

'You did. When I said do you want onions.'

'I couldn't have, I hate sausages, they're dead animals. Get off me, you're too hot.'

'Well you had one at the fireworks.'

'I never did. I couldn't eat an animal. Or onions. They've got feelings, you were the one who told me that.'

'Oh,' said Starling. The argument seemed to have lost its way. She frowned her eyes into focus and Gatta peered into the hall mirror and wiped the smudges from under her eyes. Starling yawned.

In the pause Anna said, 'I want to go home. Where's Matthew?' They both turned to her and Starling looked uncomfortable. 'Is he upstairs?' Anna asked. Starling shuffled.

She said, 'I wanted to ask Elaine and so did Steffie but Gatta said it was all right.'

'Where is he?' Anna looked from Starling to Gatta who had gone back to studying herself in the mirror.

'He's not here,' said Gatta, flicking back her hair. 'MacKinnon came looking for you again. We said you'd most likely be staying at the pub all night so she took him.'

'Is that all right?' said Starling. 'Is that all right?'

'Of course it's all right,' said Gatta. 'She doesn't look after him properly anyway, everyone knows that. I've seen what she's like. She leaves him by the river and she lets him freeze and she forgets to feed him. She'd forget all about him if you gave her half a chance …'

Anna had pushed past her, out into the night. She was running even before she knew what it was that made her run.

Christmas Morning

My baby is sleeping in my arms and I should not wake him.

If I were alone I would run. I'd run for the joy of it because at last there is no need.

It is years since I felt the wind pulling my hair and pushing its weight on me, pressing its weight on my face and my throat to slow me. It never could. I was always too strong and too fast if my children were calling.

They've not called for so long you would think I'd forgotten. But I haven't.

When I talk or eat or do the hundred other things that seem to be my life, I am always listening.

Tonight is different. The night was so quiet when I watched my husband sleep in a chair by the fire. I remembered his hands and his kiss and his long lean body that I love. How could I have forgotten?

Robert.

He looks old but I know this cannot be so.

Jack is sleeping in my arms. I will put him to bed when we are home. I need not worry for Catherine now. She was always strong and quick like me. It will not be long before I find her.

I will sleep well tonight. I will be happy.

⁓

The fire in the living room was out and the room was in darkness. Robert had gone. Isabel wondered why he'd not waited for her to come home before he went to bed. For so long, for reasons she could not clearly recall, she had gone to bed alone in their house. It had always been hard to sleep for all the noise, the fluttering in the roof, the pattering and tapping and knocking, the doors singing softly on their hinges. It was as if the place was filled with activity as soon as the lights were out.

But tonight she would slip into bed beside Robert in the quiet earth house and sleep undisturbed until morning.

It was past one o'clock. It was Christmas morning. She made a list in her head of the things she would gather together. There was nowhere for the baby to sleep in the blackhouse, so she would take bedding for him. And suddenly it occurred to her that she need never come back to this stale, restless house with its too many rooms. She would live with Robert, all of them together in the quiet and the warm of the earth house like his stories of home on St Kilda.

The baby was sleeping. She carried him upstairs to her own bed and made a crib for him with pillows to stop him falling if he woke. He was wrapped in a shawl that Elaine must have found for him and he breathed noisily. Isabel felt his face. He was hot and his skin was damp, there was chocolate round his mouth. Anger rose up in her: Anna had lied, she'd left him with those girls, they'd fed him sweets and exhausted him.

But Isabel was too busy to think of Anna for long. Perhaps Anna would not come back.

Isabel went up to the room in the attic and collected Jack's quilt and mattress from the cot. She packed some toys and clothes for him in a bag.

From her bedroom she took a hairbrush, a nightdress and clothes for herself. She reached for the picture on her bedside table but found that she could not touch it. The photograph of the river made a tightness in her head and filled her with anguish she could not understand, but she need simply let her eyes rest on the sleeping baby for a while for the feeling to melt away.

She would get everything ready and then collect him. She took the bag and the bedding down to the kitchen and put them by the back door. She gathered up the baby's presents from under the Christmas tree.

In the kitchen the supper plates, the glasses and the wine jug were piled in the sink and she pulled them out on to the draining board to find the baby's cup and bowl. She folded the wooden high chair Robert had made for him. It would take two trips or even three to carry everything across the garden but she would not wake Robert to help her, he had looked so tired when she watched him fall asleep in the armchair by the fire a few hours ago.

Suddenly there was the sound of the front door opening and banging against the wall, and footsteps running along the passage. The kitchen door flew open and Anna was staring at her, at the pile of things by the door. Isabel saw her confusion then fury so wild it stretched the muscles of her face and her eyes were black and blank as an animal's. For an odd moment Isabel had the sensation of looking at her own reflection and she despised Anna for such futile, ridiculous emotion.

'He's with Robert,' said Isabel. 'I don't want another scene.'

'I'm taking him and I'm not coming back. I hate this place.'

Isabel laughed. 'Oh, darling, that's a silly thing to say—in this weather?'

'Don't make me feel stupid. Don't, Isabel. I'll go to someone near.'

'Someone near? That would be Josef Sevier I expect. How lovely that you two have got together. I should have known you would.'

'He's ... We're not together. I don't want to see him ever again—or this place. No one's honest, no one tells me the truth, and I'm sick of it and I'm leaving.'

'He's always been a liar. I'm sorry he's hurt you, Anna.'

'You're not sorry. You're never sorry—only for yourself.'

Isabel paused. 'I must say, you look very pretty this evening, my darling.'

'You've no right to take my son and decide what's best as if he's yours. Well he's not. As soon as I can get out of here I'm going.'

'He'll stay where he's safe. I'll not allow you to wake him.' Isabel stood with her back against the garden door. 'He's with Robert and he's asleep.' Then her voice was gentle. 'I'm only suggesting what's best, darling. Stay with Josef. Sometimes we must forgive. Another woman, I expect—it's only weakness, Anna, it can't be helped. Go on now, Jack's perfectly safe with me.'

The name made Anna's heart stop.

'I'm taking him now. I'll go to Elaine.' She took a step towards Isabel. 'Get out of my way.'

She saw Isabel calculating, measuring. Her eyes flickered past Anna to the passage door.

'He's here in the house, isn't he? He's upstairs.' Anna turned. 'He's not Jack,' she said under her breath. 'And he's not safe with you.'

She did not see Isabel pick up the jug from the sink, and felt only astonishment at the flash of vicious light like an explosion inside her skull as her head hit the iron stove.

⚭

Robert's house was not locked and Isabel carried the things across the snow to his door. She went back into the kitchen, stepping over Anna and noticing a little pool of blood that had settled on the flagstones by her head. It had soaked her hair, spread out on the floor and gathered in a dip in the stone. The blood did not look real, it was too bright and too red.

Anna seemed to be sleeping, her face was rosy and her cheek rested on one upturned palm as if to cushion it. Her other hand still wore a woollen glove.

It had become icy in the kitchen with the door to the garden left open, and Isabel put on the red coat.

Upstairs in the bedroom the baby had woken and he put his hands up to Isabel's face as she bent over the bed to take him into her arms.

'My little boy,' she whispered. 'My Jack.'

As she left the house, she switched off the light and locked the kitchen door behind her.

Christmas Afternoon

'Fez,' said Constance triumphantly. 'F is four, plus E is one, plus Z is ten, triple word score, forty-five.'

'Oh, Connie, bravo!' said Lydia, clapping her hands. 'Congratulations. I'm well and truly vanquished.' She peered at the score sheet. 'Let me see. My puny 192 to your magnificent 270. And that's not counting your forty-five and minus all these letters I've got left.'

'You did very well, Lyddie, very well indeed.' Constance folded the Scrabble board, tipping the little tiles into the box. 'Time for tea I think. No. Wait.' She held up her hand: 'We shall have a small port *as well as* tea.'

'I've so enjoyed the day, Connie dear. I can't imagine how I would have got through it without you.'

Constance felt a welling up in her chest and she wanted to kiss her friend and say, *No, don't thank me Lyddie, it's the best Christmas I've had in years,* but she pressed her lips together. Her nerves were still not good, thanks to Lydia's disorganized arrival.

'I'm so glad,' she said. 'It's been very pleasant to have you here.' She went to the sideboard where the port and glasses stood on a festive doily.

Constance did not feel she'd helped. Lydia had been cheerful of her own accord even when Gerald was mentioned. Constance apologized for her carelessness the first time this happened but Lydia had said, 'Gracious, Connie, Gerald's not been arrested or run off with a floosie! There's no need to be sorry.' And they had giggled behind their hands as if they were still at Marjorie Barton's School of Dancing.

Constance could almost say she'd relaxed. After lunch she closed her eyes and drifted off for a few minutes, a thing she could never normally have done with a visitor present. It was odd that even while she dozed, with Lydia making no sound at all, Constance could feel she was not alone. The quiet of the bungalow was filled with Lydia—like candlelight, thought Constance without embarrassment as she floated in semi-sleep. Yes, Lydia glowed sweetly like the candle in the table decoration. *'Connie, how lovely, Gerald loathed anything fancy on the table. I shall light this for him, the dear curmudgeonly old ox, just to annoy him.'* They had left the candle burning and the turkey carcass on the table all afternoon.

The drama in the small hours of yesterday morning seemed not to have disrupted Lydia's stay at all, in spite of their both getting very little sleep that night on account of Isabel MacKinnon's extraordinary behaviour. Lydia had arrived back at the bungalow past eleven on Christmas Eve morning, having been up the rest of the night with Elaine, trying to pacify Isabel and coax her into returning home. They had indulged Isabel, to Constance's mind.

It was disappointing. Isabel MacKinnon was one of the few women that one could say one respected, with her straightforward and gracious attitude towards even those it was plain were not her equal. They shared values, she and Isabel, the old values that had started to slip with the Abdication and non-iron cotton.

Until now Isabel MacKinnon had not dwelt or wallowed, she had put her trouble behind her. For a while she had been erratic, it was true, but she had done her crying and got on with life. She had pluck and dignity, what more could one say? Constance had admired her.

So it had been shocking to see Isabel in such disarray, as if thirty years had simply peeled away like so much old paint, and humiliating for her to break down in front of people she barely knew. But Constance would take a leaf out of young Josef Sevier's book and

overlook it. Isabel need not fear: the incident would not be referred
to again.

And it seemed all was well now. Isabel had called on them after
lunch, perfectly happy to all appearances, with Anna's child. They
were going for an afternoon walk in the snow. Apparently she,
Anna, was staying with Josef Sevier (a fact that need not be broad-
cast, Constance thought), so Isabel had stepped in. Young mothers
like Anna are so relaxed about handing over their offspring. The
infant was very sweet in his little snow suit and his pixie hat. A nice-
looking boy, though a little tearful and fractious, and rather too
dark-skinned.

Dear Lydia had coo-eed and peek-a-booed until he stopped his
whining and Isabel had taken him off home for Christmas tea. Yes,
all in all, it had been a most successful day.

'How did you think Isabel seemed today, Connie?' said Lydia.

'Seemed?' said Constance, handing Lydia her port. 'Seemed?'

'Do you think she's ... herself? Do you think she's well?'

'She looks perfectly healthy to me. Her colour was good.'

'I know, dear, I know. She *is* healthy, but how did she seem, in
herself?'

Constance sipped her port and considered. 'Well, I'm glad to say
she was properly dressed and coherent. And I've not heard her refer
to Robert so warmly for years. I don't know what else one can say.'

'He seems a most patient man. He must love her terribly,' said
Lydia. 'But I'm not sure I would have suggested she look after a
child, not so soon, not after the other night.'

'I'm sure she's competent, Lydia.'

'I'm sure she is, Connie. It's just a feeling. It's just a feeling I
have.'

⌒∞⌒

At four o'clock the light was almost gone. Purple shadows stretched
slantwise from the trees by the river across the garden to the house.

In the slivers of sunlight the snow was livid pink, like icing on a bun. No more had fallen all day and a crust of ice had hardened the surface, spoiling the innocent new-fallen softness that invited reckless games like a giant feather pillow. Now underfoot it was sharp as grit.

In the warmth of the day the sun at its highest had made icicles along the eaves of Isabel's house and on the twigs of the trees. The trees dripped and the white slabs on the roof split and slithered. As evening came the cold flowed out from the shade and set hard the millions of diamond drips on the trees and fixed the last drops suspended on the points of the icicles.

Robert banked up the fire to warm the blackhouse, ready for Isabel and the child when they came home from their walk. He peeled potatoes and sliced some ham. Mince pies were warming in the oven, and now he had time to check on the sheep and to light the stove up in the empty house to stop the pipes freezing while they were all away.

He knew the sheep would be following the last patches of sun to the far side of the house and he set off along their tracks, following their drunken lines of dots and dashes in the snow.

He breathed in the freezing air and smiled in spite of the pain that was pressing on his chest like a fist.

It had started as he waited for Isabel to come home on Christmas Eve. At first it was only his eye and cheekbone that ached where she'd struck him, then slowly the pain sunk down to his chest as if the ribs had tightened and the space was too small for the lungs to take in their fill of air. Claws gripped under his breastbone and he moved slowly so as not to provoke them. But it did not trouble him; his heart was singing—an expression meant for poetry he thought, a metaphor for joy and a condition of the brain. But this was not always so; it could be a sensation of the body. His heart had broken free of its dogged, obstinate thudding and it fluttered in the cage of his chest and vibrated in his throat, making him breathless and high.

He had woken this morning and Isabel was beside him. He lay motionless, listening to her breathe. She was warm. Her back was turned and her hair spread out on the pillow they shared. In the half-light he took a lock of her hair in his hand and felt its texture, rolling it between his fingers. After a while she turned over into his arms. She was no different.

When the daylight came in at the window high up under the roof, he was momentarily surprised to see the lines on her face and her faded hair. But she smiled and said, 'Here I am,' as if he'd called out to her in his sleep, in a dream, and she had been there all along.

Past the tree house the tracks of the sheep blurred where they had lain down for a few hours in the weak midday sun then wandered on to the other side of the house. He found them huddled in the straw-bale shelter he'd made a few days ago and they bleated a greeting to him, a gentle, muttering sound that was both contentment and complaint. He smashed the ice on their water trough.

It was dusk when he turned towards the kitchen to light the stove. Under his feet the hoof prints of the sheep were deep pocked shadows in the snow, lacing to and fro as they must have followed each other some time earlier in the day. But there was something odd in the tracks, something that made Robert stop, bend down and reach out his hand.

The small hoofs were clear, the press and drag of each pace in the snow, the hind hoof overlapping where the front one had fallen. The tracks merged and separated leaving stretches untouched, and there in the pure white was a small human footprint, deep at the heel and the ball of the foot, the toes pressing their little fan shape in the snow.

He stooped lower and the pain in his chest tightened. His breath rasped. He did not touch the footprint for fear of spoiling it. In the twilight the shape shimmered and slipped and was just the mark of a sheep's muzzle nosing for grass. Then the impression became so clear it could only be the footprint of a child.

Robert let his eyes follow the tracks, back and forth, searching for more. There was another, and another, right up to the kitchen door. He leaned against the house. With every breath he drew into his lungs the fist pressed and the claw gripped tighter in his chest. The wall held his weight as if the world had tilted and he slid to the ground.

It was dark when the pain subsided. He was more tired than he thought it possible to be. The memory of his children that had come clear and perfect as he leaned helplessly against the house, slipped out of reach again.

He felt in his pocket for the key to the kitchen door. It would be a pleasure to turn back to the small chore of lighting the stove with the proof of Catherine and Jack there in the snow behind him.

Isabel would be home soon. He did not feel anxiety now at the prospect of Anna leaving and taking her child away. It would be different—he would comfort Isabel; he would not fail her this time.

He unlocked the kitchen door and reached in to switch on the light.

'Robert.' Isabel called to him from across the garden. 'Come and see what we've found.' She held the baby up and waved his mittened hand. 'Quickly. Come quickly.' She was laughing. Robert closed the door and walked across the garden to them.

Christmas Night

Mice pattered over the hilltop skull. They stroked the lightest touch of their tails on the slopes of the face, between the fingers' crevasses. They were soft, inquisitive mice made of air. They were neither warm nor cold.

The black sea stretched out, twinkling and frozen to the black horizon and the earth looked out from her eye, a huge fallen cyclops moon, looking out from the edge of the shore. She was solid and insensible and untroubled. The earth had always been so.

A white door opened and a child stood. The girl child looked with clear green eyes. The sun was a halo and a dress made of coloured glass. Beside her a gold-skinned boy with a quill of hair held up his hands. He had the legs of a colt. They stood against the white, empty as air.

They could have crossed the black sea, bringing the whiteness with them, right up to her, but they didn't. They could have come to her, she was ready, but they didn't. They closed the white door to black.

A thousand years and the earth slept. A gust came over the sea and there was an indigo door in the black sky. A man stood. He leaned on the edge, too tired to see, tired as the sunken moon.

The earth heaved, splitting the moon to agony but the man did not see. He turned too soon, and was gone. There was a giant's table and a giant's chair, frail and sly as splinters, and they slid away weak as air. The earth plunged like a whale sliding down, sinking deep down to the hard black bed of the sea. The black sky closed over to nothing.

Boxing Day

'Nothing,' said Steffie. 'Nothing happened. I didn't get told off because Mum hasn't seen her.'

'You will though, when she finds out.'

'It wasn't me, and *she* said,' Steffie poked a finger at Gatta. '*She* said we could say we thought we were doing the right thing and it would be rude to say no to Mrs MacKinnon about the baby.'

'But we shouldn't have said we didn't see Anna. It was stupid; we could just have said we were scared of Mrs MacKinnon,' said Starling.

'For fuck's sake don't fuss. The baby's OK, so what's the problem?' said Gatta irritably.

'I hope she doesn't hate me,' said Starling. 'Anna's my friend.'

'She's too busy loving it up with him,' said Gatta. 'She won't be thinking about anything except his dick.' They giggled.

'Like my sister,' said Steffie. 'They only come out of her room when they want food. I don't think they do it, though. Anyway, I'm going. My gran's done a big cake for us with reindeer on the top and someone's got to say it's nice.'

'Bye, Steffie.' Starling shifted along the bench and took out her pack of cigarettes.

'You should give that up,' said Gatta automatically. 'You'll get cancer.'

'What do you think I should buy with my money? I don't know if I want one big thing like a jacket or small things like earrings and a belt and a bag.'

Gatta didn't answer. She pressed her feet into the snow, making a little puddle of slush under her boots. The air was warm.

'Or a dress. Or boots. You're not listening to me.'

'I am. You said, or boots or a dress.'

'What's up?'

'Nothing. Stop going on. I'm not interested in your money.' Gatta got up. 'And you look pathetic in dresses if you must know, your legs are like chipolatas without ankles. I'm going home.'

'Why don't you come back to mine? Mum said you should have tea with us, and she's got something for you under the tree. We can watch telly if you like. Don't go home if it makes you cross. What's wrong?'

'Anna, if you must know.'

'What?'

'I don't know where she is.'

'She's with him,' said Starling puzzled. 'You said so.'

'I can't see her in there, I looked. And MacKinnon's still got the baby.'

'What do you care? You don't like Anna anyway.'

'I did. I do,' said Gatta. 'When I said she was fat I just said it, that's all. It didn't mean anything.'

Starling waited for her to explain. A car passed slowly, the first they'd seen for days. The tyres made splattering waves of sodden snow turn up their muddy undersides.

'Don't feel bad, I expect she's forgotten by now. Maybe it's all over with him—Josef—and she's crying in her room. I'd feel responsible if he hurt her, I gave him to her.'

Gatta looked furious and Starling could tell that she'd better not say any more.

'I'm going. See you.' Gatta walked off towards home.

Starling sat smoking thoughtfully and wondering if perhaps she would go for a stroll later, maybe in the direction of the pub to see if there was still some work going on New Year's Eve after all.

She ground her cigarette into the snow and turned up her collar.

She smoothed down her hair, then fluffed it at the back. She sucked her lips. Now would be a good time for a walk.

And on a bend in the lane she met Josef Sevier, his eyes fixed on the ground. He was alone except for the dog. He almost walked into her.

'Hello,' said Starling. He looked like he used to, as if he didn't want to talk and didn't really know her. 'Hello—Josef,' she said. It was the first time she'd called him by his name and it felt grown up, like speaking to a friend.

'I'm sorry, Starling, I was miles away. Have you had a good Christmas?'

'Yes, thank you.'

'Lots of presents?'

'Um. Not really. People give me money now.'

'Yes, of course. I expect you know exactly what you like.'

'Mmm.' Starling looked at her feet. She could only manage his eyes for a minute or two.

'Starling, have you seen Anna? I'm wondering how she is. I haven't seen her since Christmas Eve, and she wasn't very well.'

'She ... no, we haven't.'

'Not since she picked up Matthew?'

'She didn't. Mrs MacKinnon did. We didn't see Anna. I was wondering about New Year's Eve ...'

'Isabel collected the baby?'

'She came instead of Anna. Anna must have told her to. I'd like to help at New Year if you want.' But Josef wasn't listening.

'And Anna didn't come at all? Maybe she did and you didn't see her.'

'No, she didn't. Really. Ask Gatta. And Steffie.'

Josef looked at her and she felt herself blushing with the lie.

'I'll speak to Elaine,' he said, walking on. 'And I think we need to have a talk if you want to work at New Year—about my car ... and my lighter.' Starling sidestepped to get out of his way. His car?

His lighter? A talk? Then she realized what he'd said and she shouted at his back, 'No, don't ask Elaine! She doesn't know.'

He turned and waited for her to go on. His eyes were not friendly but a thrill fizzed in her stomach: she had all his attention.

'Elaine doesn't know that Anna came, and Steffie will be in trouble. Because Anna didn't come, we gave Mattie to Mrs MacKinnon. Then she did. Anna came after all. But she was upset, that's why we didn't say she had to Elaine. Gatta said things and she was upset, I think. About you.'

'Me?' He walked back to her. She said shyly, 'Gatta said you like her mum more than Anna. And you like me.' She added the last words so softly she wondered if he'd hear. He looked blank as if she'd said something in a foreign language, then he looked over her head and punched one gloved hand into the palm of the other over and over, absently as if he were cold. It was only when she dared look into his face again with a smile ready on her lips that she saw he was furious, saying nothing because no words would come.

'It wasn't anything much, really,' she said desperately, clutching at his sleeve. 'Gatta told her she was fat and I said she couldn't help it, and then she ran off, that's all.'

Josef started towards the village and suddenly Starling couldn't bear him walking away from her again. She ran after him and put her arm through his just as she had when he'd walked her home that wonderful evening in November.

'I'll come with you and help explain,' she said leaning close to reassure him, but to her horror he shook her away.

'No.' His voice was like ice crackling. 'I'm tired of your games— you and Gabriella.' Starling heard a squeak that must have come from her, but she couldn't speak.

'I said nothing about the car, Starling. Deliberate damage. I was going to wait until I'd talked to you to ask you myself why you'd done it—and my lighter, thieving too—but hurting Anna is more spiteful a thing than I would have thought you capable of. And I don't know what happened with Isabel, but I'll find out.' His eyes were stormy, inky blue. 'I'd thought you were a kind person, but I see I was wrong.'

He studied her face as if he were fascinated by the badness that must show like monstrous pimples on her skin. Then he looked away as if the sight of her disgusted him. He walked on and left her.

'I expect you to return my lighter—and keys if you still have them. Leave them outside on the step,' he said over his shoulder.

⌘

The tattered edges of the tarpaulin dripped and the trees poking their bare branches inside the aviary dripped, and the snow whispered and hissed like soap suds as it sunk down into the earth.

Starling had cried for so long that her stomach ached. The tears had come from deep down inside, squeezed up from her core and out through her eyes and her nose, and filling up her mouth. It was as though her insides had turned to liquid and she trickled and dripped and dribbled like the thaw outside.

The horses had been suspicious when she first came in, and they shifted uneasily to the other end of the aviary, but after a while their curiosity brought them closer until they stood over her as she sat on a bale of straw and cried.

Before Josef had gone more than a few yards down the lane, Starling had turned resolutely towards his house as he'd told her. She gripped the lighter in her hand and imagined placing it gently and lovingly on his doorstep like a posy on a grave. The thought of herself doing this made her cry so much she could hardly see.

But she did see when the sobs paused momentarily as she stumbled round the house and came upon the damaged Citroën. She saw a word scratched on the boot. At first she thought it said HAT because the E slipped away, its horizontals not touching the upright. HATE—and underneath, perfectly clear was a large

curving S, gone over and over so it made a dozen silver snakes
slithering together on the yellow paint.

Then she cried some more.

The tears did not run dry until she'd been sitting in the aviary
with the horses for what seemed hours. She felt completely at peace.
All her human feelings were emptied out and only her soul, like a
washed glass tear-drop, was left inside her. She lit a cigarette with
the lighter that she had forgotten to leave on the step and wrapped
her coat tighter. The cigarette glowed warmly and the smoke in her
lungs was soft and friendly. Her hands were shaking and she was
terribly thirsty. It was getting dark and a heavy grey sky was framed
in the doorway.

'I thought you'd be here.' Gatta's voice came out of the shadows.
She sat down beside Starling and took her hand. 'Hello, Star.
It's me.'

'He thought I did it,' said Starling and tears she didn't think she
had began to sting her eyes again. 'You put S. Why did you put S?'

'I dunno. Don't ask me.'

'You owe me. Why S, tell me.'

'It wasn't S for Starling it was S for someone else.'

'Who? Steffie?'

'Steffie? You must be joking.'

'Well, tell me who then.'

Gatta didn't say anything for a while. Starling smoked and they
both stared at the rectangle of murky sky.

'Go on,' said Starling pulling her hand away. 'I've got a right to
know.'

'The S wasn't supposed to be you,' said Gatta. Her voice in the
gloom sounded flat and tired. 'I can't really remember now.'

'You could at least try. I copped it on account of you.'

'The S was *for* you, in a way, I suppose, because he hurt you.
And my mother.'

'But *why?*'

'Because I hated him but I don't now. It goes on and off—like a switch that doesn't have an in-between. I'm like that. I go black inside. I hated him when I did it but after I did it, I didn't any more.'

'Well he thinks I did it and you'll have to tell him. You'll have to.'

'Yes,' said Gatta. 'I'll tell him it wasn't you.'

Starling hadn't expected it all to be solved so easily, Gatta didn't usually give in. But provoke further argument and she would probably take it back.

'S for Sarah,' said Starling conversationally. 'I never think of my mum as Lorraine. I wouldn't have put L if it was my mother I was scratching a car for.'

'In my head she's Sarah. I wish she was like yours but she isn't, she's Sarah.'

'She doesn't fuss like mine.'

'I wish she would fuss. She's always thinking of something else—someone—she doesn't notice a thing, whatever I do, and not even Linnet sometimes, and I think it's his fault. I know it's someone, some man, who's messed her up.'

'Well you've really messed things up for me and Josef.' Starling couldn't help herself, she still felt aggrieved.

The longer the words hung in the air the more Starling knew they weren't true. Eventually she said, 'It's because I'm too young for him.'

'Yes, you are,' said Gatta unexpectedly. 'I've never been young but you are, you're lucky.'

Starling didn't know what to say.

'I thought once he might be, you know, my father,' Gatta said. 'I knew if he was he'd look at me in a special way, and sometimes he does. That's why I don't get it. He looks at me like he knows something, like maybe I am special, but then nothing happens. He doesn't do anything. I was going to make him fall in love with me—I know I could—but I didn't because of everyone else, you for one,

and my mother. And then I couldn't because of Anna, and I didn't
want him to love me in that way anyway. For a while I thought I
looked like him, but I don't, do I?'

'No,' said Starling. She felt uncomfortable at Gatta's talking so
much, telling her all these personal, complicated things, and she
felt that in the circumstances she should be the one to talk about
her broken heart.

'Children don't look like their parents, that's the trouble,' Gatta
went on. 'That's why I won't ever work it out. Except sometimes
they do—Pete and Spike look like Dario. I wish I looked like
someone. I could be anyone's.'

'You're your mum's,' said Starling. 'Why don't you ask her?'

'I can't.'

Gatta got up and went to the door. She unhooked the lantern.

'Got the lighter?' It took a while fiddling with the glass and the
wick to get it going, but at last the flame caught and settled. Golden
light hung in the air and their faces were lit up out of the blackness.
Gatta's cheeks were streaked with tears.

'Don't be sad,' said Starling. 'I'll always be your friend, no matter
what.'

'You look like a skull,' said Gatta, and grinned.

'So do you,' said Starling, but she didn't mean it. Gatta was an
angel on a Christmas card. Her face was made of gold and her eyes
were still and shining as if she'd seen everything there was to see in
the world. Starling thought she looked more sad and wise than an
ordinary girl should ever be. Gatta wasn't young like her or Steffie,
or Pete and Spike—she could see that now.

'I'm happy when I'm with you,' said Gatta softly, and she stared
into the yellow flame, then she looked up and added in her ordinary
voice, 'but don't let it go to your head, it's only because you're as
weird as me. Come on, we're going to find Anna.'

'Where?'

'She must be somewhere, she can't have left the planet.'

'I've got to go home.'

'Let's go to MacKinnon's place; she's got to be there. I might tell her I'm sorry. Come with me, Star.'

'I'm wrecked—look at me. I'm going home.'

They blew out the lantern and Starling stubbed out her cigarette on the floor. As they walked up the lane, they splashed in puddles and sunk into the waterlogged ground. They heard the river rushing between its banks.

&

Josef did not often walk through the village, and he would have turned back and taken the river path or the track over Tye Hill, but he was already as far as Edward and Joséphine's old house. Although the temperature was rising, snow still covered the missing roof tiles and the crumbling windowsills. The cracks in the path were smoothed over and the house looked almost as it had years ago.

When he'd walked past on Christmas Eve morning with Anna, the sun on the windows had made the house look inhabited. It was as if all the lights were on—in Edward's study, in the bedroom above it that was once Sarah's and up in the little attic room that had been Joséphine's. Today the windows were dark.

Josef went on past Frank and Elaine's place, forgetting he'd told Starling he'd talk to Elaine.

The memory of Starling's stricken face was painful and he tried to banish it on the strength of the proof against her. But he was unnerved at how much he admired her reckless spite, and secretly he envied the fury and vigour with which she must have taken her revenge on his car. He could not have done it.

'You are so *English,*' the Frenchwoman had once told him. 'You make yourself a big secret, perhaps you are less interesting than you think. All men are crying, angry babies. What would happen if you let it all out? Ha! Nothing!' She laughed at her joke but they both knew she could not win. Stubbornness had always been his nature.

The real joke was that she was right. Guilt and apology seemed to hang on his shoulders like a flag of surrender, a burden and a shield in equal measure. He could never feel outrage as Starling had. She did not accept perpetual atonement as her price for existence, but he could not remember a time when it had not been so for him, and flashes of inner rebellion brought with them shame so crushing he could not bear it.

He knew now why Anna had not answered his calls and had not come back to him as she said she would—she thought him a liar and a cheat. He must accept her judgement.

Two nights ago on the path to Penquit he put down the lamp on the riverbank and they lay on the soft dry snow. Their fingers found each other through the layers of winter clothing.

They forgot Penquit and walked home to make love again in his bed. Later she got up and dressed, saying she must collect her child. There was no need for him to get cold too and he should sleep, she said—it would be only a few hours before she would return. They would spend Christmas together.

'I'll come back, I promise.'

He had lost her because he'd let her go. It would not have happened if he'd thought clearly. It would not have happened if he'd held her close and confessed. And his mind set in a groove that seemed always to have been etched there. The words of condemnation played over and over and the voice in his head was as familiar as his own, but not his own. It was low and croaking and dry as stone; he was thoughtless and bad. He was a liar.

The idea of explaining to her seemed foolish. There was no reason why she should forgive him.

⌒∞⌒

'Good afternoon, Josef,' Lydia called to him from Constance Lamb's garden gate. 'How is Anna? I do hope she's feeling better.'

'I'm afraid I've not seen her.'

'Oh?' Lydia looked puzzled. 'We thought … well, it doesn't matter.' She closed the gate behind her and waved to Constance who stood at the window with a handkerchief to her nose. 'Poor Connie has such a head cold, but I just can't stay in all day—I should go barking, as my husband would say.' She waved to the swaying net curtain. 'I was just taking a stroll to see Isabel. Are you going that way?'

'I'm not sure. I haven't arranged a visit. Anna may not want to see me.'

Lydia merely settled her hat and said, 'My dear Josef, what nonsense. We needn't stay long if she's poorly.' She patted his hand as if his doubts were dealt with. 'We can go together, how lovely. Would you mind if I join you?'

She took his arm with a sweet formality that reminded him of his mother. To his shame he said, 'I'm really not going that way, not now.' He nodded towards the steep path to Tye Hill. 'I need some proper exercise. Perhaps another time.'

His rudeness did not seem to offend her. 'Of course,' she said. 'I shall give Anna your love.'

Josef nodded. He could think of nothing more to say. When he glanced back, he saw Lydia cautiously negotiating her way between the slush and puddles.

He forced himself to run up the steep incline without stopping and the exertion cleared his head. From the top of the hill the landscape was a dreary monochrome. The snow had almost gone.

He sat down, ignoring the wet, and looked out over the sweep of the river. The only colour was the yellow straw that had been thrown down in heaps here and there on the meadows for the cattle.

There were no shadows to show that the sun was setting, only a gradual darkening from east to west like a lid closing. Even high up from this distance, Josef could hear the river. The sound made him think of Anna asleep on the riverbank when he first saw her last summer.

He had squatted down and his eyes examined her. She was curled on her side and a little cloud of gnats danced above her in the sunlight. Drops of river water were clinging to the down on her sunburned arms and legs, and where her body was white and smooth on the rounded belly and hips and buttocks, the wetness had an oily sheen like cream. The pelvis was padded with thick flesh and crisscrossed with white threads where the skin had been stretched by pregnancy. The sagging breasts were blue-veined, the nipples small and rose-pink—a girl's nipples on a woman's body. For reasons he still could not fathom he was disconcerted by the imperfections of her body. He had, nonetheless, waited for desire to stir in him, but it did not. Her helplessness and her baby deprived him of it.

He'd not thought then he would love her and later he was certain he could not. He was wrong.

Beside the silent river two nights ago they heard the trees creak and the patter of snow falling from the branches. Anna's hair was spread out on the snow and her peaceful eyes looked into his.

Two memories: in one she dismayed him, in the other he loved her with an ease and a tenderness he thought he'd feel for no one in his life but Sarah. Memories were deceitful, treacherous things, a ragbag of delusions and desires. They were a forgery that one constructed to fit with all other counterfeits in one's life until there was no way of judging the truth of anything.

But it was all there was. He longed to see her.

There was no smoke from the chimneys of Isabel's house—the fires must be hot. He hoped Anna was warm. He was glad that Lydia had probably already given her his love.

He looked westwards to his own place and was surprised to see smoke rising above it. But it was not smoke—it dissolved immediately into the air. The wisps of white did not funnel upwards but shimmered like a patch of mist that had settled in the trees. Then he saw an orange flame. It was gone so quickly he thought he'd imagined it. He stood up. Another flame fluttered amongst the trees, then another. He started running.

As he ran it came to him that the mist was steam from the soaked tarpaulin being scorched by a fire beneath it.

The flames spread so quickly he could make out the black iron arches against the blaze before he was halfway down. The aviary was lit up like a lantern in the trees.

Boxing Day Afternoon

Lydia walked past Isabel's house and on towards the bridge. She was not disappointed that Josef had refused her invitation. It was nice to be alone.

For months she had avoided solitude, disciplining her time like a drill sergeant. She devised strategies for marshalling the minutes, shoulder to shoulder, little rows of five times twelve to the hour, and the hours into seventeen immaculate regiments through the day. From the alarm at six to bedtime at eleven she was busy, and when her friends told her to rest, that she had time for herself now, she felt herself fleeing in chaos to the back of her mind.

But today, for the first time in months, she was content to wander for a while between one minute and the next. Connie was a dear friend but she pressed like a thumb on the ache for Gerald. She did not mean to, but every moment Lydia felt squeezed into Connie's routine, driven through the days on invisible tramlines laid down on the bungalow carpets.

Lydia breathed in the soft air and did not feel the emptiness she dreaded—a gap of nothingness between herself and the world—nor did Gerald's presence hang round her as he used to constantly after he retired, in the kitchen or muttering after her in the supermarket.

She was alone, just herself and the wet countryside and the birds twittering in the bare trees.

She sloshed along and wondered how Isabel would be today. A strange, unhappy woman, Lydia thought. Constance seemed in awe of her but Lydia saw only a stony frozen girl of a woman who had lost more than there was to lose. Perhaps Isabel was a lesson in what could happen if one never paused between the minutes.

Lydia stood on the bridge and looked down at the rushing water. It frothed around the stone arches and made ridges like toad's skin where it pushed against the girders that the workmen had put in. The bridge trembled beneath Lydia's feet with the tons of water forced through the narrow arches. The gushing and spluttering and roaring made Lydia want to throw things into the water and watch them being carried away. She held on to her hat, picked up a stick and threw it upstream then raced to the other side of the bridge to see it appear beneath her. It had gone, swallowed up in the frenzy, or perhaps sunk straight to the bottom.

She walked on to the station and looked idly at the timetable. Plymouth seemed another world; perhaps she need not go back. The thought made her lightheaded and she looked at all the other destinations (not many it was true) to which one could travel from Cameldip. There was a walkers' map next to the timetable with a red dot—*You Are Here*—and an arrow to its centre.

'Yes, I am,' said Lydia aloud. 'I am here.'

The lane past the station looked inviting. It curved gently up to the brow of a hill then out of sight in trees. She set off, deciding that she would visit Isabel at four-thirty, a little late for tea but it didn't matter, and be home to Constance by six. The habit of timetabling could not be abandoned entirely just yet.

❧

When a thread of smoke rose up and a tiny flame crackled into life, the horses turned their faces to the wall and their hindquarters towards the annoyance. They lifted their heads and laid their ears back, but they did not move.

The glowing end of Starling's cigarette rolled lazily one way and then the other in the draught, then came to rest. A gust through the open door almost extinguished the miniature bonfire and the flames dipped and sputtered, then recovered. One flickered up more strongly than the rest and touched the ragged corner of the bale on which Starling and Gatta had been sitting. The stalks flinched.

There was a pause as if it had failed, a pretence that the job of burning had proved too much. Feeble curls of smoke wavered, then suddenly a riot of flames burst out—the fire had merely been digging down deep, holding its breath until it came up for air.

The horses shuddered and pressed their faces closer to the wall. They shifted uneasily, their rumps collided and the shock of the rare misunderstanding sent them circling restlessly at the far end of the aviary, the fire between them and the door.

For a while nothing but the straw bale burned. It popped and crackled, and bits of burning straw floated up into the darkness. The horses barged back and forth, irritated by the sting of cinders falling down on them, and for a second Martha's hind legs swung into the flames; her tail fizzed like a fuse and she kicked out. The bale shot like a comet across the aviary exploding in a shower of fire against the wall. In an instant it was everywhere; a pile of sacks caught, then bags of feed. Stinking smoke billowed from the harness hanging on the wall and flames slid up the peeling iron-work. Flakes of burning paint danced like fireflies. The fire joined straw to straw across the floor. The horses dodged and shied but as the blaze encircled them they no longer knew which way to go. Their manes scorched and their eyes burned. With a grinding of their great hooves on the mosaic floor, they leapt blindly through the smoke and luck had turned their heads towards the open door.

They galloped full stretch across the garden, squeezing through the gate and out into the lane. With the danger behind them, they slowed to a trot.

The embers caught in their manes and tails continued to sparkle as they trotted side by side in the darkness, and they trailed behind them the acrid smell of burning hair. Fear still widened their eyes and pulled their lips back a little from their teeth. Their heads were high and their hooves hit the metalled road in perfect time.

Constance Lamb saw them pass by. She stood at her bedroom window looking out for Lydia, who was late again, and she stared open-mouthed as the two great shadow horses beat a single step past her bungalow, their manes and tails alight with stars.

Constance mopped her brow—perhaps she should sit down quietly for a while—but she forgot her head cold and found herself hurrying outside to the gate to catch a last glimpse of them. It occurred to her to telephone Josef Sevier to complain, but it was not possible that those could be his dull, lumbering beasts.

She listened to the rhythmic, marching beat fading into the distance and knew she had seen something wonderful. The air was filled with the scent of war, the thrilling metallic scald in the nostrils she'd not known since the Blitz.

The horses slowed to a walk as they neared the bridge. Drawn by the sound of the water they left the lane and slithered down to the river path past the cement mixer, the workmen's tea cabin and the pile of iron girders, then they turned instinctively downstream towards home. Where the banks flattened out on the meadows the river had become a lake and the horses splashed along the submerged path. They turned together down into the flowing water, stretched out their necks and drank deeply. The river cooled their burned legs and floated out their singed tails. They stood peacefully side by side in the rushing darkness.

⁓

Lydia could see no light on in the house. She knocked and wondered if Isabel had gone walking again with Anna's baby. The thought reminded her of the conversation with Josef—if Anna was not with him and she was ill, surely she would be somewhere in the house? Perhaps Isabel was looking after the child because Anna was poorly—but why had she said that the girl was with Josef?

She knocked again but there was no answer. Lydia stood for a moment undecided, then she followed the little gravel path round to the other side of the house, past the long sash-windows of the dining room where she cupped her hands on the glass, and then on to the kitchen door.

She tapped on the window.

'Isabel,' she called. 'It's me, Lydia. Are you there?' Her hand rested on the door handle and she rattled it to announce herself. Unexpectedly, the handle turned and the door opened. She hesitated, then leaned in and called again. Her voice sounded flat in the darkness.

The house was freezing as if no one had lit the stove for days. There was a smell of dampness, and another odour, delicate and sickening that made her recoil and want suddenly to pull the door closed and go home.

Lydia switched on the light.

At first she could not gather her thoughts or take in what she saw. A figure sat against the stove, its head leaning a little to one side.

The head was red, thick and ridged like spilled paint, filling the sockets of the eyes and congealed at the slit of the mouth. The red was dark crusted where it had dried, and scarlet where the last trickles had set. There was a patch of smooth cheek like the white flesh of a fish with the skin peeled away.

On the chest, the red had blackened to a stain down to the outstretched legs. One hand resting on the lap was a black-red paw, the fingers curled and stuck together like something burned, the other hand wore a yellow woollen glove.

Lydia pushed the door wider. She stood on the threshold and in the time that passed it came to her that she was looking at Anna. The thought started with the sight of the yellow glove and rose up to the surface of her mind slowly and smoothly like a bubble of air through oil.

She was careful to avoid stepping in the blood, not because she was squeamish but because it seemed still to be the property of the body from which it had come. It was flesh turned inside out, solidified in crimson skin on the flagstones.

Anna had tried to get up, or to crawl towards the door. There were prints of bloody fingers along the table edge and on an upturned chair.

'Anna, my poor dear child.'

Lydia stooped down and lifted the yellow gloved hand to find a pulse, but her fingers were numb with cold and she could feel nothing. She leaned close to the mask that was Anna's face to feel for breath coming from her mouth.

Suddenly she was aware of something behind her. There had been no sound, only a movement of air or change of light that she'd sensed.

Isabel stood in the doorway. She did not speak and for a moment Lydia had the odd sensation that Isabel was not surprised at what she saw.

'Telephone the hospital, Isabel,' Lydia said calmly. As she turned, her hand touched Anna's shoulder, and Anna sagged into her arms. She struggled to control the horror of the bloody head touching her face. 'It's all right, Isabel dear, just do the 999 and say there's been an accident.'

Isabel took a step into the kitchen but she did not go to the telephone; she stood over Lydia, looking at Anna as if she'd not heard. She licked her lips and she bent closer.

'Isabel!'

Isabel looked up. She gazed blankly at Lydia as though she did not know her, and clenched her hands into fists.

Fear made Lydia's voice cry out, 'Call Robert. Do it now!' and Isabel started back. She turned and disappeared out into the darkness and there was the sound of her footsteps running across the garden.

∽∞∽

Lydia wanted to ask, but the sight of Robert's ashen face made it seem pointless. She wanted to say, 'But didn't you wonder? Didn't you wonder where Anna was?' But of course they had all thought she was with Josef and it was a miracle that Isabel was looking after the baby.

Lydia sat on the floor and was no longer concerned about the blood. They wiped Anna's mouth and turned her so that she was not twisted against the stove. She lay against Lydia, cold and utterly still.

They did not try to find a pulse again, there was nothing more to be done but wait. Robert went outside and stood in the lane with a torch to wave down the ambulance.

Under the blanket they had spread over Anna, Lydia could feel blood seeping through to her own clothes. The wounds had opened again—perhaps it was a good sign that blood still flowed. There was a gash above Anna's eye and a gaping split on her chin. She must have fallen on the stove and then hit her chin on the floor. But there was another wound on the back of her head that was spreading a stain on Lydia's coat. How had she hit her head twice?

As Lydia sat waiting, she thought of the look in Isabel's eyes when she bent over Anna. The memory chilled her and to distract herself she took off Anna's glove and chafed the cold hand between her own.

'They'll be here soon,' she said. 'I'm here now, Anna dear, I won't leave you.'

The fragile, nauseating scent that had come to her when she opened the kitchen door pressed softly in her nostrils, joining her senses with a memory she had tried for months to banish. The night before Gerald died a sound brought her downstairs. She switched on the porch light and beside the overturned dustbin, within reach of her hand, was a fox.

It turned its golden eyes to her, the tapered muzzle lifted, and it panted quick soft breaths, delicately lapping the air as if to taste her. It was not afraid. It fixed her with its ancient gaze and she knew it was she who was fearful—not of its wildness but of its mute wisdom. It knows, Lydia thought, though at the time she could not have said what. The fox whisked its tail and was gone.

A furtive sweetness hung in the house for weeks. It seeped in from the porch, through the kitchen and up the stairs. It became so familiar that after a while Lydia ceased to notice, or to wonder if it was the scent of the fox or of her husband's death.

And now, here with Anna, it had found her again.

She struggled to recapture the feeling of her walk, the empty air in her lungs and the spacious sky, the astonishing delight in solitude. She told Anna about the rushing water, and the bridge shuddering under her feet like an earthquake there'd once been in Italy, on holiday as a girl with her parents.

But it felt as if she spoke to empty air and there was no one in the kitchen but herself.

Robert did not think of Isabel as he stood in the lane—he'd not thought of her since she burst into the blackhouse. She was breathless from running. She had gone straight to the baby who was crawling on the floor. She picked him up and swung him into the air and he squealed with delight.

She tipped him to her face and kissed him. 'Lydia's here, Robert,' she said, smiling up at the child. 'She wants you.'

'Lydia?'

'Away we go, flying away like a little baby bird!' She spun round, holding the child out in her arms.

'Surely it's you she's come to see?' Robert had said but Isabel didn't hear. She was laughing and the baby shrieked.

The ambulance came quickly—the roads were almost clear of snow. When it arrived, the kitchen seemed full of people and equipment and voices.

'Hop in, Lydia, love, off we go, chauffeur-driven. You're her mum, are you?' They patted Robert on the back. 'All under control now, mate. Have yourself a nice cup of tea, you've earned it,' they said, as if he'd saved Anna.

As they helped Lydia into the ambulance she said to him, 'Would you let Connie know? I'll telephone her as soon as I can.' And then just as the doors closed she called, 'Look after Isabel.'

The siren was faint in the distance. He knew as he pushed open the door to his house that Isabel would be gone.

∞

The river was over its banks, sweeping round the trunks of the trees and along the path. It flowed faster than he ran, and little waves pushed against the backs of his boots.

Robert knew he must run fast to catch up with her—perhaps there was still time—but the river at his side swept away all urgency and the noise of it filled his head.

If it weren't for the child he would let her go. Perhaps this was how he must love her better this time—he should spare her what must come next and be content with the gift of these past two days in her company. But he had relished being alive with her again and it was not enough. He forced himself to run faster.

On the meadows the flood stretched away to the distant hedges as flat as a sheet of tin. To his right where the river was, the water was ridged like a running sea.

There was enough moonlight to see his way. He switched off the torch.

∞

The girl was there. Isabel had not heard her for the noise of the river, but once when she turned knowing there was someone following, she saw the slender figure walking along the flooded path behind her.

Isabel's arms were tired and she shifted the child so his weight rested on her other hip. At first he had been wide-eyed at the spectacle and the din of the racing water but now he leaned his cheek on her shoulder and watched the girl who followed them.

Isabel did not hurry, the girl did not try to hide, and they walked like this across the flooded meadows. The girl's black coat trailed in the water.

After a while the air carried something other than the rank smell of the riverbed and sodden undergrowth, something choking and bitter. Away from the bank, through the trees, an orange light glowed and figures scurried like demons in front of it. Sometimes a fountain of sparks shot up in the darkness.

Isabel stood and stared. It was the old aviary. The roof had gone and every iron sapling pulsed with fire as if it had just been forged.

She had not seen the place for years. She remembered some other time when it had been filled with golden light, the iron trees were white and the floor was made of jewels.

Perhaps it was another place she was thinking of, or something in a dream. She walked on.

But the sight pierced her. It stabbed a pinhole in the darkness through which she saw a scene so clear she forgot the night and roar of the river. There was a table strewn with wrapping paper and empty dishes. Robert sat at her side, his hand over hers on the arm of the chair, and Catherine stood by a tree that was covered with beads of light. She wore a white dress, too large and long for her, and she held out the cotton skirt in her hands.

And there were the boys riding their bicycles in the candlelight. Josef with his dark hair long as a gypsy child's, and Jack, bigger, stockier and blond as a cherub. Jack. He was her son.

She looked at the baby in her arms. She had been sure, but now the flames and the burning iron trees made her feel weak and uncertain. It was all the fault of the woman's daughter with her pretty sneer and her grey-green eyes. She must tell the girl to go home; it was outrageous to be tracked like an animal. Under a tunnel of trees Isabel stood in the shadows and waited.

When the girl came nearer and saw that the path was empty, she stopped. She stood motionless and her long coat became part of the night and the trees.

Isabel shouted into the blackness, 'You've no right to follow me and I insist you go home.'

But for once the fury deserted her and she was frightened. She felt the soft weight of the child in her arms and the warmth of his hands on her neck.

She would have run but suddenly the girl was there, so close that Isabel could see her teeth when she spoke.

'It was you,' the girl said, although there was nothing but the thunder of the river. 'Murderer.'

❦

When Robert saw someone on the bank he thought he'd found her. She was running desperately back and forth as if searching for something in the river.

The woman wore a long black coat and it suddenly came to him that it was Sarah. As he came nearer he caught a glimpse of her face and saw that Sarah's daughter held the child who clung to her, too terrified to cry. She paused where the edge of the bank must be. She took a step, the water was over her knees and she almost fell.

Then he saw Isabel. She was in the river, pressed against a fallen tree. Debris swept round her.

Robert plunged in and the river surrounded him, solid and oblivious. He was pushed forward and down and he came up gasping to the air. The river had hurled him towards Isabel and was sucking him down again under the tree. He reached out to save himself and grasped her in his arms.

They clung together, Isabel's face against the tree and Robert's in her hair. He shielded her with his body and the water curled over their heads like the inside of a wave. The riverbed rolled beneath them and the mud was sucked away around their feet. Isabel was slipping down and he couldn't hold her, his hands were numb and the river was pushing his legs from under him.

Then the girl's voice came to him. He could not hear the words but the sound of her brought him to his senses.

He lifted Isabel. Her shoulders were up out of the water but she hung in his arms, doing nothing to help him. Her weight seemed impossible, heavier each second, and he had no voice to shout.

'Isabel, Isabel.' He did not know if he thought or said her name.

She reached out, clawing at the tree, hauling herself up. He pushed her with all his strength and she was out of the river, sprawled along the trunk, her hair and clothing streaming.

She heaved herself up on her hands and her face was desperate. Always she had obliterated him, reduced him to nothing, but now she searched for him as though her life depended on it. Although he was only an arm's length away, she could not seem to see him. It was as if he was already gone.

He tried to shout, but if he made a sound it was lost in the thunder of the river and even he did not hear it.

The girl was calling. Isabel turned away. She began crawling towards the bank.

He saw the girl drag Isabel to her feet and thrust the baby into her arms, then push her sliding and scrambling up through the trees into the darkness and away from the water. They were gone.

He sunk back. The pain in his chest made him long to be still and he closed his eyes. His face was against the rough bark and he wondered how high in the air this place where he rested his cheek once was. A part of him marvelled that he thought of such things while he fought for his life in the river. Which was his?—the mind that was incredulous at his own stupidity or the mind that was absorbed in the grain and the smell of this great ruined thing. He heard the pounding of its heart.

Something touched his hand. The girl was balanced on the tree and she leaned down to him.

He saw her face. How had he not known she was Catherine?

She hauled on his sleeves, frowning and gasping with the effort, and she dragged his hands to her shoulders as if that was how he should pull himself up. But his muscles were frozen and he could do nothing but look at her. He wanted nothing more.

Then something made her look up, past him upstream, and she let go.

There was a wall of water higher than their heads. It rolled slowly downstream, heavy with the weight of mud and broken trees, turning them over and over.

New Year's Day

It is thirty years since I held my husband's hand. But he takes it now in his and holds it so quietly in spite of all I did and said to him, and we look together at the place where our children drowned.

My mind is silent but full of pictures: my own feet running beneath me in pointed white shoes or in boots, or bare, running along a muddy path. I run past this place thinking I might still find them.

They call me and I come to them. And if I run fast enough those hours will not happen, that night will be left behind like the tail of a comet, dust that is lost in the black of nowhere, and I am scorching bright, alive again.

But how could I know I ran past them? That all the time they were in this place under the trees and not down the river caught floating by a fallen branch.

When I ran he would hold me, but I spat in his face and fought him till he let me go. We stand now, the two of us, and we look: the carcass of a boat heaved from the riverbed.

My children's boat. Its rope is coiled in the mud like a tail. The bottom has gone but two seats, one in the prow and one halfway, still span the little hull. So many years it has been hidden, until melting snow washed the river clean. What could bring more promise than the end of winter?

There is no need for words. Our children are gone but I am glad that Robert is here. I have not held his hand for thirty years.

1990

The Underground was crowded. People funnelled through the doors and up the escalators. Josef fed his ticket into the barrier, keeping time with the rhythm of machinery counting them through. He liked the dumb cooperation of city travel, it amused him—a mass of efficiency for a million secret purposes.

A busker echoed in the tunnel and the clicking of feet on the concrete steps changed tone as they came up to the open air.

He walked along the Embankment. The Thames sparkled and the breeze smelled of hot dust and fumes. People wore summer clothes and the colours were bright and coarse like an old cheerful postcard.

The flat was at the top of a red-brick block with finicky decoration and Gothic windows. It was ugly and looked like a workhouse, but the view of the river was expensive.

'Oh, yes, hello. Come up,' said the voice on the entryphone.

The woman who opened the door was neat and slim; she wore white jeans and a T-shirt. Her hair was cropped short and she ruffled it distractedly as if it were a habit. They shook hands.

'Hello, Anna.'

He followed her along a dark hall and into a white room lit up with sunlight from the river.

'It's very good of you to come to see me.' Her speech was slurred and she moved slowly. 'Would you like some coffee? Please sit down.'

There were two yellow sofas in an expanse of wood floor, a sound system, a print of orange splashes on blue. Newspapers and books

326

and toys were strewn about. He went to the window and stood looking out. He could hear her in the kitchen.

'Tom told you, did he?' she called. 'About me?'

'Yes, he did.'

She came in with a tray and knelt beside it on the floor. As she handed him the cup, coffee spilled into the saucer. He sat down on a sofa with the tray between them.

'It seems such an odd thing for me to have done, just go off by myself and live in Devon. But apparently I did.'

'Yes.'

'I remember some things. I remember Isabel—her face. Tom says she was wonderful, looking after me and the baby. She did everything for us.'

Josef nodded and stirred his coffee.

'How is she? I know her husband died; it's fine to tell me the truth.'

'She ... she's better, I believe,' he said. 'She's well.' He hesitated, trying to gauge if he should go on. Which truth should he tell? His own, with Robert gone, and the daughter he had never known. Or Isabel's? To Anna it did not matter. For her, both were no more than stories.

She was watching him, studying his face. 'I'm so sorry,' she said. 'I thought I'd remember you, Tom said we knew each other, but I don't think I do.'

He could reach out his hand and touch her.

'It will come back slowly, I expect. Don't worry.'

She got up and went to a table scattered with drawings and pencils.

'Were we friends?' she said. Her face was hidden from him. She shuffled through the sheets of paper.

He did not know how to answer. She gathered up a bundle of papers awkwardly in her thin arms and waited, her back to him.

He said, 'We didn't know each other for long.'

There was the sound of seagulls on the river and the city traffic.

'Show me your drawings, Anna. Tom told me you draw. He said you'd like me to look at them.'

Then she turned and smiled. 'They're awful, truly terrible. I have to draw with my left hand, so you must make allowances.' She sat beside him on the sofa and spread the drawings on the floor at his feet.

They were like a child's, objects all over the paper, lines and dots and mythical creatures.

'I thought you might know what these things mean.'

There was a house in a tree, a lamp and a glass covered with stars. There was a moon and a rocking chair.

'This is a cat, a bird,' she said pointing, 'and that's a horse. You'd never know but it really is. And I don't know what this is, I just drew it. I think it's a birdcage.'

'It's an aviary,' said Josef.

'An aviary!' she said delightedly. 'Where was it? Did I live near it?'

'It's gone now,' he said. 'It was just a place in the village.'

They bent over the pictures and her arm touched him as she leaned forward to point. 'All those dots are snow. I keep thinking of snow as if it's important. Looking up into trees and there being snow.' She turned to him expectantly. His heart raced.

He pretended to examine the drawing. Eventually he said, 'I don't know, Anna.'

She said, 'I'll remember one day. I'll just have to be patient.'

They finished their coffee and the sun moved across the room. They talked about London and restaurants they both knew.

'I must go.' Josef looked at his watch.

'Yes, of course, you mustn't miss your flight. You've moved to France, Tom told me, with your wife and your children. Did I know them too?'

'We're not married, and yes, you knew them. The boys are Peter and Sebastian, we call him Spike, and Linnet, she's nearly seven.'

'What a sweet name. And your wife?'

'Sarah.'

Anna frowned as she considered, but Josef could see that the names meant nothing to her. Her eyes wandered past his shoulder and she yawned. 'I'm sorry, I still get so tired.'

He followed her to the door and she held out her hand.

'Come for supper when you're next in London. I know Tom would love to see you and you must meet our son.'

He still held her hand and she smiled politely. Something flickered in her eyes for a moment and was gone.

'Thank you for coming to visit me.'

He could feel her watching as he walked along the passage, then there was the sound of the door closing.

He took the lift down to the street and walked out into the sunshine.